IN THE SHADOW OF THE BEAST

C.J. ADRIEN

Copyright © 2020 by Christopher Jonathan Adrien

All rights reserved. This book or any portion thereof may not be reproduced or used in any manner whatsoever without the express written permission of the publisher except for the use of brief quotations in a book review.

This is a work of fiction. Names, characters, businesses, places, events and incidents are either the products of the author's imagination or used in a fictitious manner. Any resemblance to actual persons, living or dead, or actual events is purely coincidental.

First Edition

Originally published in the United States in 2020 by Runestone Books

ISBN: 9798646959158

For more information, visit www.cjadrien.com

Pour mon petit Viking, Leif.

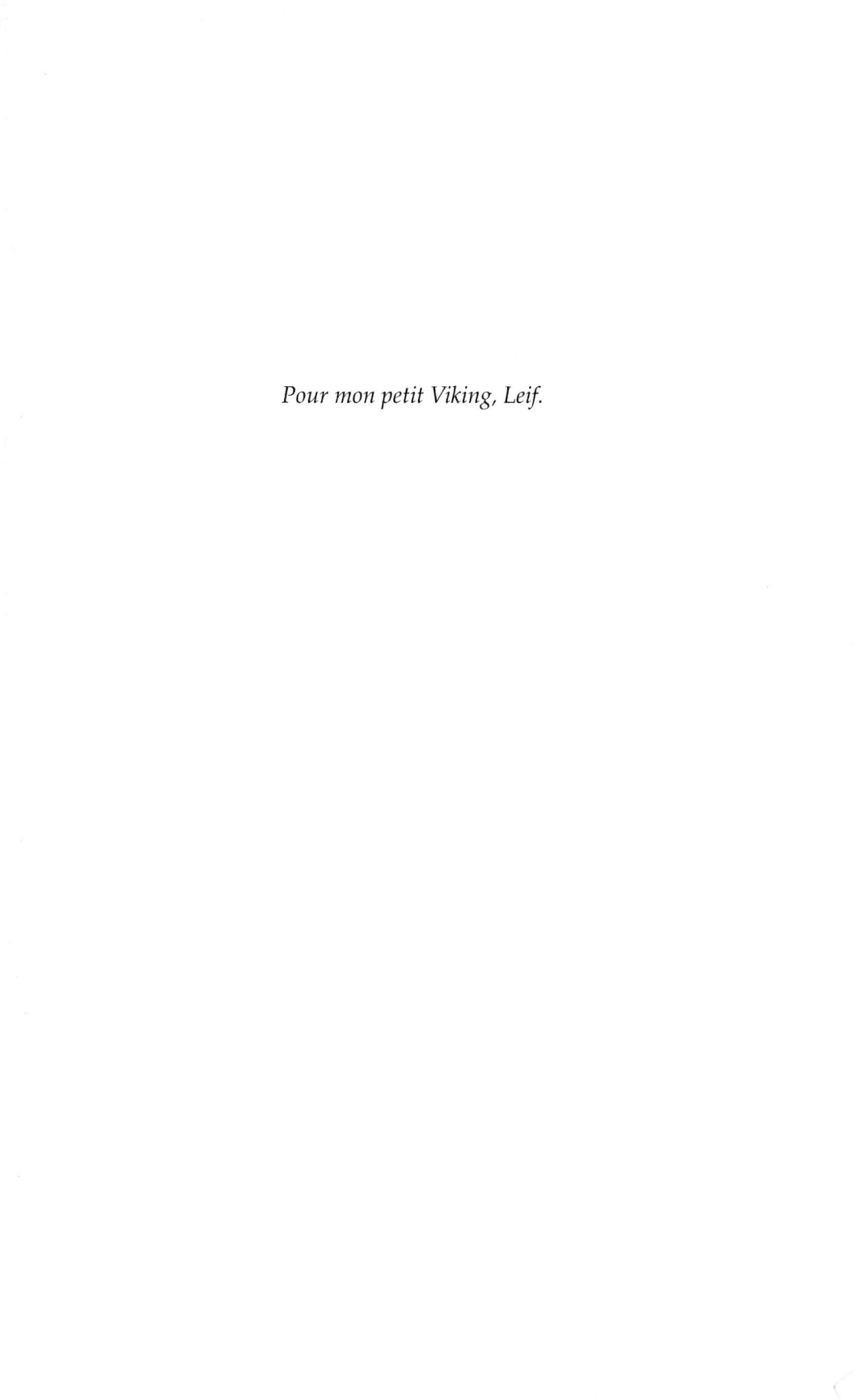

Table of Contents

Map	9
Chapter 1	11
Chapter 2	31
Chapter 3	45
Chapter 4	61
Chapter 5	81
Chapter 6	101
Chapter 7	115
Chapter 8	143
Chapter 9	159
Chapter 10	183
Chapter 11	199
Chapter 12	215
Chapter 13	231
Chapter 14	251
Chapter 15	269
Chapter 16	289
Chapter 17	305
Historical Note	319
Primary Sources	333
About the Author	337

"Pagan ships have done much harm to the islands of Aquitaine. Some of them were entirely lost. A great chastening is upon them unlike any the ancient Christian world has ever seen."

ALCUIN OF YORK, LETTER TO ARNO

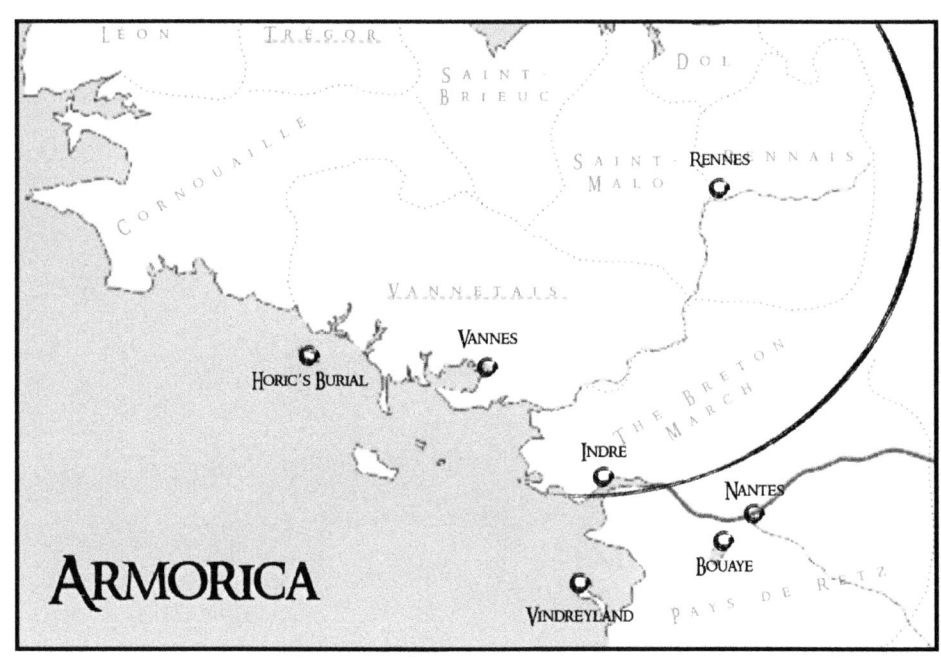

I

The Funeral

I awoke that morning to Skírlaug's agony. Bjorn and I rushed to the king's bedchamber to find her curled over him, tears of sorrow bleeding black with eyeshadow.

"Is he dead?" Bjorn asked.

"Yes, he's dead!" Skírlaug glared at him and slipped backward onto her knees, panting with labored breath. "It is my fault," she muttered. "I misread the runes. The gods warned me, and I missed it. Somehow, I missed it."

"You couldn't have known," I said.

"I should have known. It is my life's work to know," she snapped.

"What do we do now?" Bjorn asked.

"We should tell the others," I said. "Gather the ship captains for a meeting in the courtyard."

Bjorn bowed and left the chamber with hurried steps. I kneeled down and wrapped my arm around Skírlaug. She nestled her head against my bosom and wept. We remained still for a long moment until she looked up and caressed my face.

"Thank you," she said.

"I understand how important he was to you," I said.

She wiped her face with her sleeve and caught her breath before speaking again. "Horic did not tell you, but you should know," she started.

"Tell me what?"

"I am his daughter," she said.

My jaw dropped at her words.

"That is why I weep; it is not devotion but the love of a daughter."

We stared into each other's eyes for a brief moment, but she looked away before either of us could say anything more. She jumped out of my arms and to her feet, pretended to brush herself off, and pulled on her brooches to adjust her dress. I reached out my hand as if to say something, but before my mouth could produce words, she put her finger on my lips.

"I will care for Horic's body," she said. "Go to the courtyard. The worst is yet to come."

I wanted more from her. What I wanted, I cannot say precisely, but I lingered a moment too long for her liking, and she resorted to pushing me out of the chamber. She slammed the large oak door and left me in the bleak darkness of the monastery's inner hallway.

Echoes from the ground floor reached my ears; a commotion had erupted in the main hall. I took a moment to gather my strength and made my way to the stairwell. To my surprise, the echoes had not come from the main chamber but from the courtyard. Bjorn had left the front door open, which had let in the flood of voices. I emerged from the monastery to find Ragnar and all the ship captains gathered in the courtyard, pushing against Bjorn and his warriors in an attempt to enter my hall. Ragnar caught sight of me and shouted over the others.

"Does my son speak true, Hasting? The king is dead?"

I raised my hand to gather their attention. My calmness seemed to still Horic's followers. "It is true," I said in a low voice. "Skírlaug was with him all night, and she is with him now."

My words were met with sobs and murmurs. These men had traveled far in search of riches, and many of them would not have made the journey if not for Horic's reputation. Skalds sang of his daring deeds abroad, and the songs always attracted eager followers.

Without Horic, their spirits hung like straw over a sharp blade, ready to split at the slightest touch. I needed these men. For five years, I had waited patiently, playing by the Vikings' rules and building my island's strength. And all this for revenge.

"We are fortunate," I said. "Horic's völva has traveled with him, and she will guide us so that we may bury him as a king. Let us celebrate his life and his deeds. Let us cast our worries aside and join one another as brothers before the gods. Let us drink together and fight together, and let us bury our king together. And when he has begun his journey to his next life, I will lead us all to glory and riches."

A dead silence followed. When I thought all was lost, Bjorn spoke up to defend me.

"Hail Hasting, king of Vindreyland!"

But Bjorn's words fell on deaf ears. The sea captains turned to the figure at the center of us all, an enormous man who bore the same name as my father: Ragnar. Though this man's son was none other than Bjorn.

"Hasting speaks true," he said. "We should honor the king and do as the völva says. We will help the king of Vindreyland where we are able."

The tension in the air diffused in an instant, and Ragnar gave me a stern nod as he and his men left the courtyard. I sighed in relief, as did Bjorn, and we returned to the oak table in the main hall to sit and relax. Servants from the village arrived, as they did each morning, and delivered us our first meal of the day.

There were many mouths to feed, so the servants had to make several trips back to Vindavik to feed us all. After they had delivered the morning meal, more and more men joined us at the table. At first, we ate in silence, waiting to hear whatever we could from the stairwell. Not a sound came from the second level. One of Bjorn's men sat at my side—Bjarki, a stout warrior with a round face and red cheeks, his hair a mess from slumber, and his eyes still half-closed. He reached for a pitcher of milk and poured himself a cup. As he took his first sip, he looked at me and noticed my uneasiness.

"Did somebody die?" he asked.

"The king," Bjorn muttered.

Bjorn's response caused Bjarki to shrink. He sipped his milk and looked at the others around the room. I could see the thoughts ruminating in his mind as he scanned the world, searching for the right words to say. At last, he broke his silence and said, "At least it's not raining today."

A few of us chuckled, and our smiles helped to brighten the room. Bjarki had a way with humor, and he always managed to lift our spirits in our darkest moments. It did not wash away the severity of our predicament, but it at least helped break our somber mood, if even for a moment.

"You know what else is funny?" Bjorn added. "My father called Hasting a king."

"You called me a king; he was only repeating it," I said.

"A king of what? The wind?" Bjarki said. We all laughed, and he raised his goblet to keep the joke going. "Hail Hasting, the Lord of the Wind!"

No sooner had the words left Bjarki's mouth than Bjorn let loose a resounding fart that shook the bench upon which we sat.

"Hail Bjorn, the Lord of Passing Wind," I said.

At that, we howled with laughter. Bjarki fell over, holding his belly. Our cackling ceased when Skírlaug appeared in the stairwell. Behind her, Horic's men carried his body over their shoulders. She glared at us.

"I need salt," she declared.

"How much?" I asked.

"It will take many days to prepare Horic's burial, and I will need to preserve his body. We will need to encase it in salt somewhere with as little moisture as possible," she said.

"The crypt is as dry a place as any. I will have barrels of salt brought to you."

Skírlaug nodded, her face devoid of emotion, and Bjorn leaped to his feet to show her the way to the crypt. His eagerness did not surprise me. He had served as Horic's champion for over a year before he swore to me. He had loved Horic as a father.

Warriors slain in battle ascend to Valhalla with the help of the gods' servants, the Valkyrie. Still, Horic had not died a warrior's death, so Skírlaug said, and he would need to reach Valhalla on his own. Given the proper enchantments, his ship would take him there. But the journey would be long and full of perils, so he would need to take as many weapons and supplies as the ship could hold. All these things Skírlaug told us, and we listened.

The part I did not like was when she said my island's soil was too soft and sandy to make a proper burial. She would send a ship to nearby islands to find one with rich enough land for what she envisioned.

While the ship searched for good earth to bury the king, the rest of us remained on my island to make preparations. In truth, we had little to do. After a week of waiting, Ragnar's camp bustled with activity. They had set up their tents in a large circle in the field off to the west of the wetlands where I had asked them to, and as I would have expected, they had set pikes along the perimeter.

They had also erected tall wooden posts carved with the likenesses of gods and animals to form an empty circle at the heart of the camp. Each post had carved scenes depicting the gods' most famous battles and hunts. Between the emblems, a crowd had assembled, and their cheers drew my attention. I entered the camp and snaked through the tents. At the center, I found Ragnar holding the entire mast of a ship on his back and across his shoulders. His face was as red as fresh-cut beets, and the veins in his arms, shoulders, and chest bulged from his skin like worms emerging from the earth after a rainfall. He took two short steps forward and collapsed to his knees. The mast of the ship thudded as its ends landed on tall wooden crates that held it in place about chest-height. Ragnar's men cheered and rallied around him following his feat of strength, and I could hardly believe what I had seen. A few ship captains saw me standing at the periphery, and they dispersed their men to allow me to speak with Ragnar. I stepped into the circle with my hand on my sword.

"You have the strength of many men, my friend," I said.

Ragnar took a moment to collect himself. His men laughed at my compliment but quieted down when their leader approached me and said, out of breath, "I have been training for many years to carry the mast."

"It was impressive," I said.

"Do you train your body?" he asked me.

"I do. My men and I train almost every day," I replied. "Strength and stamina must be earned."

"Yes!" he cried. "What good is an ax and shield without the strength to wield them?"

He stretched his arms and puffed up his chest. While we spoke, another man ducked underneath the mast, and as he did so, the crowd around us started to cheer. It took Ragnar's attention, and he clapped and screamed to lift the man's spirit.

His chest and arms were thicker than Ragnar's. With strict posture, he looked to the sky, forced his shoulder blades under the pole, and lifted it from the crates. As he held it on his back, he took one step, and then two, and a third. Before releasing the load, he looked at Ragnar and gave him two confident nods. When the mast hit the crates, the crowd erupted in celebration.

"What is his name?" I asked Ragnar.

"That is my son, Ubba. He is the strongest man in all of the North."

Ubba walked over to us and patted Ragnar on the back. The two of them were matched in stature, but Ubba had the face of a child. His curly black hair flowed to his shoulders and contrasted with his bright blue eyes.

Ragnar smiled and said, "You've won again."

"When will you try to lift the bigger mast with me?" Ubba joked.

Ragnar shot him a sideways look.

Ubba turned to me with a grin and said, "How about you? Think you can carry this one?"

I laughed and said, "I don't need to break my back today."

Ubba slapped me on the thick of my back as we laughed together, and it jolted me forward. Once I had regained my footing, I stood as tall as I could.

As we stood there, one of Bjorn's men entered the camp and announced a ship had entered the Concha. I followed him to the port, leaving the giants behind and carrying with me a feeling of unease, at least until I took sight of the visitors' sail. My heart lifted with joy: it was Sail Horse.

It had been years since Rune had taken her back to Ireland. I had lost all hope of seeing them again. What stories of their travels did they have to tell, I wondered. At the water's edge, I called for men to tie off the ship and welcome the crew onto dry land. Rune stood at the prow with a full black beard, his hair long and flowing. Last I had seen him, he had the look of a young boy; now he was a grown man. Behind him stood Fafnir, looking tired but firm on his feet.

Sail Horse butted up against the wood-planked pier, and a plank flew over the gunwale to bridge the ship's deck to the dock. I could not contain my excitement. I grinned from ear to ear, and my eyes watered a little—just a little. Rune walked down the plank first. He wore a thick wool overcoat with fur trim and a light tunic beneath. I reached for his hand, but he leaped forward and embraced me with a kiss on the cheek. His embrace lasted longer than I had expected, and when he pulled back, he gazed into my eyes with a soft smile. Fafnir walked up behind him and patted me on the shoulder.

"Too long, my friend," I said as I released him and gathered myself.

"It is good to see you again," Rune said. "We did not know if we would find you here. There are rumors in the North that you are dead."

"Are there?" I asked. "Who would start such a rumor, I wonder?"

"It does not matter," Rune continued. "I am happy we have found you here."

It did matter. No man of any importance should ever ignore a rumor about himself. Whispers of my death could encourage an ambitious sea captain to seek out my land, and in so doing lead to a war I did not want to fight. I recognized the gravity of the news, but I kept my concern buried deep.

Other men from my first crew disembarked as we spoke, including Sten, Gørm, Torsten, Ulf, Trygva, Frode, Arne, Erik, and Troels. Behind them were many other men I did not know and who had not sworn to me.

"Whom do they follow?" I asked Rune.

"Me," he replied. "But only for the journey. They only follow me because I have told them of you."

He may have grown into a man, but his agreeableness had not left him, and for that I was thankful. I looked over all the men as they passed, each carrying a load of supplies to land. At that moment, I noticed Sten lifting and folding the sail all on his own, and I remembered how powerful a man he was. I walked closer to the ship, leaned on the gunwale, and watched him work for a moment. When he saw me standing behind him, he paused and looked back at Rune.

"If I put the mast of a ship on your back, could you carry it?" I asked him.

He shrugged his shoulders but did not say no.

"How would you like to be my champion for a day?"

I took Sten, Rune, and Fafnir back to Ragnar's camp. I explained what my guests had done earlier, and how I hoped Sten might match their strength. It was my honor I wanted to save, and the gods had given me my chance.

Sten explained as we walked that he and his father had done the mast-carrying challenge, too; it was a famous test of strength in the North. My step had a new lightness, and the others noticed. When we arrived at the center of the camp, I inserted myself, not so subtly, into their gathering.

"Ragnar, I want you to meet my champion, Sten," I announced. Sten carried his large, rounded body over to the mast as I spoke, and I glowed. "He and his father are no strangers to your test of strength."

Sten ducked his head underneath the mast and wrapped his arms around it. He pressed his shoulder blades against the wood and lifted the whole of it with apparent ease. He stepped forward four quick steps, and to all of our surprise, four steps backward to lower the log onto the supports.

Ragnar and Ubba's jaws both dropped. Sten walked back to me, as expressionless as ever, and crossed his arms over his thick belly.

Ragnar looked around at his men, and when I thought he might flee, he lifted Sten's arm in the air and cried out, "Do you see this man? Behold, the strongest man in the North! Let us celebrate him!"

Ragnar's warriors erupted in cheers and circled Sten, who grinned and took in the praise. He looked back at me and shrugged. I cheered for Sten as well; he deserved the praise.

When Ragnar found me in the crowd, I gave him a smirk. With all the commotion, Bjorn had appeared on the edge of camp to investigate. He snaked through the crowd and found me first, and when Ragnar saw him, they both froze.

Ragnar's stance widened, and his steps toward us were short and shallow. As he moved, Bjorn took to mirroring him. Their dance attracted the attention of everyone around them. Ragnar reached for Bjorn's tunic, but Bjorn cast him off before he could grasp it. Bjorn, in turn, grabbed at Ragnar's tunic, and when he had a firm grip of it, the two locked arms and jerked each other back and forth. They wrestled without ever saying a word to one another, and when the dust around them settled, Ragnar had pinned his son to the ground. Bjorn grunted as he struggled, but he had no moves left to counter.

"Few men can say they have bested Bjorn," I said with my arms crossed.

"I hope for your sake you are one of them," Ragnar replied, winded. He released Bjorn and straightened his back.

Bjorn stood and walked past his father, then shoved him. Ragnar feigned a lunge forward, which sent Bjorn into a trot in retreat. The men laughed, and Bjorn sauntered in a wide circle back to me. He pouted the rest of the afternoon.

Some days later, Skírlaug's ship returned. The sailors had an island in mind for the king's burial. When they described it to me, I understood they had found one of the islands off the coast of the Morbihan, not far from Nominoë's lands. It was a flat, circular, and grassy island surrounded on all sides by jagged cliffs, except for a single beach on its northern side. It had no trees, but given the flatness of the land, it appeared someone had cultivated it at one point in the past. When we disembarked and ascended the cliff to the grassy plateau, Skírlaug dug her hands into the dirt and smelled the soil.

"This is good land," she said. "Our king will be happy here until his ship departs."

Shiploads of goods made their way to shore first, and our men pitched so many tents that by the time they had finished, it looked as though we had built an entire city. Horic's ship followed. It took one hundred men pulling two ropes to drag it up the beach to the field Skírlaug had demarcated with smooth stones for the burial. Ragnar's men dug deep into the ground, and they took care to move the dirt they dug to one side of the hole. Servants brought them food and drink as they worked, but the servants did not help to dig; that honor belonged to the men who had served the king.

Each night, we gathered around a fire pit, placed a short distance from the tents, and drank and ate together. Skírlaug's ceremonies did not begin until the men had put the ship in the hole and loaded it with the goods the king would need for his journey.

Persistent rain delayed the ceremonies several days. While we waited for the weather to pass, we spent our time resting in our tents. We told stories, sang songs, and played all the gambling games we had learned on our travels. I was amazed by how many games my men knew.

Before the rain had cleared, one of Skírlaug's servants summoned me to her tent. My heart skipped a beat. Thoughts of what she wanted with me, and me alone, filled my mind and fed my more outlandish fantasies. Once I reached her tent, however, my fantastical imaginings faded. She had also summoned Ragnar. He had arrived before me and lounged on some furs along the side of the tent. He sipped from a wooden goblet while she spoke to him in a soft tone. When she saw me standing at the entrance, she paused and smiled.

"Come in," she said with a wave of her hand.

I ducked my head to step into the tent. Skírlaug invited me to lounge on furs opposite Ragnar, and she offered me a goblet of wine.

His grin made my skin crawl. A man of his caliber involved in my affairs made my position precarious. Vikings tended to fear one thing above all: other Vikings.

"Your oaths to Horic have ended," Skírlaug began. "You are masters of your fates."

"I am still sworn to Hakon of Lade," I interjected. "To broker peace between Hakon of Lade and Horic, they appointed me lord of my island, loyal to both but in conflict with neither."

Ragnar sat up taller with intrigue in his eye. "You are sworn to Hakon of Lade?"

"I have sworn to him a share of the salt trade, but should he call on me to fight, I am not compelled to join him," I explained.

"And he returns in the summer?" Ragnar pressed.

"He arrives later than Horic. Lade is much farther away than Ribe," I said.

Ragnar leaned back into his furs, his grin broader than ever. He took a sip of his wine and stared at the ceiling of the tent, seemingly content with himself. Skírlaug scowled and turned her attention to me.

"The two of you are powerful warlords in your own right, with many men sworn to you, but only one can rule the islands of Aquitaine in Horic's place. I hope the two of you have realized what is at stake here," she said. Her voice deepened as she spoke, and her eyes grew darker. "Horic's son will not seek to keep control of these lands. Challengers to his title will force him to look toward his own lands."

"I know all of that," Ragnar spat. "Why do you think I am still here? I could have taken my ships home, but to what? A civil war? Again?"

"I am already lord of these parts, and I am allied with the Celts and the Northmen," I said. "No Dane could take my place."

"Ragnar disagrees," Skírlaug said. "He has asked for a *holmgang*—to challenge you for your lands and the loyalty of your followers."

I laughed. "You want to fight me?"

Ragnar nodded. He gave me another wine-stained grin and winked at me.

"And then what? If you defeat me, how will you manage the salt production? Our trade with Hakon? And the alliance with the Celts that keeps the Franks at bay?"

Skírlaug reached for me, but I brushed her off, stood with fists clenched, and glowered at my new foe. My breathing quickened, and every muscle in my body tensed.

Ragnar picked at his fingernails, and without looking at me, he replied, "Your mistake is to think it won't work without you."

"It won't!" I roared.

"There will be no fight until Horic is buried," Skírlaug demanded. "We will bury the king first and settle this quarrel after."

I fought my way through the flap of the tent's entrance and stormed into wind and rain. I returned to my tent with such wrath, my men ceased their banter and jumped to their feet. They stared with wide eyes as I panted and raged. Rune approached me first, his steps light and cautious. My sodden clothes dripped and puddled at my feet. Behind me, the wind howled, and the rain thrashed.

"What happened?" Rune asked.

"Ragnar," I said.

Rune looked back at the others. They all seemed to know what I had to say. Had Ragnar's intentions been so obvious? Had I missed the signs?

Fafnir approached me and put his hands on my shoulders. "If there is a man who can defeat Ragnar, it is you," he said.

"We should stall," Bjorn proposed. "Hakon is due to arrive. He will support your claim to the land."

"Our laws are clear," Fafnir said. "Even if Hakon arrives to support Hasting, the challenge stands and must be met. It is a matter of honor."

"The gods will demand blood," Rune added.

"I will fight him, and I will kill him," I said.

"You can't!" Bjorn lamented. "He'll kill you."

"Or are you afraid I'll kill him?" I spat.

"You don't know him. You don't know what he's capable of."

"I believe in you," Rune said.

"And I," said Fafnir.

The other men in the tent also lent me their support, but Bjorn's angst did not reassure me. I took a moment to think through my situation and, in my silence, listened to the rain subside.

When I stepped out of the tent, most of the clouds had moved past the island and on toward land. They left behind a bright and pale blue sky on the precipice of darkening. Warriors emerged from the other tents and looked up as I had. No sooner had I taken my first deep breath in the open air than a horn blew in the distance. It was Skírlaug summoning us to the burial ground.

We gathered at the entrance to my tent, then trudged across the muddy field to the ship. A mild breeze sent our hair flying in every direction—at least, those of us who had hair. Trygva, the oldest member of my crew, had lost most of his and had resorted to shaving his head. The breeze did not bother him.

Two masses of warriors approached the burial ground on separate sides. To the right, my men and I formed a wall from prow to stern. To the left, Ragnar and his men did the same. The ship had been placed in a pit deep enough that the prow's top edge was flush with the ground. All that stood above ground was the prow beast, a menacing serpent head adorned with knotted carvings and fierce fangs.

A plank bridged the pit where we stood with the ship's deck below us. Skírlaug led a procession of Horic's warriors who carried his body over their shoulders on a wood-framed canvas. Two columns of warriors followed them with smoldering torches. Their frowning faces conveyed a terrible torment, one that they hoped to assuage by giving their king a proper send-off.

They lowered the canvas and deposited the king's body onto a bed of furs between mast and steering paddle. All around him were carafes of wine, baskets full of bread and cheese, and enough silver to sink Sail Horse. Skírlaug motioned to one of her warriors, and a man led three goats to the ship. He handed her the ropes that kept them, and she led them around the king's body to the aft of the deck. The goats bleated in terror and pain as she ran a steel blade across their necks, one by one. Her last victim was the most unfortunate—it had to watch the others die. Skírlaug lifted a bloodied blade in the air to show us all what she had done. The goats had joined their master.

Skírlaug waved again, and a warrior approached with a slave girl in tow. I had never seen the girl before; she had likely traveled with Skírlaug from the North. She could not have been older than twelve, and she whimpered as the völva's man led her to the king's side. Skírlaug recited a poem as they walked:

> *Odin is named All-father,*
> *Because he is the father of all the gods,*
> *And also the Choosing Father,*
> *Because he chooses for his sons all of those who fall in battle.*
>
> *He has prepared the hall Valhalla,*
> *For the fallen to feast, fight, and live,*
> *A place where they are called heroes.*
>
> *Five hundred doors*
> *And forty more*
> *Adorn the halls of Valhalla.*
> *Eight hundred heroes through each door*
> *Shall issue forth*
> *Against the wolf to combat.*
>
> *The heroes all*
> *On Odin's plain*
> *Will hew each other daily.*
> *From the fray, they will ride,*
> *And drink ale with the Aesir.*

"Horic did not die in battle," Skírlaug said. "But in life, he was a fearsome warrior. Odin will still take him if he makes the journey to Valhalla and proves himself worthy." She looked down at the slave girl and wiped the tears from her face. "You have chosen to follow your king on this journey. Do you still willingly choose your fate?"

The girl trembled. She sniffled and took in shallow, distressed breaths, and she gave a single nod. Skírlaug held her blade to the girl's chest. We all fell silent. All we could hear was the girl's breathing. The knife slid into her chest without a sound.

Skírlaug reposed her body at the foot of Horic's bed and placed her hands over the wound to cover it. Following a short pause, the völva climbed the plank to our level, and as soon as she reached the top, the rest of us began to shovel dirt into the pit. Skírlaug circled the gravesite to oversee our work. Night's relentless gallop overtook us, and before we had finished, we found ourselves in the dark.

Later that night, we ate and drank our fill, but each camp kept to themselves. Word of the duel had reached everyone, and the mood on the island had grown taut. No one dared mix with the other camp.

I paced alone behind our tent, and I raged at the laws of the Danes, that Ragnar should have the right to challenge me. Still a young man then, I had a hard time containing that rage, and as a warrior, I needed to lash out and hurt someone. I also felt betrayed. Skírlaug, as a daughter of Horic, should have had the authority to refuse Ragnar's challenge. Horic would have wanted me to stay in power; should she not have carried out his wishes?

I have often found the traditions of the Danes and the Northmen problematic or contradictory. I recalled a long-ago night in Vannes, with Nominoë, and how I had told him about some of the stranger traditions of the Danes. He had found the idea of a blood-feud, which had robbed me of my family, barbaric and revolting, and I tended to agree. What might he think of this duel?

Emboldened by the wine I had drunk, I decided to take my questions to Skírlaug. I left my tent and stomped through the mud to hers. When I burst through the flaps of the entrance, I froze. Skírlaug sat against some furs with wine in her hand and Ragnar whispering in her ear. She giggled at whatever he said. When she saw me, she straightened herself and pushed Ragnar away. I have not often felt the poison of jealousy, but at that moment it stung me like a wild hornet.

"Hasting, wait!" Skírlaug cried out as I bolted outside.

I fled into the night, toward the beach, with the light of the moon to guide me. Youth has a way of making us impulsive and out of control, and I knew if I stayed at camp, I would do something I would later regret. I had to find space to think and to breathe. After all, I might die the following day. The beach, at least, felt secluded and gave me a chance to cool my temper. It was nestled between two ridges where the rocky cliffs broke away into the ocean. I took off my shoes and waded into the water. I inhaled the salt of the sea, felt the coarseness of the sand and the cold water on my feet, and listened to the distant rumbling of waves against rocks. Standing there, I pulled myself back from the precipice of rage and into the serenity of the sea.

"Hasting," came a voice from behind me.

"Leave me alone, Skírlaug," I said.

"What you saw… I understand why you left, but you have me all wrong." She waited for my reply, but I said nothing. "Please, Hasting, hear me and what I have to say."

I turned to face her. "What is there to say? You and Ragnar… so what? You are not my woman; why should I care?"

"I've seen how you look at me," she said. "And you have seen how I look at you."

"How's that?"

"Stop playing this game, Hasting. You know what I mean," she snarled. "I have known many men, and many men have tried to seduce me, including Ragnar, and they have all failed. But never in my whole life have I met someone like you."

"And what am I like?"

"When I look into your eyes, I fall under your spell. I can't control myself. And the worst part of it is, you have no idea what you're doing."

I laughed and said, "You have been ice-cold toward me since you arrived."

"Because of how I feel," she insisted. "What happened in Ribe, I thought it was a fluke. But when I saw you again, I—I had to protect myself."

"Protect yourself? From me? Do I strike you as someone who would do you harm?" I asked.

"Yes."

We faced each other in silence, both of us breathing hard. Even in the dark, I could see the shine in Skírlaug's eyes, the contours of her face, and the shape of her body. I felt drawn to her as if the gods themselves were pushing me forward. I took a step toward her, and she stepped toward me. We both took a second step together, and a third, and when she had drawn close enough, I reached for her. She pressed her bosom against me and relinquished control. I leaned in, and when our lips touched, she kissed me with more passion than I had ever been kissed.

But in the next moment, the cold steel of a blade pressed against my neck. I released her from my grasp, and she stepped backward several steps—a dagger in hand and out of breath.

"Tomorrow, you will fight Ragnar," she said. "Don't die."

2

The Duel

The night before the duel, I sat alone in my tent while my crew feasted and drank with Bjorn's men around a campfire. They sang songs, told stories, and cheered all night. My name was mentioned once or twice in the stories Rune told, no doubt to impress those who did not yet know me for the caliber of my deeds. Several of my crew returned to the tent and offered me a drink, but I abstained. Instead, I sat in the dark with a sharpening stone and my father's sword, and I focused on the work of readying the blade for the fight against Ragnar. The leather straps that wrapped the grip had worn through, so I tore them off and applied fresh leather from hilt to pommel. Ragnar, I thought, would use an ax or a spear. Most Danes preferred such weapons. But I believed my father's sword brought me luck above and beyond my abilities, and the Celts had trained me well in the art. Swords are graceful weapons, and the skill to wield one harkens to the profession of a skald who recites the songs of heroes and gods. Most warriors, at least those I had met in the North, did not possess the finesse needed to wield one. Swords such as mine were thought of as symbols of wealth and power and not particularly useful weapons of war. The Northmen and Danes did not forge them—they were made by blacksmiths in the Carolingian empire. To gird one was to flaunt one's wealth. I hoped Ragnar thought this of me, and that my martial skill with the blade would surprise him.

At sunrise, I walked through a mass of mead and wine-soaked bodies to reach the opening of the tent, and I traveled the muddied path to the burial ground. It was a beautiful resting-place. The sea surrounded us in all her majesty, and waves headed for the Morbihan crashed and broke on the jagged rocks, spewing foam and mist into a cloudless sky.

The salty sea perfused my nostrils with every breath. A constant roar of waves and wind filled the air and drowned out the barks and moans of seals on the protected side of the island that stirred from their slumber to begin their day's hunt. Cormorants and seagulls squawked, chirped, and wailed behind me in a ferocious struggle for which of them would have the chance to feast on the remnants of last night's feast. It reminded me of the pernicious squabbling of men over the scraps of lords and kings.

The Christians say we men are different from all other creatures in Midgard, but the more time I have spent in the wild, the more I have found fault in such a belief. The birds and seals and dolphins of the sea, and the stags and wolves and hawks of the land, all seem to hunger as we do, to feel pain as we do, and to desire what they do not have, as we do. We are not so removed from them as some might want to think. We are all temporary beings caught in the same cycle of life, death, and renewal. Though men dream of life eternal, removed from the natural order, nature returns to claim what it owns. Even the Aesir, our gods, cannot escape it. They, too, will perish —not by the hand of a god-like foe but the onslaught of wild beasts unleashed upon them by nature. Their time in the great cycle must end to make room for a new order. We cannot live without nature, and we cannot survive it.

Reminded of the closeness of my death, I closed my eyes, took in the sounds and smells around me, and fell to my knees in front of Horic's burial mound. A single tear coursed down my cheek.

I wish you were here, my friend. I had not yet acknowledged what Horic's passing had meant to me. The first days and weeks after his death, my mind had focused on all the challenges ahead of me. My heart had not begun to grieve. Horic had seen something in me, supported me, and taught me how better to lead my men. Bjorn had even said he believed Horic saw more of himself in me than in his own son. I had not met his son; he had not bothered to make the journey with his father in the years since we had established our foothold off the coast of Frankland.

On that, I agreed with Skírlaug—the king's son would not bother to travel to my island to ask me to swear to him. Part of me felt anger toward the king. How reckless he had been not to settle his succession when he felt illness upon him. A king should never die with his legacy in anarchy. We Danes and Northmen spend our lives forging the stories of our adventures that will survive our death, and Horic was no different. His failure to prepare his affairs imperiled his reputation and his memory.

Had I been a skald composing a song for him, I would not have sung much beyond the chaos his death dealt to the islands of Aquitaine and my land. What wars would the Danes fight in their homeland, how many children might be orphaned, all due to Horic's willful ignorance of his own demise? Was it fear that had paralyzed him? Or arrogance?

Not long after I arrived at the king's gravesite, I heard Skírlaug's horn on the wind. The burial ceremony had ended, and all that remained was Ragnar's challenge. I looked back at the camp and saw men begin to stir. Some walked with staggered steps, while others hunched forward. I knew all too well the pain they felt. I scanned the tents for Ragnar, but I did not see him, though I did spot Skírlaug emerge from the camp with a dozen of her men behind her. She had washed and applied fresh makeup, and she had let her hair down. Her gown reached to the muddy ground, so she lifted it up at the hips. We locked eyes as she approached.

"Are you ready to die?" She smiled.

My brow furrowed at her question, and I replied, "Not today."

"Men who believe they will die have nothing to lose. It makes them better fighters," she said.

I shrugged but said nothing.

She continued, "I cast the runes this morning."

"So you know who will win."

"I may." She waited for my response, but I had none to give. She glanced away and pointed to the field beyond the grave. "We will form a circle there," she commanded.

I have never met a harder woman to read. At times, she acted as if she cared for me, as she had in that briefest of exchanges, but her tone and temper changed like the tide of the sea. I could not forget last night's kiss, and the thought of her warm, soft lips plagued my heart when I should have been hardened for battle. Now she acted as if none of it had ever happened. Her eyes were expressionless, and I wondered if she wanted to confuse me, to fill my mind with doubt so I would lose the fight. Yet I could not think of what I might have done to merit a wish of death.

I knew that if I allowed her to continue to cloud my mind, Ragnar would have the upper hand. I reached out and grasped her arm. "Have you changed your mind about me?"

She froze. Her men surrounded me, ready to strike. I understood their meaning and released her. She shrugged me off and stepped back several paces. Where I thought I would see anger, I saw a deep sorrow. Her eyes welled with tears, and she wiped her hands on her apron. Without speaking a single word, she walked past me and toward the camp.

Once the men from both camps were standing where she wanted them, she guided me into the circle with a cold callousness I had only ever known from complete strangers.

Ragnar stood across from me, surrounded by his most loyal followers. He drank from a polished horn and murmured words that made those around him laugh. His unkempt hair and twisted, braided beard gave him the look of a wild man who still lived among the creatures of the forest. He radiated confidence.

Each of us received a shield from our men, and we approached one another at the center of the circle at Skírlaug's side. The closer we approached each other, the more the men roared in support of their champion. My men's voices joined together in a hair-raising chant, and I felt inspired by their faith in me. I needed their help, because inside my chest, my heart thrashed in terror. Ragnar had made such quick work of his son when we first met, I had half a mind to think I was outmatched.

"One shield, and one weapon," Skírlaug shouted over the roars of our supporters. "Stay within the circle, else lose the contest and face banishment; do not accept a weapon other than your own, else lose the contest and face banishment; do not yield, else lose the contest and face banishment. Do you understand these rules?"

Ragnar and I nodded. He locked eyes with me, and he had a grin smeared across his face, as if in a trance. He lifted his ax and shield above his head and turned to his men who cheered louder as he walked toward them.

I turned to my men, who continued to shout in support of me, and I looked at Rune and tapped my shield with my sword. Rune elbowed Fafnir who helped to spread a message among the others. One by one, they pulled up their shields and started to bang on them with the hilts and pommels of their axes, swords, and seaxes. The banging took on a menacing rhythm and, coupled with a chant led by Rune, it drowned out Ragnar's men.

Skírlaug stepped out of the circle, and as she did, all the banging of shields and chants and cheers turned into a muddled fracas. The fight had begun.

Ragnar stood relaxed on the other side of the circle. He took another drink from his horn and tossed it into the arms of his followers.

I took notice of the carelessness of his movements. I wanted to rub dirt between my hands to prevent my sword from slipping in my grip, but the ground had not dried since the rain. I lifted my shield and held it against my breast, and the rawhide trim pressed against my chin.

I glanced at Bjorn where he watched from the front of the crowd, his neck craned. He had a death grip on his ax's shaft.

A gust of wind swept across the field, and it pulled at my shield, but I held firm. It tore at Ragnar's shield, too, but the strength in his thick, veiny arm prevented it from moving much at all. Our duel served as a test of skill and grit, so neither of us wore armor—only simple short-sleeved tunics and baggy trousers wrapped around the calves from ankle to knee.

I lifted my sword to signal my intention to approach, and Ragnar responded by pointing his ax at me. It had a long, curved blade of blackened iron, and the wooden shaft had runes carved from head to handle. My heart fluttered again, telling me to withdraw, but I put one foot before the other, as I had done in every other fight, and moved closer to my foe.

Ragnar responded by charging at me in full sprint. His sudden burst surprised me, and I staggered my feet to repel him. He screamed wildly with high and low pitches and leaped forward like a bear closing in on its prey. His ax bore down on my shield, slid upward, and its curve locked onto the rim. With a quick jerk, he pulled my shield away from me and jabbed his shield at my face. I do not know how, but I ducked out of the way and saved my teeth.

I pranced backward, trying to stay light on my feet. Ragnar slowed to catch his breath. He had put tremendous energy into his first move, and his fatigue did not pass unnoticed. Yes, he was large and powerful, but he lacked stamina and speed. I circled and forced him to keep moving. He growled and charged again.

With a spring in my step, I parried his slashes, swipes, and lunges. I was a scavenger bird, circling my weary prey and waiting for my moment to strike. By his third charge, my confidence returned to me. He had played a good game of intimidation by rattling Bjorn's feathers, but he did not have the skill with a blade to back it up.

I had fought several men who relied on size and strength to win fights, but a lack of consistent training and skill always defeated them in the end. Lifting a mast upon one's back and wielding a blade are two different things, indeed.

Ragnar charged once more, and I knocked his ax clear out of his hand with my shield and struck him hard on the head with my pommel. He fell back onto his rump, dazed, and as he tried to scurry backward, I pressed the tip of my blade against the notch at the base of his neck. Blood dribbled down his face from where my pommel had cut his scalp. I looked into his eyes and, although I saw fear, I knew he had no intention of yielding. He nodded as if to tell me to finish the deed, and I nodded back.

"No!" Bjorn cried from behind me. "Stop! I beg you!"

Skírlaug leaped into the circle and shouted, "How dare you interrupt this sacred ritual!"

Bjorn stepped into my line of sight, behind his father, and said, "Ragnar is an honorable man and a great warrior. It is too soon for him to die."

"You know the rules, Bjorn. Either he yields, or he dies," I said. "He challenged me, and now he must pay the price."

"I do not yield!" Ragnar growled with his chin pressed against my blade.

"Please, Hasting… brother. I beg you to spare him."

"The gods demand blood," Skírlaug barked.

"I do not care what the gods want," I said. I looked into Bjorn's sorrowful eyes, and I could not bring myself to refuse him. I glanced around the circle at all the blank faces of the men whose futures rested on my decision. "Help me take him," I said to Bjorn.

I lifted Ragnar by the arm, and Bjorn joined me, and we helped him outside the circle. Bjorn stayed with him while I returned to Skírlaug.

I shouted for all to hear, "Horic is dead. Ragnar is defeated. I am your king now!"

My men cheered, but Ragnar's remained silent. I kept my gaze on Skírlaug who scowled and crossed her arms. She hated Ragnar; I could see it in her eyes. That I spared his life upset her. She took my hand without looking at me and raised it above our heads.

"Hail Hasting," she cried out, "the king, chosen by the old gods!"

After her words had a moment to settle, I stepped forward.

"I wish to speak to all the ship captains who swore an oath to Ragnar," I said. Fifteen or so men stepped into the circle to face me. "Ragnar is banished. The rest of you have a choice: swear to me, or sail home with him in disgrace."

One of the ship captains spoke up. "Why should we swear to you if you cannot kill a man who dishonors you?"

I frowned and opened my mouth to reply, but Skírlaug touched me on the shoulder and said to them, "Do you see those who follow him? See how they show love for him? Did you ever show such love for Ragnar, or only fear?"

"And yet you dishonor them by letting Ragnar live," another said. "Your honor is their honor."

"No!" I spat. "I honored my champion by allowing his father to live. Is that not proof of my devotion to those who follow me?" My words stirred their chatter, but I continued. "And see how they are dressed and the arms they carry. Vindreyland, my kingdom, is rich and grows richer each day. Swear to me, and you, too, will enjoy the fruits of these lands."

Not a single man stepped forward. I looked at Skírlaug who remained icy and distant. She shook her head.

"What would it take for you to swear to me?" I asked.

My question appeared to confuse them. They murmured among one another for a moment, but low enough so I could not hear. Their gestures spoke of angst and uncertainty, and some of anger. At last, they all turned their backs and walked away. They returned to their side of the circle and led their crews back to camp to pack. Two of them helped Ragnar to his feet and walked with him back to his ship.

Bjorn joined me as they left. "Good riddance," he said.

"Good?" I growled. "If they leave, who will take our salt this summer?"

"We still have Hakon," Bjorn said.

Skírlaug glared at me. I could tell she thought letting Ragnar live was a mistake, and I did not understand the consequences that would follow.

"The gods were promised blood," she muttered again. "And they will have it."

We packed our ships, and the two fleets sailed their separate ways. Ragnar's fleet set north with no salt, and we returned to my island with no silver. Left with four ships and a shrinking retinue of perhaps five dozen warriors, I feared what the summer might bring. It would not take a vast army of Northmen or Franks to challenge us for the salt trade.

For days I sat in angst on our journey home, stewing over what fate had in store for me. Skírlaug did not help. She kept repeating that the gods demanded blood, and I had deprived them of it. We stayed apart during the journey home. She sailed on her ship with the warriors who had accompanied her from Jutland, and I remained on Sail Horse with my old crew. Despite the distance, I kept looking out toward her ship to catch a glimpse of her.

My heart sank when we took sight of Vindavik. A column of smoke reached from the village to the heavens, scattered in the sky by the wind. It was not smoke from their hearths; a fire had run through it. We had to wait for the tide to rise again before entering the inlet to the Concha. The longer we waited, the more I raged. I sensed my men's distress, but I could not tell if it was from the smoke or my boiling anger that I did not try to contain.

At dusk, the water had risen enough for us to row to port. No sooner had Sail Horse's hull butted against the pier than I sprang from gunwale to dry land and raced up the beaten path to the village.

A fire had roared through the houses, leaving behind crumbling timbers and smoldering coals. There were a few slain throughout the town, some burned and others maimed, but most of the villagers had vanished. I hunted for survivors but found none. Rune and Fafnir joined me, but they too found nothing. A short while later, Bjorn arrived in the village out of breath and terror-stricken.

"They've taken everything," he said. "The salt reserves, the wine, the silver—all gone!"

"And the villagers," I added.

"Could it have been Ragnar?" Bjorn asked.

"Impossible," I said. "They could not have beaten us here. It was someone else. There are Vikings nearby, and somehow they knew we would be gone."

Skírlaug appeared unannounced, as she often did, and surveyed the destruction around us. She closed her eyes, took in a deep breath, and opened her arms wide as if to embrace the sky.

"You see? The gods always reap what they are owed," she said.

"What will we do now?" Bjorn asked.

"Ragnar's men have abandoned you," Skírlaug said, "and soon will those who still follow you."

"Quiet!" I snapped at her. "I've had enough of your quips for one day."

My outburst enraged her, and she stood next to Bjorn and glared at me scornfully. Bjorn stepped back as if to leave but stopped when I drew my sword and pointed it at him.

"Do not dare," I snarled. "If you had not pleaded for your father's life, none of this would have happened. You will help me climb out of this hole, or I will kill you myself."

"What do we need?" Rune asked in an attempt to defuse the situation. "What needs to happen to make things right again?"

"We need laborers to farm the salt," I said. "And supplies to last next winter."

"Sounds simple enough," Rune suggested. "All we need to do is raid for slaves and supplies."

Taking and owning slaves continued to make me uncomfortable. After all, I had been a slave, and the first Viking I had sailed with, Eilif, had shown distaste for the slave trade. Though Bjorn had initially taken the villagers on my island as slaves, I had given them their freedom and asked for their loyalty in return. The arrangement had worked well, particularly since they had nowhere to run—Vindreyland was an island, after all. Our entire way of life required someone to toil, and under the constant threat of war and invasion, the strongest of us had to devote our time to training in the skills of war. On my island in particular, I had no community, no pool of natives from which to draw labor, nor could I bring any from the North to do the hard work of salt farming, so we were under tremendous pressure to take slaves.

Without salt, I had nothing to trade, and without trade, I had no wealth—without wealth, I believed, my men, even Bjorn, would abandon me for another chieftain. I needed wealth for the army I hoped to raise to fight and kill Renaud, the count of Nantes, and the man who murdered my first love. Revenge remained ever-present on my mind. In this way, I was a slave to my success, always pushed to do things I did not particularly want to do, to pursue my revenge.

It was the same when I had sailed with Eilif. Though he had not wanted to take and sell slaves, there came a point where trade alone could not make the wealth his followers expected him to provide. He had to betray his instincts to survive another day, lest a challenger rise to kill him and take his place.

"Raid?" I balked. "I haven't raided in years."

"Raiding is no one's favorite thing to do," Fafnir added, "but often, as it is now, it is necessary."

Rune and Fafnir spoke true. The way to mend the damage done by whomever had raided Vindavik was to start anew and raid for slaves and supplies. Raiding was a terrible business, but it had to be done. In the years I had controlled Vindreyland, I had not needed to raid—as part of our arrangement, Horic and Bjorn had done the raiding on my behalf. Raiding stirred awful feelings of shame and guilt that I harbored from my first raid with Eilif and Egill. I thought back to the helpless man on the beach who they'd forced me to behead. The mere thought of it made my stomach turn with disgust. I understood, however, why we needed to raid. My entire life's work teetered on the edge of a blade, and for the first time in the years we had spent in Vindreyland, my revenge felt out of reach.

"Where will we raid?" Bjorn asked. "The coasts are deserted. Our kindred have devastated the beaches of Frankland for decades; they will know how to evade us."

I looked at Skírlaug as I thought, and she straightened herself and said, "The hungrier the wolf, the more risk it will take to capture prey."

"Haven't the gods seen enough blood?" I asked her.

"They have had their fill," she said.

"Then tell them to stay out of my way."

3

Proving my Worth

It was in these early years of my time as a Viking that I learned the act of acquiring wealth was as important as the wealth itself. Warriors wanted wealth, yes, but they also wanted the chance to fight alongside men of great deeds whose skaldic songs might include a small mention of the men who helped them.

Not every man is destined for greatness. What separates warriors of fame from all the others is hard to define. Only the gods know, and the best a man can do is hold his nerve in the face of mortal danger. It is an easier task for a young man than for the old. Young men are arrogant and foolhardy, and Bjorn and I were no different. With few ships, and faced with the need to launch a successful raid against the most powerful empire in the known world, we chose to try our luck in the Loire Valley. No Dane or Northman had ever raided past the fortified bridges, and everyone who followed us knew it.

Bjorn had grown quieter since my duel with his father. He obeyed every command I gave him, almost subserviently, which I took as his way of giving me thanks for sparing his father's life. But his quietness made him hard to read. He had lost a father figure in Horic, so I could not blame him for his grief, but I would have expected him to show a little more responsiveness. I had gambled nearly everything to acquiesce in his request to spare Ragnar. Now we risked the lives of everyone in our fleet to remedy the consequences of his plea.

We navigated the mouth of the Loire and dashed as fast as we could upriver. In the years since I had sailed with Eilif, the villages on the riverbank west of the fortified bridge had all been abandoned. Once, the Franks would have known of our arrival from far away, but now we could sail the first leg of the river with impunity.

Our first obstacle was the fortified river bridge. It had sunk several Northman fleets over the years, and it had shown no sign of waning in strength. But we had the advantage of knowing it was there, and we had a plan.

We came ashore downriver, and that night Bjorn and I led separate raiding parties up each bank to cut off the soldiers on the bridge from the road. We could not allow a single man to pass through, else they would call up the Frankish cavalry.

I scaled the thick underbrush of the riverbank with two dozen men at my back, and we tiptoed up the road to the bridge. Two stone walls as thick as a man's breast flanked the bridge, with a wooden roof and walls build between them. The fortifications overlooked five massive stone archways in the river that were blocked off with chains and logs. Faint torchlight emanated from the space between the wood planks of the walls, and we could hear murmurs and soft laughter from within. We had caught them by surprise.

Our plan was simple: barge through the doors and kill everything that moved. Before my men and I reached the door on our side of the bridge, I heard a horrible clank and crash, and the cries of Bjorn's warriors and the screams of their victims. The lock on the door on our side of the bridge wiggled, and the door was flung open. Without looking, I charged toward it with my sword held forward. It met with the flesh of a Frankish soldier who had tried to escape. The others behind him attempted to run past me, but my men gobbled them up as water does a flame. Inside the building, Bjorn took a torch and studied the workings of the logs and chains that blocked our passage.

"How do we lift the log and chain?" he asked.

I shrugged. Bjorn lowered his torch near a porthole to study another part of the mechanism, when a small ball of dried thatch caught fire. It dropped down where we could not reach it and put off heavy smoke. The embers below teetered on the sill of a barrel. I had seen such barrels before, and I knew what was in them.

"Run!" I shouted as I darted backward.

Smoke filled the building as we scurried away. No sooner had our last man passed through the doors than the lower level burst into flame and engulfed the whole structure. Red and yellow flames rose into the night sky like a beacon to alert the Franks we had arrived. I exhaled in a long sigh, knowing we had no chance of surprising our enemy beyond the bridge, no way of overwhelming their defenses.

Bjorn put a hand on my shoulder and said, "I am sorry, brother. But how did you know it would ignite so?"

"The embers of your torch landed in a barrel of tar and oil used to burn ships," I said. "It was bad luck, is all."

"Bad luck, indeed," Skírlaug added from behind us. She emerged from the darkness and stood at my side to watch the fire, foreboding written across her face.

"I thought you told the gods to stay out of my way," I said.

Skírlaug laughed. "The gods are not so petty as to follow your every move."

As the fire burned, the pulleys that held the logs and chains weakened and snapped, and we heard them drop into the water. We would not know until daylight if the river would still be navigable. We retreated to our ships and rowed downriver away from the bridge to avoid any entanglements with the Franks.

At dawn, my ship led the journey to the bridge, and, to my surprise, the stonework had remained intact. Three of the five archways were clear, so we took down our masts and passed through them unhindered. An eerie quiet preceded us; the river had no other boats or barges fording from bank to bank. A half-day of rowing later, we took sight of Nantes, its white limestone walls glimmering in the morning light. Among my men, I alone had ever set eyes on the city or entered it, and I saw the same wonder on their faces as when I had first seen it. Danes and Northmen did not build such things.

The river split into two around the island of Nantes, flanked on both sides by towering walls. The branch of the river to the north was much broader and slower than the one to the south. We rowed along the northern outer bank, beyond the range of their archers. On the wall's ramparts, crossbowmen in their shiny coned helmets and blue overcoats stared us down through their sights. They did not fire on us, but they were ready.

From the aft of my ship, I signaled for Bjorn to follow, and he gestured to the others behind him. We rowed on, passing under the bridge to the city gates and into the river beyond. The walls felt as though they continued forever, and it took a good long while to row to the other end of the island.

And there I saw her.

On the ramparts overlooking the eastern shore of the river, a tall, slender woman with long blond hair flowing in the wind looked out from her perch at our passing ships. I squinted, but I could not see her face. My heart leaped as if I had seen a spirit from another world. I sat on a chest at the aft of my ship. Rune noticed the sway in my shoulders and my sudden collapse and hurried to my side.

"What is it?" he asked.

"I thought I saw something… someone," I whispered. "It cannot be."

"Who?" Rune asked.

I did not answer him. Instead, I held his face and said, "You are a good and loyal friend."

I hopped to my feet as if nothing had happened. The last thing I needed was for my crew to question my state of mind. We had raiding to do, and the men would need me at my best. Still, what I'd seen stirred a whirlwind in my gut, and the feeling lingered most of the day. All our ships passed the city without a single crossbow bolt fired. The Franks had apparently locked themselves in for a siege after seeing the smoke from the bridge, but we had no way of besieging them, so we navigated the river out of their range. Bjorn's ship rowed up beside mine, and he leaped across the gunwales to meet with me.

"What now?" he asked with a loud sigh. "Have you ever been beyond the city? Do you know what is out there?"

"No," I said. "But the empire is vast and filled with wealth. And upriver, they won't know we are coming—at least, not for a while—nor will they expect us."

Bjorn bared his teeth and looked at me sidelong. He leaped back across the gunwales to his ship, and they veered away to give us the lead. I had no idea what we might find further inland. Undeterred, I stood at the aft of my ship, cupped my hands to my mouth, and shouted to Bjorn, "Give it two days!"

How long would it take for a lord to muster an army to chase us down like wild dogs? The thought made me quiver, but I remained undeterred. We would find a village or monastery, I believed, and we would take wealth and slaves.

After dusk on that first night, we made camp in the forest with a single fire in a large pit, and everyone assembled around it as night fell. We did not gather around the fire for warmth; summer was at our doorstep and, so far inland, the night did not cool down as much as it did on my island.

I walked the camp with Bjorn to assess the morale of the men, and as we walked, we heard whispering. A tense mood had taken hold of my army. Some of Rune and Skírlaug's men who did not yet know me felt betrayed by what I had done but had no recourse. My streak of bad luck, from the loss of Vindavik to the burning of the bridge, had not passed unnoticed. Whispers flowed. Rune had relayed to me that some of the men spoke of a curse. I knew too well what such rumors could mean; if the men believed me to be cursed, it was only a matter of time before they killed me to cleanse the group of it. I had to take hold of the situation. I approached a small group of Sail Horse's new crew and pulled one of them up by his collar.

"There is no honor in whispers," I growled.

"We would not whisper if you had any," one of them said, and the rest laughed.

My anger turned to rage. "A cleaved head does not plot."

"Good thing you do not cleave heads," another said with a chuckle.

"Hasting..." Bjorn started.

I drew the dagger that I had used to kill Hagar and drove its point into the man's neck. I did not know his name, but his insolence put everything I had built over the past few years at risk. Never have I thought of myself as a rash man, but at that moment I lost all control.

The man's allies drew their weapons and leaped up at me, and I drew my sword to meet them. The dark made it hard to see their blades, so I parried backward toward the fire. With the light at my back, I could see them breathing hard and in utter fear of the next stroke of my blade. Perhaps I should have said something to them;

maybe I could have saved them. But something took over as if a force from another world had possessed me, and I charged at them with an enraged cry.

I parried, I blocked, I stabbed, and I lunged, and before I knew it, three more of Rune's recruits lay on the ground, bleeding onto the decaying leaves of the forest floor. One of them squirmed as he bled, his eyes filled with terror. I knelt at his side and grasped him by the hair.

"You asked for blood," I said so everyone could hear, then ran my sword across the man's neck. Blood gushed with the rhythm of his heart until it stopped. I stood and faced the others who looked on in shock. "Who else questions my honor?"

None answered. The whites of their eyes glimmered in the dim firelight. Even my own men held their breaths. They had never before seen me act in such a manner. Pain has a way of digging deep into our hearts, and no matter how much we ignore it, the world around us always finds a way to draw it out.

The impetuousness of the men had struck a vein, and something deep within me lashed like a beast from the wild. My loss of control felt good, as if I had scratched an itch. Bjorn stepped between me and the others and put out his hands to calm them. He shot me a look I will never forget, one of fear and dread, but also approving, as if he had been waiting for that side of me to emerge for a long time.

In all our time together, I had shown great calmness and restraint, almost to a fault. Still, we lived in a world of struggle and pain that required swift action, impulsion, and violence. Above all, we were Vikings, and as their leader, I needed to remind my followers what I was capable of. The quality that they respected the most was my prowess, my ability to kill another man.

"You are a man, after all," Skírlaug said.

"What is that supposed to mean?" I snarled.

She smiled and slipped back into the crowd behind her. Her words enraged me even more, and I chased after her into the woods. My men split apart to allow me through, and they watched with blank faces as I vanished in pursuit of the völva into the dark. Tree limbs snapped and crackled as I pushed my way through the forest's thick undergrowth in search of her. I had no thought of what I would do or say when I found her. All I knew is I wanted to make her feel the pain I felt.

"Who are you, Hasting?" Her whisper seemed to come from all around me.

"Why these games?" I asked in reply. "You accused me of playing games, but ever since you arrived, you have toyed with me and tried to unsteady my nerve."

"Yes," she said. "You have learned to hide what you really are; I thought perhaps you had forgotten."

"Forgotten what?"

She wrapped her arms around me from behind and said, "Who you are, or should I say, what you are."

"What am I, then?"

I grasped her hand and twisted it down and around and caught her in my arms. She pushed herself up against me and latched on like a leech. Her touch felt familiar, and when I tried to push her off, her lips met mine. My desire to harm her faded away, and I picked her up off the forest floor and pressed her against the trunk of an oak tree.

She held me around the neck with one hand, and with the other reached down between her legs. I pushed up her dress to expose her naked legs and thrust my pelvis against her. Her hand guided me where it needed, until we were joined together.

She breathed into my neck and whispered, "More, faster."

My nails sunk into the soft flesh of her hips as I held her, and the more I dug in, the more she bit into my neck. I thrust harder and longer until she moaned and howled into the night. She then wrapped her arms and legs around me and squeezed. When she reached the height of her pleasure, she went limp with a tremble in her hips and a twitch in her legs.

"The one you fear most lives deep within you," she said in a hushed tone.

"Enough with these riddles!"

When I turned my back for but a moment to adjust my trousers, she vanished into the forest. Unnerved, I returned to camp to find the men resting by the fire. When they saw me reappear, they got to their feet with palpable angst. The bodies of the slain had been moved, and the forest floor where they had bled out was clear. Bjorn met me with a warm embrace.

"I have had words with all the men," he said. "You have proven your worth. They will follow you."

"Good. Tomorrow, we will raid."

As I stood near the fire with Bjorn, I spied Skírlaug walking the periphery of where the light touched. She did not move closer, but I sensed she wanted more from me, and I left again to join her. We walked to the edge of camp where she had made her tent, and she invited me to stay with her in her bed. We settled into each other's arms and slept until dawn.

My fleet rowed another half-day upriver and, as I had hoped, we arrived at a small port with a road leading to a stone monastery in a large clearing. The first people to spot us fled the dock toward the monastery, and they left all their wares behind. We donned our arms and armor and prepared for a fight, even though I felt confident we would encounter no resistance.

Skírlaug's ship was the last to arrive, and her men stayed behind to watch the other boats while Bjorn and I led the raid with sixty men at our back. She called me over before we were off and took my hand from the other side of the gunwale. She pulled me in and we kissed for a short but satisfying moment, and then I left to join Bjorn at the head of the raiding party. We marched with the confidence of conquerors at first, then slowed as we approached the monastery grounds.

"Skírlaug is your woman now, eh?" Bjorn asked through his blackened iron helm that was skirted in maille.

I could not see his face, but I knew he was grinning.

I had no time to laugh. Within a stone's throw of the monastery's front gate, the ground rumbled. We had walked into a clearing with nowhere to take cover, and the Franks had sent horsemen to meet us. I looked to the west and saw them gallop around the tree line and lower their spears. We had to act fast or be ripped apart.

"Form a wedge!" I ordered. Bjorn looked at me, confused, and I said, "Trust me, my friend."

The Celts used wedges to disperse cavalries, and it often worked. Where horses barreled through or jumped over straight lines, they tended to disperse around well-angled spearheads, or at least that is how I had seen it done when I had fought for Nominoë.

I goaded my men to form the wedge. One row knelt and set their shields on the ground, and another row held shields above the first and leveled their spears between them. We completed the spiky formation just as the horsemen reached us. Some of their spears slammed into our shields, but their force split apart as I had hoped they would, and they galloped on.

As they passed, I counted their numbers—they were fewer than fifty. Rather than turn for another charge, they circled the field to the east and paused to study us. They had not expected to meet such an organized foe, and I wanted to use it to our advantage.

"Who is our best spear thrower?" I asked Rune.

"Easy, it's Torsten," he said.

Rune understood my meaning and wiggled his way through the mass of bodies to find his man. Torsten moved up behind me with his spear in hand. He was a quiet man from my first crew—a talented sailor and Sten's closest friend. I had not known he could throw a spear, and I looked forward to seeing him in action.

"Do you see how they gather around that horseman there?" I asked him.

We gazed at their small troop and focused on the man near the front who faced the others and spoke to them. He wore expensive armor with a broigne of metal scales, a shiny conical helmet trimmed with a cloth band along the rim, and a round painted shield hanging from his left shoulder. The other horsemen also wore helmets and shields, but instead of maille, they wore blue cloth tunics with leather padding to protect them.

"I see him," Torsten said.

"Good, I need you to kill his horse. Whatever you do, don't kill him."

Torsten nodded, and when the horsemen charged at us again, he readied his spear. Again, a few of their spears slammed into our shields, and they flew past our formation in a thunderous gallop.

Their leader rode in the middle of the fray, and Torsten launched his spear with all his strength. The spear flew too high and glanced off the man's shield, but they rode so close together that the spear struck the horseman behind him in the shoulder and knocked him off his horse. After their second charge, they stopped downfield from us and turned to study us again. Their horses danced and neighed in excitement, and they appeared winded from their two charges.

"I have failed you," Torsten said with a lowered head.

I patted him on the shoulder and said, "It was a good throw."

"How do we stop them?" Bjorn interjected from the other side of the formation. His patience was wearing thin.

My men looked panicked. They had never fought a cavalry before, and the horses frightened them. There were no magnificent steeds in the North, only small workhorses for carrying goods up steep mountains. Frankish horses were tall, muscular, and powerful, and they could kill at a gallop. The key to defeating them, I knew, was to take away their advantage.

The cavalry charged again, but this time they had throwing spears of their own, and they launched several dead in the middle of our formation above our shields. At least a dozen of my men fell. When they had passed, the horse whose rider Torsten had wounded broke away from the rest and trotted toward the monastery on its own. I needed to do something to break the stalemate. I tore out of our huddle and ran for the horse. It backed away from me closer to the wall, and for a moment I feared it might run away and leave me exposed to the next charge. I slowed from a run to a walk, and I made the clicking sound the Celts made with their tongues to call it to me, hoping the Franks used some of the same training techniques. The beast looked petrified, but it did not run. I reached for the reins, and as I did so, the horse reared its head a few times but acquiesced.

With the reins in my hand, I mounted it and took a moment to remember how to ride. The Celts trained their horses differently from the Franks, but the core movements were the same. At first, the horse bucked and hopped as if to throw me off, but I stayed steady in the saddle. The next charge had begun, and a small group of horsemen broke away from the core group to charge at me. I screamed at the horse and swatted it on the rear to get it to run, and it kicked a few times before we galloped away from the Franks toward the back of the monastery. To my relief, they did not give chase that far. It took another short while for my horse to cooperate with my commands. Once it did, we trotted around the far side of the monastery and back to my army. They had not moved, and the Franks stared them down from the field beyond. With the confidence of a king, I rode up to my men and stood at their side.

"You can ride one of those things?" Bjorn cried.

I smirked and said, "Watch and learn, my friend."

With a kick of my horse, I galloped off toward the Franks. I had the advantage of surprise—never could they have imagined a Dane would mount a horse and challenge them. I heard them cry out in their language and holler at their horses to turn and give chase.

I kicked my steed again and rode forward, steering around the back of the monastery. The more we rode on, the more their horses tired. They broke off their pursuit when I reached my army again, and I positioned myself behind the wedge, to the cheers of my men. I drew my sword and held it in the air.

"I am Hasting, King of Vindreyland, and I accept your challenge!" I called out to the Franks in their language.

The cavalry charged at us once more, still confident they had the advantage. My men readied, and I led my horse in a circle in the back to gather momentum for a run. I took sight of their leader and charged at him. His spear was pointed for my chest, but Torsten and two others threw spears at him, and he pulled up from his aim. I pulled my left leg over the saddle and rode on a single stirrup before launching my whole body at him as I passed, and I tackled him off his horse and into the waiting arms of my men.

As I landed, my head smacked against one of my men's shields, and I rolled on the ground in pain. What I had done had sent the enemy running, and my men broke their formation. Some made for the monastery right away, while others stayed behind to see if I had been mortally wounded. Bjorn kneeled beside me and examined my head.

"You'll live," he said. "For now, relax. We won."

I closed my eyes to rest and did not fight the men who carried me back to the ship. Skírlaug then took me under her care. She had me lie down on some furs and placed padding under my head. I fell asleep almost instantly, exhausted by all that had happened.

I awoke on my ship to Skírlaug's soft voice humming to me as she passed a wet cloth over the wound on my head. She saw my eyes open and smiled. Someone had carried me back and lain me on soft furs near the steering paddle. We were still docked near the monastery, and across from me, the Frankish leader was bound and gagged. Up the path to the monastery, my men were returning with crates of goods.

"How long have I been out?" I asked Skírlaug.

"A while, but not too long. How do you feel?" she said.

"I am hurting," I said.

She looked back and forth into each of my eyes. "The blow to your head was hard. I will need to watch you closely in case you start to swell. I have seen men die in the night after a blow like that."

"Comforting."

I sat up and put my hand over my eyes to block out some of the daylight. The brightness seared inside my skull. Once I'd steadied myself, I crawled over to my prisoner and removed his gag.

"What is your name?" I asked in his language.

He said nothing in reply.

"You are a nobleman?"

I balked at him when he remained silent, and I sat back on my furs. We glared at each other, and had I not felt as much pain as I did, I might have beaten the answer out of him.

He was a young man, perhaps around my age, with dark hair and silvery eyes and a long, thin face with a pronounced square chin. Skírlaug shot him a few glances —at first, I thought, to keep an eye on him, but then I understood she thought he was handsome. To my relief, he in no way reciprocated.

"Do you know what happened after—?"

"The horsemen fled," she said. "Your men are singing songs of your victory today."

"And slaves?"

"The grounds were deserted. Bjorn says they found plenty of silver and wine, but the monks fled during the battle."

It all made sense. The Frankish cavalry had not sought to defeat us; they had meant to delay our attack so the monks could escape. Their leader had not counted on me riding a horse and throwing myself at him the way I did. I now had a valuable prisoner, but to whom could I ransom him? To know what to do with him, I needed to know his name and rank. Despite several attempts to ask him, he never said a word.

Our raid had proved successful. The men loaded our ships to the brim with loot, to the point of almost sinking. We even had to leave some of what we had taken at the docks. If I had wanted to continue upriver to find slaves, they would never have fit on the ships, so our success left me with one choice: to return home.

We rowed downriver and passed by the city again, and as we did, my prisoner's eyes lit up with hope. When we passed without stopping, he glowered. His expressions told me he had some kind of relationship with the city, and I hoped that Count Ricwin would pay in silver for his return. As we passed Nantes again, I looked to the ramparts but did not again catch the apparition I had seen on our way upriver. Still, the Franks had mustered no soldiers to the walls, and not a single person crossed the bridges. It had the look of an abandoned city.

The journey home proved uneventful. My men celebrated our victory and rejoiced at my heroic deed of capturing our prisoner. For the time, I felt secure as their leader. Yet my stomach turned, and sleep evaded me. The salt trade and wealth of my island remained in shambles. How would I produce salt in the summer without slaves?

4

Nominoë's Bargain

My friend Váli once said that I am a lucky man, and luck is what I had when a large, bulky cog appeared on the horizon north of my island. I had expected someone to come. After all, I had taken an important prisoner, and the Frankish nobility would not leave him with us to rot. Part of me hoped Renaud was on the ship, but he would not be so reckless.

It took the better part of a rainy late-spring day to reach the Concha, but their lack of speed did not surprise me. Cogs are built to carry cargo, not outsail our longships.

We girded our weapons and met the vessel at the wood-planked pier along the water's edge. On the squared aft flew a burgundy banner with the emblem of a fox's tail. These were Vennetes, Celts from the Vannes region of Armorica, and friends of mine, but not at all whom I had expected. Seeing their banner filled my heart with joy.

The cog took care to maneuver past the longships but nearly nicked one on the gunwale and butted up against the pier. Brown-bearded sailors with disheveled hair and salt-worn faces tossed us their ropes, and we helped them tie off.

Bjorn stood behind me and craned his neck as they put down a plank and soldiers disembarked to face us. The soldiers wore bronze-crested helmets and held gold-painted shields that gave off a crimson glimmer in the afternoon sunlight. These were no ordinary conscripts;

they were professional warriors who belonged to Nominoë's elite personal guard. Behind them, a man in a burgundy cape and cap walked the plank to the pier. He smiled and opened his arms to embrace me.

"Hasting, my friend!" he cried out in our language. It seemed he remembered the little I had taught him.

"It's good to see you," I said in the Celtic language. "Nominoë, this is Bjorn, my brother-in-arms and a nobleman in the North. Bjorn, this is the king of Armorica, Nominoë."

Bjorn gave him a small bow and said, "Hasting has spoken often and well of you."

Nominoë seemed to have understood Bjorn and nodded, then stared past us at Sten. "By God, that is a large man," he said. "What do you feed your children in the North?"

I laughed with him and translated what he had said for Bjorn. Bjorn chuckled, but crossed his arms.

"Come, we must drink to celebrate your arrival," I declared.

Nominoë put out his hand and said, "I prefer to stay near my ship. It's nothing personal, Hasting, but I must take precautions."

"Of course." I forced a smile, then called for our servants to bring up a table and a tent, as well as plenty of bread, cheese, and wine.

Nominoë's men brought up his furnishings. They included a large oak chair with armrests carved in the likeness of lion heads, and a burgundy pillow sewn into the frame. Once the tent and table were set, Bjorn, Nominoë, and I sat together in the shade. We poured wine from a simple wooden carafe into ornate silver chalices from the monastery.

Nominoë scrutinized his goblet and glowered when he saw the Christian cross embossed on its base. He took a cautious sip, and from behind the lip of the chalice his eyes scanned the monastery grounds.

"Who lives in the monastery?" He wiped a streak of wine from his upper lip.

"I do," I said.

"Hmm."

I sensed he had more to say, and I believed I knew what he wanted to say, but I did not want to hear it. "What brings you to my island?"

Nominoë frowned. "Word of your recent foray into the Loire has traveled far, my friend. And you have taken someone important to me. I have come to ask you to release him."

"My prisoner?" I asked. "He is one of yours? But he rode with the Franks…"

"Has he told you who he is?"

I shook my head.

He chuckled and continued, "He's as stubborn as his father. Well, I am here to tell you that you unwittingly captured Lambert the Younger, son of the last count of Nantes."

"A nobleman?" I laughed. "That is wonderful news. The Franks will pay a good ransom for him."

"Not exactly," Nominoë said. "You see, his father Lambert, then the count of Nantes, backed the wrong player in the last rebellion against Emperor Louis, and the emperor replaced him with Ricwin. Lambert, the father, died of the plague while in exile with the emperor's son Lothaire; Lambert the Younger came to me for help. His father and I had been good friends, you know. I managed to convince Charles of Neustria to grant Lambert lands east of the Pays de Retz and keep him in mind for the countship if and when Ricwin dies."

"And if Ricwin dies, you want Lambert, who is friendly to you and your cause, to be first in line for the countship of Nantes," I said, putting all the pieces together.

"Precisely," Nominoë said with more vigor.

"So Ricwin will not pay a ransom for him."

"It would be more convenient for him if Lambert never returned," Nominoë said. "He wants Renaud to succeed him."

The name made me quiver. Hearing it evoked a memory of Asa's lifeless body, robbed of the child she carried for him, and her severed head abandoned in the slime and mud. Seldom have I said that I hated another man, nor have many of the deeds of my life as a warrior been driven by hate. I have known cruel men, but Renaud stood apart to me as the most irredeemable, vile wretch of them all. As far as I was concerned, the man did not have a moral bone in his body. If what Nominoë said proved true, it would serve me as much as him to return Lambert.

"I can't release him for nothing in return," I said. "My men fought hard during the raid. Some of their brothers in arms were slain."

Nominoë took another sip from his goblet and scanned the land around us. "You are so few this summer," he said. "Where are your kin?"

He had a penchant for uncovering the truth, whatever it was, and I knew it would not take him long to extract the information he wanted from me. We had fought together and bled together, and I trusted him with all my heart. Still, I did not want him to know how disastrous my summer had been to that point, since he bought salt from us and expected a regular shipment in late summer.

Bjorn glanced at me with blank eyes—he had understood nothing of our conversation. I had asked him to learn more about the other languages of the region, but he lacked the patience for it. Where Bjorn lacked patience in skills of the mind, he more than made up for them in his physical prowess. Still, I longed for him to have the ability to participate in negotiations with me. He might have had a creative way to dodge Nominoë's question that I had not considered. I knew I had to be honest with my old friend, not because he would see through me, but for my own honor.

"It has been a hard spring," I said.

Nominoë listened. I told him of Horic's death, of my duel with Ragnar, and of the raid carried out on Vindavik in our absence. He sipped from his goblet, eyes wandering from time to time across the landscape behind me, and he did not interrupt. When I had finished recounting my most recent hardships, he leaned forward with one hand on his knee and spoke in a hushed tone.

"I think we both knew the arrangement you had with the Danes would not last forever," he said. "I am sorry to hear of your king's death. Though I never met him, I know him for an honorable man to have earned your trust and respect."

"He was." I crossed my arms and leaned back in my chair. Bjorn mirrored my movements.

Nominoë continued, "As I am sure you remember, salt is an important resource for us as well. My people would suffer if we did not have the salt you send. Since the loss of the island, the count of Nantes has diverted all the production from Guérende to the empire. He has also withdrawn his trade agreement with us. Without you, we would have almost no salt at all."

"As of now, we are in no position to make good on this year's shipment," I said.

Nominoë put down his chalice and wiped his lips with his sleeve. He took in a deep breath and surveyed the marshlands that surrounded the monastery and village. His eyes found their way to Bjorn, and he took to stroking his scruffy chin.

"Shame," he said. "Tell me, Hasting, when is Hakon due to arrive? You have so few ships here, he must have been delayed this year as well."

I gave Bjorn a distressed look and said, "We have heard nothing from Hakon or Halldóra."

"I see," Nominoë said.

The news did not seem to shock him in the least. "Do you plan to produce salt for him?" he asked.

"Yes."

"How?"

"We'll work," I insisted.

"Do you really think your friend Bjorn and his warriors will enjoy farming salt?"

Bjorn looked at me with utter confusion. I translated what Nominoë had said, to which he laughed and replied, "We will take more slaves."

"And how many slaves have you captured so far?" Nominoë asked. "And since when do you call them slaves? I thought you had sworn off the practice."

Bjorn stood and left the tent in anger when I translated what Nominoë had asked. For a man with so much experience in diplomacy, he had exercised little caution in his line of questioning. As for me, I too felt anger, but I understood where he wanted to take our conversation. Rather than challenge him, I remained silent and held his eye.

"I have a proposition for you," he said.

Nominoë had an air of confidence about him as if he'd known what he had wanted to ask me long before we'd sat down to drink together. Seldom had I seen him leave anything to chance. In the years since we had last met, he had grown even more cunning, perhaps driven to it by the constant war of spies between his people and the Franks. In no uncertain terms, he had heard of how few ships we had taken into the Loire and understood we had raided out of necessity.

"By what you've told me, it is evident Vikings still find it worthwhile to raid this island, despite your supposed ownership. They have robbed you of the manpower to farm the salt, and your allies in the North who are willing to travel this far to trade with you are dwindling in number."

"Where is this leading?"

"I need salt, and I have the manpower to put toward its production. However, I fear the men and women I could send here would soon succumb to a raid."

"I would protect them."

He had dangled bait in front of me, and I had shown myself far too eager to take it. He had a way with words and knew how to lead someone, even me, where he wanted.

"Would you? And how did that work for you this past spring? No, I'm afraid you and your men would find an excuse for a far-off adventure, and my people would be left exposed to another attack."

"Biting words," I growled.

"But true words." He looked at me with unblinking eyes and impeccable steadiness in his gaze. "You have told me enough about how a Northman ship operates to know that you will not last long as their leader if you do not give them what they want: wealth and glory. I propose to give you the former, and to free you to pursue the latter."

I leaned forward to rest my elbows on my knees and bobbed my head in thought. His proposal was vague, but I had a good idea of the question that would follow. He spoke true. I stood in a precarious position with those who had sworn to me. Without Horic to back my legitimacy, I had to prove myself to them on my own merits.

Thoughts of the raid on Vindavik also passed through my mind—whoever had carried it out either thought me dead or wanted it. Rune's news that rumors of my demise had emerged in Ireland did not improve my situation. In a world where reputation stands as the foundation of the loyalty between men, stories have the power to kill. Moreover, Nominoë had struck a chord when he evoked our lack of excitement. The winter had proved bitterly dull, and even I had found myself longing for more adventure. Yet, a part of me wanted to live such a life, one of comfort and ease, and one unsaddled by the burden of having to kill or be killed.

"I would prefer to stay and make wealth through trade," I admitted to him.

"I know," he said. "And one day, perhaps, you will. Your heart will always be of Armorica, and you are always welcome in my home should you need refuge and respite."

I sat back in my chair, wiped at my eyes, and said, "How do we make this work?"

Nominoë smiled and took a long sip from his goblet. "I will send the manpower to farm the salt, with a company of soldiers to protect them. They are not slaves, Hasting; do not treat them as such. We will take control of the village and marshes. My scribes will draft a royal charter, giving you a land grant to name you the owner of the island; you will be the owner of the island in title only. I will require you to maintain amicable relations with or fight off Vikings who might think it wise to raid here. In return, we will offer you ten percent of the salt production to do with as you wish."

"And the Franks?" I asked.

"Let me worry about them," he replied. "Although I do expect you to return Lambert to me."

After a short pause, I said, "I accept your proposal, but I will only return Lambert to you once your people have arrived to work the marshes. I have to show my people that we have made a fair trade."

Nominoë leaped to his feet and embraced me. He stood back and exhaled with relief and took another drink from his chalice.

"Excellent!" he rejoiced. "Now, I do have one last piece of news to share with you." Nominoë handed me a letter. "The emperor and his sons struck a peace agreement at Crémieux. With the civil war over, I thought the Franks might try to invade Armorica, but instead, they have made an offer of peace. I received this invitation from our friend Renaud d'Herbauges before I left."

I opened the letter and read it. Most of it contained the usual references to God, but the last few sentences struck me like the clap of Thor's lightning bolts.

We invite the emperor's Fidelis Nominoë of Vannes to witness the baptism of the Lord of the Rennais' son, Renaud II, with his parents Renaud and Anne, and under the protection of Ricwin, Count of Nantes.

"He took another wife quite fast," I said with trembling hands.

"The letter struck me as odd, so I had some of my spies look into it. Anne is indeed Renaud's second wife, but his first died in childbirth over ten years ago," Nominoë said.

"You don't think Anne is…?"

"I do."

My hand quivered. A part of me refused to believe what I had read and heard. When a man sees the woman he loves depart for the afterlife, he does not expect her to return. The pain from Asa's death still stung, though the years that had passed had allowed my grief to lessen some. If she was alive, whose body had I burned on the pyre? Over whose cleaved head had I wept? I could not believe Asa would have approved of murdering an innocent woman to fake her own death; there is no honor in such a thing.

"She died," I whispered.

"That is what they wanted you to believe, I would think," Nominoë said.

"But why?" I asked with force behind my words. "Why the deception? What purpose would it serve?"

Nominoë shook his head and replied, "Deception, my friend, is Renaud's greatest strength. I am not the man to answer your questions. However, there is someone here on this island who has spent a good amount of time in Ricwin's court. Perhaps he will have answers for you."

I remembered I had a Frankish nobleman shackled in the monastery crypt. Our conversation had taken such a turn, I had put him out of my mind.

Bjorn had remained nearby with some of my crew, and I left the tent to approach him and ask that he fetch Lambert. His scowl told me he remained displeased with what Nominoë had said to him. Despite this, he patted me on the shoulder and gave me a nod. As he left, I tapped him on the arm and smiled as a sign of thanks, but I knew he saw the sorrow in my eyes. It was the shortest of glimpses, and his eyebrows pulled down into a slight frown. He did not utter a word—he nodded and bolted off to the monastery to do what I had asked.

I have always admired his unquestioning loyalty. Throughout my life, I have had the good luck of meeting and sailing with men who saw more in me than I saw in myself, and who, despite my fears, chose to trust and to follow me, but none more than Bjorn.

Meanwhile, Nominoë had poured himself another cup of wine. He took the liberty of topping off my goblet, and when I sat to rejoin him, I saw he had filled it to the brim. He raised his cup and insisted I join him.

"Let us celebrate our renewed and continued friendship," he said.

I raised my cup to meet his. We both took hearty gulps and sat in silence. A breeze had picked up again, but not so much that it shook the tent. The sun circled overhead and cooked the ground around us. The heat spilled into our shade, and I felt thankful we had a cover overhead to keep us cool.

The grass around us came alive with the chirruping of crickets that echoed across the land, broken by occasional birdsong. Soon I found myself closing my eyes to take in the sounds and smells and the warm breeze on my face. No sooner had the chirping in the field stopped when I opened my eyes again to find Bjorn with Lambert in tow.

"Not a scratch," Bjorn said as he pushed Lambert toward Nominoë.

My patience for my guest had worn thin, and with all I had on my mind, I could not sit still. Nominoë stood to embrace Lambert and patted him up and down to ensure he had no wounds. Lambert smiled for the first time since we had captured him, and he rubbed his wrists where we had clamped them in irons.

"Thank you," Nominoë said to me. "We will sail home forthwith. Look for a fleet of our ships on the horizon within a fortnight to deliver the labor you need." As he left and his servants started to pack his belongings, he turned back one last time and said, "And Hasting, if at any point you feel the impulse to attend the baptism, you know where to find me. I will be happy to take you with me."

Bjorn took Lambert back to the crypt while the Celts sailed away, carried by a late-day wind from the south. I watched them from the Concha in silence, holding the invitation to the baptism in my hands, and ruminating over its implications. As I watched them drift out of the bay, I felt a warm presence approach.

"Where have you been?" I asked Skírlaug.

"A völva's work is for the gods to know, and the gods only," she replied, her face a marble statue. She nodded at the letter in my hand. "What does it say?"

"It is for those who read, and those who read only," I said.

Her cold stare melted away, revealing the eyes of a woman wounded by my words. She tried to take my hand, but I withdrew. When I moved to catch up with Bjorn, Lambert in tow, she followed, but at a distance.

I walked up beside our prisoner and said to Bjorn, "Take off these irons; this man is not our enemy."

Bjorn looked angry, but rather than argue with me, he tossed me the loose ends of the shackles. "Do it yourself," he snapped.

I took Lambert back to the monastery, sat him at the feasting table, and offered him all he could eat and drink. He chomped through the meat and cheese and bread we gave him like a famished bear. Skírlaug sat with us, her concern apparent and suffocating. When Lambert had eaten his fill, I slid the letter Nominoë had given me across the table to where he could read it. He glanced at it and then looked at me.

"Do you know the people mentioned in this letter?" I asked him.

He nodded.

"Have you met them all?"

He nodded again, his eyes wide with fear. I had not meant to frighten him, but I was a ship at full sail heading to port, and there was no stopping me.

"Anne, mentioned there, do you know where she is from?"

Lambert shrugged. I took his silence as a refusal to speak. I stomped around the table and clamped the irons around his wrists again. He looked up at me with his shoulders slumped forward and his hands between his legs. I called for two of my warriors to take the prisoner back the crypt.

Skírlaug scurried up behind me and tried again to take my hand while I spoke with them, but I shrugged her off before she could say anything. She glared at me from the doorway as I called for servants to bring food and drink to my hall for a feast.

My men trickled into the main entrance in short order, and it took little convincing to get them to eat and drink. Most of them had remained in a festive mood since our victory on the Loire. Out of caution, I had abstained from joining them, but given the gravity of all I had learned that day, I acquiesced to the pull of my desire to lose myself in the bliss of a raucous feast.

With little left to do but wait, we rested, played, and drank heartily. The Christians say idle hands are the devil's workshop, and we lived it during that fortnight. At first, it seemed harmless fun. But soon, those with less of a taste for debauchery sat out the onslaught.

Bjorn was among the first to remove himself, but he did not object to those of us who continued. In fact, he seemed amused by it. Since we had met, he had known me for my strict discipline and relentless dedication to self-improvement in everything from garnering loyalty from my men, to sailing my ship, to practicing the martial skills of war. He had known me to do things that would advance my reputation as a warrior and sea captain and had never witnessed a moment where I lost myself in something trivial. As I let my guard down, Bjorn started to talk more and laugh more freely. Skírlaug, on the other hand, disapproved, but she said nothing to stop me. She watched us from afar, continuing whatever it was she did to commune with the gods in private.

When the fortnight came to a close, I alone sat on the mead bench the morning following one of our feasts, still drinking. I had out-played, out-drunk, and outlasted them all.

That morning I will never forget. Skírlaug entered the chamber and sat at my side. She caressed my face and pulled my goblet of wine away from me.

"I know you are in there," she said.

I scoffed and looked away, but she pulled my chin toward her and gazed into my eyes. Where I thought I would see fear, I saw strength, and she took my hand and led me up the stairwell to my bedchamber. Her servants brought up clean water, fresh linens, and plenty of bread. In the corner of the room, she had accumulated some herbs and flowers in a bowl and placed them on a small wooden writing desk in the corner. As she tried to sit me on my bed, I reached around and groped her. She shoved me back and slapped me.

"You are not yourself, Hasting!"

"It's only a bit of fun," I insisted.

"You are lost," she said in tears. "I knew it would happen. The gods told me as much."

"Would happen what?" I slurred.

She gave me another shove, and I fell into my bed. "We will talk again when you have slept this off."

She left the room, and a key twisted in the lock. I leaped to my feet and worked the handle, but she had locked me in. An inexplicable rage possessed me, and I roared insults at her while kicking and banging at the door. I was still too drunk to put any real strength behind my strikes, but I am sure they terrified Skírlaug.

It did not take long for me to tire and collapse into bed. When I awoke again, night had fallen. A dim light from the moon shone through the small window in the opposite wall. The night was clear, and the moon was full; its light illuminated the island and the sea to the horizon. Any other night, I would have admired the beauty of it, but finding myself without a drink, a burgeoning angst grew in my stomach and heart, and my hands and feet had a feverish tremble. My mouth felt dry and dirty, so I reached for the water Skírlaug had left me.

I heard no sounds from downstairs, not a single voice singing or outburst of laughter. Utter quiet had enveloped the monastery. I returned to bed, and as I lay back, the room started to spin around me. My stomach twirled, and although it was empty, I turned to look for a chamber pot. Skírlaug had thought to leave one by the writing desk, and I crawled to it and dry heaved for a long, uncomfortable while.

Skírlaug must have heard me, because she unlocked the door and entered the room with a candle in hand. She had two of her warriors behind her, and behind them I caught a glimpse of Bjorn and Rune who craned their necks to see me.

"Go away!" I snarled between heaves.

Skírlaug set her candle on the desk, took some of the herbs, and crushed them with a stone mortar and pestle. She mixed the product of her work with a dash of mead and gave the final concoction to me to drink. I gobbled it down as a starving wolf would a cut of meat, not for the herbs, but for the mead. In an instant, I felt a wave of fatigue wash over me. I returned to my bed, no longer sick, and fell asleep again.

I dreamed a terrifying dream that night, filled with ghostly, ghastly figures seeking to rip the flesh from my bones. They had trapped me in a hole, and they swiped with their mangy claws when I tried to climb out. A giant wolf circled behind them, prowling and growling, and I knew it wanted me for itself. Behind the wolf was a stone wall, tall as a mountain, with a woman looking down at me from the top. I could not make out her face, but I could see her hair drifting on the wind, and her voice echoed through an endless sky.

She called to me and begged that I climb the wall to save her. But the wolf stood in my path, massive and imposing, daring me to try.

The following day, I awoke to find Skírlaug sitting at the desk, preparing another potion. No sooner had I opened my eyes than she put down her tools and sat at my bedside.

"How are you feeling?" she asked.

"I'm fine," I said.

"Are you?" Her eyes pressed for a real answer.

I did not have one to give, except to tell her my dream. She listened, and she nodded at everything I described as if she had heard it all before.

Finally, she placed her hand on my leg and said, "Tell me the story of how you met the wolf Fenrir."

It was a strange question, but I did not refuse her. I told her of the storm that had overtaken Sail Horse on my first voyage with Eilif and Egill, of how Bjorn and I had been thrown overboard, and I described for her the encounter with the wolf.

Under the waves, the ocean had felt still, and I'd floated between the light of the surface and the impenetrable blackness of the deep. A shadowy beast raced through the water as if across a grassy field, and the closer it drew to me, the larger it seemed to grow. It opened its jowls as if to devour me whole. On its first charge, it seemed to have missed me, but when it turned around again, it ran at something else—it ran at Bjorn.

I reached for Bjorn and pulled him out of the wolf's path, and at that moment, I felt Egill's powerful hands grasp me and pull us both to the surface.

"Egill believed you saw the wolf Fenrir," Skírlaug said.

"And I believed it, too," I added.

"Perhaps you did have contact with Fenrir, but contact with beings from the worlds beyond ours defies the senses. You did not physically see him. So close to death, your soul briefly crossed the threshold that separates us from them," she said.

"Why would he choose me?"

She laughed and said, "Do you really think so highly of yourself? He didn't choose you. You chose him."

I stood with clenched fists and paced to the other side of the chamber. My mouth was dryer than ever, so I took a quick sip from the goblet she had left on the writing desk and swished the water in my mouth. My hands, arms, and legs felt jittery, and waves of anxiousness gripped me and subsided. I realized I was not in control of my own body. It thirsted for wine.

"How could I have chosen him?" I snarled.

"When Odin created Man, he created us in his likeness, with his qualities as much as his faults. Like him, we are all of two essences. The first lives in the light, allows us to love, to create, and to live as the gods in Asgard. The second is the shadow that is cast when we stand in that light. It is a darkness that dwells within us and harkens to a more primal time when we were not yet separated from the wild. Those of us who are more familiar with the gods know that Fenrir is Odin's shadow. Because he refuses to acknowledge it, to acknowledge the darker parts of himself, the beast will emerge in the end to destroy him. Ragnarok will not be the destruction of the world, but rather the reconciliation of its two parts.

"Fenrir is your shadow, too. Your proximity to death the day you fell into the water forced you to reach deep into yourself to find the strength to survive. He helped you, and ever since, you have looked to him for your strength. To become a Viking sea captain, you hid away your more womanly side—of tenderness, empathy, and affection—to live in the shadow of the beast. In fact, it seems you have become your own shadow. You have gazed into the abyss and encountered a part of yourself most men will never know or understand. But you are also in grave peril. Fenrir is a voracious beast. Everlastingly hungry if left unchecked, capable of consuming all that you are—he has brought you to the brink of your own demolition."

Everything she said resonated with me. I felt a part of myself yearning to boil to the surface, and another holding it in. It was as if the gods and the Jotún had chosen my heart as their battlefield. With a heavy breath, I sat beside Skírlaug and lowered my head into her lap. She stroked my hair and caressed my face.

"Is that what you saw in me when we first met? You saw the beast?" I asked her.

"Yes. The man you show yourself to be in the light is admirable. You are honor-driven, fair, loyal, and generous. Your shadow is raw, seductive, and ambitious. I could not resist the temptation to immerse myself in it. To know it is to know Fenrir, and to know Fenrir is to know a part of the Allfather that even he does not know."

"Back then, I was in control. What has changed?"

"Whatever was in that letter reopened a wound that weakened you and allowed him to take control. Will you tell me now what you saw?"

I sat back up and reached for the parchment Nominoë had given me. Skírlaug looked down at it with curious eyes. As I unrolled it, she placed her hands over mine. Somehow, I sensed she already knew what it said. Tears streamed down her face in black streaks, and she leaned forward to kiss me on the lips.

"Just tell me," she said.

"Asa might be alive, or at least Nominoë thinks so," I said. "He invited me to join him to see for myself."

"Do you think she is out there, Hasting?"

"I do."

"Then you must go and see what she has become. To tame the beast, you must first heal the wound that has festered, and to heal the wound, you must find closure over what happened," she whispered.

"What do I do once I have found her? How do I heal the wound?"

"I can only show you the path," she said. "It is you who must follow it."

5

An Unlikely Friendship

In the time it took me to feel myself again, Nominoë's ships had returned to the island with dozens of families and a cohort of soldiers, as he had promised. They took up residence in the village under Bjorn's instruction and set to work fixing up the abandoned buildings. Their operation was self-sufficient. Their ships would sail the salt to Vannes and return with supplies for the laborers.

We Danes did not need to lift a finger to earn a portion of the wealth they would make. When I saw how well my new arrangement with Nominoë had turned out, I could not believe my luck.

That luck did not last.

Skírlaug's servants prepared Lambert for the voyage to Vannes by cleaning him and feeding him a hearty meal. I sat with him that morning, and we ate together. His demeanor told me I made him uncomfortable, but his face glowed at the prospect of escaping my island.

As we ate in silence, Bjorn entered the hall and sat at my side. I had not seen him in days, nor had I expected to see him at the monastery so late in the morning. His frown made me squirm. A pallor in his face expressed all I needed to know. Skírlaug had warned me the day before that he would visit me, but she had given me no inkling of what to expect. My behavior of late and subsequent absence, I presumed, did not sit well with the men.

"There is something I must say to you, my brother," Bjorn began.

I sat back with a mouth half full of bread and stared him down.

He gulped and continued, "There is nothing easy about this, and if I had the choice, I would not say it. Please know that I love you as my brother."

He looked around the room as if he might find someone to help him spit it out. Lambert could not understand him, yet he stopped eating and watched with his big, dark brown eyes.

Bjorn's hesitation took so long that I turned my shoulder to him and kept eating. He fumbled over a few words before he formed a full sentence again.

"We want you to step down," he said.

"What did you say?"

Bjorn cleared his throat and said, "Step down, I beg you."

"If you want to take my place, make the challenge, man!"

"I do not want to challenge you. None of us do," he explained. "We all look up to you and admire what you have done. But we have also seen a troubling side to you. What would have happened if Hakon had arrived last week and attacked us when you were drunk?" His voice started to rise. "Or worse, when you locked yourself away in your chamber, so ill you could hardly walk?"

"How dare you," I cried.

"Hasting, you are not yourself," Bjorn shouted back.

"No!" I dragged my arms across the table and knocked everything in my reach onto the floor.

"That is not the Hasting I used to know," he said. "You are walking a path we cannot follow."

"We are Vikings," I hissed. My nerves were still frayed from not drinking, and I struggled to contain my rage. "This is what we do—we raid, we kill, we drink, and we fight. I have done nothing except grow our wealth and give words to the skalds to praise us in their songs."

"That is not who we are, and you know it," he growled back. "We are guided by the example of our gods, to honor and to glory. How you have described us sounds very Christian."

"What are you saying, Bjorn?" I asked.

"You have never been one of us, not entirely," he replied.

"Is that what this is all about?" I scoffed. "You think that because I was raised by the Celts, I am not enough of a Viking for you?"

"That's not what I meant. I only—"

"You only what? You only meant to discount everything I have done for you?"

Skírlaug appeared in the stairwell at the end of the hall. She hurried over to us and put a hand on each of our shoulders. We had been so impassioned by our argument that neither of us had realized we had both stood and faced off. Never had we come so close to blows outside of training. The more I stared him down, the more nervous he looked.

"Sit, both of you," Skírlaug spat.

We complied with her order.

"Need I remind you of your kinship?" She turned to me and looked into my eyes and said, "Hasting, do you even know what he is asking of you?"

"He's trying to take my place as king," I said.

Bjorn shook his head and scoffed, and Skírlaug explained, "Not at all. If you could look past your anger, you might see that he only wants to help you."

"He is asking me to step aside," I snapped.

"I am," Bjorn said, "but only for a while, until you are well."

"That's not how things work among the Danes," I insisted. "If I pull back even a little, I'll be overthrown, and you and yours will kill me."

"On a ship full of fresh recruits who do not know you, that might have been true, but not with us. We are professional warriors and we honor our oaths," Bjorn said. "Hasting, you are the only one here capable of achieving what you have achieved. Horic saw it; Hakon saw it; I see it. We all want wealth and glory, and we believe you will give it to us. But this past winter, and then after Horic's funeral, you changed. We've all seen it, and we are all terrified of what it means for us."

I looked at Skírlaug, who nodded in agreement, and I said, "All right, what do you want from me? Spit it out."

"There has been grumbling among the men. It started before Horic's funeral, and I wanted to ignore it, but I saw what they saw, too. And I am sorry I asked you to spare my father's life; it did not help your cause. I should have known what it would do, but I could not bear losing him."

"I did not want to kill him, either," I said.

Bjorn continued, "You are not the man you were even a year ago. Something has been eating at you from the inside, and it has become more and more obvious. Skírlaug told me a little of what she thinks has happened, and what she thinks needs to be done to remedy it. I want to help."

I tilted my head to the ceiling and laughed. When I felt I had control over myself again, I said, "Tell me what you have in mind."

Skírlaug put her hand over his mouth and said, "Go find her, heal the wound, make yourself whole. We will wait for you here."

Bjorn pushed her hand aside and said, "Yes, that."

My friends had rebelled against me, and now they asked me to abandon my place and title of my own will. My mind and soul were still too blinded to see the generosity and empathy of their offer. The life of a Viking is unforgiving, and in any other company, I would have had a sword run through me or an ax cut me down. That Bjorn and Skírlaug had agreed together to give me the time to heal spoke of their deep loyalty for me. I was still angry, but as I considered their words, I no longer had the word *betrayal* on the tip of my tongue.

I agreed to their terms.

Rune and Fafnir stayed with me at first as I prepared my provisions for a journey to the mainland. I wore the same cloak and jerkin as when I had left Vannes. On my belt, I girded my father's sword and a leather satchel full of silver deniers. I asked Rune and Fafnir to give me some time to sit and rest before my journey. In truth, I wanted to sneak away so as not to upset those who had sworn to me.

We shared a last long look, and each of them gave me a nod. I sat on my bed and reflected. Where I thought I had hidden the less honorable parts of myself, everyone else had evidently seen the truth. They understood that if we had any hope of rising to the wealth we had enjoyed under Horic, I would need to heal the wound in my heart so that I might have the strength to lead them against whatever challenges lay ahead. As I walked alone from the monastery to the port, I noticed a crowd gathered at the water's edge. When I approached them, Bjorn stepped forward and embraced me.

"We've come to see you off," he said as he held my shoulders. I looked past him at the gathering of warriors who gazed back with sorrowful eyes. "Our oaths to you still stand. May you find that which will make you whole again, and when you return to us, we will follow you."

"What will you do?" I asked him.

He glanced back at his men and said, "Rune and Skírlaug will stay and wait for you. But you know me; I refuse to sit still." He smirked and wrapped his arm around my shoulders. "I think I will take my ships and see what trouble I can get into back in Jutland. Just for a while."

As we walked together toward the Celts' cog, the crowd split apart to form two columns leading to the plank. They reached out to shake my hand as I passed, and each of them offered their own words of praise and support. Most of them wished me luck. So far as I could tell, they had all recognized my faults of late, and they all wanted to see me well.

I struggled to understand what I was witnessing at that moment. I'd always believed that if I showed weakness as their leader, they would rise up to kill me and take my place. That is how it had been on Eilif's ship, and even on mine with my first crew. Here, my followers did not take advantage of my weakness but instead lifted me up through it. I learned from them that the best leaders are not those who rule with prowess alone. They are those who have won over their followers' hearts with hope for a better future—if they are patient enough to wait for it. I had thought myself trapped by the social constraints I had witnessed with Hagar and Eilif. Instead, I had developed a more meaningful relationship with those who were sworn to me. What had made the difference? I did not yet know, but I thought back to my father who had said reputation is everything. Somewhere, somehow, consciously or unconsciously, I had forged a reputation that mostly shielded me from the damage of my faults.

Rune and Skírlaug waited for me by the plank. Sten and Fafnir were there too, and a few of the others from Sail Horse's crew. They embraced me in silence, some longer than others, and Skírlaug left me with a soft kiss on the cheek.

With a heavy heart, I boarded the cog and waved to them all as the Celts set sail for Armorica. Somehow, I felt at ease on my own, whereas the days and weeks before I would have abhorred it. My heart had experienced a significant shift, and the decision to leave the island in search of myself felt right. When the cog crossed over into the open sea, I settled on a bench along the wall to the upper back deck. The sailors had cut Lambert loose and given him total freedom, and he walked back and forth along the wood planks to stretch his legs. We had not given him much room to roam at the monastery, and for that I felt some guilt. The crypt's ceiling hangs low, such that even the shortest men must stoop.

For days the cog crawled across open water, rocked by wind and waves. Its crew sailed with masterful skill, but even the greatest masters of their craft can do nothing without the proper tools. Unlike our ships where we suffered the weather above deck, the cog had a large area below where they cooked, ate, and slept.

I had never slept so well at sea—the wood-framed cot they gave me, the top of a double bunk, was dry and warm. For what they lacked in speed, they made up for in comfort. At night, the ship sailed on, where we Danes would have preferred to make landfall and camp. A separate crew manned the ship at night and returned below to sleep during the day. By first light, it seemed we had traveled as far as we would have on a longship, or perhaps further, since we did not sail the extra distance to reach land for the night.

On the second day, Lambert still had not spoken to me. He kept to himself and ate alone beneath the gunwale, while the rest of us gathered near the mast to talk. It struck me how at ease I felt with the Celtic sailors. They felt at ease with me too, and they had much to say. I gleaned from the beginning of our conversation that the Celts seemed to regard Lambert with suspicion. They even accused him of being a clever traitor.

"I don't see it," I said to Loïc, the man who oversaw the day crew. I looked back at Lambert who stared into the sky.

"See what?" Loïc asked.

"That he's clever," I said with a chuckle.

"Well, I heard he backstabbed his own father to get to the throne of Nantes. That's why he was exiled by Louis," another sailor added.

"You think so?" I said.

"Bah, they're just stories. Our king knows what he's doing. If he wants the kid back, then that's his right," Loïc said.

One of the sailors sitting to my left sat forward and stared at me. He tapped his foot on the deck, and I nodded for him to say what he wanted.

"Is it true that you speared Tristan at Pontivy?" he asked.

"It was a javelin, and yes," I said.

They murmured to each other excitedly after I answered him.

"I remember seeing you fight," Loïc said.

"You were there?"

"On the front line," he said. "I lost my brother in the trench."

"I'm sorry," I said.

"No, don't apologize. You fought like a god, as did Nominoë. I wouldn't be here if you hadn't taken Tristan down with your throw," Loïc said. "You all should have seen it. Tristan rode his horse over the trench, and he looked as if he might kill Nominoë. Hasting jumped in front of him and confronted the horse. It knocked him over and drove its hooves into the mud. But Hasting dodged, and when he scrambled to his feet, he found a javelin and hurled it at Tristan. I've never seen a man move like that."

"It was luck," I said. "If I had to throw it again, I am sure I would miss."

"Perhaps, but you succeeded when it counted," Loïc said. The other sailors were frozen in place, absorbed by his storytelling. He would have made a good Skald in the North.

"I take it that story has made its rounds in Vannes, then?" I asked.

"You don't know?" one of the sailors asked me.

I shook my head.

"You're the Hero of Pontivy. Our warriors still sing songs about your courage."

"I had no idea," I said. "And what do they say about my being a Viking?"

Both sailors shrugged.

Lambert was glaring at me from the sidelines. It had taken me a while to notice. The sun was setting, and the light of day had nearly gone. My companions drew my attention back to them with their goblets raised in a toast.

"To Hasting, the Hero of Pontivy," they said.

"I can't wait to tell my wife I met you in person," one of the sailors added.

That the crew embraced me, even celebrated me, seemed to leave Lambert unnerved. In every story he had heard, I am sure, the Vikings played the villains, so to see one fit in so well with the crew and act human must have been at odds with his preconceptions. Whatever churned in his mind, he worked up the courage to sit beside me on the gunwale one afternoon after the midday meal. After saying nothing for the longest time, I decided to help him.

"I hear your father was a count," I said.

He nodded.

His timidity stood contrary to what I had seen on the battlefield, or even in captivity. He had shown himself to be a strong, willful young man throughout, but when pressed to speak, he struggled. Why anyone would fear to talk after enduring what he had suffered in the past month made no sense to me. And then I heard it.

"You have, um," he began. He took a deep breath and lowered his head. It seemed he struggled with a severe bout of nervousness. As he tried to speak again, he bobbed his head, and he had a quiver in his wrists.

"It's all right," I said to put him at ease. "Don't hurt yourself."

He had a soft voice and a peculiar accent I could not quite place. He took in a deep breath and tried again. Whatever he had to say, I was confident, was of great significance if it took so much effort. I leaned closer.

"You have something in your… in your teeth," he said.

"Oh." I rubbed my finger on my teeth and grinned at him. "Is it still there?"

He nodded.

I reached into my pocket and drew out my ivory toothpick. After running it through all the gaps in my teeth, I asked him again, "How about now?"

"It's… it's gone." He sighed in relief when the last word left his lips.

"Thank you for pointing that out," I said with a crooked smile.

He nodded, and we laughed together. A large wave rocked the cog, and we both grabbed at ropes overhead to steady ourselves. Lambert nearly fell overboard, and I caught him by the collar just in time.

Despite the comfortable sunshine and warmth, dark clouds gathered over the horizon, and the wind had started to blow with more force. One of the sailors perched atop the mast and called down that he had spotted land. Our journey had reached its end, although it would be at least another day before we arrived in Armorica. As the commotion settled, Lambert and I relaxed a bit.

"Do you have a stutter?" I asked him.

"No, not a stutter," he said. "When I was a boy, yes. But now, I simply feel very nervous talking to people. I can't help it."

"So, you are afraid of talking to people?" I said.

"Yes."

"But you lead men in battle. Are you not afraid of fighting?"

He shook his head. "No, I am fine when I am fighting."

"It's just talking to people that makes you nervous."

"People I don't know," he added.

"Of course," I said. "And… what do you feel when you talk to a pretty woman?"

Lambert's eyes widened and he shook his head again.

"So, you can charge into battle like the bravest among us, but where you break and run is if I sit you in front of woman? You need to work on that."

"The priests say it is not so out of the ordinary. It's something to do with the humors," he said.

The more we talked, the easier it became for him, it seemed.

"I don't think it's that," I said. "But I am glad you finally talked to me. I can see it took a lot of courage."

"Where are you from?" he asked me.

"That's difficult," I said with a chuckle. "Where do I begin?"

I told him how I had been born in Jutland but grew up in Ireland as a slave. He was intrigued by how much time I had spent in Vannes with Nominoë, how I had fought with him, bled with him, and then left in search of Asa. I told him of how I had recruited men to sail to the ends of the world in search of Eilif and Egill and returned to Ribe without a scratch.

After a long while of storytelling, Lambert's eyes drifted. I paused for a moment.

"You, erm—" He grinned. "You like to talk, don't you?"

"I suppose I do," I laughed.

Afterward, I asked him about his place of birth and how he had ended up in Ricwin's service. He did not have much to say, but his manner made it a long story, and at times a difficult one to follow. What Nominoë had told me rang true—Lambert's father had been the count of Nantes, and their whole family had left in exile at the end of the last civil war.

What Nominoë had failed to mention was that Lambert's mother was a Celt from Priziac, and the daughter of the chieftain Morwan, who had rebelled against the Franks after Charlemagne's death. No wonder Nominoë wanted him as the next count of Nantes. A man with both Celtic and Frankish ancestry could ease the tension on the Breton March and allow Nominoë to push for independence.

"I hope you will forgive me for imprisoning you," I said when he had finished speaking. "Understand that we were desperate for some kind of leverage after the raid that decimated my village."

Lambert nodded.

I stared across the ocean toward land, wondering how Nominoë might receive me. As far as I knew, he had no idea I would arrive with Lambert, and I hoped he would not see it as a bad sign. I reached into my pocket and pulled out the invitation to Renaud's son's baptism. I rubbed the thin parchment paper and fixated on the name *Anne*. It seemed impossible that I could have mistaken the body discarded by Renaud after his retreat.

More than ever, I found myself doubting my senses and my memory. Never had I felt such disillusionment. I looked over at a group of sailors who sat around a small table anchored to the deck, talking and laughing over a cup of spirits. I nodded my head in their direction to invite Lambert to join me. Skírlaug had warned me not to indulge, but the draw of drink pulled me to my feet and led me to their table. Lambert and I sat with them, and they offered us our own cups. We told stories, we laughed, and one cup turned to many.

Lambert shook me awake to say that we had arrived. The final day of sailing had flown by like the flight of a raven, and I awoke to the taste of stale spirits on my tongue. I had made it back to my bunk to sleep, though I did not remember how. Lambert helped me to my feet, and we walked together up the stairs to the main deck.

It was late morning with a low overcast sky and less than a hint of wind. Men unloaded bags of salt onto the pier, while others carried it back to the city. I stepped down the plank with Lambert and led him along the path to Nominoë's hall.

Since I had left, they had rebuilt the church and repaired the buildings damaged in the raid. The city bustled more than ever with artisans and trade. New construction lined the outer wall, and entirely new districts had arisen where there had once been empty land. Where perhaps four thousand people had lived there before I had left, there were now more than eight.

No one guarded the entrance to Nominoë's hall, and the front door was locked. Lambert nudged me and pointed at the church. It occurred to me that we'd arrived on a Sunday morning during Mass. We approached the entrance to the church and pulled on the lever to unlatch the doors. A booming clunk echoed within the stone walls, and all the heads in the pews turned to stare. At the front stood Conwoïon, who paused in the middle of his sermon. He smiled when he saw me.

"Please, come in. There are seats here for you," he said, pointing to the pew nearest him at the front of the church.

We drifted to the front, with all eyes on us. As we passed several of the rows, I saw many familiar faces. Nominoë smiled and nodded, and to my astonishment, the lord Ratvili of the Rennais was present. His black beard had doubled in size and thickness, something I would not have thought possible. Sitting next to him was an angelic young woman with dark brown hair and light green eyes. She had thick, well-kept eyebrows and a pronounced cleft chin—she was clearly Ratvili's daughter.

Ratvili glared when he noticed my eyes lingering on her. She blushed and looked away, her hands placed flat in her lap. Lambert tugged at me to keep me moving, and when we sat, Conwoïon continued.

"To finish what I was saying, Jesus warned us through his sermon not to look outside of ourselves for salvation, but within. God breathed his divinity into us, and it is of us. But cast from Eden, and faced with the harshness of the world, we men have split our souls into two. One half draws us to the divine, the other to the excesses of this world. Because we are of this world, we tend to topple toward physical opulence and exigencies. As we do so, we lose touch with God, and the result is sin. I turn now to the parable of the prodigal son."

He stepped back to a table near the altar, placed his finger on the page of an open Bible, and read:

> *And Jesus continued: "There was a man who had two sons. The younger one said to his father, "Father, give me my share of the estate." So he divided his property between them.*

Not long after that, the younger son got together all he had, set off for a distant country, and there squandered his wealth in wild living. After he had spent everything, there was a severe famine in that country, and he fell into need. So he went and hired himself out to a citizen of that country who sent him to his fields to feed pigs. He longed to fill his stomach with the pods that the pigs were eating, but no one gave him anything.

When he came to his senses, he said, "How many of my father's hired servants have food to spare, and here I am starving to death! I will set out and go back to my father and say to him: Father, I have sinned against heaven and against you. I am no longer worthy of being called your son; make me like one of your hired servants." So he got up and went to his father.

But while he was still a long way off, his father saw him and was filled with compassion for him; he ran to his son, threw his arms around him, and kissed him.

The son said to him, "Father, I have sinned against heaven and against you. I am no longer worthy of being called your son."

But the father said to his servants, "Quick! Bring the best robe and put it on him. Put a ring on his finger and sandals on his feet. Bring the fattened calf and kill it. Let's have a feast and celebrate. For this son of mine was dead and is alive again; he was lost and now is found." So they began to celebrate.

Meanwhile, the older son was in the field. When he came near the house, he heard music and dancing. So he called one of the servants and asked him what was going on. "Your brother has come," he replied, "and your father has killed the fattened calf because he has him back safe and sound."

The older brother became angry and refused to go in. So his father went out and pleaded with him. But he said to his father, "Look! All these years I've been slaving for you and never disobeyed your orders. Yet you never gave me even a young goat so I could celebrate with my friends. But when this son of yours who has squandered your property with prostitutes comes home, you kill the fattened calf for him!"

"My son," the father said, "you are always with me, and everything I have is yours. But we had to celebrate and be glad because this brother of yours was dead and is alive again; he was lost and now is found."

Conwoïon lifted his head, looked at his congregation, and said, "The prodigal son was drawn to a life of sin, perhaps out of boredom, or out of some culpability. It took him losing everything to understand that the key to his salvation was in his heart all along. Thank you, everyone, for coming; let us finish with the Lord's Prayer."

The whole church joined in reciting the prayer and they ended with an enthusiastic *Amen*. I recalled reading the story of the Prodigal Son when I had studied the Bible with Conwoïon. At the time, it did not resonate with me—I had no father, and I had not inherited any sort of wealth from him. Given my recent trials, I now understood the story in a much different way. It had nothing to do with the relationship between son and father. It was instead about a conflict inside the son.

I saw my own inner conflict in him, and I lost myself in reflection, gazing at the cross on the wall behind the altar while the parishioners cleared the room.

"You came." Nominoë took a seat next to me. "I didn't think you would."

Without a word, I reached into my pocket and pulled out the invitation he had given me on the island. He scowled. Lambert glanced at the letter, puzzled, and he looked back up at Nominoë. Nominoë took the message and handed it to Lambert. The chamber continued to clear out, and when the last of Conwoïon's congregation had departed, Nominoë's tone turned dark.

"You did not need to come," he said. "I showed you the letter because I thought you should know. But I suppose I should have known better. Of course you would come. It is who you are…"

Conwoïon observed the exchange and approached us after he had put away his Bible. He had grown fatter since I had last seen him, but he had not bought new clothes. His habit stretched around his enlarged belly, tied off by a corded belt he no longer needed to hold everything in place.

"Here we are again, reunited," he said in a hushed tone. He saw how comfortably Lambert and I sat next to one another and asked, "Are the two of you friends now?"

Lambert and I both nodded.

I stood and embraced Conwoïon. He had been my closest friend while I lived in Vannes, and he had taught me the most. Under his tutelage, I had learned to read and write in several languages, a skill I should have done more to keep up. With him, I had learned all about the Christian faith, read its stories, and discussed their meaning. He had almost made me a Christian and had even convinced me to let him baptize me. My heart, however, had always remained devoted to the gods of the Danes.

"I wish this were a joyous reunion," Nominoë cut in. "But I'm afraid Hasting's arrival is going to be a problem. I need to speak to him. Alone."

The others did not question his command—they left the chamber through the main doors. In the courtyard outside, several people had gathered to wait for something. When Conwoïon opened the door, they craned their necks to catch a glimpse of me. The door shut behind them, and Nominoë and I sat alone in the church. He had seen the crowd beginning to gather, too, and smiled.

"You made quite an impression on the people here," he said. "The Northman who was tamed, and who became one of us."

"But I left," I said.

"You did," Nominoë agreed.

"I had to—"

"You are among friends here, Hasting." He put his hand on my knee. "Relax."

"What is it you wanted to say to me?"

He chuckled. "Such directness; it never ceases to impress me." He took a deep breath and sighed. "I know why you are here. It's my fault. I shouldn't have said anything. The wine, you see, it clouded my judgment. Getting you into the baptism—it's going to be nearly impossible."

There was fear written on his face. "I can't risk another war with the Franks. If you make the slightest mistake, it could mean years of suffering and death for my people," he said.

"I won't disappoint you," I said. "I never have before. I only want to know. I need to know."

He peered through the thin veil of my quest for knowledge and clearly knew I still wanted revenge on Renaud. I had to convince him to take me along, so I told him. "I saw her."

"You what?"

"I saw her. When we rowed upriver to raid, I could not see her face, but I swear it was her staring down from the top of the wall."

"My spies confirmed Renaud's wife is not of noble birth," Nominoë added with a sigh. "But they have not said where she is from."

"I need to know if it's her," I said.

"And then what? What will you do if it is?"

"I don't know. I do know that if I try to ignore it, it will tear me apart."

"I want to help you, I do, but you are too unpredictable, too dangerous." He crossed his arms and leaned back.

I slipped off the bench to my knees and clasped my hands together. "Please. Take me to the baptism. I have to know."

He looked down at me with wide eyes and his mouth agape. Never had he thought to see me so vulnerable, and it seemed to have changed his mind. With a furrowed brow and a deep frown, he touched me on the shoulder and nodded. I breathed a sigh of relief, but before I could embrace him, he stood and stepped between the pews toward the door. He waited for me to gather myself —my eyes had watered, but I'd stopped short of crying— and when I joined him, we made our way to the courtyard.

The crowd that had gathered outside was not large, but in it I saw many familiar faces. Some of the men who rushed forward to shake my hand had fought with me at Pontivy. Others I had met in Vannes, including the tavern keeper whose candles I had made for a year. Ratvili embraced me. He had saved us, in the end, from inevitable defeat against the Britons. His daughter stood behind him, her hands clasped in front of her, eyes averted.

"Hasting, I want you to meet my daughter, Morgana," he said.

"A pleasure to meet you," she said first with a slight bow. "Will you be joining us on our journey to Nantes?"

Nominoë nodded, so I said, "Yes, it seems I will."

She smiled up at me. Ratvili stepped between us and said, "Yes, yes. Fine, fine. We will sort it all out tomorrow."

"Tomorrow?" I asked.

"Yes, we leave tomorrow. You arrived just in time to join us," Ratvili said, his tone low and sardonic.

"Lucky, as always," Nominoë added.

A few more people approached to greet me and shake my hand, and then when the crowd dispersed, I followed Nominoë back to his hall. We entered through the oak door at the front and climbed the winding stairs to the upper level. The hearth roared, and his servants had set the tables with a lavish feast of meat, bread, and even some early berries. Lambert followed us in and sat next to me at the table.

"I am glad to see the two of you have gotten along," Nominoë said. "Please, eat and drink. You must be tired and hungry after your voyage. We have a long journey ahead in the morning."

Nominoë turned his back on us and walked off toward the stairs.

6

Lost but not Forgotten

We left Vannes at first light the following rainy morning in a single-file line of covered wagons flanked at each corner by an armed escort on horseback. An army of mules and horses followed, carrying all the supplies to make camp along the road. Lambert rode in Nominoë's wagon, and I rode beside them in the downpour, wearing the arms and armor of a Celtic warrior.

We had decided that I should dress and act as one of Nominoë's personal bodyguards to gain entrance to the city and the baptism. I even left my father's sword behind to fit the part. Once again, I found myself in the service of the king of Armorica. Yet from the moment we greeted each other that morning, I felt he wanted to put some distance between us.

At first, I understood his cold demeanor to fall in line with the plan we had devised—he should treat me as one of his soldiers, and not as his friend. Later in the day, when Vannes had almost vanished from sight, I rode up to his wagon and tried to say something, but he turned his back to me. Lambert indicated with a shake of his head that he did not want to speak, so I pulled away.

It took three long days to reach Nantes, and the entire way I stayed with the other soldiers. I ate with them, slept in their tent, and rode in position behind the wagons. Some of them remembered me from when I had trained with them under Yann. Others took an interest in the story of how we had defeated Tristan and Conomor. Though I had been shunned by my friend, I could not have asked for better treatment from his followers. We reached the bank of the Loire opposite the city in the late afternoon. While the servants and soldiers built a camp, Nominoë and Lambert walked across the bridge with three other soldiers and me behind them.

The towering wooden gates remained open, and the city bustled with activity. We saw no guards at the entrance or on the wall, and it seemed the Franks had not noticed our arrival. How reckless they appeared as they prepared for the baptism of one of their lords. My fleet could have torn the city apart if we had known to strike during a festival.

After we stood at the gate for a good long while, a man wearing a silky blue tunic and elegant pointed shoes scampered over to us with a leather ledger in his hands.

"My lords, welcome!" He gave us a quick bow and continued out of breath, "Forgive me, I do not yet know the faces of all the lords in the region. You are?"

"Nominoë of Vannes, and I have brought the count a gift."

"Oh," the man said. "Yes, yes. You came… you are here… wonderful." He opened his ledger and sifted through the pages until his finger stopped in the middle of one of them. "Nominoë of Vannes."

"And who are you?" Nominoë asked him.

"I am the count's new steward," he replied without looking up.

"Is there a problem?" Nominoë asked.

"No," the man cried out. "I mean—no, no problem." He put on a forced grin. "Will you need lodging in the city during your stay?"

"No," Nominoë replied. "We have set up camp on the other side of the river."

"Good," the man said. "I will inform Lord Ricwin you have arrived. He will send a delegation to meet with you at your camp and discuss the details for this week."

"So we wait," Nominoë said.

"Yes, in your camp," the man insisted.

He had not given Lambert a second look, which told me that he had not long held the title of steward. His hurried speech and nervous demeanor suggested the preparations for the baptism had not unfolded the way his master would have wanted. He followed us out as far as the bridge, then scurried back inside the walls out of sight.

Nominoë scowled and stormed back to camp. A man of his title should have been better received, and I could see in his eyes he had not enjoyed the treatment he had received from the count's steward. Celts had always felt mistreated by the Franks, and it did not take much of a slight to enrage them.

Back at camp, Nominoë sat in his tent with a goblet of wine in his hand, and he warded off anyone who tried to join him. I stood guard outside, and it took everything in me not to enter the tent to speak with him, but he had made his intentions clear. While standing guard, Morgana walked by and paused to look at me.

"You're the Dane," she said, smiling.

"Shh," I whispered.

She understood my meaning, bowed, and moved along. As she passed, she shot me a playful look out of the corner of her eye.

Poor girl, I thought; she had no idea what peril lay ahead. Still, I felt a slight boost of confidence from it, as I always did when a beautiful girl paid me any attention. Conwoïon would have chastised me for my vanity, but what harm could come from such a thing? After everything that I had lived and seen, I could use a little distraction. After she walked out of my line of sight, I noticed several dozen Franks crossing the bridge toward our camp. Most of them were soldiers, but I recognized the man who led them well enough.

"Ricwin is coming, my lord," I said into the tent behind me.

Nominoë emerged, wiped his hands on his green tunic, then put on his burgundy cap and cape. He walked toward Ricwin with the confidence of a king, so I clutched the shaft of my spear and followed.

I hoped the long, decorated cheekpieces of the bronze helmet would conceal my face enough so no one on the Frankish side would recognize me. We met them in the clearing between camp and bridge, and the two men stopped a few dozen paces from each other, each with a retinue of soldiers at their back.

Ricwin's black hair had greyed a great deal since I had seen him last, and he wore a light, scruffy grey beard. Renaud stood behind him, his straight black hair a little shorter than before, and his pronounced square chin had a light scruff. To me, he had the look of malicious beast, and he might as well have had fangs.

"Nominoë, old friend, you came!" Ricwin said.

"You extended the olive branch; I merely took it," Nominoë replied.

"So you did," Ricwin said. "My steward tells me you brought me a gift. Is it what we agreed upon?"

"It is." Nominoë waved for the soldiers behind me to bring up Lambert. "I have returned what you lost."

Lambert emerged from the camp with two soldiers at his side, and they walked him across the gap between the two parties to deliver him to the Franks. Ricwin looked at Lambert with astonishment and said, "How did you do it?"

"It took some negotiating, but it turns out the Vikings are agreeable enough when the price is right."

Ricwin patted Lambert on the shoulders and looked him up and down. "You look well," he said.

"I am well," Lambert said.

"Thank you," Ricwin said to Nominoë. "As agreed, I have brought you yours as well."

The Frankish soldiers pushed a young boy forward, and when he saw Nominoë, he sprinted across the clearing and embraced him. The boy had hazel hair and big brown eyes, and for a moment, I thought he could be Nominoë's son. The king picked the boy up and held him tight. When he put him down again, a servant took the boy's hand and led him back to the king's tent.

"Now for the baptism," Ricwin said. "Truth be told, we did not expect you, nor did we think you would arrive with an army at your back. It's making the people of this great city nervous."

"I brought my personal bodyguard," Nominoë said.

"We've counted over two hundred spears!"

"I have many enemies," Nominoë said.

Ricwin huffed and sighed, then put his hands on his hips. "I'm sorry you've come all this way, but I can't let you in."

"That is… unfortunate," Nominoë said as politely as possible.

"At least we can say the prisoner exchange went well. That's an improvement from last time," the count said.

Nominoë nodded but said nothing more. He bowed and turned back to return to his tent. It took a moment for me to realize what had happened, and when I did, I felt compelled to act. We had been barred from the city, and I had no chance of finding Asa if she still lived. Yet there stood Renaud, not a javelin's throw from me, and exposed. I knew I could take his life, then and there, with a throw of my spear. For a moment I hesitated. Striking at Renaud would betray Nominoë and realize all the fears he'd had in bringing me along.

He had given me his trust, and I was contemplating breaking it. Alive or not, this was my chance to avenge Asa. My stomach cramped and my shoulders tensed, and without thought, I pulled off my helmet. I looked back at the Celts behind me with the briefest of thoughts about what they would say when the deed was done.

Undaunted, I took aim with my spear. My hand gripped the shaft of the spear so hard my knuckles turned white. An ache gripped my chest, and my jaw clenched so hard I thought my teeth might crack. As I took a few steps forward to launch my weapon, the Franks took notice and lifted their heavy iron shields over their lords.

"Hasting, stop!" I heard Nominoë scream, but too late.

The spear's rough shaft bent and straightened as it left my hand, the vessel of all the rage and hate in my heart. It struck hard on the rim of an iron shield so close to Renaud's face, I would not have been surprised if splinters had burrowed into his cheeks. Seeing the spear had missed its mark, I drew my short sword and marched forward. Frankish soldiers threw themselves at me in defense of their lord, and I ran the first few through with lethal precision. With a brief glance back at Nominoë's men, I saw they had formed a defensive wall with their large bronze shields and spears. Even if I had wanted to break and run, I knew they would not let me through.

More Frankish soldiers rushed at me, and the more of them I faced at once, the harder it became to strike them down. I parried their clumsy blows and felled two more, and the speed with which I moved caused them to pause. There must have been two dozen of them, each yearning to make their lord proud by being the man to take me down. They swarmed me like a hive of angry bees, without strategy or order, a mass of bodies leaping at me all at once, and I found myself fighting for survival.

I felled two more men, and their deaths caused the swarm to back off. I stepped back toward the Celts as if to escape. The Celts made it clear with small jabs of their spears that they had no intention of helping me.

A horn blew from the gatehouse, and a flood of soldiers poured out from the city. The reinforcements surrounded me, and I reluctantly fell to my knees and dropped my sword and shield. I was trapped with nowhere to run. My anger turned to sorrow; I had just betrayed one of the men I trusted most, and perhaps embroiled him in a war he did not want to fight. Nominoë stared on in horror from behind his warriors' wall of spears, and with a single look he conveyed more than could ever be spoken. Tears welled in the corner of his eyes, but before I could say anything, the butt of a spear cracked against the back of my head.

I awoke with my arms wide like Jesus on the cross and my wrists chained tight to the chill wall of a dark, damp dungeon. Water dripped rhythmically onto the stone floor and echoed across the entire chamber. Someone had stripped the clothes from my back, and blood had dried down my chest and to my right leg. My head ached and my shoulders throbbed.

I tried to pull at the chains, but I did not have the strength to even wiggle my fingers. Both of my arms had gone numb and my hands had turned dark purple.

Light from the surface broke through a manhole in the ceiling. It illuminated a small part of the chamber overlooking a dark pool of water that swirled with a mysterious current. Threadlike green moss covered the walls halfway up, which told me the room often flooded. The pool, I thought, must have been connected to the river in some way. My body took to shivering, my naked legs covered in goosebumps.

"It could be worse," I mumbled to myself.

"What could be worse?" a deep, sinister voice called out from the blackness.

"Who's there?" My voice should have also echoed off the chamber's stone walls as his had, but I had grown too weak.

"A friend, a foe. I am both, and I am neither," the voice said. "Do you know where you are?"

"A wine cellar?" I suggested.

A shadowy figure in a thick hooded cloak stepped into the light. He removed his hood to reveal a face deformed by burns. The man grinned through half-rotted teeth and said, "I am the executioner, and you and I will be spending lots of time together."

Two days passed before the executioner returned to visit me, or at least it felt that long. I had developed a cough and found it much harder to breathe. My captor did not seem to notice. He inspected my body, for what reason I cannot say, and he spent a good deal of time cleaning me with a dampened cloth afterward. He hummed a song to himself the entire time. When he finished cleaning me, he returned to a workbench on the far side of the chamber, illuminated by a small lantern, and continued to work on something. He knew I was watching him.

"Who is Asa?" he asked without turning to look at me.

"Who?" I asked as if I had not heard him.

"Who is Asa? You said her name when you were asleep."

"She's no one," I said.

"No one? I have been through this with many men, my friend, and never has anyone uttered *no one's* name while chained to my wall. So, I'll ask again: who is she?"

I refused to respond. He waited for an answer for a long time, and when it seemed he had forgotten about me, he turned from his work desk and approached me with a bowl full of a dull grey paste. He dipped a spoon in it and raised it to my mouth.

"Are you hungry?" he asked.

"Not for whatever that is," I said.

He looked at me with pleading eyes and said, "You have me all wrong. They pay me to keep you alive, so please, eat."

"I thought you said you were the executioner?"

"Do you see an ax in my hands? No, of course not. I execute on execution day."

"And when is my execution day?"

"Has anyone ever said that you ask too many questions?"

I chuckled and said, "Actually, yes."

"Eat," he urged.

I took a bite of the paste and swished it around in my mouth. All things considered, it tasted like food. The mixture had a hint of oats and honey, and when it reached my throat, I swallowed.

"There, you see?" he said. "Nothing to fear from me."

The executioner fed me the entire bowl, and when he finished, he loosened the chains that held me to the wall, which allowed me to relax my arms and sit.

Whatever he had fed me did not sit well in my stomach. My belly grumbled, and a sharp pain stabbed at my lower abdomen. Before I could ask what he had done, he left the dungeon and let the door slam behind him. I spent the entire night in agonizing pain. It felt as if a snake had somehow found its way into my guts and thrashed around, trying to escape.

Not long before daybreak, I expelled the questionable meal out of my rear with an explosive but satisfying release. Some of it dribbled down my leg to my ankle, and the smell sickened me. But at least the pain had subsided.

The executioner returned the following day and pulled the chains tight again, pulling my arms back against the wall and forcing me to stand. He looked me over, saw the mess I had made on the floor, and splashed water from the pool to clean it. He took another damp rag and washed me again. His strange little ritual unnerved me, and I wondered when the torture would begin.

It took another week for anyone else to visit me. The door to the dungeon clinked and clunked as it opened. Three men walked down the narrow spiral stairwell and crossed the main chamber to me. When they stepped into the light from the manhole above, I saw their faces—it was Ricwin, Renaud, and Lambert. They stared at me as if they had caught a coveted wild animal in a trap.

I shot Lambert a questioning look, wondering why they had brought him along. He acted as if he belonged among them and looked at me as if we had never met. Ricwin did not favor him, or so I had understood.

"Are you here to torture me yourselves?" I asked them.

"So quick to temper," Renaud said.

"He's like a mangy dog," Ricwin said with a chuckle.

I pulled hard at my chains and lunged at them with a bark and a growl. All three men jolted backward as if I had broken loose. The chains clamored and echoed in the chamber, and the executioner bolted over to pull me back to the wall. He pulled hard on the shackles to give me as little slack as possible and rewrapped them on the post that held them. My whole body ached, and I grimaced in pain when the chains pulled my arms out and against the wall.

Renaud scowled at Ricwin for inciting me. "Not another word," he commanded.

"But—" Ricwin started.

Renaud cut him down with his eyes. If I had not known any better, I might have mistaken Renaud for the count of Nantes, not Ricwin. He appeared to be the one pulling the strings. Ricwin pulled at Lambert's arm and they stepped back into the shadows to watch. As he faded into the darkness, Lambert looked at me, his eyes full of sorrow and concern. Renaud pulled up a wooden stool and sat on it in front of me. He nodded to the executioner, who loosened my chains and let my arms down.

"I have dreamed of this moment for a long time," he said. "You've been quite a nuisance for me. For years, your name has rolled off the lips of men and women alike, in both fear and admiration. 'Hasting this' and 'Hasting that.' You're a damned hero, and you're on the wrong side!"

I smiled at him, mocking his every word.

Dismayed, he crossed his legs and leaned back with two hands clasped around his knee. "The emperor remembers you, too. He asked about you last time I saw him. You made quite an impression on him. 'The Reformed Northman,' he calls you."

"Did you come here to compliment me to death?"

Renaud scowled. He did not like to be mocked. "Don't overestimate your importance to me, boy. I could just as soon cut your throat."

"What are you waiting for, then?"

"You are testing my patience," he said.

"Careful, Renaud. You have a job to do. Don't blow it with one of your tantrums," Ricwin said.

I saw the anger in Renaud's eyes. He swiveled on his stool and looked at Ricwin. Whatever look he gave him, the count hushed and said nothing more.

"So why keep me alive?" I asked him.

"Leverage," Renaud said. "The emperor has called us to war; another of his sons has rebelled. We leave in three days. I needed a plan to contain the... situation with the Celts. They are in open revolt—which was to be expected—and I cannot stay to defend my city. Nominoë, however, will not threaten the city if your life is at stake. As we speak, a letter travels to him to explain that if he attacks during my absence, you will be publicly beheaded."

"And after you return?" I asked.

Renaud bared his teeth with a malicious smile and leaned forward. "Oh, the terrible things I wish I could do to you. They say revenge is unchristian, but it would feed my soul to see you suffer after all that you've done."

"Renaud," Ricwin warned.

Renaud leaned back again and adjusted his tunic. "It will have to wait. Until then, the executioner has his orders. If Nominoë attempts to take the city—"

"I hope he does," the executioner blurted out.

"What makes you think Nominoë would let my death stand in his way?" I asked.

"I don't," Renaud sneered.

"So that's it? You came all the way down here to tell me about your plan? You could have just left me here."

"Where's the fun in that?" Renaud smiled. "I want you to suffer, both spiritually and physically. I've come here to deliver both."

He reached out to Ricwin, who handed him a long whip. The executioner turned me to face the wall and patted me on the back. I heard the whip drag across the floor, and then Renaud took a deep breath. A booming crack echoed in the chamber, followed by a sharp, burning sting across my back. I howled in pain and panted to catch my breath.

"Will you hurry this up?" Ricwin said.

Renaud lashed the whip several more times in quick succession, and he moaned with pleasure each time I cried out. When he'd had enough, he threw the whip's handle at the executioner and spat at the ground. I slumped to the floor and convulsed in pain.

"That is just a taste of what's to come," Renaud said as he turned to leave the dungeon.

"Wait!" I cried out. "The baptism… the woman, your wife—"

Renaud stopped in his tracks. "What about her?"

"Is she… Asa?"

"What?" Renaud laughed. "You thought my wife Anne was Asa?"

"The two of you were married, weren't you?"

"You pathetic fool. Whoever told you that misled you. Asa was my mistress, one of many, and nothing more." He paused a moment to regard me, and then he laughed. "Don't tell me it was *her*. She told you we were married? Oh, that's too funny!"

"Stop," I pleaded.

"No, Hasting, I will not stop. Do you want to know what happened that night? The night she returned to me after visiting you in the forest? Let me tell you. She thought she had me fooled, wrapped around her little finger. I knew where she had been. I could smell it on her. I was already livid that she had set you loose. Oh, yes, Hasting, I knew it was her. She tried to tell me she had gone riding, on her own, as if that were a normal thing to do on the eve of battle." He sat again on his stool. "First, I choked her. You should have seen those beautiful blue eyes of hers fill with blood as I squeezed her neck. I enjoyed watching her turn red, then purple, then blue. I cut into her neck and severed all the veins to her head. The moment she died, the child was born, and I gave it to my men to toss into the cesspit. I sawed through her spine and took her head because I knew you would want to keep it."

"Stop!" I howled.

He struck me with the back of his hand, and I fell against the wall. "Is it too much for you to hear,

Northman? Have you lost your appetite for blood because your little girlfriend died the way so many have died because of you? This is war, Hasting, and if you can't handle it, you should have stayed home."

Renaud adjusted his tunic and spat on the ground beside me before returning to the stairwell with Ricwin and Lambert.

I released my wild rage into a roar. "I'll kill you, Renaud! I'll kill you!"

His reply came from the shadows. "Not this time, Hasting. You fell into my trap, and like any good hunter, I plan on skinning my catch and mounting its head as a trophy."

7

Apostasies

Starvation is the worst way to die. A blade kills swiftly, as does drowning, but hunger consumes a man relentlessly, slowly.

After Ricwin and Renaud left to join the war, the only person I saw was the executioner. He fed me a single bowl of mush each day, and some water. Sores developed where my skin rubbed against the stone floor, and over time they healed into leathery patches of boils. I struggled to keep count of the days, and when I asked the executioner, he shrugged. I knew it had been weeks if not months when my wrists shrank so thin my captor had to replace my shackles with smaller ones.

We talked now and then, but he kept his distance, never revealing anything about himself or his life outside the dungeon. Other prisoners passed through from time to time, but the executioner gave them a cell with a bed and chamber pot. It wasn't until the third or fourth prisoner that I realized they had barred cells on the far wall where I could not see.

Captivity is a strange thing. It takes time to settle down and find the patience to remain calm. During my first few weeks in the dungeon, I screamed a lot, and I cried out for help. The more noise I made, the more the executioner beat me. He had a long narrow stick that bent back as he swung it, and it snapped on my skin like a whip. My arms bore innumerable lacerations from my beatings.

After a while, I stopped trying to resist. Eventually, I ceased speaking and obeyed whatever commands the executioner gave. I would never have expected myself to bend to the will of a captor—I had always considered myself indomitable—but time has a way of breaking us all.

The man I had been outside of captivity faded away, and I started to live for my mealtimes, a prisoner to my more animalistic instincts. Perhaps it is the spirit's way of coping with the bleakness of isolation and the agony of starvation. It is a fate I would not wish on my worst enemy, even Renaud, and that he had thrown me in the dungeon to rot while he fought a never-ending war spoke of his cruelty.

I could not say how long I stayed chained to that wall, but however long it was, it robbed me of everything I was and everything I had been.

One night, the executioner brought in a man and put him in a cell to sleep off his intemperance. The next morning, before my captor returned, the man looked out into the dungeon and saw me chained against the wall near the pool of water. Light from the manhole shined over me and obscured the rest of the chamber, but he could see me. I must have looked like a wild beast, caged and beaten, with scars covering my back and arms. My hair and beard had grown out to where I could not tell where one stopped and the other began.

"You there." The man's voice echoed across the chamber.

He was the first person to try to speak to me in a long time. Though I heard him, my mind remained absent, and I had no words to reply.

"Yes, you! What do they have you in here for?"

I could hear in his voice that he was still a little drunk from the night before. He rattled the bars of his cell to make some noise, and after a short time, I raised my head and looked in his direction. "There you are," he continued. "You look like shit! Who did you piss off?"

I opened my mouth to speak, but when I tried to say a word, my voice crackled. My lungs tickled from the vibration, and I coughed until my abdomen cramped and caused me to curl up on the floor. Still, I tried to speak again, and after a few tries, I mumbled, "Renaud."

"Oh," the man said. "I've heard about him. Not good things, mind you. I'm Léon. What's your name?"

"H… Haaaa… Hasting," I said.

"Hasting? You mean, *the* Hasting, the Hero of Pontivy?"

"You… are… a Celt?" I asked. He had been speaking to me in the Frankish language.

"Did my name not give it away?" He chuckled. "I heard you were dead."

The door to the dungeon creaked open, and footsteps echoed down the stairwell. My captor walked over to me and untied me. He helped me over to a stool and sat me on it, and he began his daily ritual of wiping me down with a dampened cloth and feeding me the tasteless paste. Léon watched on with his hands on the bars of his cell.

"What are you doing with him?" he asked the executioner.

The executioner looked up at him and smiled. "I am keeping him clean for the execution."

"Why don't you bathe me like that?" Léon joked.

The executioner did not laugh. He instead continued his duty and ignored the interruption. Léon, however, would not leave him alone.

"Aren't you afraid he'll try to escape?"

"He's broken," the executioner said. "He is but a sack of skin and bones. I've made sure of it."

"I don't think you know who you're dealing with. That man has done things you wouldn't believe. He's a damned hero," Léon insisted.

When Léon said those words, something woke up inside me. I suddenly remembered who I had been before my captivity, and I clenched my fist fully for the first time in months. These were the hands that had vanquished Tristan and Conomor. They had killed Hagar. My hands had made me famous, and they were powerful.

The executioner noticed nothing, and while he dipped his cloth into the bowl of water at my feet, I put my wrists together and raised my hands up. With all the strength I could muster, I swung down and slammed my iron clamps into the back of his head. To my astonishment, the blow stunned him, and he fell forward. I looked back at Léon who waved at me to tell me to run for it.

With heavy steps, I lumbered toward the stairwell. My feet ached as if they had both broken, and my legs could hardly hold me up. Paces away from the first stone step to the surface, I heard the crack of a whip and felt the sting of the leather tip slice through my flesh.

"Nice try," the executioner said.

The blow knocked me over, and I rolled on the ground. My captor carried me back to the stool, sat me down, and then cleaned my wound. For the first time, I heard him growl.

"Any other man, and I would have killed you just now. But I will not let you steal my pleasure of taking your life on the chopping block."

When the executioner left, I found myself shivering in pain on the floor. My escape attempt had taken all the strength I had left, along with the final shred of hope that I might survive my captivity. When I rolled over, I could make out Léon still standing at the bars, staring at me. He knew my name. Perhaps, I thought, I had not seen the true opportunity the gods had given me.

"Do you live here, in the city?" I asked him.

"No," he replied. "I'm a merchant. I sell wine."

"How long do they have you in here?"

"A few days, I think," he said. "Public drunkenness is usually two days. Happens when I get a few days away from the wife." He chortled at his own joke.

"You said you know who I am."

"I do."

"What do you think about helping me out of here?" I asked him.

"I'd lose my head."

"Nominoë would pay you," I said.

"How much?"

"I don't know, but I'm worth a lot to him. I'm sure it would be worth your while," I said.

"Out of the question," Léon snapped. He released the bars and slipped back into a dark corner of his cell.

The following day, the executioner released Léon. I was alone again, and my mind went blank. More time passed, days or perhaps weeks. It all melded together into what seemed like one long night. My body continued to whither, and though I should have thought about my death, I had no way of knowing how much longer I might endure. Death felt inevitable.

On a night no different than the others, the door to the dungeon creaked open, and footsteps made their way down the stone steps. A figure in a dark cloak knelt at my side.

"It's me, Léon," he whispered. "I am sorry it took me so long. Here, take this." He shoved some bunched herbs into my mouth and offered me a drink to wash it down. "These will put you to sleep and trick the executioner into thinking you are dead. When they send you out to be buried, I'll come to find you."

I fell asleep before I could thank him, and calmness washed over me. My head rested against the cold stone floor one last time, and I drifted off with shallow breaths. I had a vision that night of the light shining through the manhole. It illuminated the entire chamber, and in it I saw an angelic figure walking toward me. She knelt at my side, her face radiant and bright, and she whispered in my ear.

"Let go," she said.

I looked up into Asa's face.

"Let go," she said again.

"I can't."

"You can. You will."

She touched my shoulder and caressed my face, and I realized I had taken the form of a black, mangy wolf. Her hand passed through my fur, and she leaned forward to breathe her essence into me. I felt her warmth. I felt her love. We floated above the ground together, light as a feather in the wind, and rose to the surface. Past earth and cloud, we climbed high among the stars. She looked at me with pure, innocent eyes, and kissed me on the head.

"To be the man you were meant to be, you must tame the beast inside you," she whispered.

Her hands wrapped around my neck and head in a soothing embrace. At first, I snarled and growled at her, resisting her affection. She continued to stroke me, and when I calmed down, I transformed back into a man.

Ours hands met, but she continued on toward the heavens while I drifted back toward the earth. I turned to face the fields below and saw all the land as the gods see it, and I fast approached the ground and landed with a violent thud.

I jolted awake and found I was not where I had fallen asleep. Part of me thought I was still dreaming, since dream and reality had become indistinguishable. Someone had put a blanket over me, and the floor beneath me rocked and shook. A squeaking and grinding ruckus echoed from all sides. I flipped onto my back and opened my eyes to find a bright blue sky overhead, and a fresh, warm wind blowing over me. A beautiful voice hummed a soft melody not far away, and for the first time in a long time, my ears took in the sounds of birds tweeting and crickets chirping.

Was I in Fólkvangr, I thought? Had I died and passed to the next world?

"He's awake," a man's voice said.

The humming voice stopped. "He's what?" a woman asked.

"His eyes are open," the man said in a panic. "What do we do?"

"Hit him with a shovel," the woman said.

"I can't do that," the man said.

"I don't know what you want me to say. The executioner said to bury him. That's what we'll do."

"But he's alive, Gwenaëlle. There's been a mistake!"

"Whoever he is, Corentin, he must have been a bad man. Why else would they have given him to the executioner?"

Corentin crawled into the back of the cart and craned his neck over me. He had black, wavy hair in a bowl cut, and a thick black mustache. He pulled my eyelids down and stared at me. I looked back at him, and when my eyes moved, he jolted.

"He's definitely alive!" he cried out.

I reached my bony hand out and murmured, "Help."

My voice had not returned to me, so my utterance must have sounded like a moan. He scurried to the front of the cart and sat by Gwenaëlle. She glanced back at me, then pulled on the reigns to stop the horse that drew us.

"He said 'help,' my love. He's asking for help," Corentin pleaded.

"I'll sort this out," she said. She pulled back her curly brown hair, put on a headscarf, and rolled up her sleeves before climbing into the back of the cart. "God, he stinks."

She picked up my wrist and inspected the laceration scars from the shackles. My arms had nothing but skin on the bone, and the rest of me must have looked the same. Corentin circled the cart and lowered the tailgate to have a look at what she was doing.

"It looks like they tried to starve him to death," she said. The cross she wore around her neck dangled over my head.

"That doesn't sound right," Corentin said. "I've never seen that before."

"What's your name?" she asked me. I was too weak to respond. "Maybe we should take him back."

"To the executioner? That'd be a wasted trip. I'm guessing he'd just kill him and send us back this way."

"We should finish him off ourselves, then," she said. She let out a long sigh. "They don't pay me well enough to kill people."

"What if we help him?" Corentin suggested. "Look, I was raised a certain way, and when someone needs help, I—"

"And that's why I love you," Gwenaëlle said. "All right. He's too weak to be a danger to anyone. And maybe he's important. There's a war on, you know, and prisoners can fetch handsome ransoms. Besides, the executioner already paid us; we may as well go home."

"I would have settled for helping him," Corentin said.

Gwenaëlle reached for a gourd of water and held it for me to drink. She fed me small pieces of bread and some chestnuts she had stowed in a basket in the front, and when I ate all I could—it wasn't much—she tucked me into the blanket to keep me warm.

She and Corentin sat again at the front, and she whipped the horse onward. We traveled the rest of the day along rocky dirt roads until we arrived at a village. The thatch-roofed houses formed two columns up to a small church built with uneven, moss-covered stones and a black tile roof at the center.

I was too weak to walk, so the two did their best to carry me to their house. Several of their neighbors saw them and offered to help. They placed me on a cloth tarp on the ground, and four people picked it up at the corners to carry me inside.

It was a small house with a single room and a fire pit in the center. The ground was compact clay and ash, and the place smelled of lingering smoke.

For days, they fed me and gave me water, but the frailty of my body seemed too progressed to reverse. They called their priest, a man named Bertin, who took care of the church all on his own, and he recited prayers for me. I struggled to understand why these people, to whom I was a stranger, fought so hard to save me when I had given up and wanted to die. During my first few days in their home, I slept a lot, comforted by the softness of the blankets beneath me. During the day, they left for work, and the priest visited the house to care for me. Most nights, they did not return until after I had fallen asleep.

It took over a week for me to feel strong enough to walk again, and when I did, I took the liberty of leaving the house on my own. I limped into the daylight, and, while it hurt my eyes at first, I basked in the sun's rays. Bertin saw me from the church and came to meet with me. He stood a head shorter than me, but his shoulders were wide, and he had a pointed chin and nose with narrow eyes and thick, bushy eyebrows that gave him an unintentional severity.

As he approached me, he smiled and said, "God is good."

I nodded and tried to speak. My voice grumbled in the back of my throat, and I croaked like a frog. It took a moment to clear it out, and with a raspy voice, I said, "Thank you."

Bertin took my hands in his and rubbed them together. "We almost lost you there," he said. "Tell me, what is your name?"

I looked at him with hesitation and said, "No one."

"Ah," Bertin said. "I see. Well, to be expected from someone released from the Nantes dungeons."

"I'm not a criminal," I said.

Bertin smirked and patted me on the shoulder. "Whatever you were, that can all change now."

"It already has," I said.

"Do you have a home? A place you could return to now that you are well?"

I gave his question some thought. At first, I thought of returning to Vannes, but after what I had done, I knew Nominoë would either cast me out or kill me himself. My lack of patience and self-control had torn apart the relationship he had sought with Ricwin, and I did it for my own selfish reasons. My spear had missed its mark, and my heart still yearned to kill Renaud. And there was Skírlaug, and Bjorn, and Rune, and the Danes who had followed me. They had to know that something had happened to me, and even if I wanted to return to them, what of it? They had asked me to leave, and I did not believe I had learned the lessons I needed to take my place among them again.

I looked at Bertin and said, "I have nowhere to go."

He looked at me with pensive eyes. "If you're going to stay, we'll need to call you something. *No one* won't work for most people here. I understand you want to leave your old life behind, but you'll need to share some things with them to gain their trust, and with that accent, it won't be easy. What if we call you René? It means 'Reborn.'"

"I like it," I said.

"Good. Well, I know Gwenaëlle and Corentin would like to speak with you. They are good Christians for what they did. I am sure God will recompense them for their effort. In a time of war and killing, there are too few people like them anymore."

"Where are they?" I asked.

"They left for the city this morning," Bertin said. "They used to be farmers, but these days there's more money to be made as gravediggers for the city. Oh, and I suggest you pay a visit to Mathilde in that house over there. She made those clothes you're wearing. It wouldn't hurt to thank her."

He rubbed my hands one last time and returned to the church. I looked around the sleepy village. A single dirt road passed through the main square and vanished into a thick forest of oak and ash intertwined with holly and climbing ferns. They had a blacksmith who lived behind the church and pounded away at a piece of iron, and a carpenter next to him sawing blocks of wood. Both men appeared long past their prime but still worked with youthful vigor.

I wandered nearer the house Bertin had pointed out and saw a woman in the window sewing together some clothing on a table. She wore a light cap on her head and a simple brown farm dress with a work apron. As Bertin had suggested, I paid her a visit and knocked on the door. I heard a gasp when I knocked, and she moaned when she saw me standing at her door. She invited me in with a bow—I had to duck to pass through the doorway—then sat me at the table with a scowl and brought me a mug of cider.

"Bertin says you made these for me." I pulled at my simple white tunic. "Thank you."

"It was no trouble at all," she said.

She sat across the table from me with her hands wrapped around a wooden cup. Her fingers were swollen and wrinkled, and she had small bandages on both thumbs. When she forced a smile, her eyes wrinkled like crow's feet, and the dark color and leatheriness of her skin spoke of a lifetime of labor.

"What is this place called?" I asked.

"Our village? It's called Bouaye. It means 'wooded place.'" She paused and gave me a sideways look. "That's a strange accent you have. Where are you from?"

"It's a long story," I said.

"You will soon learn that things do not move quickly here."

I looked around the village and understood her meaning. It felt strange to have nothing to do, no defenses to build, no ships to repair, and no war to fight. There was no looming threat to my life or reputation. It occurred to me at that moment that I had lived at a breakneck pace, with no time at all between each new crisis. The life of a sea captain demanded constant action, and the higher I'd risen in the ranks, the more life had demanded of me. For the first time since I'd left Hagar's hall, I felt released from the burden of Viking life; the weight of it lifted from my shoulders. As far as anyone I ever knew was concerned, I was dead. With that, I had no responsibility weighing on my spirit.

"If I told you everything, you wouldn't believe me," I said.

"Perhaps not, but I would like some idea of who you are. Forgive my bluntness, but I would prefer not to waste our charity on a criminal, if that's what you are. We've suffered enough as it is."

"I am not a criminal," I said.

"You came from the dungeons," she snapped.

"Thank you for the clothes," I said as I stood to leave.

"At least tell me what to call you," she insisted.

"René," I said.

"René? All right. Those clothes were not cheap to make, and I spent time making them. I will not ask you to repay me, but know that what I did pales in comparison to the time and resources Corentin and Gwenaëlle have put toward saving you. I hope it will have been worth it, and that we can count on you to treat them how they deserve."

"I have nothing to repay them with," I said.

"Yes, I know. But there are more important things than money."

I bowed and darted out of her house with an uncomfortable feeling. Rather than explore more of the village, I returned to Gwenaëlle and Corentin's house and hid away from the other villagers.

Before I knew it, word of my renewed health had spread, and heads poked in through the windows. I could not believe the impunity of their intrusiveness. Where I was from, prying eyes were swiftly punished. To hide from them, I pulled my blanket over my head and rolled into a corner. Eventually Bertin came to my aid and asked the villagers to leave me alone. He entered the house with a basket full of food and a gourd of water.

"Would you prefer wine?" he asked me.

"No," I blurted. "Thank you."

He sat on a stool near the fire pit and started to unpack the basket. "I heard about your conversation with Mathilde," he said.

"What of it?"

"She says you thanked her. It warms my heart to know you took my advice and showed her gratitude. You still need time to heal, but a young man such as yourself could be a great help to us."

"What do you have in mind?" I asked.

"Gwenaëlle and Corentin have land in a clearing not far from here. They haven't tilled it since their three sons left to fight in Louis' war. If you tilled it for them, it would be a great help to all of us."

As much as I did not enjoy the prospect of working the land, I saw little choice in the matter. None of the fighting I had done in my life would help me to pay back these poor villagers, and I wanted to pay them back. The idea of working also made me anxious since I had lost all my strength during my captivity.

Bertin left me to eat on my own, and I waited until nightfall to build a fire. Gwenaëlle and Corentin had not yet returned from the city, so I closed their rickety wooden shutters and tidied up some of the mess I had made. A little later in the night after I had drifted off to sleep, they arrived home and slumped straight into bed. The following morning, Corentin nudged my shoulder to wake me.

"I heard you were walking around yesterday," he said.

"I was."

"And you've found your voice! You should come with us to Mass this morning. Bertin says he has a good sermon planned."

"Don't you have to go to the city today?"

"Not on Sunday," he said.

I took a moment to gather my strength before sitting up while Corentin mixed up some oats and barley with honey in a bowl and gave it to me to eat.

"Quickly," he urged, "or we'll be late."

We walked to the church together to find all the other villagers gathered in the pews facing the altar. They stared up at me as if they had seen a giant. My shadow eclipsed Corentin, whose age and stature were similar to Bertin.

Bertin stood at the front with an open Bible and some candles lit underneath a large silver cross, which was decorated with an intricate floral pattern. The windows were small and let in almost no light, so the priest had set candles on small tables along the walls leading to the chapel, giving the chamber an amber glow. Wooden beams crisscrossed overhead to hold up the arched roof where birds flapped from perch to perch and chirped at the people below them. Corentin led me to the front where we joined Gwenaëlle.

Bertin led his flock in song, interrupted by short sermons and readings from the Bible, and ended with a prayer. The villagers stood as soon as it ended and left the church. I followed my hosts like a stray dog, and they led me back to their house.

"I want to thank you for saving me," I said.

They looked at me with wide eyes but said nothing.

I put my hands on my hips, stared out the window at a cloud drifting across the azure sky, and said, "I want to find a way to repay you."

"We were hoping someone you know would pay a ransom for you," Gwenaëlle said.

I frowned. "I'm sorry to tell you that no one out there will want me back." The two of them looked dismayed. "But I want to pay you back for what you've done for me. Bertin says you have a field that needs tilling?"

Corentin scoffed and said, "It needs to be plowed, but our oxen were taken for meat by Renaud's army. You'd never manage on your own."

"I'll find a way," I said.

"How about you start by helping us around the house here," Gwenaëlle suggested.

The remainder of the day, they set about doing chores and tidying up their household. I helped where I could, and by late afternoon, I found myself with idle hands. My energy had begun to return to me, so I made my way to the church to find Bertin. I found him in the back, pulling weeds in his garden and whistling a tune to the birds. As I approached, he straightened with one hand on his lower back.

"René!" he said with open arms.

"I was wondering if you needed help around the church."

He gave it some thought and said, "The help I need, I doubt you could do."

"Perhaps I'll surprise you."

Bertin scratched his head and glanced around the garden. "The one thing I could really use help with is making candles."

I could not believe my luck and exclaimed, "I've made lots of candles!"

That night, I returned at dusk to Corentin and Gwenaëlle's house. They welcomed me with wide eyes and quick, nervous nods at first, but they relaxed when I presented them with a gift. I pulled a single silver coin from my pocket and placed it on their wooden table. They looked at the coin and at each other with astonishment.

"How did you—?" Gwenaëlle started to ask.

"I have skills your priest finds valuable," I explained.

"Thank you." Corentin took the coin and put it somewhere in a dark corner of the house.

"Don't thank me yet," I said. "That's the first one, and it doesn't come close to repaying you for what you did for me. There will be more."

The next day, after Corentin and Gwenaëlle had left for the city, Bertin showed me to their field on the other side of a grove of trees behind the church. Rain had soaked the land and the ground had recently flooded. They had grown wheat and barley there, Bertin told me, and Corentin had helped his father farm that land, and his sons had helped him. Bertin showed me an old plow with a rusted share, and he lamented how it had fallen into disrepair.

I looked out over the field and wondered how I could ever turn it back into arable land if experienced farmers had given up. Weeds had overrun the soil, and the ground was thick and rocky. As we stood there, I had an idea. I had seen Bertin tending to his own garden, so he knew something about farming, and he needed help with making candles.

"What do you think about helping me?" I asked him.

"I don't see how," he said.

"I'll need some help to plow the field, and you need help making candles and other small things around the church. What do you say we work together on both?"

"Oh, no," he said. "I have too much to do and too little time." He paused, and while he did, my heart sank, but then he turned away from me and continued, "But I might know someone."

"Who?"

"An old war hero with too much time on his hands."

Bertin led me back into the woods in the direction of the village, but before we reached the church grounds, he took a sharp right up a beaten path to a small house nestled within a thicket. Smoke rose from a chimney that protruded from a thatched roof and fresh mortar walls. A chicken coop stood in the back, with an open shed that had a wood roof, and a lattice fence around the front to keep the chickens in it. Raindrops plopped on the leaves all around us, drowning out our footsteps.

The priest approached the door and lifted his fist to knock, but before his knuckles touched the door, it opened. An older man with long, greying hair and a patch on his left eye stared us down.

"What?" he snarled.

"It's good to see you, too, Evroul," Bertin said. "May we come in?"

Evroul examined me with a suspicious eye but shuffled aside to let us through the doorway. He had a limp in his step— he had a wooden peg for a left leg. We sat at a small table by the fire, and he brought over a carafe of wine and three goblets. He poured wine for Bertin, but when he offered some to me, I put my hand over my cup. He shrugged and poured himself a full cup.

"Why are you here?" Evroul asked Bertin.

"This young man is called René, and he plans to plow Corentin and Gwenaëlle's field to repay them for helping him," Bertin said.

"How is he going to plow without animals?" Evroul asked.

"I'll pull it," I said.

Evroul laughed. "You're thin as a broomstick, boy. I've seen men twice your size try and fail."

"I'll pay for your help," I said.

"I don't need money."

"Do it for your sister," Bertin said.

Evroul stared into his goblet of wine and sighed. "What good would I be to you? I only have one leg."

"I have an idea on how we'll make it work," I said.

"Excellent!" said Bertin. "I will let the two of you get to know each other. I look forward to seeing how this works out."

Evroul growled in protest, then took a hearty drink of his wine and said, "Because I owe *you*, Bertin."

The priest left me at Evroul's house to talk, but Evroul did not seem keen on learning much about me. We agreed on when to meet next, and I returned to Gwenaëlle and Corentin's house. It took another week to restore the plow to working condition. I used the silver from helping Bertin around the church to pay the blacksmith for a new share, and the carpenter to repair and replace some of the wooden parts. I also had him rig up the front of the plow with a crossbar instead of the harness for the animals so I would have more leverage to push.

It is strange to say, but I enjoyed myself during this time. I remained focused on the here and now rather than dreaming of the future or plotting my next adventure. It was an unexpected and fundamental change in me, and a freeing one. Evroul helped me where he could, and he scolded me when he disliked my manner of doing things. When the plow was ready, I positioned myself behind the crossbar, while he took the handles in the back to guide the share. I lunged forward with all my strength, but the plow would not budge. Again and again I tried to move it forward, but the share remained stuck in place. Evroul tried to help by pushing forward a little, but nothing helped.

"I told you, boy," he said to me. "You're not strong enough."

"If you won't help me, then get out of my way!" I snarled. "Just leave."

He lowered his head and hobbled off.

My anger subsided soon after, and I sat against the plow and gazed at the sunset. Stars began to appear as the sun vanished behind the horizon. The cool of night washed over the land. The stars reminded me of my dream, of Asa drifting into the heavens and telling me to let her go. I heard her voice urging me to move on with my life. Without her, I had no purpose, no reason to be. I started to cry, feeling lost and adrift in a world where I did not belong.

Life has no meaning, I thought; *there are no gods, and there is no reason for any of it*. As these thoughts passed through my mind, I heard Asa's voice clear as day: *Do you always think this way?* Her voice jolted me awake—I'd drifted off while watching the sunset.

Footsteps approached from behind the plow. I turned to find Evroul, who had returned to see me.

"I am sorry," he said. He saw the tears drying on my face and clasped his hands in front of him. "Why don't you come to my home tonight and eat with me?"

I accepted his invitation, and we returned to his home in the woods. He cooked up a hearty soup with lentils, peas, and shredded chicken meat, and we ate in silence. After he had filled his belly, he sat back with a cup of wine and asked, "Who are you?"

"Bertin told you. I am René."

Evroul shook his head and said, "Who are you really? You're not fooling anyone, you know."

"I will tell you when I'm ready," I said.

"A man who hides his name is a man who does not know himself," Evroul suggested.

I nodded at his peg leg and asked, "How did you lose it?"

He looked down at it, too, and smiled. With a hand under his knee, he lifted it onto the table and said, "Everyone thinks I'm a damned war hero because of it. They all think I lost it in some glorious battle. In truth, I wore boots two sizes too small, and my toes developed a pus on a long march. The pus ran up my leg, and they took it off before the sickness moved any further."

"Why don't you tell everyone the truth?" I asked him.

"Oh, I have. They refuse to believe it. Sometimes, people need to believe certain things about you to make themselves feel better. Let them live in their fantasy, I always say."

"I never thought of it that way."

"What would you do?" He laughed.

I understood that is what I had spent my life doing. Everything had to be within my command, and when something spiraled out of my control, I spiraled out of control. Though he had not seen much of the world, Evroul possessed a kind of wisdom I had never before appreciated. My thoughts turned to Asa again for a brief moment, and I was overcome with sadness.

"How do you manage without such an important part of yourself?" I asked him.

From the empathetic expression on his face, we both knew the conversation was no longer about his leg.

"You must learn to live with it," he said. "The question is, do you live with it here, in the calm of the village, or out there, in the world that took it from you?" He bobbed his head in thought, then took a long sip of wine. "Do you want to try again tomorrow?" he asked.

"I think tomorrow I'll pull the plow without the share, to practice," I said.

"I'll still join you in case you need me."

For the next fortnight, I spent the morning pulling the plow by myself without digging into the ground, to strengthen my body for the task. Evroul watched me from where he rested upon a log. He encouraged me to keep working, to push harder, and to not give up. Some days my arms and legs and chest and back ached so badly I could not stand without help, but each day I returned to the plow and pushed harder.

"Was your father a farmer?" Evroul asked me once while we snacked on some salted fish between efforts. He had traded one of his prized chickens for it with a trader who had passed through town the day before.

"I don't know," I said.

"You have a farmer's hips—wide and sturdy. I think he was."

"I did not know my father very well. He was killed when I was a boy," I said with a solemn frown.

"Shame. Fathers have so much to teach us." He chuckled as if remembering his own father, then continued, "Mine once told me, 'Watch me, son, so you will know what not to do when you're older.'"

"He sounds like a flawed and wise man," I said.

We laughed together, and Evroul even snorted. "He was, rest his soul," he said. "Do you remember anything your father told you?"

"Yes, he said to me once, 'Reputation is everything.'"

"Mm, reputation is essential," Evroul agreed.

"I've spent my life trying to build mine up, working to mold it as a blacksmith molds a sword," I said.

"In my experience, we can control what others think about us as much as we can control the weather."

I thought about what he said, and I agreed with it. "But if reputation is so important, how can a man leave it to chance?"

"I didn't say it should be left to chance," he said. "If you are true to yourself and you do the things you are meant to do, and do them well, reputation will follow. I think more than anything, living in service of others, and not yourself, is what endears. Your father would have told you that, I think, if he'd had the chance."

His words stayed with me for the rest of the day.

In the afternoons, I continued to work for Bertin, and he saw the change in me more than I saw it in myself. On several occasions, he visited us in the field to see our progress. Each time, he brought snacks and drinks. On the day I planned to pull the plow with the share, he brought bottles of wine in case a celebration was in order.

Evroul grasped the handles at the back, and I steadied myself at the front and readied to push. I lunged forward with all my strength, and on the first try, the plow did not move. I took a deep breath to steady myself and searched within for the will to give it my all. Rather than lunge again, I fell to my knees and sighed.

"What happened?" Evroul asked.

"I think he broke," Bertin said.

Evroul limped over and kneeled next to me. "What's wrong?"

"I… I don't know why I'm doing this," I said. "Why am I so determined to plow this field? There's no reason for it. There's no reason for anything."

Evroul's brow furrowed. "I think your reasons are obvious."

"They are?"

"Yes. You are plowing this field to help Gwenaëlle and Corentin, to pay them back for caring for you," he said. "You are also plowing this field to save yourself." He put a hand on my knee. "You could have worked for Bertin for a few weeks, paid them back in silver, and been on your way. But you saw that they needed help with this field more than they needed the silver. This tells me you have a deep desire to do good in the world. I have sensed that your former life put you at odds with this part of yourself, so you hid it away. I know what that's like; I was a soldier once, too."

His words cut through me like the sharpest of blades. "I had to hide it," I lamented. "I had to hide it to survive. Showing any weakness would have been the death of me. And I couldn't die, because I needed to save *her*."

I wept. Evroul and Bertin looked at each other with concern, and they both put a hand on my shoulder to console me.

"What happened to her?" Bertin asked.

"Renaud killed her," I snarled. "He murdered her."

Evroul worked up his courage and asked, "Who are you? You have been hiding your name from us, but we need to know if we hope to help you."

"My name is Hasting," I said.

Both men gasped.

"You are a Northman?" Bertin asked in horror. "God save us."

"Wait," Evroul said. "You fought with Nominoë in the war of the three kingdoms, yes?"

"How do you know about that?" I asked him.

"This town used to be part of a Celtic kingdom. What happens in Armorica ripples across the whole of our land."

"So, you are a Celt?" Bertin asked.

"I am both," I said.

Both men struggled to take in what I had told them. The revelation that I had spent time in a Christian kingdom put Bertin more at ease. Still, he kept his distance when he said, "Tell us more about the woman."

"I loved her more than anyone or anything," I explained. "When I lived in Vannes and fought for Nominoë, she was taken from me. I would never have left if the Northmen had not taken her. I became a Viking sea captain just so I could find her."

"It has the ring of a beautiful love story," Evroul said.

I explained everything that had happened in my life, from my enslavement in Hagar's village to my rise in rank and reputation among the Vikings. The two of them listened, and they seemed shocked at first to hear of what I had done.

"God will find a use for you," Bertin said. "Whatever his plan, you will play an important part, I am sure. He did not bestow you the gifts of language, diplomacy, and prowess for nothing. I caution you: whatever path you take next, do not lose yourself again in the man you were before. The man you are in your heart and the man you were with the Vikings must come together as one. Only then will you be open to receive God's love and His will."

His words struck a chord with me and harkened to what Skírlaug had said. She had spoken of a splintering of my soul, between the great wolf and me, the man. She had also talked of bringing the two together to make me whole. It occurred to me, sitting in that field, that the worlds of the Danes and Northmen and Christians were not so different from one another. In the end, we share something more fundamental than faith and religion; we share a collective human spirit.

"Now that I know Asa is dead, I have no purpose," I said. "If all I did was for her, how can I go back now?"

"You cannot," Evroul said. "At least, you cannot go back as you were. Life goes on. You must find a new purpose."

"Might I propose you start with Gwenaëlle and Corentin?" Bertin said. "There is no greater purpose than to serve others."

"And when it is done?" I asked. "What purpose will I have then?"

"God will show you one. You must trust him," Bertin said.

"But I'm not a Christian," I said.

Bertin smiled and said, "You don't need to be." He and Evroul helped me to my feet and placed my hands back on the crossbar. "God is not out there." He pointed to the horizon. "The spark of the Divine lives within you, in all of us. To let Him work through you, you only need to stay out of your own way. You need to let go."

I glanced at Evroul, who had taken his place back at the handles, and he nodded to say he was ready. Slowly, I pressed forward with my hands gripped tight around the crossbar; I savored the woodgrain pressed into my skin, the tension in my arms, shoulders, and chest, and the cold late-morning breeze that caressed my face. With a deep, controlled breath, I lunged forward, and the plow moved with me.

Step by step, we carried the plow ahead, and the ground rumbled beneath our feet. Bertin cheered, and he intoned a prayer as we passed by, thanking God for giving us—me—the strength to plow. Despite my newfound power, I did not have the stamina of a pair of oxen, so we stopped soon after we had started. Each day, we plowed a little more, and each day, I could pull the plow farther and longer. When we arrived at the last patch of soil to plow, Evroul and I sat and admired what we had done. It was nothing short of a miracle, or so Bertin would have had us think.

The following Sunday, Evroul and I invited Corentin and Gwenaëlle to join us after church. Bertin came as well, and he brought more wine to celebrate. When we arrived at the field, Gwenaëlle clasped her hands at her mouth and fell to her knees. Corentin fell with her, and they embraced each other with tears of joy over what they saw.

Sprouts had begun to break through the soil, and there was time enough left in spring and summer for the plants to provide a good yield in autumn. Bertin embraced both Evroul and me, and he helped the couple back to their feet. They turned around and grappled me about the chest. I put my arms around them while they sobbed into my bosom. What I felt then was unlike any feeling I'd ever had—greater than any victory I'd known in battle, and more meaningful than any treasure I had acquired.

"I am proud of the man you have become," Bertin said. "May you continue to work as God's servant."

Even as we rejoiced together, even as I was renewed—as if reborn as a new man—the pull of my old life lingered in my heart. Asa had moved on, and I had needed to let her go, but the injustice of her death remained. What kind of man would I have been if I had abandoned my desire to kill Renaud? Where I had failed the first time, I understood, was in wanting to kill him for my own selfish reasons. In helping the villagers of Bouaye, I saw a higher calling. I would not kill Renaud only for

Asa, but to avenge all those he had wronged, and I would do it in service of something more than myself.

8

Reunification

During my time in Bouaye, I had come to understand the toll that the repeated civil wars among Frankish nobility had taken on the commoners of the region. Renaud had bled the villages dry to feed his army and robbed them of their means to support themselves. When we had finished plowing Corentin and Gwenaëlle's field, I knew it would only last for a single season. They did not have the animals or the manpower to work the fields again the following year. Yet I knew I could not stay.

What they experienced in their village was widespread, and the man at the center of it all needed to be stopped. Now that my body was healed and my spirit healing, it was time for me to leave. Bertin had said God would find a purpose for me, and killing Renaud seemed like a good start.

On the day of my departure, I thanked Evroul and Bertin for all their help, and they accompanied me to the wagon. We shared a long, tear-filled farewell.

Gwenaëlle and Corentin had agreed to take me as far as a bridge on the Loire, southwest of Nantes. I was sure they meant the bridge Bjorn and I had accidentally burned down, but I did not mention it. They waited for me by the wagon as I said my goodbyes to the rest of the village. I waved for a long time to the small crowd of villagers who had gathered to see me off.

Our wagon soon turned a corner out of sight, and it was over. I slumped back into the cart on a bed of blankets and settled in for the long ride ahead. Gwenaëlle and Corentin remained silent. They did not want me to leave, but they understood my reasons.

By midday, we had reached the river and said our goodbyes. I crossed the stone bridge into the charred wood of the old guardhouse. Once on the other side, I turned and waved to the people who had saved my life.

"I will never forget you!" I called out from across the river.

"Neither will we!" Corentin shouted back, one arm tight around Gwenaëlle.

I continued on the path feeling comfortable on my own. It would take another three days to reach Vannes, and even then, I did not know if they would let me in. As Bertin had taught me, it was all in God's hands, or the gods' hands, and all I could do was follow the path. It did nothing for me to speculate and worry. Enough perils lay on the road ahead. I needed to remain fixed in the here and now. Wolves and bandits stalked the land after dusk, and without a weapon to defend myself, I had to remain vigilant.

By nightfall I reached the old Roman road to Vannes. Out of the question for me to stay in an inn or tavern along the way—I had no money and no desire to work off any debts. Instead, I snuck into a village and found a comfortable haystack behind a stable. Settlements, at least, warded off the perils of the road, even if the villagers could prove dangerous if they discovered me. At daybreak, I scurried back to the road, snacking on some bread and chestnuts from my knapsack, and sauntered on my way.

The rest of the journey proved uneventful. I arrived at Vannes in the afternoon, and from the looks of it, they had closed off the city. They had fortified the palisade on the edge of town, and soldiers patrolled the watchtowers that stood over the gates. The Celts were nervous, and Nominoë had gone to great lengths to protect his city. The afternoon sun was in their eyes, and they did not see me approach the gate at first. When they did, there was a commotion on the other side, and the gate opened. Two soldiers emerged with their hands clasped around sword hilts. They examined me from head to toe.

"A wayward traveler?" one of them asked.

"I am here to see Nominoë," I explained.

"Are you, now?" the other sneered. "Why would a pauper think Nominoë would want to see him?"

"Tell him an old friend has returned from the dead," I said. "And tell him my name: Hasting."

They had not recognized me with my long hair and beard, and they both gasped when they heard my name.

"Send a messenger to Nominoë. Tell him it's Hasting!" one of them called to the watchtower.

Not long afterward, a horseman galloped out from the city. I regarded him and said, "Aren't you going to let me in?"

"You've caused us a lot of problems, Northman," the man said.

We waited a long time before anyone returned to the gate from the city. I knew I had erred, and their ambivalence toward me spoke to the gravity of my wrongs. Whatever the consequences, I had to face them.

A cohort of horsemen rode up to the gate. The king of the Celts led them with Conwoïon close behind. Nominoë wore his bronze breastplate and golden conical helmet decorated with feathers. They were ready for a fight. The horses passed through the gate and surrounded me.

"Whoever you are, whatever trick this is, know that we will not spare you any punishment," Nominoë barked.

I raised my hands to show I had no weapons. He steered his steed to the side and dismounted, then drew his sword and approached me with great caution. Leading with the point of his blade, he drew nearer, and he pressed the tip against my chest.

"Look at me," he said.

I looked up, and we locked eyes.

"I can't tell you how sorry I am," I pleaded. "I was arrogant, self-centered, and foolish. Forgive me."

Though I had changed, and so had he, he recognized my face and my voice, and he wept. He sheathed his sword and turned to his men.

"It's him," he cried.

Conwoïon led his horse forward and said, "We will fetch a robe to clothe him, and slaughter a goat to feed him. This son of Armorica was dead and is alive again; he was lost and now is found."

Nominoë stood me up and held me tight. Some of the men behind him cheered, and others wept. They had all thought me dead.

They welcomed me back into the city and took me to the king's hall where they fed me all I could possibly eat and gave me a silk tunic with golden, embroidered trim—clothes more fitting of a warrior of my former status. With Conwoïon sitting to my left and Nominoë to my right, I felt I had returned home. My belly full, I sat back in my chair and gazed at the fire.

"What happened to you out there?" Nominoë asked.

So much had happened, I did not know how to express it all so they would understand. I started to weep as I spoke. "They took everything from me; everything I was, every trace of my humanity."

"There, there," Conwoïon said, rubbing my back.

I went on to explain how I had almost starved to death, and how the reason I escaped the dungeon was that they thought I was dead. Conwoïon seemed intrigued by what I had to say about the people who had saved me. I spoke of Gwenaëlle and Corentin, Bertin and Evroul, and the spiritual journey I had taken with them. When I finished, there was a long silence between us.

"I like this Bertin," Conwoïon said. "And he's right, there is no greater reward than to live in the service of others. The question is, will you follow your new purpose here with Nominoë, or out there with the Vikings?"

Nominoë squirmed in his chair. "Our esteemed priest assumes too much," he said. "Look, Hasting, you are welcome to stay here as long as you need. I love you as a brother—we have fought together and bled together. But you betrayed my trust when you tried to kill Renaud at the baptism. I don't blame you, it's natural to be self-serving, even for your kind."

"Haven't you listened to a word he's said, Nominoë?" Conwoïon clasped his hands and leaned over the table. "He's a changed man, can't you see?"

Nominoë flicked his hand in dismissal, then leaned in and said, "I appreciate the ordeal you have lived through, I do, but it doesn't magically make you a saint."

"I never said I was a saint," I said.

"Why did you come back here? Why not stay in Bouaye?" he asked me with a firm tone.

"I could have," I said. "I came back because I care about you, I care about Armorica, and I want to help. I saw what harm Renaud has done to his people, and I do not want the same for you. You fight for the wellbeing of your people and the wellbeing of all people who suffer under Renaud's rule. I was given a choice to hide away from the world and live in peace, but that's not who I am."

Conwoïon clasped his hands together and cheered. "What more could you ask?" he said.

Nominoë leaned back and crossed his arms. "I will need assurances of your loyalty."

"I understand."

Nominoë darted from the hall unexpectedly, leaving Conwoïon and me alone to talk. When he returned, he carried a long, thin object wrapped in a blanket and put it on the table in front of me. He unwrapped it to reveal my father's sword, which he had kept sharp and clean. I stood and put my hand on the hilt.

"I've kept it safe for you these past four years," Nominoë said.

"Four years?" We had not discussed how long I had spent in the dungeon, and the revelation struck me like a horse at full gallop. "It can't be. I couldn't have been gone that long."

"You were," Conwoïon said.

"So much must have happened," I mumbled. "Tell me everything."

Together, they explained the events that followed my capture. Nominoë had sued for peace and for my release. But Ricwin, Renaud, and Lambert had all left to fight in the emperor's new war, and they had left no one behind with authority to negotiate. The steward of the city had proven fickle about the whole ordeal. He'd insisted he had no knowledge of my whereabouts, even though he had threatened to put me to death if they tried anything. Nominoë sent spies to find out where they kept me, but to no avail. Eventually, they'd received word that I had died, and the Franks had buried my body in an unmarked grave south of the Loire. When Nominoë spoke of the message, his eyes watered.

While my ordeal seemed bleak, the greater world at large had crumbled into chaos. Emperor Louis had defeated his sons but fallen ill on the eve of his victory. His death brought renewed warring between the Frankish nobility. No sooner had he taken his last breath than his sons declared war on one another over their inheritance. They had assembled their vast armies at a place called

Fontenoy and fought a three-sided battle the empire had never before seen.

What made the campaign different, Nominoë explained, was that it was the bloodiest of them all. In a typical battle, when a lord fell, his opponents apprehended him and ransomed him back to his estate. At Fontenoy, the emperor's son Lothaire gave the order to kill and not capture, and his brother Charles, who faced him, did the same. More noblemen perished at Fontenoy than in any other battle in the history of the empire. The Frankish nobility had been obliterated. Ricwin was among the slain —he would never return to Nantes.

"What about Renaud?" I asked.

"He backed the victors at Fontenoy." Nominoë grimaced. "And Charles, the new king of Francia, has named him count."

"What about Lambert? Where is he?"

"He broke with them after the emperor died; he was convinced Lothaire, who had won so many battles against his brothers, would prevail. I supported his decision since the emperor's grandson, Pepin, who is the king of Aquitaine, supported Lothaire. I've never liked Charles. He is a spoiled, arrogant man-child, and that he won at Fontenoy puts me in an uncomfortable position," Nominoë explained. "To answer your question, Lambert is with Pepin in Bordeaux."

"What does that mean for Armorica?"

"Nothing good," Conwoïon cut in.

"It means we are at war with Charles and at peace with Pepin, and tomorrow it could be the opposite." Nominoë scowled at Conwoïon. "For now, the Celts are free from Frankish rule, and we intend to remain free."

"And then there are the Vikings," Conwoïon said.

Nominoë scowled again and said, "They are the least of our problems." His eyes drifted over to the fire. "That woman you left in charge has ruled over the island with grace and wisdom. We have taken to calling her the queen of the sea."

"But you called her a problem."

"I suppose I did," Nominoë admitted. "The problem is that her power increases each day. My troops on the island are now outnumbered ten to one, or so they have said in their letters. For now, I can do nothing except watch and profit from the salt trade."

"It sounds like they have gotten along without me just fine," I said.

"You asked how you can help," Nominoë said. "I want to echo what we told you before: you are welcome to stay here with us. But, if I am honest, I could use your help with the Vikings, because I am sick at heart to think of the horrors they might bring to Armorica if left unchecked. The queen has not been helpful in repelling raids on our coastline. Just last week, there was a raid in Quimper, not a four-day ride from here. The decision is yours. You do not need to make it now."

As we spoke, a young man with curly chestnut-colored hair, a round face, and big brown eyes entered the hall. He sat in a chair without speaking to anyone or asking permission and began eating. We stared at him, waiting for him to say something. It was then I recognized him—he was the boy Ricwin had traded for Lambert, but almost grown.

"Hasting, I would like you to meet my son, Erispoë," Nominoë said.

Erispoë kept eating without a word. I shot a questioning look at Conwoïon, and he offered me an exasperated shrug.

"It's an honor to meet you." My words were answered by a loud lip smack. I said to Nominoë, "You are not old enough to have a son his age."

"I had him young."

"Who is his mother? I never knew you to be married."

"She died in childbirth before we met. I left Erispoë in the care of his mother's family until Renaud captured him. Now he lives with me." He paused to watch his son eat with an air of disgust. "It's been challenging."

We ended our meal, and I retired to the dormitory on the lower level. It smelled familiar, and memories of my years as Nominoë's prisoner flooded back. I did not know it then, but I had lived a simpler life among the Celts than as a Viking. A battle raged in my heart over what to choose. The Vikings thought me dead, and they had likely moved on. If I never returned to them, they might never know what had happened to me. The thought of a simple life, like the one I had lived in Bouaye, called to me. I fell asleep with the candle at my bedside still lit, and it burned until the flame reached the bottom of the wick.

The following morning, Conwoïon asked me to help him at the church. In two weeks, he said, they would receive guests from all over Armorica to celebrate the festival of Saint John. Saint John's celebration took place on the same day each year, June 24, in honor of the birth of John the Baptist. All of Christendom observed the occasion, and when I had lived in Armorica, it seemed civilization lapsed for an entire day to celebrate. Conwoïon put me to work cleaning, arranging, decorating, and making candles. It was exhausting work.

Visitors from other towns in the Vannetais trickled in the days before the festival. By the time we had finished our preparations, the city busted at the seams with people. On Saint John's eve, I had dinner in Nominoë's hall, where I had the happy surprise of seeing Ratvili and his daughter Morgana.

Ratvili gave me a warm embrace and squeezed me against his thick, powerful chest. His oiled beard slopped against my face, which made the embrace much less enjoyable for me. Morgana took my hand and bowed.

"We are happy to see you alive," she said.

"Me too," I replied.

We sat next to each other at the table, and while the others talked and feasted, she and I exchanged quiet, flirtatious regards. She was as beautiful as I remembered, and I feared I had grown disheveled and barbaric-looking. To my relief, she seemed not to mind. When the meal came to a close and we all returned to our bedchambers, her smile lingered in my thoughts.

The following day, Conwoïon asked me to help fill the pews in the church to make sure everyone would fit for his sermon. Up and down the city boardwalk, merchants had set up stands to sell food, trinkets, and other wares. Flowered garlands hung overhead between the buildings, giving the streets a colorful glow in the morning sunlight. Masses of people entered the church, all wearing their most elegant clothing and perfume.

I directed groups to sit together and make room for others. Conwoïon did the same on the other side of the main walkway. When the pews filled up, people had to stand along the walls and beside the pillars. Children sat on the floor below the altar, cheering and giggling as they waited for the ceremony to start. Their feet lingered under the shadow of the cross. The church had filled to the point that I was unable to find a place of my own. I surveyed the crowd from the entrance, but rather than squish into the throng, I closed the doors and waited outside.

"I see what you did there," Morgana said from behind me.

"I'm sorry—I'm sure we can find a spot for you."

"Please, don't," she pleaded. "It's a miracle I ducked out of my father's sight. I won't be so lucky twice."

I smirked. "Are you skipping the sermon on purpose?"

"Spare me," she said. "You're skipping it, too."

Without giving it much thought, I asked, "Would you take a walk with me?"

"I'd love to," she said.

She took my arm, and we walked underneath the garlands toward the edge of town. I led us out the back gate to the beach, keeping one eye behind us to see if anyone followed. We skirted the water's edge until we reached where the dune turned to rocks, and we took a beaten path into the fields above.

"I've always loved the coast," she said. "Oh, there's a beach south of here you would not believe. The sand is white as my dress, and the water clear as crystal."

"It sounds wonderful," I said.

"You've sailed a lot. What was the prettiest beach you ever saw?" she asked.

"The Giant's Throne," I said.

"What's that?"

"It's far, far to the north—a dark place, and a sad one in my memory, but I will never forget how majestic it was. Towering slabs of grey stone plunge into the clear blue water. There is a purity there I have not found elsewhere."

"I would like to see it one day," she said.

I smiled and said, "I don't think I will ever go back. The journey nearly killed us." My harsh words dampened the mood for a moment. "I see you haven't married."

She lifted up her ringless hand and said, "Actually, I have. My father married me off to a Frankish nobleman's son a few years ago."

"I see."

She laughed at me and said, "I only met him once. He ran off to war the day after we were married. We never even... well, I suspected after the wedding that he fancied men, because the night we were to, you know, he took off with his friend."

"What happened to him?" I asked.

"He died at Fontenoy." The cheerful glint in her eye vanished for a moment. She paused, and after some thought, she asked, "What about you? Have you been married? Do Vikings even marry?"

I chuckled and said, "Yes, Vikings marry. And no, I've never—"

"Have you ever loved?" she interjected.

I could tell she had wanted to ask the question and had worked up the courage to do so.

She saw the sour look on my face and said, "I'm sorry. I'm nosy."

"It's fine," I said to put her at ease. "It's an interesting question to ask a man you don't know. It makes me wonder where you're headed with it."

She stopped us in the open field and took both my hands, her eyes gazing into mine with a burning desire. "Armorica needs more men like you, men with passion and honor. My father said you might be staying with Nominoë for a while." The more she went on, the more she strung her words together in a nervous jumble. "He likes you, you know; he says you're a loyal man. I'm an only daughter. My father has no heir. I'm not getting younger, either, and I need—"

"Relax," I snickered. "Don't hurt yourself."

We laughed together, and she took my arm again and squeezed it a little harder than before. My cold, calloused skin had not felt another's touch in so long, I nearly pulled away. It took a few deep breaths for me to relax and enjoy the affection. Her attraction to me felt undeniable, and I found myself imagining what a quiet life in Brittany might offer me. I could escape the hardships of the sea and settle down in the tranquil, serene Armorican countryside with a beautiful wife, a small family, and a simple home. Rather than fight, I could farm, as I had done in Bouaye, and the fruits of my labor would feed my family and neighbors—no more war, no more killing. I had to admit, the thought was tempting.

We stopped again after only a few steps. I pulled her close and held her in my arms, and we gazed into each other's eyes. Asa was gone and I had to let her go. Skírlaug undoubtedly thought I had died in Francia, and I was sure she had moved on. All considered, I was unattached, and I had before me one of the most beautiful women I had ever met. The more we gazed into each other's eyes, the more the distance between our lips shortened. Her breathing quickened. The skin on her neck and cheeks flushed. I could almost taste her lips.

"We should get back." She jerked her head to the side before we could kiss. "We don't want to make them suspicious."

She pushed me away with a light but determined touch. To fix her dress, she turned to face the beach, and she froze when she saw what had crept up behind us.

Two men dressed in rusted maille and dull iron helmets emerged on the path ahead with spears in hand. By the shape and make of the shields, I knew they were Vikings. Were these the men who had raided Quimper?

There were a half-dozen longships out in the Morbihan, about one hundred warriors in all, rowing past the islands closest to the city. The two men before us had arrived on a smaller ship to scout the area before the main raiding party arrived, as my men and I had done countless times. I stepped in front of Morgana to shield her. I did not have my sword on me—Conwoïon had forbidden me to wear it during Saint John's festival. I whispered a small prayer before facing them. They froze in place and both gaped at me.

"Hasting?" one of them asked.

"Yes," I replied.

They looked at each other in astonishment. "You're supposed to be dead."

I opened my arms, glanced down at my body as if to verify, and said, "As you can see, I am not."

"What in Hel's name are you doing here?" the other asked.

"I live here," I said.

"Think of the reward our captain will give us if we bring him *the* Hasting as a captive," the one muttered.

"Do you serve someone who wants my head?" I asked.

"He will when he learns you are alive," the other said.

I had no memory of the two men and no idea whom they served. Whoever they were, they had made it clear they had no intention of letting us go.

The first man lunged at me with his spear. I parried the blow and grasped its shaft. The other man stabbed at me before I could wrestle his companion's weapon away from him. The point grazed my tunic. Morgana shrieked in terror. I had both shafts in front of me, and I pressed them into the ground to disarm them.

The men released their spears and drew swords. With a swift motion, I wrested and twirled one of the spears, then brought it to my hip as I faced them. We stared each other down for a moment, and it gave me time to breathe. I channeled all the rage and hate in my heart, and my grip on the spear tightened.

The two men charged at me at the same time, but I warded them off with quick, repeated jabs. Their shields blocked my strikes, and their blades whirled forward. I swung the spear around and struck at the man on my left with the butt of the shaft and lifted the other end to block the second man's sword. He hit me hard with his shield and sent me staggering backward. I had stunned one of them and could focus on the other.

We circled each other, teeth bared and growling like wolves. I attacked first by lunging forward. He brought his shield around and blocked me. I staggered back again, looking for a weakness in his armor. His helmet glinted in the sunlight and made it hard to see his eyes. Eyes always betray a man's intentions. He charged at me with his shield forward, and he swung at my legs with his sword. His blade missed my leg, and I kicked up hard against his shield, sending him rolling onto his side. He opened himself to me for the briefest of moments, and I drove my spear into his chest. His throat gurgled as he howled. When the other man saw what I had done to his companion, he fled in terror. My rage took control of me, and rather than let him escape, I held up my spear and hurled it at him. It struck him in the middle of his back, and he thudded to the ground.

"Are they dead?" Morgana asked.

I turned to her, and I knew in that moment she had seen the beast.

"My God," she whispered.

It took me a moment to calm myself, and when I did, I approached and held her. Her whole body quivered, and she struggled to walk in a straight line. As we passed the corpses, she croaked in disgust.

We hurried back to the city to find open, unguarded gates, and packed streets full of festivalgoers and merchants. It was, after all, the festival of Saint John, an occasion where the whole city opened up to welcome visitors, even in a time of war. Our distress passed unnoticed. In front of the church, Conwoïon stood idle. His hands were clasped in front of his habit, and he smiled at passers-by. He glanced in our direction and knew something had happened. Without pause, he brought us into the church and sat us at one of the pews in the front. He brought a chalice of wine and a blanket for Morgana, whose face had turned pale.

"She must be in shock," he said. "Here, my child, drink. It will help."

Ratvili must have seen us enter the church, because he burst through the doorway soon after we'd sat Morgana in the pews.

"What's happened?" Ratvili barked.

"We were attacked," I said. "Vikings."

"God, save us." His own face drained of color.

"We ran into their scouting party," I explained. "It won't be long before the others arrive. We need to warn everyone."

Ratvili sat by his daughter and swatted my arm off of her so he could embrace her instead. "Where were you when it happened?"

"Near the beach, outside the city wall," I said.

"You took her outside the city wall?" he snarled.

"I'm sorry," I said. "I didn't think—"

"He killed them," Morgana whispered. "Such ruthlessness."

"I had to," I said.

I tried to put my hand on her lap, but she pushed it away and screamed, "Don't touch me!"

"It's okay, my dear," Ratvili said. "He's right. They would have killed you both."

"She'll be fine," Conwoïon said to me. "Go find Nominoë. Go!"

I left the church and weaved through the crowd to the outer wall, then climbed the ladder to the nearest watchtower. It was a simple platform with a wood-planked roof and a waist-height railing. Each watchtower had a large bronze bell in the shape of a coin used to alert the city to approaching danger.

Across the bay, the ships were rowing with terrifying speed toward the beaches of Vannes. I picked up a long-shafted hammer from the corner and rang the bell.

9

The Call of the Sea

Panic spread through the city like lightning through a night sky. Masses of bodies crowded into the church, all hoping God would save them. Many others hid away in the shops and houses along the main street. Though the bell had rung out, few soldiers answered the call. It made sense. Most of Nominoë's warriors had taken the day to spend with their families. They'd never dreamed of an attack during the festival of Saint John. At least, they'd never dreamed of an attack from the Franks on such a holy day, despite being at war with them.

I returned to my dormitory in Nominoë's hall for my sword, and once I had it, I made my way back to the gates. I hoped I had not arrived too late and had time to close them. Through the southern gate, I could see the longships running ashore and hordes of warriors leaping over gunwales with their shields, axes, spears, and seaxes. The quality of their arms and armor spoke to their master's wealth, and I knew with a mere glance that we were dealing with a powerful warlord. I pushed with all my might to close the first door of the gate, and it dragged in the sand and dirt, making it grueling to move. Several men visiting from elsewhere in Armorica saw me struggling to close it, and they leaped to my aid. We heaved with all our strength, but something had blocked off the hinge and kept the door from closing. The Vikings' swift charge reached us before we had a chance to ready ourselves. Once again, death seemed inevitable.

"Out of the way!" Nominoë screamed from behind me.

He had assembled several dozen horsemen and charged through the gates with their lances aimed forward. A whirlwind overtook me as they passed, forcing me to back up against the palisade wall. I drew my sword, much to the surprise of the men who had helped me, and charged out behind the horses. The cavalry cut through the Vikings' line as a knife cuts through a herring's belly. Some of the horsemen launched javelins at their foe, while others cut them down with their spears and swords. A horse gives a man an unmatched advantage over his enemy, and whoever had launched the raid had not expected to be thronged by a mounted counterattack.

Panicked, the Vikings fled to their ships, covered in their retreat by their archers. Nominoë and his men chased the stragglers and cut them down. He returned to the city as soon as the ships had pushed off, offering a confident nod as he trotted by the gate. I followed him back to the stables on the north side beyond his hall and waited as he handed off his horse to a stable boy.

"That was close," I said.

He turned to one of his soldiers and said, "Captain, call your men and prepare a ship. Those Vikings will strike elsewhere in the Morbihan, and our people there will need our help."

The captain nodded and marched off toward the barracks.

Nominoë turned to me next with vehemence in his eyes and asked, "Do you know who that was?"

"No," I said.

"Are you sure? Your friends on Herio are supposed to be keeping an eye on other Vikings."

"It's an impossible task," I insisted. "New sea captains set sail every year; there's no way to keep them all in check."

Nominoë turned to the soldiers around us and barked, "Keep the gates closed, man the walls, and ring the curfew bell! I want a watch all day and all night, and not a soul enters or leaves the city until we know the Vikings have gone."

We walked back to the church to inform the people there of what had happened. Nominoë knocked on the door. While we waited for an answer, he glanced at me with his head half-cocked. He had never been one to hold his tongue around me, yet at that moment, I sensed precisely that from him.

No one answered, so he tried again with a more forceful knock. A latch clinked on the other side, allowing us to push the door open and enter the church. The people inside stood shoulder to shoulder, every one of them with fear written in their eyes.

I followed Nominoë, and the sight of me caused many murmurs to dance around the room. Ratvili had not moved from his seat at the front of the pews, his arms still wrapped around a sobbing Morgana. Conwoïon welcomed us and led us up the altar steps so we could address the whole crowd. Every person in the room held their breath as Nominoë readied himself to speak.

"We've chased them off," he said to an eruption of cheers. He smiled, taking in the gratitude of his people for fending off a near-calamity. He paused for a moment and turned to the side to cough several times. "For those of you with relatives living in the islands of the Morbihan, we will send ships to find and help them if they need it. But we must wait for the danger to pass. For now, the city is safe, and you may leave the church. To our guests, you may stay as long as you like, and you may leave as soon as you like. The choice is yours."

We stepped down from our perch to join those we knew in the front. Morgana had calmed since I had left her, but she could still hardly look at me. Ratvili, on the other hand, could, and his scowl made me squirm in my skin. Conwoïon embraced Nominoë, and afterward, he embraced me as well in thanks.

"Today is a dark day," Nominoë said. "We are on the cusp of complete freedom from the Franks, and now Vikings have attempted an attack on the heart of Armorica, on our capital city, on one of our holiest days."

"They've raided here before," I said. "The fleet that attacked us today was small, and they fled."

Conwoïon put his hand on my shoulder and said, "I'm sorry, Hasting, but I did not fully disclose the severity of the raids of late. They have struck every province by the sea—Léon, Trégor, Cornouaille, Saint-Brieuc. They have cast a shadow over all of Armorica," he explained.

"What about Renaud?" I said.

"Renaud has been raiding my lands," Ratvili said. "He is still a threat."

"Hasting," Nominoë began with a heavy heart, "I need you to do something for me."

"Anything."

"No," Conwoïon said. "It's too soon!"

"You want me to go back to the island to stop the raids," I said.

Nominoë nodded.

"Why didn't you say that's what you needed me to do from the start?"

"Part of me wanted to give you respite after what you'd been through, and part of me hoped you might stay with us," Nominoë said.

Conwoïon stepped forward to protest. "What can he do against the relentless tide of raiders? He is but one man."

"He was their king, once," Nominoë said. "If we have any chance of stopping the raids, it's with him. It is only a matter of time before a raid on Vannes succeeds, or one on Herio for that matter. The captain of the garrison there, Loán, has sent letters saying even the Vikings on the island have had to repel raids from their own kind. God gave us a gift when he returned Hasting to us. We would be fools not to use him."

Morgana found the strength in her legs and stepped away from her father. She said, "Wait, you want to send him away? Will he come back?"

"He has a way of returning home," Nominoë said with a chuckle. "And this time, he has sworn fealty to me."

"You're still in shock," Ratvili said. He reached for Morgana's arm, but she shrugged him off.

"I'm not a child," she hissed. "Hasting, I want to give you my thanks. I am sorry I did not show it before, but I am grateful to you for saving me today."

"You're welcome," I said.

She stepped toward me and said, "Perhaps we can continue our conversation when you get back?"

"I would like that," I said with a smile.

Our short exchange drew the disdainful regard of her father. He took her arm and walked her out of the church. The rest of us remained silent for a long while until Nominoë said, "She needs a husband, you know."

"Don't tell him that," Conwoïon sneered. "Now, he'll never come back."

Our laughter released some of the tension we felt. Nominoë's laugh turned into a rasped cough that he covered with his tunic. I wiped my eyes with my sleeve and said, "I'll be back. I still need to kill Renaud, so I'll be back."

"I know you will," Nominoë said.

One week later, I was a passenger on a cog headed to Herio, or as we Danes called it, Vindreyland. With as many Vikings stalking the coast as my Celtic friends suggested there were, I feared an attack as we left the

Morbihan. To my relief, we saw no other ships the whole of our journey—nothing but blue skies and flat waters.

As we approached the island, it struck me to see several other cogs already moored in the Vindavik harbor. They were tied off alongside several dozen longships. Above the docks on the hill, the wooden palisades around the monastery had two long white banners draped over them on both sides of the gate. Both had black ravens stitched into them. When the cog butted up against the pier, I dashed down the plank and made my way up the hill.

There was no welcoming party; in fact, the entire village seemed untroubled by our arrival. The grounds appeared well cared for during my absence. The boardwalk over the moat and through the palisade gates was a mixture of colors and tones from where older, darker wood had been replaced with bright new boards. Fresh boards were spattered along the wall as well, and some additional supports had been installed to reinforce the gate.

Inside the monastery grounds, the entirety of the courtyard soil had been cultivated, with narrow paths through each plot. The plots had started to yield their fruits, with flowering stems in the earth, towering vines supported by tall, thin stakes, and plump berries hanging from young shrubs.

"Who are you?" a voice called out in the language of the Danes. It came from one of the plots to my right. I looked around until I spotted a person's head peering out from a grove of dangling pea pods. "Yes, you!"

"I am here to see Skírlaug," I said.

"That's not what I asked you," the shrill little woman said. She wore a baggy brown farm dress with tight-fitting straps and gloves on her hands. Her long grey hair, tied behind her head in a thick braid, spoke to her age.

"My name is Hasting. I used to live here," I said.

My name seemed to have struck the woman's heart with horror. She gasped and fled into the monastery without saying another word. I stepped closer to the open doors but could not see the dark chamber inside with the sun overhead.

In short order, several warriors emerged with hands lingering over weapons, ready to draw. Skírlaug stepped into the light and faced me. She had plumped up since I had last seen her, giving her a much fuller figure and a more rounded face.

"You had better make this quick, stranger," she barked. She held a hand up to shield her eyes from the bright afternoon sun.

"I am not a stranger," I said. "It's me, Hasting."

"You're the third Hasting who has come here this summer," she sneered.

Her words gave me pause. How could she not recognize me? Perhaps it was the length of my hair and beard, which had grown far too long during my time away, or perhaps it was the sun. My eyes darted around the grounds before I said, "Third?"

"Yes. Now tell us what you came here for and just as soon be on your way, along with whomever brought you," she said.

"The Celts brought me back," I said. "But—third?"

Something about how I spoke changed her stance. She took her hands off her hips and stepped closer, giving her warriors an open-palm wave to wait. Her gaze pierced through me, as it always did, and she stepped closer still. When she could reach out and touch me, she grabbed at my beard, pulled back my hair, and gasped.

"You're dead."

"That's what I keep hearing," I said with a smirk.

"How? The gods showed me; they said you died."

"In a way, that's true."

She leaped into my arms and clutched me in a long embrace. I felt her heart beating in her neck and chest, and the relief in her breath. When she pulled back to look at me again, tears streamed down her face, streaking some of her eyeshadow. She dabbed her eyes with her apron, adjusted the brooches at her shoulders, and turned to say, "The hero Hasting has returned to us!"

The Celts cheered, but the Danes remained muted. These were not the men who had followed me, although they did seem to know my name.

The old woman emerged again from the garden and stood at Skírlaug's side.

"Hasting, this is my mother, Ingrid," she said.

"Your mother?"

"Yes, she came to live with me, to help me with—" Skírlaug was interrupted when a little girl with long, braided blond hair skipped out of the hall toward us. "With her."

"You have a daughter?" I asked.

"Yes. She turned four years old this past winter," Skírlaug replied.

My heart leaped into my throat. The little girl skipped up and stood by her mother. She had Skírlaug's eyes, and she examined me with that same piercing regard.

"Who is the father?" I asked.

Skírlaug exchanged a wary look with her mother, then said, "You are."

I smiled and looked down at the little girl. She stared up at me with a quizzical look and said, "My Amma said you came back from the dead. What's it like to die?"

"Your Amma?" I asked.

"Yea, my Amma." She pointed to Skírlaug's mother.

I knelt down and said, "I didn't die, so I don't know. What's your name?"

"Um," she said with a twirl of her dress, "Ulfrúna."

"Ulfrúna, that's a pretty name," I said. My compliment made her smile. "My name is Hasting."

"Oh," she said. "My father's name is Hasting."

Before I could say anything more, Ulfrúna darted off into the monastery. Her mother and grandmother continued to gaze at me as I stood up and grabbed at my aching back. I shot them a sideways look before Skírlaug invited me in. We entered the monastery under the close supervision of her warriors and sat at the mead table.

When I had left, the table had innumerable goblet stains strewn across it. Since then, someone had reworked the surface and restored it to an almost-new condition. Servants presented us with silver chalices and carafes of wine to drink. Skírlaug leaned forward the moment the carafes hit the table, as if to observe my reaction. I looked up at the servants, and before I needed to ask, they brought more carafes filled with clean water and milk. We filled our cups with our drink of choice and raised them to give thanks to the gods. Ulfrúna hopped up on my bench and stood over me, burning with curiosity.

"Ulfrúna, my little rabbit, will you go play with the other children? We have grown-up things to talk about," Skírlaug said.

Ulfrúna ignored her mother. It did not take long for her to face the consequences of it. Her grandmother stood and clapped her hands and chased her outside. I laughed at the child's boldness. Once they had vanished from sight, Skírlaug slid along the bench toward me and put a hand on my knee.

"It's good to see you," she said with a warm smile.

"The feeling is mutual."

"Still cold to the outside world, I see," she murmured.

"I could say the same of you."

"What took you so long to come back?"

I told her everything. She focused on my words, and I knew exactly what she wanted to hear. She wanted to see if I had faced the beast, and if I had, how I had managed. My dream about being a mangy wolf spoke to her; she leaned close as she listened to how I had turned back into a man and fallen to the earth. To my surprise, she welcomed what I told her about Bertin and Evroul, and Gwenaëlle and Corentin. She smiled when I told her what they had taught me about service and sacrifice, and about letting go of the past and the future, giving both over to God or the gods, and focusing on the present. I also admitted that I had been selfish and self-absorbed in my desire for revenge. Though I still wanted to kill Renaud, I would need to do so in service to a higher cause: to help the people of Armorica and Vindreyland. Skírlaug's eyes offered a kind of understanding I had not expected.

"Has anyone told you the story of how Odin learned to read the runes?" she asked me. "A long time ago, before Man's creation, our gods fought a bloody war with another race called the Vanir. Odin and his kin were outmatched—the Vanir possessed skill in battle that made their victory inevitable. Odin knew this, and he feared it. He searched the world for something, anything, that would help him in the fight. Upon Yggdrasil's trunk, the great ash tree, he discovered the runes. They had been carved by the Norns, but none of the Aesir knew their meaning, and they did not know how to speak them.

"Here is where you must listen carefully, Hasting. Odin did not know what the runes could do or how they could help him. All he knew was that if he did nothing, the Vanir would destroy him and his people. To learn the runes, he hanged himself from the great tree for nine days until his life ended; he gave a sacrifice of himself to himself. Through this sacrifice, the runes revealed themselves to him. They contained more power than he could have imagined, and they even brought him back to life. The runes gave him strength, vitality, wisdom, and patience; they gave him protection, healing, virility, and prowess; they gave him mastery over earth, fire, water, and air. When the Vanir saw the Aesir's newfound strength, they sued for peace."

"Death and rebirth," I said. "While my fight is the same, my near-death opened my heart to the greater purpose of my life and gave me the tools to face it."

"Your near-death opened your heart; it's those people who helped you to see rightly with it," she said with relief. "So, New Hasting, how will you embody what you have learned when you return to your life as a Viking? I am sure you have thought about it. I fear it may push you back into the shadow of the beast."

"I fear it too," I said. "I cannot do it alone. I need your help."

Skírlaug sat back in thought, running her hands through her matted hair. She examined the clothes I wore —all of them were of Celtic make—and tilted her head to say, "Where do you believe you belong?"

"I don't know what you mean," I said.

"Are you one of us or one of them? Does your loyalty lie with your people, the Danes, or with Nominoë and the Celts? Are the Danes even your people now?"

No one had asked me that question before, and I had never had to think about it. My heart belonged to Armorica. The beauty of the land, the strength of her people, and the majesty of her long history drew me in. The Celts of the Vannetais had a way about them that I admired and wanted to emulate. On the other hand, my destiny kept pulling me toward the Danes, my father's people, and the sea also called to me. It was my father's words that spurred me to action, to achieve the reputation I believed he would have wanted for me. Skírlaug presented an impossible choice, as if to embrace one was to abandon the other.

"I am both," I said. "I am neither."

Skírlaug took my hands and said, "You can be both." She smiled and continued, "You are allowed to be both."

She rested her head on my shoulder as she caressed my back, her breaths slow and long. Part of me wanted to pull away from her. I understood that my impulse to resist my feelings stemmed from the man I was before I had left, the man reluctant to expose his softer side for fear of what it might do to his reputation. I wrapped my arm around her shoulders and held her against my breast. Our hands clasped together. The soft touch of her skin sent a wave of warmth through my body that put my fears at ease.

It did not take long, however, for Ulfrúna to reappear and interrupt us. Her energy impressed me—she never walked, she ran, and when she ran, she titled her large head forward and led with it. She jumped up onto the bench, breathing hard, and tugged at my tunic.

"What is it, my little rabbit?" Skírlaug said, her words muffled by my tunic.

"I want to play with my new friend," Ulfrúna said.

"Your new friend?"

"Him!" Ulfrúna exclaimed, her little finger drilling into my shoulder.

Skírlaug laughed as Ulfrúna peered over me with her big, brown eyes, and her chin resting on my shoulder. "Give us a little longer, my rabbit. When we are finished, he will play with you."

Ulfrúna gave a deep frown and darted back out into the courtyard, leaving a cloud of dust motes in her wake that drifted in the sunbeam through the open doorway. Skírlaug sat back to fix her hair. I looked around the chamber, wondering about the supposed number of warriors Nominoë had mentioned. Since I'd arrived, I had seen two men who stood guard over the monastery entrance, but no others. They had entered the chamber with us and now sat at a knee-high table with what appeared to be chess pieces. They sat opposite one another on short, rickety stools, and they hunched over their game. The game pieces clattered when they moved them, but outside of that, the two did not make a sound.

"Now that you have returned to us a new man, what is it that you want? Do you want to take back your place and title?" Skírlaug edged away from me and crossed her legs beneath the table.

Her change in tone put me on guard, and I replied, "No. I don't even want to be a ship captain."

Skírlaug chuckled and said, "False modesty does not suit you, Hasting."

"It's not false modesty," I tried to explain, but she brushed me off.

She leaned over the table a little more and scratched at the wood grain with her fingernail. "We need you," she said. "You're the only man who can make things right here. No true Dane could do it, and no true Celt. Vindreyland needs a king who is both."

"What about you?"

She scoffed at me before answering, "I've held things together, but… I can't," she said.

I considered her words before speaking again. "How do you want to handle the child?" I asked. "Should we marry, or something?"

"Could you at least pretend to feel something?" Her eyes watered but she had a curl in her lip. "By our law, our daughter is your charge. You are responsible for providing us the wealth we need. But, Hasting, I cannot marry you."

"Oh." I exhaled a relieved breath. "Is it because you are a völva?" I asked. She shook her head, and my heart sank. "You mean, you do not love me anymore?"

"I still love you. But it's been too long, and I fell in love with someone else after you left."

"You did?"

"Yes," she whispered.

"Who is he? Where is he?"

She wiped her eyes with her apron and scooted away from me on the bench. Her breaths quickened, and she picked at the wood grain on the table again. She focused on her fingers, and each time she opened her mouth to speak, her lip quivered, and she withdrew.

"Do you need some time?"

She nodded and sank her head into her hands. "Ulfrúna is waiting," she said through her fingers.

I left her in her hall—it was *her* hall now—and joined Ulfrúna in the courtyard. She had a small hand net she was using to try and catch butterflies. They seemed to have all evaded her, but that hadn't dampened her spirit. When she saw me step out of the monastery, she jolted toward me. Her grandmother stopped her labor in the garden to watch over us.

"Do you know how to catch a butterfly?" Ulfrúna asked.

"I've never tried," I said.

"Oh—I'll show you."

She took my hand and led me into the garden. When we neared the inner palisade wall, she tugged on my tunic for me to kneel next to her, then she whispered in my ear.

"Be very quiet."

"All right," I whispered back.

"No. Quieter than that."

I could not contain my laughter. Ulfrúna placed her hand over my mouth to keep me quiet. Then she grasped her net with both hands and tiptoed toward a small blackberry bush. An arm's length away from it, she paused. With a sudden, violent stroke of her arms, she swung her net at the bush and struck it hard. Leaves and berries flew off, as did a few butterflies. Ulfrúna swiped at the sky but missed all of them.

She turned to me, jumping up and down and brimming with excitement, and said, "Did you see? Did you see it? I almost had one!"

"May I try?"

She nodded and handed me her net. I followed the butterflies a short distance, and, when I drew near enough, I swiped at them. Ulfrúna shrieked with joy when she saw me bring the net to the ground with two butterflies in it. We both hovered over the net to observe them.

"I like the white one," Ulfrúna said.

"I do, too," I said.

"No, you're supposed to say you like the black one."

"I like the black one too." I laughed. "We can both like both. How about that?"

Ulfrúna agreed. She reached down to grab one of the butterflies, but before she could touch it, I stopped her and said, "If you touch it, it will die."

"Why?" she asked.

"Well, because they are fragile creatures," I explained. "When they are flying on their own, they are strong and beautiful. But if you try to grab them and hold onto them, they fall apart."

I could see her mind working hard to grasp what I had said. She seemed sharp for a four-year-old; brighter than I was, I think.

"What should we do with them?" she asked.

"I think we should let them fly again."

I lifted the net so the butterflies could float off into the garden to join the others.

We sat in the dirt together and watched them for a while, admiring their grace and their beauty. The longer we stayed still, the closer they flew to us. Some of them flew so close as to almost land on us, and Ulfrúna marveled at them. I admired the glint in her eye and the innocence in her curiosity about the world around her. She had never taken the time, it seemed, to observe the butterflies. In doing so, she discovered a new way of enjoying them that did not involve a hand net. Over time, the butterflies all flew away from us and our fun ended.

"Why did you leave my mother?" Ulfrúna asked.

Her question sent a shock through my body. It took me a moment to steady myself and find the words to answer her. "I had something I needed to do," I said.

She looked me in the eye with a face devoid of emotion. Already, she had her mother's ability to ice over like the coldest of winters.

"Your mother let me go, like how we let the butterflies go. I needed to fly on my own, and if she had held onto me, I might have fallen apart."

How well she had understood me, I cannot say. Children of that age seem to understand more than they do in some instances and in others quite the opposite. She squinted at her grandmother through the bright afternoon sunlight. Ingrid was bent over and working a plot of soil near the entrance to the grounds.

When it seemed Ulfrúna would not speak again, she asked, "Will you stay awhile?"

"Yes."

Ingrid suddenly craned her neck over the garden and called for Ulfrúna. The tone of her voice was dark and shrill. The little girl complied, a stark contrast to how she had ignored her mother's orders in the monastery. Something or someone had put them all on edge, and it did not take long for me to see why.

A group of men walked through the palisade entrance into the gardens. They wore simple tunics and tightly woven britches, and each wore his hair differently. Some wore beads and rings in their beards; others did not. I did not recognize any of the men, nor did any of them know me. A few looked in my direction as they passed, heading for the monastery's main chamber, but they paid me no attention.

Skírlaug met them at the doorway. She spoke to their leader, a stern-looking man who wore eyeshadow, same as her, and whose long hair he bunched in a knot atop his head, with the sides of his scalp cut short, almost shaved. His blond beard started at his ears and reached clear to his chest, and it was tied into two ringed braids below his chin. I guessed that he'd wanted it to have the look of a serpent's tongue to intimidate his enemies. The man next to him was identical, except he wore his long blond hair down, blended with his beard. I had never seen two men look so alike.

"Hasting, I want you to meet someone," Skírlaug called.

I stood and wiped the dirt from my trousers. Why I felt so nervous in that moment I could not say. However, I had always felt anxious about meeting new Danes and Northmen. They stared at me with curious eyes from across the garden, and when I approached, their leader crossed his arms and smirked. He scanned me from head to toe and shot mocking looks back at his followers. They, too, put on crooked smiles.

"Hasting, this is Grjotgar and Kjartan, twin brothers from Trøndelag," Skírlaug said.

"From Trøndelag? What is your relation to Hakon and Halldóra?"

Grjotgar chuckled and said, "They are our parents."

A wave of relief washed over me. The Northmen from Lade were allies, and it appeared they had helped Skírlaug continue the salt trade.

"Wonderful to meet you." I extended my arm, and he took it. "I am a great admirer of your mother. She is a brave and tenacious woman."

My enthusiasm surprised the brothers, and in a way, it helped to put them at ease. "Thank you," Kjartan said. "We have heard many stories about you, as well."

"Good stories, I hope?" My humor seemed to have shot past their heads like a stray arrow. "So, you have taken up the salt trade for your parents; that is excellent news. I've been gone so long, I'm still trying to piece together everything that has happened."

"I think the gods are playing an awful trick on us," Grjotgar said firmly. "You are smaller than what the skalds would have us think, and skinnier. How could such a frail man have done all the things you supposedly have done?"

"The biggest and the strongest are not always the best fighters or the bravest," Skírlaug interjected.

"It is true, I have grown quite thin," I said. "Given time, I will regain the strength I once had."

"We don't have time," Grjotgar spat. He turned to Skírlaug. "You said the gods had sent us a great gift. This man can't help us."

"Help you with what?" I asked before Skírlaug could answer.

Grjotgar took in a deep breath as if holding himself back from wanting to kill me. His brother stepped between us and said, "Forgive my brother; he has a hot temper." He looked at Grjotgar with black eyes, and Grjotgar stepped backward. "News of your death has been spreading, and now there are many who have vowed to fight us for this land. Our parents have asked us to protect the salt trade. We trade the salt with the Ruotsi, our kin in the East, and it is making our kingdom wealthy. But with so many claimants, it seems an impossible task."

I cleared my throat and said, "Who has vowed to fight you?"

"My half-brother Horic the Younger had vowed to reclaim what our father lost and sail here with a fleet this summer," Skírlaug said. "And they said my uncle Rurik, who lives in Frisia, has also put a fleet together."

"Don't forget Thor," Kjartan added. "He has said he wants to take the island, too. He told me last autumn when we passed through Dublin on our way home."

"Thor of Dublin? What makes him think he can—"

"There's more, Hasting," Skírlaug said. "Your friend Rune is now a powerful sea captain in his own right. Last he and I spoke, he had taken possession of Veisafjǫrðr and two other longphorts along the southern Irish coast. He, too, has claimed rights to Vindreyland as your first and most loyal follower."

"I suppose next you'll say Bjorn has become a chieftain, too, and is putting together a fleet to take the island?" I scoffed. My words were met with solemn silence. "You must be joking!"

"Bjorn and his brother Ubba have joined together, although they have not said they want to fight us for the salt trade," Skírlaug said. "They have been raiding south of here for several months now."

It took me a moment to understand the gravity of what they told me. Every sea captain of any importance, it seemed, wanted to take possession of Vindreyland for themselves. A relentless tide of invaders loomed on the horizon, seeking to consume the whole of the island's wealth, and we did not have the men to stop it. No wonder the monks had abandoned the monastery. What chance did they have against such a relentless tide?

"Was it you who tried to raid Vannes a few weeks ago?" I asked the twins.

"We have not raided at all this year," Grjotgar said.

"There was a raid nearby?" Kjartan's eyes filled with concern.

"That's why I am here," I explained. "The Celts are at war with the Franks, and they asked my help in stopping the raids."

"If there are raiding parties so close, they will attack us here sooner than we expected." Kjartan turned to Skírlaug with a furrowed brow. "I urge you to reconsider my proposal. You will be welcome in Trøndelag and safe. We must abandon the island."

"But we have Hasting, now," she insisted.

"What good is one man?" Grjotgar asked.

Skírlaug took a harsh tone and said, "He is more important than you know. When the others learn he is alive, many will flock to him. Already, I can tell you Bjorn and Rune will follow him. They will not abandon their oaths."

"Did the gods tell you this?" Kjartan jeered. "Like they showed you that Hasting was dead?"

Skírlaug slapped him across the face.

He stepped back and held his cheek. His skin flushed, and the vein in his neck pulsated like a drum. "No wonder they all abandoned you," he growled.

He tugged at his brother's arm, and they turned their backs on her. Their men walked away with them, disgust written on all their faces. Skírlaug stood tall, too proud to admit she had made a mistake.

"Go on, then!" she cried. "Leave, cowards!"

Kjartan turned and moved toward her with clenched fists. I stepped between them and put out my hand.

"Tell your little hero to step aside before I break his wrist," he said.

"This is your chance to leave in peace," I said.

"She offended me. I have a right to answer," Kjartan insisted.

"Answer her, then," I said. I knew he had meant to strike her.

"Do you even know our laws?" he asked.

"I do."

"I don't need your help, Hasting," Skírlaug whispered behind me.

I ignored her and said to Kjartan, "And in my view, you are a coward for leaving."

Kjartan's eyes opened wide with surprise. He looked back at his men, their mouths agape. I wrapped my hand around the hilt of my sword and drew it far enough so they could see the glint of its steel.

"Is that a challenge?" Kjartan barked.

"For less of a coward, perhaps, but for you, it's an observation," I said.

"Hasting, what are you doing?" Skírlaug asked in a panic.

It was a good question. What was I doing? I had never challenged a man by insulting him before. Yet, I knew what I needed. Kjartan and Grjotgar wanted to leave, and if I had any hope of sparing Armorica from Viking raids, I needed all the men I could muster, including them. They did not know my plan. Frankly, I did not fully realize it in that moment, either. But I knew I needed their help and their loyalty. Warriors understand one thing above all: strength.

Kjartan looked down at my sword. He growled, and he drew a dagger from his belt and lunged at me. I parried to the side and ducked out of the way of his blade. He sprung like a serpent from its coil, and I did not have time to draw my sword. With one hand raised shoulder-height for balance, he jabbed and stabbed at me with the other.

To my dismay, he was much better trained than I had expected. His strokes were short and fast, and he did not open himself up to a counterattack. I skipped backward to put some distance between us, but he pounced to close the gap and keep me from unsheathing my sword. Finally, he lunged a hair too far, caught his toe on a rock, and offered me a chance to throw him off-balance.

His knife swiped a finger's width from my shoulder, and I grasped his wrist and used his momentum to keep him moving. His body lurched forward, his back exposed to me, and I kicked him in the rump. He fell into the dirt, and when he turned around, he stared wide-eyed down the cold, steel shaft of my blade.

"Move, and I'll kill you," I said. "Speak, and I'll kill you. You will listen to what I have to say. The only way to make this work is to work together. Right now, I need you more than you need me, I know, but if you stay and we prevail, I will make sure the skalds sing your names to the ends of the world."

Kjartan looked over at Grjotgar, who, despite the terror in his eyes, nodded in agreement.

"We will swear to you," Kjartan said.

"No," I said. "Not to me. To her."

Skírlaug looked as surprised as the rest of them. She adjusted the brooches on her dress and glared at me.

"I can't swear to a woman," Kjartan cried.

"What about your mother? Men swore to her," I reminded him.

"No, they didn't," he said. "They swore to my father. They followed her because she was his wife."

"The way I see it, you have two choices: either die now—which is what you were trying to avoid by leaving—or swear to Skírlaug."

"This is your land, Hasting. My father gave it to you," Skírlaug said. "They will follow you because of who you are and what you've done. I have no such deeds to boast."

"I can't," I insisted. "I didn't come here to lead you."

"You can. You must," Skírlaug pleaded. "This island will never have a firm footing in the world until you take your place. My father saw potential in you. He saw that you alone could form a bridge between the Vikings and the Celts. This island was forsaken by the gods, and now they have sent you back so that we might live here in peace."

"What is it to you?" I snapped. "Why do you want to stay here?"

"Because I have nowhere else to go. In Jutland, my brother will have me killed. Anywhere else, I'll be the woman who had a child out of wedlock. Men will not touch me; communities will shun me," Skírlaug said. "Here, at least, I have a chance of giving my daughter a good life."

"Why did you come back to us if not to reclaim your place and title?" Kjartan asked.

"I am here to get the Vikings off the Celts' backs so I can return and help Nominoë fight his war against Renaud," I explained.

"What good would you be to him in Armorica as one man?" Skírlaug demanded. "He asked you to come here, didn't he? Do you think he expected you to smooth his Viking problem over so quickly and then go back to fight at his side? No, Nominoë is far too cunning for that. He sent you because he needs you to take your place as our leader again. You will be far more useful to him with an army at your back. I know you want to live out your days in Armorica, but you have a higher calling, and you need to take it."

"I don't want it."

"That is what you were missing before," Skírlaug said. "A good ruler does not rule for himself. He serves those he rules. Now that you have tamed the beast inside you, you can see it rightly. You asked for my help, and this is how I can help you: by making you a king." She stepped toward the others and opened her arms. "Who will swear to him and join his hird? Who among you will be the first to serve the king of Vindreyland?"

Grjotgar and Kjartan seemed at a substantial loss for words. They gave each other a second look as if communicating without speaking, and then, in unison, they blurted out, "We will."

10

Reputation is Everything

A fleet of thirty ships appeared on the horizon two weeks after I arrived. They sailed straight for the Concha, wasting no time in running ashore and rushing the village. The warriors' painted shields made for a colorful display, with no two painted the same. A king's warriors would carry identically painted shields gifted to them by the man to whom they'd sworn loyalty. These men fought for someone far less powerful.

The dozens of warriors who raided the village soon ceased their screaming and yelling. We had sent the villagers inland to hide, protected by Nominoë's soldiers. They had taken most of their belongings with them, so there was little left to destroy except the houses. The fighting men had stayed behind, and we were ready.

The attackers stared up the hill at the monastery and Skírlaug's ravens that hung from the gateway. A line of archers with arrows nocked stretched the whole length of the palisade ramparts. Underneath them at the bottom of the wooden wall, a row of pikes jutted out from the moat like menacing shark teeth.

More warriors arrived from the shoreline and gathered at the docks. We could not see their leaders from the palisade, but we knew what they would do next. It felt strange standing on the battlements the Franks had built to protect the monastery. I remembered what had happened to them, and I hoped we had done enough to prepare ourselves so that we would not share their fate.

Several dozen warriors broke away from the lead group and strolled toward our defenses flying a white banner.

"We wish to speak with your leader, the pretender named Skírlaug," one of the warriors said, projecting his voice so all could hear.

Skírlaug peered down at them. She wore a leather breastplate the men had fashioned for her out of a man's jerkin, and she had loose-fitting linen britches tied off at the knee like the rest of us. She reminded me in that moment of Halldóra, the only other woman I had met who wore men's clothing. Necessity demanded it.

"Hello, Ragnar," she sneered from above, her arms clasped behind her back.

His name sent my heart into a flutter. I had not expected him, but it did not surprise me that he would join the long line of warlords seeking to invade my island. I could not believe my luck. Ragnar owed me his life. I watched from my hiding spot below as Skírlaug spoke with him. Our plan was underway.

"This was King Horic's land," Ragnar declared, "and he gave it to Hasting. Hasting is gone, and with him any claim to the wealth of this land that you think you retain. We have all waited for his return. What has it been, five years?"

Skírlaug taunted him and said, "I have more claim than you ever will. How dare you come here and threaten me? I could send word to my brother and tell him what you're doing. Or what about Hakon of Lade? These are his sons, Kjartan and Grjotgar, and Hakon and Horic shared this land. I know of no one else with more of a claim than us."

"No one needs to die today," Ragnar continued. "You are outnumbered, surrounded. Surrender to me and I will allow you to leave in peace. Hasting isn't here to save you this time."

Skírlaug looked down at me from her perch. She vanished behind the ramparts and descended one of the ladders. An uncomfortable silence gripped the battlefield, broken by the coughing, spitting, and grumbling of men clearing their throats. When she reached the bottom, she started to laugh.

"What's so funny?" I said.

"I can't believe it's him," she said.

I shrugged. "He's brought more men than we can fight off."

"Yes, but it's *him*. Not Rurik or Thor or Horic the Younger, but *him*. The gods really are watching over us."

It took her a moment to stop laughing. She fixed her hair, adjusted her jerkin, and said, "Of all the men who could have attacked us first, we are lucky it's him. He's been in love with you ever since you spared his life. Bjorn and Ubba couldn't stand being around him because he wouldn't stop singing your praises. That's why they went raiding south."

"What are you suggesting?" I asked her.

"This is our chance. You could take control of his fleet." She took a step closer to me and squeezed my hand.

"I knew you would suggest that I kill him."

"No!" She slapped her hand to her mouth, as if she could catch the words before they reached my ears. "Walk out there and meet with him. Win him over. He won't fight you; I know he won't. And when he asks what you can give him in return for his loyalty, show him the crypt."

I nodded, and Skírlaug climbed back up to the ramparts and shouted, "I have a gift for you!"

I gave the men who stood by me at the gate a nod, and they set their shoulders under the crossbar and lifted it out of the way. They returned to the gate and pushed it open, letting in the afternoon light which shined on my face. I stepped forward onto the boardwalk that crossed the ditch and drew my sword. My eyes took a moment to adjust, but as they did, I heard a man cry out, "It's Hasting—he's back from the dead!"

I have never seen such fearsome warriors act so skittishly. When my eyes adjusted to the light, I focused on their leader, frozen in place, his mouth agape.

"But... you're dead!" Ragnar howled.

Without uttering a word, I swung my sword around and marched toward him. His men scattered in fear.

Ragnar did not try to defend himself. He dropped to his knees, clasped his hands, and said, "How is this possible? We were all sure you were dead."

Seeing him in such a vulnerable position, I had an idea of how to remind him of our previous encounter. I pressed my sword's tip against the dimple in his neck and said, "This feels familiar."

"It's good to see you again." His hands were shaking. "I wish Bjorn and Ubba were here; they would be overjoyed that you are well."

I bared my teeth and said, "You owe me your life."

"I know," he stuttered. "Believe me, I wish there was a way to repay you."

"Swear to me," I said.

"What?"

I leaned forward to put a little more pressure on his neck.

"Yes. It would be my honor to swear to you. But, my men, you see, they might not like it."

I sheathed my sword and crossed my arms, waiting for him to utter the words I had asked. Still on his knees, he shot a glance back at his army. Had he been a younger man, he might have tried to leap at me, but he held his knees in pain, and he knew he did not stand a chance to turn his situation around. Seeing that I was made of flesh and blood, his followers inched toward us again. They knew if they tried to fight me, I would kill Ragnar, and my archers would kill them.

"Come closer," I called to them. I brimmed with confidence. "Come hear your chieftain swear an oath to his new king—your new king."

Several muttered, but none answered me. None of them dared approach any closer; they hunched on bent knees, ready to run. That I'd asked their leader to swear to me did not seem to upset them. What made them so cautious, I believe, was that they still thought some dark magic had brought me back from the dead.

"I'll do it. I'll swear to you," Ragnar said. He took a deep breath before starting the oath. "I will make known my forebears so you may know me. I am Ragnar, son of Sigurd, hirðman to King Svein of Zealand. I myself have taken my own land and have sworn to no other before you. I swear to never forget the wealth you give me; to fight for you when called; to wrest glory from your enemy; to not flee while your heart still beats; to avenge your life should it be taken, or die trying. This oath I make now and for the duration of the raiding season until the time that I must return to my land in the North. And I swear, should you seek my loyalty thereafter, I shall give you preference over any others."

When he finished, I took a silver arm ring from my wrist—a decorated piece made in the shape of Nidhogg, the serpent that gnaws at the roots of Yggdrasil, the world tree—and tossed it to him. Ragnar stared at the arm ring for a moment, his expression perplexed, and then he looked up at me with a smirk. The men behind him looked on with dropped jaws.

"Having me swear to you means you will have thirty ship captains swear to you. They will all want payment and the promise of wealth for serving you. Do you have the wealth to afford it?" he asked.

"Skírlaug has been a good steward of my land," I said. "And the salt trade has been good. That's why you're here, isn't it? Because you heard just how good it has been."

I invited Ragnar to join me in the monastery alone, and his men stayed where they stood, still as statues. As we walked through the gates, Kjartan and Grjotgar protested bringing him in, but Skírlaug pulled them back. We made our way into the monastery and descended the stairwell behind the chapel into the crypt. I took a torch to light our way and ducked through the first low stone archway. Ragnar marveled at what he saw.

"Skírlaug, it turns out," I said, "is not a big spender."

I lowered my torch to illuminate the wealth she had stowed away in the crypt. Piles of silver chalices and bowls, carafes brimming with silver coins, rings, and necklaces lined the walls and glinted faintly in the torchlight.

"The Celts pay us in silver to protect the villagers who farm the salt. Even then, they make more than their ships can carry, so Grjotgar and Kjartan take the rest home to their father, Hakon, who trades it with the Ruotsi." I pointed my torch at a chest full of silver coins with mysterious inscriptions. "They tell me these come from a land far to the east where the sun shines hot and the people's skin is dark."

"I am familiar with the silver hordes the Ruotsi bring back from their travels," Ragnar said. "How many pounds of silver do you have down here?"

"Thousands," I said.

"What a treasure."

"I look to you for guidance." My statement seemed to surprise him. "How much should I give each sea captain for his oath, and how much should I promise him when we are finished?"

Ragnar scoffed and said, "You want to give this all away?" He put on a crooked smile that bared half his teeth; he was transfixed by the wealth.

"I don't need silver," I said. "I need men."

"You will have them," Ragnar said. "I will speak for you, Hasting. My men will follow you."

We hauled several crates of my wealth out of the crypt and across the ditch into the clearing under my archers' watchful eyes. Ragnar returned to his army to gather the sea captains, and while he did so, I sat on one of the crates to wait. I was joined by Skírlaug, who seemed more than content with herself.

"I can't believe this worked," I said. "A fortnight ago I was a pauper, and now I am a king."

"A good reputation is priceless," she said. "Your former deeds will follow you wherever you go, and men will flock to you and swear oaths to you."

I thought back to my time on Eilif's ship when I'd learned the importance of oath-taking in the fabric of our culture. An oath binds a man to another, whether he is a jarl, a ship's captain, or a friend, and a man who upholds his oaths earns wealth and reputation. Oath-breakers face the wrath of the gods, whose judgment falls by the sword or ax, or however the oath-keeper sees fit. The Aesir, our gods, swore oaths to one another, and it formed the fabric of their laws; so too do the oaths of men make the fabric of our laws. An oath, I remembered, is the most divine gift a man can give to another.

Ragnar would keep his oath, I assured myself, as would his men. He returned with all of the ship captains. They formed a line to take their oaths one by one, and I gave each man who swore to me as much silver as he could carry in his hands. It felt strange to receive oaths from men I did not know, but they knew me. They knew my name, and they knew what I had done and what I promised to do for them in the future. That is the power of reputation—it allows men to know others without ever meeting them, to inspire trust, and to command action. Reputation is everything.

When the last of them swore to me and took his silver, I sat on the empty crate and breathed a sigh of relief. Ragnar took them back to the port, and they traded their weapons for tools to make a camp in the field where we asked all visiting fleets to stay. Skírlaug joined me with a smug smile.

"You look happy," I said.

"I am," she replied. "We are alive, we have an army, we have wealth. Your return has helped more than you know."

"When I spared Ragnar's life, I was convinced his men had not followed me because they thought I was weak."

She started to laugh but sucked it back in with a sigh. In forced seriousness, she said, "Sometimes, Hasting, you impress me with what you know, and other times with what you don't. No, they did not swear to you because, with Ragnar still alive, their oaths to him still stood."

"If I had killed him, they would have sworn to me."

"But you had already promised Bjorn you wouldn't. I can't believe how badly you misread that situation," she said with a disparaging smile.

"What part of 'I spent my childhood as a slave' did you not understand?" I jeered. "I missed things. I'm still learning."

She put her arm around my shoulders and leaned into me. "Next time, I'll explain the whole thing to you with plain words so you can make better decisions."

We laughed together, and I said, "Help me carry these crates back in."

The more time we spent together, the more I felt something for her. It was not the kind of love that would spur me to launch ships for the icy desolation of the Giant's Throne, the distant fjord on the edge of the world where I had sailed in my quest to find Asa, but it was love. I trusted her implicitly, and I felt I could confide in her.

She seemed desperate to win me back over; it was evident in her over-attentiveness. Part of it, I knew, was that she had settled back into the role of advisor to the king, a position she had enjoyed with her father. Having grown up as a Dane and living all her life in Jutland, she had a better sense of cultural nuance that I had ever learned. Her advice was crucial, and through her I learned many of the things I had done with my first crew that could have landed me in trouble—and they had, unbeknownst to me. Her presence helped me keep Grjotgar and Kjartan happy, and I would also look to her to help me with Ragnar's men. I did not, however, listen to the so-called will of the gods when she divined it. She had been wrong about so many important things, I doubted she had any ability to commune with them at all.

We invited the ship captains to my hall to feast and to drink later that night. It was my first real test since I had returned to see how well I would manage myself when thrust back into the wolf's den. I felt the powerful pull of the beast clawing at my heart to pull me back into the shadow. But I resisted.

The entire night, I sipped on a blackberry and cherry juice Skírlaug had set out for me, and that looked like wine. As king, I did not have to share my personal carafe, nor did anyone in the room try to fill my cup with theirs. And here I found myself with another strange feeling—I had never thought of myself as ostentatious, but Skírlaug had insisted I dress in a manner that told everyone in the room how much wealth I had. She dressed me in an elegant silk tunic with a thick leather belt and draped a bearskin over my shoulders. These had been

Horic's clothes, and it surprised me that they fit so well. I had not yet gained back all of my strength and size.

Skírlaug also decorated my beard with silver and colored beads, and she put rings from all over the known world on my fingers. She applied dark shadow over my eyes, same as hers, and when she finished, she presented me to Grjotgar and Kjartan, who both laughed and marveled at my new flair.

"He looks pretty," Kjartan laughed.

"I feel ridiculous." I sat at the head of my table in all my new adornments, stiff and uncomfortable.

"Everyone wants to look good, Hasting," Skírlaug said. "The Celts may have told you to take that part of yourself and hide it at the bottom of a bag, but you need to let go. Have fun!"

My whole life, I had been a man behind a mask, acting the way I thought others wanted me to. At the feast, I felt I should carry myself a certain way, but it made me rigid and unappealing to my new followers. Skírlaug was right. I needed to let go and be how I wanted to be, or at least as much as was tolerable.

Ragnar had no trouble being himself. He seemed to have nothing holding him back—no expectations, and no unreachable ideals to chase. During the feast, he sat several places over to my right, his face lit by a well-placed candle. When he spoke, he spoke from the heart, and his passions drew the attention of the others in a way I'd never before observed. His stories sounded half-cocked, made up, but he spoke with such liveliness and authenticity that everything he said seemed believable. Though I had defeated him in a duel, he had far and above mastered the skill of leadership, and I had an opportunity to learn from him. Few men could say they had lost a duel and could still inspire thirty ships to follow them. At first, I resented him for it. He embodied those traits that Skírlaug said I'd shoved to the bottom of a bag, and because I still did not know how to let them out and accept them, I was jealous. The longer I kept those traits hidden away, the more power the beast would have to drag me back into his shadow. I still had much to learn, but my journey, I believed, had put me on the right path.

Ragnar had started to slur, and now he shifted his attention to me. "Hasting! What comes next? Hm? You've earned my… our loyalty, so what will you have us do?"

"Patience, Ragnar," I said. "There will be plenty of fighting to come."

Kjartan leaned in and whispered, "Do you think he knows about the others?"

He made a good point. Ragnar might know about the other fleets. I sat back in my seat and crossed my arms. "What do you know about Horic the Younger and Rurik? Were they planning to sail their own fleets here when you left?"

Ragnar paused. He gazed into his drink and swirled the liquid with a twist of his goblet. "They were," he said.

"Did you think you could fight them off?"

"We did not sail here to take the island," Ragnar admitted. "We were on our way to find Bjorn and Ubba who are raiding south of here. I never intended to fight Skírlaug, only to scare her enough to pay us off in silver and salt. It would have been a good victory to start off the raiding season."

Skírlaug scoffed at him, skin flushed, and glared. "That's all we were to you?" she snarled. "A casual raid?"

"It's what we do, darling." Ragnar raised his cup to her.

I could see she wanted to reach across the table and strangle him, but I intervened and said, "Well, you got much more than you bargained for; you've embroiled yourself in the coming war."

"All the same to me," Ragnar said. "Raids are a nasty business, and you're never sure what the payoff will be. At least fighting for you, I know you will deliver on the wealth you promised—I've seen it with my own eyes—and I've seen you fight. Our chances of victory are high."

He raised his cup again, and more than half the men at the table raised theirs to cheer with him. When the ruckus quieted down, there was a loud knock at the door. I looked at Skírlaug, who dug her fingernails into the table. No one should have knocked. We had warriors guarding every entrance to the grounds to greet visitors, and so late in the night, no one should have arrived by boat. Two of Skírlaug's men walked over and unlatched the doors. When they swung them open, a tall, dark figure in a black hooded cloak stepped into the candlelight.

"Is he one of yours, Ragnar?" I asked.

Ragnar shook his head, his face white as the full moon.

"What is your name, visitor?"

The man pulled back his cloak. I did not know him, but Ragnar and his men did. They gasped at the sight of him. He had a square face with wide eyes and a pronounced forehead, and his chin and scalp were shorn down to black stubble. A golden hilt girded beneath his cloak glinted in the faint candlelight.

"I had not expected to find so many ships in the harbor," he said in a low, raspy voice.

"What is your name?" I demanded.

The man's eyes were daggers when he looked at Ragnar, and then he laughed. "What in Hel's name are you doing here?"

That the man refused to tell me his name angered me. I stood up, my chair grinding across stone, and pounded my fist on the table. This caught the man's attention. He examined me a moment, then stepped forward. Ragnar's men dispersed around him, and he stood at the opposite end of my table to face me. His eyes drifted over to Skírlaug, who also seemed to recognize him. She had frozen in place with a scowl on her face.

"How did you sneak past our guards?" I asked him.

"Sneak?" He pulled back his cloak to show a dagger tucked under his belt without a sheath, its blade stained with fresh blood. "I don't sneak."

"Who are you?"

"I should ask you the same thing. Who are you to speak to me first when it is my niece who governs this place? Are you her new lover?"

"You must be Rurik. I am Hasting."

"Hasting? You're supposed to be dead."

"So I keep hearing."

"That is ill news indeed." Rurik muttered with a scratch of his chin. "I have heard about you. I wonder if the stories are true."

"What stories?"

Rurik poured himself a cup of wine and sat at the table. Though I had not invited him to do so, his relaxed stance seemed to put everyone in the room at ease. When he spoke, he addressed everyone.

"My nephew, Horic the Younger, still tells the story of how you bested his father's champion in a duel, and how that champion was so impressed by you that he swore to you."

"You mean Bjorn," I said. "It wasn't a duel; more like training."

Rurik nodded and continued, "I also heard you killed Hagar, one of the most famous duelists in all the North."

Grjotgar butted in and said, "Our mother was there; she saw it. Hagar fought Hasting with an ax, and Hasting had a fisherman's knife."

As the list of my deeds went on, my confidence grew.

Rurik nodded again and said, "Lastly, I heard you handily defeated Ragnar in a duel and further insulted him by letting him live." He smiled, shook his head, and added, "Savage."

"What are you getting at?"

"This would all have been easier, Hasting, if you had not returned. I came here alone to challenge my niece and her champion to a duel. I prefer not to risk my warriors when I am confident I can win on my own. But I see now I am perhaps outmatched. How can I hope to defeat a legend? Especially one who has returned from the dead?"

"You are wise not to fight him," Skírlaug spat.

Rurik stood and walked toward the door. Skírlaug's warriors stepped in front of him to block his way.

"Why should we let you leave?" Skírlaug said. "We could kill you now and sever your army's head from its neck."

Rurik took one step back and gave us a sideways look and said, "If you do that, my men will seek revenge, as is their right for murder, and they outnumber you three ships to one."

Skírlaug raised her hand as if to tell her men to kill him but waved it instead to allow Rurik to pass. He fled into the night, guided by the half-moon's light.

"Grjotgar, Kjartan, follow him back to his camp. I want to know where they are and why we did not see them arrive," I commanded.

The twins bolted from the table, leaving their meals half-eaten and their wine half-drunk. Ragnar breathed a sigh of relief and gathered his men to return to their camp. He left us with a crooked smile and a shaky bow. Before we knew it, Skírlaug and I were alone at the table. We sat in silence, thoughts on the fighting ahead. She reached across the table and took my hand.

II

Under the Frankish Yoke

How Rurik's army had made landfall on the north side of the island without us knowing, I could not say, but by the time we realized they were there, it was too late to move against them. They had made camp on the backside of a flattened dune that fed into a patchwork of rocks half-submerged in the water. We supposed from the fact that they had siege weapons already assembled and ready to move across the marshes that they had arrived several days before Rurik's visit. Outnumbered at least two to one, we still debated meeting them in the field rather than letting them come to us. I summoned a war council, the first I had ever called as a king, to create a plan we could all agree would maximize our chances at surviving the summer. Rurik was the first of a long list of potential challengers to arrive, and we had to defeat him with as few losses as possible. If his army outmatched us in number, I feared what might follow him even if we prevailed.

I welcomed my closest followers into the main chamber of the monastery, and we gathered around the oak table in the center. Skírlaug's servants had removed the benches so we would all need to stand to see the plan as I had laid it out.

Kjartan, Grjotgar, Ragnar, and Skírlaug formed the core of the group, with half a dozen of the more influential ship captains standing with them. As I spoke, I pointed to ivory *tafl* pieces I had placed on the table to represent the armies. They sat on a stretched cloth with the island's rough outline sketched with black paint.

The representation helped me visualize the countryside, but I knew the Danes would have trouble reading it. In Vannes, Nominoë had shown me many maps of his lands—where the rivers flowed, and how far his influence stretched. Vikings did not draw such things; they instead used landmarks to guide their way, some written in the rocks of the coastline, others in the night sky. Knowing this, I made sure to point out landmarks they would recognize and added them to my map.

"This is us, in Vindavik." I pointed to a drawing that resembled a house. "Over here is Rurik. Between them and us are numerous marshes and abandoned pastures. The rough terrain will take time to cross, and their two rams should slow them down. If we wait here, there's a chance one or both of the rams won't make it to our gates. If they do make it, however, we won't last long."

"Could they be fake?" Ragnar asked. "The rams, I mean. Rurik is a cunning man; the rams could be bait to draw us out. It is hard for me to imagine they brought them knowing the palisade would be here. And he must know the marshes will stand in their way."

"I don't think so," Kjartan interjected. "They looked real enough, and they rolled when pushed. I saw with my own eyes."

"What I don't understand is what they are waiting for," I said. "They have the rams, they have the men, but they're not moving."

"Rurik did say he had not expected to see so many ships in the harbor." Skírlaug's arms were crossed and she was glowering at the table.

"She's right; he will be more cautious now that I have joined you. For all he knows, we have more allies on the way," Ragnar said.

"I wish Bjorn was here. We could use him now," I lamented.

Ragnar took a hearty drink from his cup, wiped his lips on his sleeve, and said, "Too late now, boy. It would take weeks to find him and bring him back."

I stared at the table, waiting for a suggestion from one of the others. The last thing I wanted was to fall into a trap, and everything about how Rurik had arrived and prepared his army told me that was what we faced. I looked to Skírlaug, who held her chin in thought. She had little to offer in the way of ideas. None of the other men seemed to know what to do either, and as I looked to them for advice, they looked to me for the solution.

"What about the Celts?" Grjotgar asked, breaking the silence.

"They are protecting the villagers," I said. "We can't risk pulling them away."

Since Rurik had made his unwelcome appearance, I had ordered the Celts to evacuate the village a second time. They made camp in the pine forest on the western edge of the island, in a clearing where Northmen had once lived but had fallen to Renaud's sword. I knew little about the people who had lived there, but Asa had told me her father had ruled over them, and Renaud had wanted them gone.

Something about that place felt otherworldly, as if the spirits of the dead watched over it. The first time I was there, a mysterious old woman named Oddlaug had helped me find the Northmen's treasure. Without it, I could never have done what I had done since.

That Oddlaug had vanished into the forest without a trace haunted my dreams on occasion. Sometimes I imagined her roaming the far side of the island where no one lived. Whether she did or not, the forest served as an ideal place to hide the villagers and the garrison of soldiers from the perils of war. My mind drifted with thoughts of the forest, but I caught myself daydreaming and brought my attention back to the council.

"Remind me, Skírlaug, where is Rurik from?" I asked.

"Frisia," she answered.

I rubbed my face and leaned over the table. "How did he end up there?"

"He used to raid there, and the Franks invited him to rule over some of their lands along the river to fight off other Danes," Skírlaug explained.

I did not know if I had missed that detail or not, but the revelation changed the conversation in my head in an instant. If Rurik ruled over Frankish lands by invitation, he would have sworn allegiance to one of the Frankish kings. Charles had taken possession of Francia and Frisia after his father's death, so I could assume Rurik had sworn to him in some way.

It seemed strange that such an established lord would waste his time fighting abroad when he had no need for it. In fact, he should have stayed home to defend his land, since the Danes had a nasty habit of raiding in that part of the world. If Horic the Younger had set sail from Jutland to head our way, he would not have hesitated to attack the Frisian coast for supplies. Why would Rurik take such a risk in leaving? What benefit did my island give him?

"To whom does he owe allegiance?" I asked.

Everyone in the room shrugged. They had all assumed, as I had, that he fought for himself, but the more I thought about it, the more certain I was that he had sailed to our shores at someone else's behest.

"If Rurik is a vassal of King Charles of Francia," I said, "then we could commit all our strength against him."

Ragnar leaned over the table and said, "Tell us what you are thinking, Hasting. You seem to know something we don't."

"I could be wrong," I started, "but Rurik would not have left Frisia without assurances from Horic the Younger that he would not raid his lands. The Franks and the Danes talk, you know. My friend Nominoë told me as much."

"So, you think Rurik convinced my brother to abandon his claim to this island?" Skírlaug asked.

"Not Rurik—Charles."

"That doesn't tell us anything about why they are waiting," Ragnar spat.

"No, it doesn't," I said.

As we talked, a warrior burst from the stairwell to the bell tower out of breath and with a furrowed brow. "Ships on the horizon, my lord," he said with a bow.

Skírlaug and I looked at each other with dread. Perhaps Horic the Younger had arrived after all. I stepped away from the table and followed my man upstairs with Skírlaug, Kjartan, and Grjotgar in tow.

We made our way up the winding stone steps to the second level, then the third, and stepped into the bell tower above. Since I had taken possession of the monastery, there had never been a bell. Vikings had seized it in the first raids. Its absence gave us plenty of room to fit, but we had to negotiate a narrow walkway over a significant gap in the floor to the second level. We looked out toward the east, across the water between island and mainland, where a fleet of ships was gliding across the water. I had poor vision at a distance, so I relied on the others to tell me what they could see. There were two dozen ships in all headed for the inlet to the harbor.

"Checkered sails," Skírlaug said. "Blue and silver."

"Blue and silver?" I asked. "Do we know who that is?"

"We know who it isn't," she replied. "Horic the Younger's colors are red and white. Thor's are green and black."

"What are my colors again?" I asked Skírlaug half-joking.

She looked at me with scorn and said, "You haven't chosen any yet."

Her words and the way she said them made me feel small.

"Those are Rune's colors," Kjartan said.

"Rune?" He had been my most loyal follower, and he had my ship, *Sail Horse*. "What great timing."

"Should we make room for him at the docks?" Grjotgar asked.

"Hasting, he's here to fight us, like the rest of them," Kjartan warned. "I advise caution."

Kjartan spoke true. Rune's name had floated around with the rest of the warlords who sought to take control of the island. We had to treat him carefully. But, as with Ragnar, Rune knew me, and more than that, he had sworn an oath to me.

"He can't dock; the tide is out," I said. "But I know where he will go. Kjartan, I thank you for your caution. Make preparations as you see fit in case we fight."

By the time Rune's ships had run aground on the longest beach below the oak forest, clouds had formed overhead, carried by wind that never ceased. The forest loomed above colossal sandstone slabs that were cracked and smashed by deep roots and the unrelenting ocean. Dark caves formed where the stones overlapped. I stood at the edge of the forest where the sandstone broke apart and crumbled into the water below.

The lead ship was *Sail Horse*. Rune had landed where Halldóra, Grjotgar and Kjartan's mother, had run aground to carry out her raid on the monastery. Fifty of us gathered above them, and Rune did not notice us until he tried to climb the rocks from the beach to the forest. He stared down the shaft of a nocked arrow and gulped. Several of his men found themselves in a similar predicament farther down the beach. Dozens of men milled about below us, and as more ships ran aground, hundreds more would disembark. If they wanted to fight, we would not keep them down for long.

"I wish to speak with your headman," he said.

Two of my men pulled him up and stood at his side while the others prevented any more of his warriors from climbing. Our ambush had taken them by surprise. I walked over from my perch to face Rune, but he looked past me as if looking for someone else. It was evident he had not recognized me, and I did not blame him. My long hair and beard would have looked out of place to a man who had followed me since the beginning. Rune scanned all our faces, and when his eyes returned to me, he paused. His eyebrows arched, and his scowl became a brief smile.

"Hasting!" he rejoiced.

I stepped forward and extended my hand to greet him, but he pushed it aside to pull me in for an embrace. "I can't tell you how happy I am to see you alive."

"Careful, Hasting," Kjartan said from behind me. "Remember what he came here for."

"He's right." Rune took a step back. He and Kjartan seemed to know each other, and not in a good way. His jubilance soured, and he rested a hand on the hilt of his sword. "I came here to take this land and add it to my kingdom, not to make friends with the dead. I mourned you, Hasting, I did, but I am now a king in my own right, and my men will not be satisfied unless we claim what we sailed here for."

"Get in line," I said. "Rurik of Frisia is camped north of here with one hundred ships."

"A hundred?"

I crossed my arms. "To be honest, I have half a mind to let you take the monastery so he can rip you apart instead of me."

My men and I laughed at Rune's expense, and I could see it displeased him. He shot quick looks at all the men around me, though he lingered on Ragnar, Kjartan, and Grjotgar. He continued scanning the forest to count our warriors, and when he realized our strength, he relaxed his stance and released the hilt of his sword.

"Still lucky as ever," he muttered.

"It took a lot of bad luck to get here," I joked.

A few men laughed, and Ragnar was the loudest.

"With so many men, and defenses to boot, you stand a good chance of fighting Rurik off," Rune said. "Perhaps I should challenge you to a duel to take your place. None would need to die among our own that way."

I laughed and said, "Don't be ridiculous."

My laughter sent him into a rage. He fixed on me and widened his stance. "I am a king now and one of the deadliest dualists in all the North. I could kill you with ease."

His sudden change of spirit dampened my own, and I asked him, "What happened to you?"

He had changed. Somewhere in the years since we had parted ways, he had grown into a bitter, battle-hardened shadow of his former self. I almost pitied him. He had so much potential when we first met. Part of me felt guilty for whatever had happened to him. After all, I had recruited Rune and, in a way, groomed him. For a brief moment, I saw myself in him.

Everything about how he carried himself told me he had taken to shaping his reputation as I had, to cultivate the stories of his deeds, and to reach the top, whatever that was, at any cost. He had lost himself to the way of the Vikings, as I had, and the same dark shadow that had lingered over me enshrouded him and cut off his heart from the world. Had I acted so insolently toward others before my departure for Nantes? Had I seemed so calloused and out of touch with reality before my return?

"I told you," Rune bellowed, "I am a king now, one of the great Irish Sea Kings. And I don't abandon my people to chase after a dead girl."

He had meant to insult me, and I knew it. His words drew the gasps of everyone around me. His slight to my honor compelled me to respond. Perhaps they saw him as the warrior he had become, but I still saw the young, innocent face of the boy I had recruited in Dublin.

In the time we had spent speaking, a familiar figure had hobbled up the rocks. Fafnir, the most skilled navigator I had ever known, had stayed at Rune's side. He had aged. His head had gone bald, and his long and scraggly beard had turned grey, but he looked well. I commanded my men to help him up, and when he saw me speaking with Rune, his eyes lit up, and he opened his arms to embrace me.

"Hasting? We thought you were dead!" he exclaimed.

"Not yet," I said.

He gave me a warm embrace and held onto my shoulders. His rejoicing diffused the tension their arrival had created. After lingering a moment, he stepped back and saw Rune standing there, his fist closed and breathing labored.

"I see," Fafnir muttered. He faced away from us, brought his shoulder level with Rune's, and whispered in his ear. Rune nodded at whatever was said and whispered back. Fafnir scoffed at him and spoke with a raised voice, "Well, he's not dead, and your oath to him isn't null."

Rune brushed off Fafnir's words. He stepped forward as if to make good on his challenge, but then dropped his shoulders with a heavy sigh.

"I thought I could, but I can't," he said. "I still love you."

Fafnir gawked at all the men we had brought to the forest and said, "You never cease to amaze me, Hasting."

He then knelt in front of me, wincing as he did so. "My oath to you still stands, if you will have me. As does Rune's."

I gave him a soft smile and helped him to his feet. "Nothing would make me happier," I said.

"Why did you come back?" Rune tilted his head, eyes searching. "You could have stayed in Armorica and escaped from it all. What compelled you to return and take your place among us?"

It was a difficult question to answer, or at least it would have been before my captivity in Nantes. Without overthinking it, I replied, "I live to serve those around me so they may have a life worth living."

My cryptic answer did not seem to satisfy him. "This is all about Renaud still, isn't it?"

"In a way, yes," I said. "In so many others, no."

"Hmm."

Rune still seemed dissatisfied with my answers. I knew the feeling. It was not so long ago that I would have demanded a more precise explanation, as Rune had.

"Hasting will have to be involved in the politics of the region if he hopes to build a thriving kingdom here," Fafnir added. "Like you must do in Ireland."

"True," Rune said. "My worry is he will become too involved and leave us again."

"I understand it will take you time to trust me," I said. "But we could use your help. I'm asking you as an old friend."

"What's in it for us?"

"Rune, enough!" Fafnir snapped. He turned to me more calmly and said, "Hasting, we would be honored to join you and we trust in you to bring us glory and wealth."

"Thank you, Fafnir. I will see that you are rewarded."

Kjartan and Grjotgar grumbled behind me. They did not want to give up any of their share of the salt trade, and they knew that was all I had to offer. It also occurred to me that I did not know how much wealth the salt brought my kingdom, though the silver in the crypt told me I had plenty to spare. Whatever I decided to offer him, I needed to take care not to overpromise and over-leverage my wealth. How I would have loved to draw up a written agreement, as Nominoë had done with me, to make clear what each party was owed, but Vikings did not write such things. Agreements were made orally and fulfilled by honor.

"Today I can offer you silver and the promise of a trade negotiation, if we prevail," I said.

"We do not need a new agreement," Fafnir interjected. "By our laws, and for our honor, we are still sworn to you. That is enough."

"Fine," Rune said with hands on hips.

In the middle of our exchange, we were interrupted by one of Kjartan's men who came up behind Rune and said, "There's an army marching up the old Roman road from the south. They're Franks."

"I knew it," I blurted. "That's what Rurik was waiting for."

"Waiting for what?" Kjartan asked.

The others had not made the connection. I explained my suspicion that Rurik was conspiring with the Franks. His allegiances lay with the Franks in the same way mine lay with Nominoë.

Renaud had admitted to me that he knew of our alliance with the Celts. With Nominoë in open rebellion, it made sense the Franks would seek out new allies. Charles had a long road ahead to consolidate his power, and reclaiming the island's salt trade through his new Viking friends was where he'd decided to start. Renaud controlled Guérande, the other salt-producing region of Armorica that had once supplied the Celts. Taking Vindreyland, or as they called it, Herio, would weaken Nominoë's war effort and strengthen Renaud's.

What had Renaud and Charles promised Rurik, I wondered, to convince him to sail south with so many of his ships? The same thing I had used to convince Ragnar and Rune to join my cause, I thought—a share of the salt trade and plenty of silver.

"I'm not the best at counting, but I would say the odds have shifted in their favor," Ragnar bellowed.

Rune scowled at him and crossed his arms. "This is no laughing matter."

"What will we do?" Kjartan's eyes were filled with worry.

"We will do what we can do," I said. "Gather your men and lock down the monastery."

The castrum was never meant for a long siege. We fit as many tents as we could in the courtyard and along the perimeter of the monastery. Still, many men had to sleep in the halls and gather like sardines in the chambers.

Skírlaug seemed the most distraught. Her daughter—our daughter—had spent days with Ingrid in the forest on the other side of the island in hiding with the other villagers. From Skírlaug's perch in the bell tower lookout, she could see clear across the flat marshes. None of the Franks or Vikings had bothered to venture that way.

In the time it took us to finish our preparations, the Frankish army marched into the village below and waited. It did not take long for Rurik's troops to arrive and meet them.

To my astonishment, Rurik's soldiers did not look like Danes, but Franks. At least, a large portion of his army looked that way. They carried heavy iron shields and wore conical iron helmets and blue overcoats. The distance between us made it hard for me to see, but Kjartan, who had become my most helpful and eager follower, described what he saw with his fresh, young eyes. He confirmed that many, if not most, of the men who marched with Rurik, wore Frankish arms and armor. I asked how he had missed that detail during his scouting, to which he had no answer except the embarrassed blush of a young man who had made a mistake. It reminded me how young he and his brother were, in both body and spirit.

The Franks did not bother to send a messenger to speak with us. Instead, they set to digging a trench around our defenses as a means to trap us inside our own fortifications. It occurred to me when they started their work that they had far more experience in sieges than we did. I had expected to fight Vikings who would have found it dishonorable to starve us out.

Though I did not show it to my followers, I feared the days to come. We had enough supplies to last a few weeks, but with the castrum so overcrowded, I feared flaring tensions between the different factions among my own men more than the threat of starvation. Northmen and Danes have a long history of not seeing eye to eye, and, to that point, Ragnar's men and those of Lade had not said a word to one another.

I soon realized I had made a critical mistake. Skírlaug joined me on the battlements and watched with me as more and more soldiers joined the effort to dig us in.

"Well, at least we won't have to fight today," I joked, but Skírlaug did not find me funny.

She peered around the curve in the palisade to see how far the line of enemy soldiers stretched. They had us surrounded. Her eyes wandered back over to our side of the palisade as she observed our own warriors. The rift between the three factions was evident, and the more the Franks dug in, the wider the division grew. She took my hand, and pulled me close, and said, "Don't let us die here. Not like this."

When darkness fell, the land around us was aglow with firelight. We could hear the Franks talking, laughing, even cheering—all night, as if they needed no sleep. Skírlaug joined me in my bedchamber that night. She was afraid, and for once, she had trouble hiding it. Ragnar's men had not been shy about making unwelcome advances toward her—she had mentioned to me that she had been groped more times than she could count. Her servants had complained of the same problem, but she had not grasped the severity of it until they had left with her mother and daughter. Never before had she felt so uncomfortable. Then again, never before had she lived among men who did not know or care that she was Horic's daughter.

We lay hip to hip in my bed, but she did not want me to hold her or touch her, only to be with her.

Inside the monastery and within the palisade, we maintained utter silence. We jolted awake with every loud crack or bang, fearful the Franks might try to attack us in our sleep. Restful sleep evaded us. Not until first light, when the first rooster from the village crowed—I was surprised he was still alive—did I fall asleep.

One of my men pounded at the door to wake me. I rubbed my eyes and drank some water. Skírlaug continued to sleep, and I let her. I met my man at the door with a whisper and slipped out to walk with him.

"Kjartan wants to see you," he said as we walked. "It's Ragnar. He's lost his mind."

His foreboding words did not sit well with me. We descended the spiral staircase to the main chamber where we met with Grjotgar and Kjartan, and together we marched to the courtyard entrance.

Outside, we found all of Ragnar's men dressed for battle, holding their shields and drinking wine to invigorate their spirits. Kjartan led me to the palisade gates where we found Ragnar and several of his ship captains passing around a gourd of wine. They looked ready to do battle.

"What are you doing, Ragnar?" I asked him.

"I'm going to fight," he said.

"You'll be killed the moment you step out of those gates," I snarled.

"Better than to die of hunger in here, or worse, be killed in my sleep by one of those damned Northmen," he slurred.

He pushed me back with his meaty, powerful hands, away from his circle of close friends. I should have killed him on the spot for his insolence. Instead, I patted Kjartan on the shoulder and said, "You know what? I think we should let them do what they want. In fact, let's help them."

Kjartan understood my meaning and smirked. He joined me at the gate to lift the crossbar and carry it off to the side. We pushed the gates open, and I stood on the wooden walkway across our moat and presented the enemy's defenses to them. The Franks' trench had pikes aimed chest-height, and they had dozens of mantlets stacked side to side behind it where their archers sat and waited for us. When our gates opened, we saw a few conical helmets peak over the mantlets and vanish again. If Ragnar had wanted the element of surprise, he would not have it.

Ragnar glared at me with a furrowed brow, annoyed by my assistance. I think he wanted to drink more, but now that I had opened the gates, his men wanted to push through and fight. That was their one advantage—they desired to fight.

"All right, Ragnar, see how far you can get," I taunted him.

12

Ragnar's Sortie

Arrows whistled like the howling of wind, followed by thunder knocks as they struck Ragnar's shield wall. His front row had interlocked their shields facing forward, while the second row raised theirs over their heads at an angle to block out the rain of wood and steel launched by the enemy. Crossbowmen shot straight and true, hitting the shields from the front, while archers lobbed their arrows toward the heavens to strike at them from above.

Undaunted, the Danes pressed forward, one step at a time, closer and closer to the pike-filled ditch. What Ragnar planned to do once they reached it, I did not know. Although we could not escape the grounds, the Franks could also not send their cavalry against us, giving the men who had joined Ragnar a fighting chance, at least, to withdraw.

"He's mad." Skírlaug joined me on the battlements to watch their ill-conceived attack.

I glanced back at the empty courtyard and, for a moment, thought it might work out better if the Danes never returned. We would last longer in a siege with fewer men, and the risk would decrease of us killing each other before the Franks ever stepped foot inside the monastery. The trouble was, I needed Ragnar, and I needed his men. If we survived the siege, Kjartan, Grjotgar, and Rune would return to their lands in the North, leaving me with no warriors to defend my new kingdom. Ragnar, at least, lived his life to rove, and so long as he had enough silver to shower his men in largesse, and enough wine to drink, I could count on him to stay at my side.

"They'll turn back once they see how stupid an idea it was to attack," I said.

Sudden movement on the other side of the trench drew our attention. The arrows ceased, and Ragnar's shield wall halted. A man on a white horse wearing a blue overcoat and cape signaled to those in front of him as if urging them to move forward. Though I could not see his face, his black, wavy hair and the way he carried himself on his horse told me this was Renaud.

A taut standstill ensued where neither Ragnar nor Renaud made a move across the trench. A wall of shields faced a wall of mantlets, waiting, bating, in a game of courage, wits, and patience.

On the other side of the grounds, a terrifying rumble and boom, akin to a tree uprooting in a windstorm, struck fear in my heart. We had been so distracted by Ragnar's sortie that we had not thought to keep an eye on the enemy's movements elsewhere along the trench. I asked Skírlaug to stay on the battlements with the archers and to keep an eye on Ragnar.

I slid down the ladder to make my way across the courtyard and around back. Before I even turned the corner around the stone wall, I heard the echoing of steel striking steel, and the grunts and cries of men in a struggle to stay alive. I drew my sword and quickened my steps.

At the source of the sound, I found Grjotgar and a few of his warriors pulling debris from a collapsed woodshed the Franks had built against the inner wall of the defenses. It appeared one of our men had lost his footing on the battlements and fallen onto the roof.

"Everything all right?" I asked.

"Just an accident," Grjotgar said. "There's nothing to see here apart from a drunken fool with a broken leg."

"Have you seen any movement on this side?"

"Nothing," Grjotgar reported.

Relieved, I sheathed my sword. As I watched them pull the man from the broken shed, I noticed that the ground underneath had sunk several feet, as if it had been built on top of a hole. I pressed my foot into it and found it unusually soft. I knelt down and dug into the muddy ground until I'd uncovered half-rotten wooden planks lapped side by side.

"What's wrong?" Grjotgar asked.

"There's something under there," I said. "I don't think that man fell. It was the ground that collapsed under him. Help me move it."

The men at my side helped to pull away the debris, while one of them cared for the man who had fallen. Once we had removed most of the cracked wood and fallen thatch, Grjotgar and his warriors used their axes to break apart the wood planks in the soil. Whoever had built the shed had placed the planks against the beams of the palisade, making them hard to pull off.

"It's a hole," Grjotgar said.

"What for?"

"Looks like a fine place to hide a body. Bet a denier there are bones at the bottom," one of Grjotgar's men said.

"I'll take that bet," Grjotgar said, and they shook on it.

"I'm going down there," I said. "Someone fetch me a torch or something."

Enough daylight shone into the hole that we could see the bottom, so I sat and slid along the edge to allow my legs to dangle. With a quick twist, I plopped onto my stomach and skated backward, clawing at the ground to break my momentum. When my hands reached the edge, I slipped inside and hit the ground with a muffled thud.

Grjotgar's head appeared over the aperture, blocking out the already dim light, and he said, "That's deeper than I thought it would be."

He withdrew, then lowered a small makeshift lantern—a frame of wood and linen with a candle inside. I grasped the leather strap and held it forward. My light illuminated a long tunnel, hand-dug through dirt, limestone, and sand, and propped up by rows of wooden beams as far as I could see. To my relief, the tunnel seemed to go deeper than the trench the Franks had built.

I ducked forward and started down the passage, avoiding hitting my head on the rocks that protruded from the ceiling. The tunnel led deep underground to a large, cavernous chamber with limestone walls and tree roots dangling from above. On the far side of the cave was an opening wide enough for a single man to pass through, and daylight shone through it. I made for the hole, but something glinted in the darkness to my right. I turned the lantern to find a gold signet ring with a red intaglio protruding from a sizeable earth-covered tarp. Beneath the tarp, I discovered an immense pile of silver deniers spattered with a few other gold signet rings.

We'd always wondered where the monks had hidden their wealth, and I had found it. I pulled the tarp back over the treasure to protect it and continued on to the cave's entrance. As I crawled through the narrow, triangular hole, I took sight of the bay between the island and the mainland. The passageway led to the rock-laden beaches where Rune had left his ships. I had known about the caves, but never would I have dreamed one of them might have a secret passageway into the monastery grounds.

In the distance, I could hear the echoes of men roaring and screaming, and the clatter of steel on steel. Ragnar, I assumed, had broken formation and attacked. With no time to admire the beauty of the oak forest I had so seldom explored, I crawled back into the cave and returned to the monastery with my lantern. To my relief, Grjotgar and his men had waited for me the entire time. They pulled me up from the hole and helped pat the dirt off my tunic and trousers.

"What did you find down there?" Grjotgar asked.

"Hope," I said.

I wasted no time in returning to the battlements to find Skírlaug and Kjartan; they were watching as Ragnar's sortie drew to a close. Skírlaug cracked her knuckles and clenched her jaw. Wounded men carried each other back through the gates, and they looked up at me with blood and mud spattered on their faces and shock in their eyes. Ragnar's charge had broken through the pikes and pressed into the first row of mantlets, but the Franks had surrounded them with spears and crossbows, and they had fallen back to our side of the trench. They raised their shields to defend themselves against ongoing volleys from crossbowmen and archers.

The whole ground beneath them had darkened from the thicket of arrows that had rained down on them. It was a hard fight for them to crawl back to the gates. By the time the last of them had made it through, they'd left behind a spattering of abandoned shields, axes, and spears across the land that separated us from our enemy. The Franks made no attempt at a counterattack, though I'd guessed they would not. They wanted us to starve and to turn on each other.

Later in the day, we sent men to fetch the bodies of the slain, but the Franks fired arrows upon them, so we left the corpses to rot in the sun.

Skírlaug's servants tended to the wounded as best they could. Some they cleaned and bandaged, while others whose wounds proved too severe to heal they left alone to die. One man had his entire forearm bolted to his shield by two arrows. The arrows had pierced through the shield, and the jagged tips had lodged into his bones. Ragnar's men had to cut through the arrow shafts to pull them free, and they burned the holes on both sides of his arm to keep them from festering. Skírlaug thought we might need to take off his whole arm if he hoped to survive.

In the aftermath of the sortie, I walked the grounds to give my support to those who had fought. I found Ragnar drinking in my hall. He was licking his wounds and lamenting their failed attempt to break through the enemy's defenses. I joined him at the table with Skírlaug at my side, and we waited for him to speak first. He kept drinking in silence, irked that we had been in the right.

"Stop gloating," he said.

"Neither of us is gloating," Skírlaug snapped.

"We're still trapped," Ragnar lamented. "We have no way out."

"That's not entirely true."

My words caught his attention. His eyebrows lifted and he looked at me with pouting lips. Before I spoke, I waited for the others I had called to arrive. Grjotgar and Kjartan, Rune and Fafnir, and several ship captains from Ragnar's camp filtered through the doorway and joined us at the table. They took seats where they found room, all of them scowling at Ragnar. He shrank a little as they stared, knowing how foolish his decision to attack had been. I did not need to scold him. His guilt did that for me.

"Now that this morning's excitement has passed, I will share my plan to fight back Renaud and Rurik." I stood to address the room. "Grjotgar deserves some credit here—he and his men helped discover the key to our victory."

Grjotgar crossed his arms and smirked, alone among his kin in knowing what I had found.

"We discovered a hidden passageway this morning," I went on, "that goes underneath the Franks' defenses to Rune's ships."

"You want us to run away?" Rune scoffed.

I laughed at him and said, "If that's what *you* want to do, don't let me stop you." The others laughed with me, and Rune shrank. "What the passageway gives us is free movement around their defenses."

"Lucky as ever," Fafnir added with a smile.

"To be honest, if Ragnar had not attacked them, the Franks might have been drawn to the sound of the shed collapsing, and our passageway might have been found out," I said.

Ragnar beamed. His attack had not been for nothing.

"That isn't to say what you did wasn't stupid," I added.

"How do you want to use the passageway?" Kjartan asked.

I turned to Skírlaug. She viewed the discovery of the tunnel as a gift from the gods, and I believed if she, as my völva, impressed that on the others, it would inspire their courage and lift their hearts.

"I believe the gods caused the collapse of the shed," she said with a booming voice. "They want us to have this land, and they have shown us the way. Tonight, we attack."

Something about the way Rune carried himself made me uneasy. I had not won him back as I had Fafnir, and I feared what he might do if given a chance to shift his allegiance. On the eve of battle, while the others prepared their arms and armor and prayed to whatever god they preferred, I invited Rune to the bell tower—alone.

When he arrived, the ocean skyline was still painted in red, gold, and violet hues as sunset chased horizon into night. Rune inched toward me, his hands clasped behind his back.

"I feel like we need to start over," I said.

Rune said nothing. He wore a deep sorrow he had not shown before, and a willingness to listen.

"I understand your anger toward me," I said. "What I did, or at least what I thought I needed to do, was reckless. I regret that I did not have the strength or wisdom to have done things differently."

Rune unclasped his arms and put a hand on the stone sill of the window. A soft breeze played in his long, black hair, and he threw the strands that had fallen over his face back over his shoulder. With a deep sigh, he said, "I mourned you. When they said you were dead last year, my world collapsed around me."

"I'm sorry."

"I know you are, but I don't think you understand why I am so angry with you," he said. His eyes welled with tears. "I… I can't believe I'm going to say this."

"You can tell me anything," I reassured him.

He placed his other hand on the sill and stared out into the darkness gathering over the mainland. Stars had appeared overhead, and below them we could make out the faint firelight of distant villages. Rune took several deep breaths before speaking again.

"Since I've known you, you have been chasing after one woman or another. First Asa, then Skírlaug, and now who knows," he said. "Remember how you felt when you found out Asa had died? That is how I felt when I heard you had died."

At first, I did not understand what he meant. He looked at me, but his eyes were obscured in the waning light.

"That is how I would feel if you died," I said.

"No," he spat. "You still don't understand… I love you the same way you love Asa."

I took a step back and gasped. He turned his whole body toward me and took a step forward. "Now, wait, I—"

"Now do you understand? It was a blow to hear you had died, but it almost felt worse to see you alive again, and to face once more that you will never love me the way I love you," he cried.

I tilted my head. "Hm," was all I got out.

To his relief, I am sure, I did not feel anger or any impulse to violence, as other men might. That I did not react harshly invited him to inch toward me even more, though I kept sliding back little by little.

He was right, I could never love him the way he loved me. I had heard once about men such as him. The Danes call them *ergi*, or men who desire other men the way they should want a woman. Magnus had accused Egill of such a thing the last time I visited Ribe. Having never lived in the land of the Northmen or the Danes, I did not know the laws that might help guide me through such a delicate situation.

"I know exactly how you feel," I suggested. "I know what it is like for the one you love to be out of reach. Before she died, I briefly held Asa in my arms, only to see her leave for another man. She was alive, and I couldn't have her. It was the most pain my heart has ever felt. Worse, even, than when she died."

"I see," Rune said.

"Rune, I still love you as a friend. You have done well for yourself without me, and I am proud of you. I need your help, and I hope we can find a way to have you stay with us and fight by our side. If the pain is too much for you, I would also understand if you decided to leave."

He looked back out into the darkness. Our enemy had reignited their torches and fires, flooding their camp in a circle of light. From our perch, we could see them patrolling the perimeter of the defenses, watching for any sign that we might try a sortie at night.

"All I ask," he muttered, "is that you say nothing to the others. It is my secret, and if anyone were to find out, I could be killed. I don't know if you know this, but in Ireland, man-lovers are put to death the moment they are found out."

"Not a word," I promised.

Rune nodded. We seemed to have an understanding, but before we could discuss it further, a column of firelight rose up behind the mantels facing our gates. A row of archers stood behind the knee-high flames, dipped their arrows in the fire, and raised them to the sky. A volley of steel, wood, and fire whooshed at our wooden walls, striking the ground feet away from our moat. Their archers were still out of range, but the fire took to the dry grass and spread at a gallop, spurred by the wind. I patted Rune on the shoulder and fled down the stairwell.

Back at the courtyard, my followers had already formed a line from the well to the battlements. They passed buckets of water to one another with surprising speed. As the fire burned closer to our defenses, we drenched all the wood with water, keeping the danger at bay.

Later in the night, when the enemy camp fell silent, we made our move. I led Rune and Fafnir and their men through the tunnel first, followed by Grjotgar and Kjartan and their men. Ragnar remained in the monastery grounds awaiting our signal to attack, while Skírlaug stood atop the battlements with our archers in case the Franks attempted anything during our absence.

It took a long while to gather all our warriors in the dark forest beyond the enemy's defenses. At long last, the final man emerged from the cave and confirmed no one had followed him.

Everyone gathered around as I held up a linen lantern and said, "From here, we move in the dark. Offer them no quarter, show them no mercy. Remember that they would show you none."

We moved through the forest like a pack of hungry wolves narrowing in on our prey. The first group of Frankish soldiers we encountered slept around their campfire on the backside of the monastery. Their watchman seemed to have heard our footsteps, but he could not see us moving in the darkness beyond the light from his fire. Grjotgar stalked him, and the watchman had no time to scream. He reached around his prey from behind, cupped his mouth, and ran a blade across his throat.

As the watchman's body fell to the ground, Grjotgar's men slaughtered the others in their sleep. By the time we arrived at the edge of the enemy's camp, we had nowhere left to hide. Their torches and campfires illuminated the rest of our way, and they would see us coming. I drew my sword and swung it over my head to signal the attack.

Our warriors stormed into the enemy camp howling, hacking, and slashing at anything that moved. We rushed forward like a horde of locusts, consuming whatever lay in our path. When we reached the heart of their camp, we used their own torches to set their canopies ablaze. Men emerged from the tents, exhausted, half-asleep, confused, and with no time to prepare for a fight before we cut them down.

A horn blew a warning in the distance, but too late. The slaughter had begun. I looked for the most massive tent in the camp in the hopes of finding Renaud, and I seethed for a chance to kill him. Moving through the field, I pulled back the entrance flaps to several tents and peered inside. In one of the tents, several men had taken up their weapons and fought me back. One of their blades grazed my leg. Rather than fight them, I called over some of my men with spears, and they encircled the tent and stabbed into it until all the men inside stopped moving.

I paused my search for Renaud to give the signal for Ragnar to attack. Kjartan took one of the enemy banners and dipped it into a campfire, then raised it high above his head and waved it in a circle. Ragnar's men responded with a bone-chilling war cry. With their help, our victory seemed all but certain.

As we continued through the camp, our fortunes changed. An arrow whizzed by my head, while others found their mark. Dozens of my warriors fell in an instant. Behind the arrows, a horde of Viking warriors charged at us from the darkness beyond the camp. Their howls matched our own, and they crashed into our line with the force of a tidal wave.

In the chaos of the battle, I lost track of where all my warriors had gone. We had dispersed to carry out the slaughter, and Rurik's army now split us apart and fought us back. The tents prevented them from forming a line, same as us, so we fought man to man, shield to shield. Hacking and slashing and punching and stabbing, I fought through a sea of enemy warriors.

Kjartan saw me cornered and brought a few dozen men to push back against our enemy. The battlefield became hard to read—where the Franks wore distinctive armor and colors, Rurik's men were hard to discern from our own. At times I did not know if the men I fought were his or mine, or if at that moment it even mattered so long as I killed them before they killed me. As we fought, I wondered where Ragnar and his men had wandered off to, or if they had made it across the trench yet. Before I could find out, a man called my name.

"Hasting!" Rurik roared.

His men split apart as he walked toward me, both hands gripped around the long shaft of a Dane ax. I had heard of such weapons but had never come up against one. Bjorn had told me once never to fight a man wielding a Dane ax; the deadliest of all warriors use them.

Rurik's face was obscured by the dark, and against the firelight behind him his silhouette seemed larger than it should. He swung the ax around in a circle and twisted it in his hands to demonstrate his mastery, and then he charged. I lifted my shield and held my sword to the side, unsure of what stance to take to repel him.

The beard of his ax swung down from overhead and locked against the rim of my shield. I tried to un-lodge it with my sword, but he ripped my shield away from me before I ever had the chance. He pulled back the ax to swing at me again, but one of my warriors leaped at him and threw him off balance. One of Rurik's men threw himself at me, and we both had to fight off another warrior before resuming our duel.

The man who attacked me dropped his shoulder to parry one of my blows, so I swung my sword around and stabbed him in the neck. When I turned to face Rurik again, I saw he had hacked my warrior's arm clean off. I gulped at the sight of it. The Dane ax proved heavy and hard to block, with a blade so sharp it could have sliced the Norn's weave.

Rurik charged at me again, his ax's head swooping close to my head, neck, and chest. I parried his lunges, ducked away from his swings, and dove into a roll to my right to dodge a mighty hack. When I lunged at him, he swung the ax's shaft around and blocked every stroke of my sword. His speed matched mine.

Twirling the long pole around, he jabbed at me with the blunt end and struck me in the stomach, sending me pacing backward in agony. He wasted no time to press his attack and swooped the ax in an impeccable circle, and I felt the blade trim the tip of my beard. I felt my neck in a panic, but everything was intact.

In an act of desperation, I charged while he caught the ax's momentum behind him, and I tackled him. We rolled apart, and when we stood again, he laughed.

"Impressive," Rurik said darkly. "Until we meet again."

He gave me a half-bow and fled as Ragnar and his men rushed up behind me, not a moment too soon. They chased him and his men into the darkness but broke off pursuit at my command. Relieved I had survived the duel, I knelt down to catch my breath. Ragnar found me and patted me on the shoulder.

"That was close," I said through labored breaths. "He almost killed me."

"No matter how good you think you are, there is always someone better," Ragnar said.

I stared out across at the camp, at the burning tents and squirming bodies of the slain on the ground, and I remembered why I hated war. My hand quivered as memories of my previous battles and the men I had killed flooded my mind. Ragnar continued to pat me on the back, waiting for me to gather my wits and stand. I took a deep breath and accepted his hand to help me to my feet.

"We need to find Renaud," I said. "If we don't, he'll come back and we'll have to fight this battle all over again."

"If he was here, he is probably dead," Ragnar said.

Rune appeared from the fray and embraced me as soon as he saw me. He smiled from ear to ear. Grjotgar and Kjartan soon joined us as well, and we stood together with few words to say, but with a laugh of relief here and there.

"Do we have any prisoners?" I asked them.

"Lots," Grjotgar said. "They will make good slaves."

"I would speak with one of them," I said.

We walked over to a campfire where Kjartan and Grjotgar had gathered some Franks and sat them on the ground. They all looked terrified of what might happen next.

I knelt down, stared at each of them in turn, then asked, "Where is Renaud?"

For a moment, none of them dared to reply. Each man averted his eyes. After a moment, one man in the back blurted, "Renaud is in Nantes."

I stood up to have a better look at him and said, "Who led you?"

"Captain Goscelin," the man said.

"Where is he?" I asked.

"Dead," the man said.

I looked back at Rune, Kjartan, and the others and said, "He did not dare come here himself."

"What happens next?" Kjartan asked.

"I think it is time to take the fight to him," I said.

"How can we? The city's defenses are impossible for us to overcome," Rune scoffed.

I stepped away from the prisoners and looked out into the night. "There is only one man who can help us defeat Renaud and sack the city. And that man is Nominoë."

13

The Return of Ironsides

Life in Vindreyland found a measure of normalcy in the aftermath of the battle. We still feared Thor's arrival to contest ownership of the salt trade, but with Ragnar, Rune, Kjartan, and Grjotgar, and with how well they had fought, I had no doubt we could repel almost any Viking fleet that thought it wise to challenge us. Rurik had fled in shame, but I had a feeling I had not seen the last of him. He had proven himself a formidable foe in a duel, and I dreaded facing him again.

Once we had cleaned up the bodies of the slain, we invited the villagers to return to Vindavik and resume their lives. To keep them focused on farming salt, I commanded my warriors to dismantle all the fortifications the enemy had built and to fill in the trench. I ignored their grumblings and kept thoughts to myself about how strange it was that they prided themselves on physical prowess and yet abhorred physical labor.

There was also the issue of the treasure I had found in the cave. To my relief, no one else had noticed the tarp among the rocks, and I wondered how I could bring it back to the crypt without drawing attention. The Danes and Northmen did not like the passageway. They found it creepy. In the stories of the gods, Skírlaug told me, caves often contain dark and dangerous creatures. All the better for me, I thought, as no one would go snooping. The treasure could stay where I had found it for a time.

The rest of the summer passed without any further attacks on my land. To keep my agreement with Nominoë, and to keep my warriors busy, I sent fleets of ships to patrol and explore the coast of Armorica and Francia.

I had primarily sent the fleets to repel raiders, but what I received in return both surprised and impressed me. Whenever Rune returned from his week-long voyages, he would sing songs to describe the coastline and landmarks of specific areas so he could remember how to navigate them again later. He taught the songs to other ship captains, and they to others, and in that way, all of the men who sailed the treacherous coastlines of Armorica and Francia knew how to avoid the perilous rocks and where to find safe harbor at night.

Where the Celts would have used a map, the Vikings used their voices and memories. I found the song describing how to sail to the Morbihan and Vannes most intriguing:

A king does slumber,
In Aegir's hold.
The mast and the prow,
Buried deep beneath.
When Sòl flies high,
But begins her fall,
Follow in the shadow of the prow beast.
Half a day's sail,
Njord's breath to follow,
Until her armor, sail.
When reached her grasp,
Keep watchful eyes,
Her fingers reach in threes.
Past her grasp,
she'll welcome you,
Her legs spread for you to enter.
Fear not the water,
It welcomes you,

Armorica's favorite new lover.

With the end of summer in sight, I was uneasy at the prospect that a majority of my men would sail home for the winter. The warriors loyal to Skírlaug would stay—they were Danes who had moved their families to the island to escape the in-fighting in Jutland after Horic's death, and they lived in the village with the Celts.

Skírlaug had only a handful of ships, and I feared what might happen if an enemy fleet arrived in spring before the return of those loyal to me, if they returned at all. Ragnar had taken to boasting about the wealth to be had in England. So, it seemed he and his men would leave us for good, or at least until they decided sailing to Vindreyland might earn them more wealth. Ragnar, however, had come to understand by how I had taken to governing that Vindreyland would prove perilous and not particularly profitable for him. I saw it too, and I did not blame him.

Grjotgar and Kjartan were the first to sail home. Their journey to Lade took the longest, and they needed to leave before the winds changed. I recalled my adventure to the Far North with *Sea Fox*, my first ship. How foolish we had been to take such a dangerous journey in the middle of winter. I still shuddered at the thought of the mist freezing to the sail and gunwale, building and building until the weight of the ice nearly sank us. The men from Lade loaded their ships with salt to take home to Hakon and Halldóra, and they departed at first light when the tide was high.

"See you next summer," Kjartan said as he leaned in for a warm embrace.

Grjotgar wrapped his arms around me next. "We will sing songs of your victory back home."

"Give Thor my regards," I said, knowing they would stop in Dublin on their way. "And if he grumbles about wanting to take my land… well, you know what to tell him."

Grjotgar and Kjartan laughed and stepped over the gunwale to board their ship. We waved to each other a good long while as they rowed toward open ocean, their black and gold shields obscured by the distance. It was early and others had not yet awoken, so I stood alone on the docks to watch them go.

Once they passed the sand bar and raised sail, I wandered off along the Roman road for a relaxing stroll. I found a lonely oak tree on the edge of the marshes and sat in silence to observe the land around me—my land—and I basked in the warm sunlight. I closed my eyes and sat in place for the rest of the morning, breathing the fresh morning air and listening to the birds chirping and singing. Listening to the sound of the natural world helped to put me at ease—it still does— but that day, those sounds were eventually broken by distant shouting.

I opened my eyes and blinked at another fleet rowing into the port from the south. Their checkered sails of blue and gold fluttered in the wind as they worked to lower them. One of my men hurried down from the monastery in a panic to warn me of the arriving fleet. Their lead ship had reached the boardwalk by the time he arrived, much to my dismay. We should have spotted them from much farther off.

Skírlaug joined us as well, without any of her warriors.

"Friends of yours?" I asked.
"It's Bjorn," she said.
"Bjorn?"
She smiled. "He'll be happy to see you, too."
"Where did he get those fancy sails?"

When I had first started to sail, the one person whose entire fleet had matching colors was King Horic. Other fleets were akin to Ragnar's, where each band of warriors and ship captain had their own colors and designs. The same had once been true for Bjorn, but times had changed. The more wealth a ship captain has, the more he can buy for his followers.

"Bjorn's reputation grows," Skírlaug said.

"More than mine?" I joked.

She nodded, and my smile faded. I looked her over as she gazed into the distance at Bjorn's ships, her hand in a fist against her chest.

"It's him, isn't it? He's the one you fell in love with after I left?"

With eyes wide and lips pursed, she said, "We... I... no."

I put my hands on my hips, smirked, and said, "Don't lie to me."

Skírlaug blushed and lowered her head. "I wanted to tell you before," she said, "but I did not know how you would take it."

I was almost jealous. In the time we had spent together since my return, I had started to feel a little something for her again. She knew the ways of the Danes and the Northmen far better than I, and she had proven indispensable. A romantic relationship with Bjorn was a dangerous thing, I thought.

"When did it start?"

"Last summer," she said.

"Should I be worried? Is he going to challenge me for my land, like everyone else? Whisk you away and rob me of my closest advisor?"

Skírlaug giggled and said, "You know him better than that."

Bjorn's ships maneuvered in the receding waters of the Concha and ran aground in the mud below the pier. I sent men to catch their ropes and tie them off for when the tide returned, and we brought ladders for them to climb up to the boardwalk. Several men ascended while the rest passed them crates of supplies.

After they had finished, Bjorn appeared, his chest held high, and with the widest of grins smeared across his face. He opened his arms to embrace Skírlaug, and she reached around his waist and squeezed him. It was then that he looked at me and tilted his head. It took him a moment to recognize my face, but when he did, he bounded forward with an excitement I had not expected.

"Hasting!" he cried out, his eyes welling with tears. "You're alive; how can it be? The Celts said you died in Renaud's prison."

"A little grit and a whole lot of luck," I said.

Bjorn wrapped his meaty arms around me and lifted me up in celebration. While I had lost weight over the years, he had gained it. Since we had last seen each other, he had packed on some serious size in his arms and shoulders.

"You've been training with Ubba, I see."

"Oh, yes. Ubba and I are true brothers now. His ship is that one over there." He pointed to the third ship in line arriving at our docks. "We call our fleet 'The Sons of Ragnar.' What do you think?"

"I think a lot of people in the North will wonder who you are talking about. Ragnar is a common name," I said with a chuckle.

"That's right. Your father was named Ragnar, too," he jeered. His eyes lit up with even more excitement. "You could join our fleet, and we wouldn't need to change the name."

We were interrupted by a shout from the monastery.

"Speaking of Ragnar," I said.

"Bjorn!" Ragnar stomped his way down the hill toward us. "Bjorn, my boy, it's good to see you."

Bjorn shrank in embarrassment. "By the gods, what is he doing here?"

I laughed and said, "He's sworn to me."

"He swore to you? But how—" I could almost smell his shock. "We have a lot to talk about."

"Relax, Bjorn. All is well."

"It's just… he's just…" Bjorn lowered his voice. "Ever since you spared his life, he's been so awkward. I used to fear him, but now he's a bit of a joke."

It seemed strange that Bjorn did not respect his father. I saw nothing wrong with how he carried himself, and his followers admired him. Since I had never known my father, I could not pretend to understand how Bjorn felt.

"At least you still have your father," I said.

Bjorn looked at me, surprised, then patted me on the shoulder. "I'm sorry, brother."

Ragnar flexed his knees and parried in an arch around us, his shoulders level with his neck and his hands held forward. Bjorn shrugged off his fur overcoat and matched his father's movements. They scuffled around, reaching and grasping at each other's tunics. Their wrestling match felt familiar, except this time it ended differently. Bjorn managed to grab one of Ragnar's arms and twist it around his back, and then he shoved his father into the dirt. Ragnar laughed.

"You've been wrestling with your brother," he suggested.

"And winning," Bjorn said.

Bjorn released his father, and when both were back on their feet, they embraced. I marveled at how much Bjorn had changed. He had more confidence than ever, but it was controlled and did not feel like arrogance. I found myself drawn to him, and had circumstances been different, I could have seen myself following him.

As the dust settled from their bout of wrestling, Ubba climbed to dry land and joined us. Ragnar wiped the dirt from his tunic and trousers and opened his arms wide. Ubba had kept his size and gait, and he sauntered over to meet us.

"Look who's back from the dead." Ragnar motioned in my direction.

Ubba looked at me and gave a sharp nod. He did not seem to remember me at all.

"So, who is in charge of this place?" Bjorn asked.

"Hasting is king," Skírlaug said. "And he's earned it. We escaped destruction at the hands of the Franks and their new ally, my uncle Rurik."

"Rurik of Frisia?" Bjorn asked. "He was here?"

"Hasting dueled him," Ragnar said.

"And you won?" Bjorn asked.

"Not exactly," I said.

"More of a draw, I would say," Ragnar added, and I agreed with him.

"The Sons of Ragnar salute you," Bjorn said with a slight bow.

Skírlaug glared at me, and at first I did not understand her meaning, but when Ragnar and his sons started to talk without me, I realized that as king, I needed to assert my authority. Bjorn and his brother were welcome visitors, but given the fraught political situation among the Vikings, I needed to know his intentions and whether he would renew his loyalty to me. If not, I risked creating yet another adversary.

"What about your oath to me, Bjorn?" I interjected. Their conversation ceased in an instant.

"What about it?"

"We are not the young adventurers we once were, my friend. Our benefactors, Horic and Hakon, will no longer protect us. I am king now, and I need to know where your loyalty lies," I said.

Bjorn turned to face me, his face stern and stoic. "I owe you my life, Hasting. I am with you and always will be. In fact, I have brought you a gift. It was meant for Skírlaug, but since you are back, I will give it to you."

He signaled to his men unloading the ships and made a small circular motion around his face. His men brought up three slaves in tattered linens, with brown caps on their heads. We all marveled at them. Their skin was as dark as the night sky, and their hair thicker and curlier than the underbrush of a wild forest.

"What are they?" Ragnar asked.

"They are men," I said. "I've seen their kind before, when I was a boy." Indeed, during my first sea voyage with Eilif and Egill, I had seen men with such dark skin in the market in Nantes.

"We bought them in a land called Al-Andalus," Bjorn said. "In the North, there are people who look like the Celts. They are surrounded by these dark men who conquered the rest of their land. The Celts called them Moors. We did not sail so far as to see their kin, but one of the cities we visited had these three as prisoners, and they were happy to just give them to us.

"The one on the left is quite clever. He has learned much of our language since we took him on board. He says he was a warrior among his people."

"A warrior?" Ragnar said. "I would like to see him fight."

"Perhaps later," I said. "For now, have your men join Ragnar's camp."

"I will have my men take the slaves to our hall and have them cleaned," Skírlaug said.

"Your hall?" Bjorn asked. "The two of you are together?"

"I meant *our* as in I live there. I am Hasting's völva, nothing more," Skírlaug said coldly.

Bjorn sighed with relief. I pretended not to have heard the exchange and made my way back up the hill ahead of everyone else.

We returned to the monastery with my gift in tow and sat down to celebrate Bjorn's return. I took my usual place next to the head of the oaken table, leaving the most honored seat to Skírlaug. It paid to honor the one closest to the gods, for she could influence their will, or so my men believed. I supposed I thought so too. Though she had been wrong several times, she'd always found a way to show that the gods had not lied to her—she had just misheard them.

Ragnar, Rune, Fafnir, and several others joined us at the table, all of them overjoyed to see Bjorn. Servants filled our goblets with wine, except mine, which they knew to fill with cow's milk. The Celts boiled the milk and skimmed it, so what they sent us tasted far better than the raw goat milk Skírlaug's servants made, though I never told her so. Seeing the servants pour my drink from a separate pitcher, Bjorn leaned toward me with a crooked smile.

"Not drinking, are you."

"No, I am not drinking," I declared.

Bjorn slid back, stretched his neck, and said, "Good, it didn't suit you."

We sat for a long while listening to Bjorn's stories of his adventures in Al-Andalus. He talked of a king who ruled over the mountain lands of a northern kingdom called Asturias. The leader feared above all that the Moors would one day conquer his country as they had conquered the lands of his forebears farther south.

The king of Asturias had offered Bjorn a significant sum of silver to raid the Moors in Al-Andalus, but he refused. He had not assessed the Moors' strength and so could not risk sailing his ships up their rivers. He recalled how the first Viking ships off the coast of Francia had made the mistake of attacking inland too soon and with too few men. We had sailed together on one such unfortunate vessel. There was still a deep purple scar near my groin to remind me of that ill-fated voyage.

When Bjorn finished recounting his travels, he asked about what had happened in his absence. Skírlaug told him of how I had reappeared out of nowhere when she had needed me most. He had not known about all the warlords who wished to take my place upon hearing of my death. Had he known, he assured her, he would have returned to defend her.

"If Hasting had not returned, your father would have done us in," she insisted. "As would have Rune. And they only had thirty ships each. Rurik arrived with one hundred ships, bolstered by an army of hundreds of Franks."

Bjorn marveled at me for a moment and said, "So you come back from the dead, and immediately those who followed you before rally behind you. Remarkable."

"Not without a little arm-twisting," I said.

"Is there anyone left?" he asked. "Who would want to fight you, I mean."

"Thor had wanted to sail here, but he decided against it," Rune interjected from down the table. "I spoke with him before I left. He said, 'If you go out there with Hakon's boys, I won't bother. And anyway, I fucking hate Francia.'" Rune's impersonation of Thor was quite good, and all of us who had met him roared with laughter.

"So, you have fought off your enemies, and now you are king," Bjorn continued.

"Not quite," I said. "Renaud is count now, and he will not stop until we are destroyed. He told me as much. If we hope to keep this land, we will need to kill him."

"Won't another take his place if we kill him?" Bjorn asked.

"Not if we do it the right way. Do you remember the prisoner we took from the monastery on the Loire?"

"Yes, Lambert was his name, wasn't it?"

"It turns out his father was the count of Nantes before Ricwin, and he's in league with the Celts. If we eliminate Renaud, Nominoë can get him the title, and we would have an ally in charge of the whole region."

Bjorn scratched his chin and said, "This is on a whole new level for us."

"Never have our people been so involved in a foreign land," Ragnar said.

Rune cleared his throat. "Actually, in Ireland we are even more involved."

"I said *our* people, the Danes," Ragnar clarified, and Rune glowered at him.

"We have the puppet, and we need to get him on the throne," Bjorn said to interrupt them. "What's the plan?"

"We should sail to Vannes to speak with Nominoë," I said. "Without him, there is no plan."

As we spoke, Skírlaug's servants brought in the Moors whom they had washed and dressed. I had no idea what to do with them, so I had the servants sit them against the wall and wait. Bjorn seemed proud of himself —the Moors were an exotic gift, demonstrating his largesse as a ship captain. Their arrival had interrupted our discussion and drawn the eyes of everyone at my table.

"Do you mind if I bring one up to the table?" Bjorn asked.

Skírlaug scoffed and said, "You may not! This table is not for slaves, it is for the king and his guests."

"It's all right," I said, putting my hand on hers. "I would like to meet one of them."

Bjorn called over one of the Moors and scooted to the side to give him room to sit. The man stared at me with dark eyes, his spirit seemingly undaunted by his captivity.

I put on a smile for Bjorn, trying to show some measure of enthusiasm for his gift.

"What is his name?" I asked.

"My name is Tariq," the Moor replied.

"You have learned some of our language," I said. "That's good."

"I do out of necessity."

"Tell us, Tariq, what can you do? How can we use you?" Skírlaug asked him. She had owned many slaves and knew far more than I about how to manage them.

"Among my people, I am a warrior," he said.

Bjorn laughed and patted Tariq on the back. "You hear that? He was a warrior!"

"I wonder how they fight," Ragnar cut in, his mouth full of bread and wine.

'Yes, I would like to know." I stood and raised my goblet. "I would like to see how Tariq fares against one of you. Any takers?"

After a long, awkward silence, Bjorn spat out, "I'll do it, you cowards."

We moved our party into the courtyard under the midday sun. From horizon to horizon, the sky shone a deep, beautiful blue without a single cloud. Bjorn took a sip of his wine and grasped a shield and wooden training stick, and we gave Tariq the same.

Tariq felt the weight of the shield and smiled as if it seemed light to him. The rest of us gathered in a circle to watch them spar, and Bjorn gave his shield a tap to signal to his opponent that their match had started. Tariq floated on his bare feet, gliding above the ground with the weightlessness of a butterfly, while Bjorn circled around him with heavy shoulders.

At first glance, Bjorn had him outmatched in size and strength, but he struggled to keep his shoulders facing Tariq. Bjorn engaged first, launching at his opponent with a fierce hack and slash with his stick. He also jabbed with his shield to ward off a counterattack.

Tariq parried the blows but missed ducking out of the way of the shield and was pushed back. He stayed on his feet and hopped forward with a counter, and he used his shield to knock away Bjorn's.

Bjorn shifted his weight to his back foot, and Tariq swatted at his legs with quick, successive strikes. Bjorn blocked the blows and swung his stick so hard it knocked Tariq's clear out of his hand. Rather than withdraw, Tariq twirled his shield around and smacked Bjorn with it in the lip. Bjorn staggered backward. He felt around where the shield had struck, and his fingers came away bloody.

"Damn," he said. "He's almost as fast as you."

I clapped my hands and laughed. "Well done, both of you," I said. I looked at Tariq and added, "Let's end it before you make him angry."

Tariq's quick breaths and wide eyes told me he was in the fight for his life, whereas Bjorn was having a little bit of fun. Nonetheless, he had held his own, even if for a moment, and for that, he had earned my respect. I looked at Bjorn, who had already traded out his stick for a goblet of wine, and said, "I think we should give him an earned name."

"An earned name?" Bjorn jeered. "Those are for free men." He saw the look on my face and scowled. "But I suppose you were never one to keep slaves."

"I tried having slaves once, and it tore me apart. I've seen both sides of it," I explained. "I can't change our laws, and I know slaves are necessary for many places in the North, but I will not have them here."

Tariq followed our conversation. His head bolted back and forth as we spoke, his hand still clasped around his shield.

As we talked, Ulfrúna darted out of the monastery, her grandmother chasing after her. She ran through the courtyard without a care in the world, and when she strode in front of Tariq, she tripped over his foot and fell forward. Tariq dropped his shield and stick and reached out his arms to catch her. He pulled her back up, set her on her feet, and patted her on the head.

"Where are you from?" she asked.

"I am from the South," he said.

"Do you miss it?"

"Every day," he said.

"My Amma says it's important to make guests feel welcome," Ulfrúna said. She tugged on his tunic to pull him forward, and when he leaned over far enough, she gave him a peck on the cheek and darted off.

"I think she likes you," I laughed.

Skírlaug grimaced at me. "I think we should move back inside."

Bjorn's warriors took Tariq by the arms and dragged him back into the monastery. That they felt the need to treat him so harshly bothered me. Our party followed and returned to the oak table, everyone eating and drinking with cheer. Skírlaug held onto Ulfrúna at the table, not wanting to let her go, and I gave my usual seat to her mother.

Once Ingrid sat beside me, I noticed Ragnar eyeing her as if he knew her. Ingrid had not spent much time among us. Most of her days were given to watching over and teaching her granddaughter, and Skírlaug had asked her to keep the little girl away from the warriors. Though we had grown in number, the Vikings living in Vindavik were almost all men, and often they did not set the best example for a young child.

I wondered how we might change that. The men who had sworn to me remained attached to their homeland by their families, so at the end of summer, they would leave. Grjotgar and Kjartan had gone first, and Rune and Ragnar would soon follow. Bjorn, with his shiny new fleet, might do the same. If I wanted my kingdom to last, and to play a more significant role in the region, I would need to anchor my followers to the island. With my silver reserves dwindling, I could not pay them off as mercenaries forever. It occurred to me that I had the tools to begin attracting more Danes and Northmen to settle permanently on the island, and it would start with Bjorn.

"Such beautiful women," I said as Skírlaug caressed Ulfrúna's head. I took a sip of my milk and winked at the little girl. "Don't you agree, Bjorn?"

Skírlaug's eyes widened and she bared her teeth at me. "What are you doing?" she growled.

"Nothing," I said. The others had stopped talking. I leaned over the table and stared at Bjorn.

"Why are you looking at me?"

"You didn't answer my question." I nodded in Skírlaug's direction.

Bjorn took the hint and looked at Skírlaug, his mouth agape. "But you said—"

"I know what I said," she spat.

"Why did you lie to me?"

Skírlaug's eyes welled with tears. She stood, her daughter still in her arms, and her mother followed her up the stairwell to their bedchamber.

Bjorn turned to me with pleading eyes. "How did you find out?"

"I figured it out," I said.

"But how?"

"A feeling."

Ragnar butted in, his cheeks red from the wine, and roared for all to hear, "Figure what out?"

I raised an eyebrow at Bjorn as I said, "He and Skírlaug are lovers."

Ragnar put down his drink and glared at Bjorn. For a moment, I thought he might leap across the table and strangle his son. Rune, who sat beside him, scooted down the bench, pressing into Fafnir. Bjorn's face lost its color. Ragnar belched a hearty laugh and slammed his fist on the table several times, coughing and trying to catch his breath.

"You're doomed," he cried with laughter.

I waited for Ragnar to quiet down before speaking again. He had to shift in his seat to look away from Bjorn, and every time he looked back at him, his laughter grew louder. It was infectious, and though the rest of us had not found what I had revealed to them funny, we found ourselves laughing too, all of us. Our laughter spread like madness, infecting each man it touched. I wondered for a moment what Skírlaug and her mother must have thought as our voices echoed through the monastery.

"I did not bring up the subject to mock you, Bjorn," I said between bouts of laughter. "But I do want to talk about it."

"What is there to talk about?" Ragnar jeered, and I must have shot him a menacing look because he shrank.

"Bjorn, my brother, I know you have dreams of far-off adventures, to go a-Viking, but it would be an empty endeavor if you did not have loved ones to return home to," I said. "You have a chance to build a life here, one where you could have your adventures, but also have a home, a wife, and perhaps children of your own to shower with gifts upon your return."

"What about Ulfrúna? She's yours," Bjorn said.

"I will always make sure Ulfrúna is cared for. But if you and Skírlaug marry, you will be in her life," I said.

Bjorn took in a deep breath and sighed. "I don't know, she has seemed so cold since my return. Perhaps it was only meant to last the one summer."

I clasped my hands over the table. "I saw her watch your ships enter the harbor. She held her heart with relief, the way no woman has ever done for me. Look, I don't know what happened between the two of you after I left, but whatever came of it is still there. She had feelings for me once, yes, and I know she keeps room in her heart for me, and always will, but we are not meant for each other. But the two of you—"

"What should I do? I've never loved a woman like this before. I'm... I'm nervous."

"Come on, Bjorn," Fafnir bellowed from the other end of the table. "Where's that legendary courage the skalds sing about, hm?"

"Go to her," I said.

Bjorn looked at the others at the table, took in a deep breath, and bolted for the stairwell.

"I see what you're doing," Ragnar said once he thought Bjorn was out of earshot. He grinned and patted me on the shoulder.

"What am I doing, Ragnar?"

"You're trying to get him to stay. And I think it will work for a little while, at least."

"What about you? Will you stay?" I asked him.

"Oh no, you and I agreed on silver, and that's what I'll take. Don't even think of offering me land," he said.

I smirked as I took a sip of my milk, and with my face half-covered by my goblet, I muttered, "I wouldn't dream of it."

Everyone at the table laughed at my retort, and it lightened the mood. What he had said, however, stuck in my mind. I had never been a king before, nor did I consider myself one, and I wondered what he had meant by offering him land. All this time, I thought the men who followed me wanted silver and salt. Ragnar had implied something different.

For the rest of the gathering, I sat in silence, contemplating how to best manage my land. Skírlaug, I was sure, had plenty of ideas, having served her father, a true king. As midday came to a close, and we all contemplated a pleasant nap, a man scurried through the courtyard to the main hall. He barged through the doors without any hindrance from the warriors who guarded it. They knew him, and I knew him. The man's hair and beard were wet and disheveled, the sleeves of his tunic were sliced and tattered, and blood ran down his arm to his wrist. It was Grjotgar.

I jumped to my feet. "What's happened? Why are you back so soon?"

"It's Rurik, my king. His fleet is still out there."

"Where is your brother?" I asked. "Where is Kjartan?"

Grjotgar fell to his knees, his legs robbed of all strength, and he wept. "Rurik killed him."

14

The Black Viper

Within a day, we had mustered our ships and our men to respond to Skírlaug's uncle. If he still sailed the seas north of the island, I had no doubt he would attack the coast of Armorica for supplies, and I had promised the Celts our protection.

Rune's fleet of thirty ships set out first, their hearts hardened by a thirst for revenge. The Northmen had loved and admired Kjartan, and his death required a bloody response. The Danes on the other hand, with the sixty ships belonging to Ragnar and Bjorn, were not so keen to fight their kin, but they joined without protest because they knew if they tried to sail home, Rurik would pick them off one by one. Our combined fleets barely made us an even match for Rurik's fleet of one hundred ships.

We waited for the late-afternoon tide, and as the water rose, the first of our ships rowed into the open ocean. Bjorn and I were the last to leave the monastery grounds. He went to say goodbye to his small family while I put on my new armor. Skírlaug had kept one of King Horic's sets, replete with thick leather bracers, shin guards, a full maille shirt, and most impressive of all, a fanged helmet with a golden visor and spine that gave me the look of a sea serpent. It seemed far too expensive to wear, but Skírlaug had insisted that Horic would have wanted me to use it.

As we left the monastery, my helmet under my arm and Bjorn at my side, we passed the Moorish slaves who had helped the other servants clean and organize after our feast. Tariq saw how we were dressed and skipped up to me with no fear at all.

"You are going to fight?" he asked.

Bjorn lifted his hand as if to strike him, and I caught it before he had the chance to bring it down. The other two Moors cowered as they watched, but not Tariq. I admired his boldness. Bjorn glared at me, and he shrugged off my grip.

"We are," I said.

"I wish to join you," Tariq declared.

I smirked. "We are going to fight Danes; I'm not sure you could handle it."

"You allow women to fight—why not me?"

I raised my eyebrows at his question and followed his eyes to the back of the chamber where Skírlaug was dressed in her breeches and padded leather jerkin. Bjorn's mouth fell agape. He marched over to her, wagging his finger.

"You can't come with us," he snarled. "It's too dangerous. You need to stay here with Ulfrúna."

Skírlaug slapped him across the face as soon as his cheeks were within her reach. She pointed her finger back at him and tapped deridingly on his nose.

"Tell me what I can and cannot do one more time and I'll cut your balls off," she said through gritted teeth. She walked over to me and ran her hand down the linked rings of my maille shirt. "It fits perfectly," she said. "Come, you and I will take my ship."

"What about me?" Tariq cried out.

Skírlaug and I looked at each other, her head shaking in disagreement and mine bobbing.

"I think we should take him," I said.

After a deep breath, Skírlaug answered with a single word: "Fine."

At her command, her servants darted up to my bedchamber to fetch some clothes for Tariq. They brought back linen breeches, a long-sleeved tunic, and a wool overcoat.

Tariq marveled at what we offered him. He threw on his new clothes, and as we left for the docks, we handed him a spare shield. Bjorn moped the entire way, embarrassed by how Skírlaug had put him in his place. He had evidently not spent much time among sharp-tongued women, and her injurious words had shaken his confidence. She, on the other hand, did not pay him any attention; she remained focused on preparing the fleet to leave.

Bjorn parted ways with us to join his impressive warship of sixty oars—*The Bear's Claw*. It was twice as long as his old ship, with a much larger sail and a far more frightful prow. The prow had the head of a beast that resembled the unholy union of a serpent and wolf. His crew had painted the beast's fangs red to warn anyone or anything that dared attack them that they had spilled blood. Skírlaug's ship, *The Riveted Serpent*, was smaller, with twenty-six oars and a coiled snake on the prow.

We rowed out to open ocean and set sail. Vikings do not like to sail at night, so the fleet hugged the coast until the sun set over the horizon, and before dark, we made camp on a beach Rune had scouted. The following day, we left again at dawn. We sailed as far as we could before reaching another cove Rune had found during his many explorations of the area, and we camped again.

In this way, we continued for days along the coast of Francia and Armorica, searching for the man who had slain one of the heirs of Lade. Their fleet was a day ahead of ours, and they did not know we were coming, or at least that is what we thought. Still, none of the ships that led the fleet had taken sight of our enemy's sails. A tense mood gripped my army. We wondered and feared where Rurik had taken his fleet. Though we were the hunters, I could not help but feel as if I was being hunted.

After some five days of sailing, we made camp late on a well-protected beach below a rolling hill that split apart into two jagged rock faces and crumbled into the sea. Some of our men camped on the grassland above, while others preferred to set their tents under the rock faces to keep out of the wind.

Some of Rune's men thought they spotted sails in the distance, but low-hanging clouds and growing waves had made it hard to know for sure. We were close, I thought, and I readied myself for a hard fight ahead. My dreams were filled with Rurik and his Dane ax, an unbeatable foe who had thwarted my best moves and withheld his full wrath against me.

I had become so distracted by this dread that I did not notice a growing rift between Bjorn and Skírlaug. His attempt to stop her from joining us had unnerved her, and she had not spoken to him since we'd left Vindavik. What had begun as a lover's quarrel grew into something worse. Where I had thought my situation might improve after defeating the Franks and Rurik, I found myself buried in challenges to my plans. I needed Bjorn to stay the winter with me, and I needed to convince more Danes and Northmen to bring their families to Vindreyland if I hoped to form a long-lasting kingdom rather than a foothold for Vikings to raid south.

Skírlaug stayed with me in my tent as she had done the other nights, but that rainy night Bjorn decided he did not like how much time we spent together. She had grown into my closest ally, my indispensable confidant and advisor, and I could not envision life without her. We spent most of our time together, but as she and I had established upon my return, we had no future as a man and a woman. I loved her, but not the way Bjorn loved her. Yet his jealousy boiled over, and he entered my tent to confront me, moments after Skírlaug had left for the cesspit.

"I've had enough of this," he growled with clenched fists. His clothes dripped from the rain.

"Of what?" I asked as I poured myself and Tariq a cup of fresh water.

"You and her, always spending time together—is there something going on between the two of you?"

I looked around my tent at empty furs and linens and said, "She's not here now."

"You're mocking me," he said.

"I'm not mocking you." I paused to consider how serious he was. Tariq stood at my side like a statue. "You are her lover, Bjorn, and I respect that. You have nothing to worry about, I promise."

"Why is she ignoring me then?"

"You know why," I said. "You tried to control her. She's your lover, not your property. I don't know what's gotten into you, but I think you need to take some time to relax. When you've cooled your head, I would recommend you start by apologizing to her, and perhaps then she'll talk to you again."

Bjorn marched over to one of the chairs by the furs and plopped down. He held his chin in his hand and leaned back, his eyes full of angst. "I've never felt this way about a woman before. I'm afraid I'm blowing it."

"You are blowing it." I started to laugh, and so did he. Tariq chuckled with us, but he kept his voice soft and tempered. "You're overthinking it. Clear your mind, have a drink, Skírlaug still loves you, and she's not going anywhere."

"You're right," Bjorn said, wiping at tears of laughter.

Skírlaug ducked through the entrance flaps and froze. She shot daggers at him, and he shrank in his chair.

It took him a moment to gather himself, and when he did, he stood up and took a deep breath.

"I'm sorry," he said.

I noticed that Tariq and I stood between the two of them. With a soft smile and a quick bow of my head to each of them, I tugged at Tariq's tunic to tell him to follow me. We took several long, awkward steps toward the flaps and slipped through them to leave the lovers to resolve their quarrel.

Outside, I took in a deep breath, feeling the chill of the breeze in my chest, and decided to take a walk around camp. Sailing and rowing had exhausted the men, so most had retired for the night, but a few fires still flickered, drawing us to them like a mosquito toward a candle. The first fire we found had no one around it, and the light drizzle had snuffed it out. The next fire still roared because it had a tarp set above it, although it fluttered so much in the breeze it did not keep out all the rain. Under the tarp, I found Rune sitting alone, ruminating over something.

"Out for a late-night stroll?" he asked.

"Er, Bjorn and Skírlaug are... making up."

"Oh." Rune waved at the logs around the fire and said, "Please, join me."

Tariq and I sat across from him, leaning forward to avoid the dripping edge of the tarp. The drizzle soon turned to rain and all we could hear was the plopping of water on canvas.

"Have you seen Ragnar?" I asked. Rune shook his head. "I wonder where he's gone off to."

"Probably sleeping," Rune said.

I nodded. Since he'd admitted his feelings for me, our conversations had become uncomfortable. In the dim firelight, I could not see his eyes all that well, but I assumed he was looking at me the entire time. It was when I noticed Tariq staring back at him that I realized. With slow, deliberate movements, I scooted away from Tariq on the log, and Rune's eyes did not move with me.

"So, Tariq, do you have a wife back home?" Rune asked.

"No," he said.

"A lover?"

"No."

Tariq and Rune's eyes remained locked.

"Hmm," I said. "I think… I think I'll head to the water for a piss."

I left the two of them alone and walked down the grassy slope to the sandy beach. The rain did not bother me, nor did the wind. My thoughts kept returning to Rurik, and to how he might kill me the next time we faced each other. No man had ever scared me so much, not even Hagar. I turned my back to the wind and pissed into the breaking waves. The surf crawled up the sand and covered my feet, and the cold water chilled me to the bone. Above me, stars shone through a break in the clouds. The moon also glimmered through to illuminate a small patch of tumultuous ocean, mountainous waves colliding with offshore rocks.

Caught in the faint rays of light, something moved over the water—the square shape of a sail fluttering in the dark, suspended in a moonbeam. Rolling waves rocked the ship, crests breaking white against the hull, and the relentless pull of wind lurching it forward to the next valley between.

Larger and larger waves rolled in from the open ocean, each one tipping the ship a little further on its side until it capsized. The break in the clouds closed, and the ship sank away into darkness. The light surf pulled at my feet, and I was relieved that our cove had the protection of a rock reef to break apart the largest of the storm's swells. What fool had thought it wise to sail in such weather, I wondered, and at night, no less. I returned to my tent, thinking about Rurik, and thinking about that ship. Bjorn and Skírlaug had gone, and Tariq had not returned. For the first night in a long time, I slept alone.

The following morning, I awoke to the cacophony of the camp breaking down to pack for the next stretch of our journey. Men chattered and laughed as they worked, and I lay in my furs for a while, resting and listening to them. Not long after I opened my eyes, Skírlaug snuck through the flaps of the tent and set about cleaning up the table and other beddings she and Tariq were supposed to have used. I sat up and stretched my arms over my head.

"You're up," she said without pausing in her work.

"So, you and Bjorn made up?"

She blushed and nodded.

"That's good; I'm glad."

Tariq barged through the flaps of the tent, out of breath. He said, "Hasting, I'm sorry, I—"

"It's all right," I interrupted him. "I'm happy you made a new friend."

Ragnar burst through the flaps next, eyeing Tariq and gripping the ax handle at his belt. "Hasting, I caught this *thing* lurking around camp just now," he said. "I'm not comfortable with it wandering around without supervision."

"Tariq was with Rune," I explained. "If you like, I will ask him why he was allowed to roam free around camp."

My response seemed to appease Ragnar. He nodded and said, "My fleet is ready."

I rubbed my eyes with both hands and looked around for my water. Tariq found it first and handed it to me.

"You are a good man," he said so I alone could hear him.

I looked up at him with a smirk and said, "You don't know me that well yet."

Skírlaug shoved all of the bedding into a large wooden chest and dragged it to the entrance. She ducked through the flaps for a moment, and when she entered again, two of my men followed her to carry the chest to our ship.

I could tell she had something to say but wanted to wait until the two of us were alone. Tariq saw it too, and he nodded to her and stepped out of the tent. As I watched him leave, I felt a little guilty. Ragnar had not even treated him as human when he complained of how I had let him walk around camp. How many others felt the same way, I wondered. Skírlaug interrupted my thoughts by kneeling and then sitting beside me in the furs.

"Bjorn asked me to marry him," she said.

"Admittedly—and please don't hit me—it was a little bit my idea," I said.

Skírlaug shot me a quick glance and continued gathering up all our things.

"Look, I still need you by my side. I would not be a so-called king if you hadn't given me that title and urged the others to swear to me."

She said nothing, and her silence made me uncomfortable, so I kept talking.

"I thought if you and Bjorn rekindled your affection, he would stay here, with me, and I had hoped to attract more Danes to live in Vindreyland, to farm and to trade, to raise their children. And it could all start with you."

"So, that is what this is all about?" she growled. "I'm just a pawn in your political games now? To be used as a tool for your own self-gain?" She sat on the lone remaining stool in the tent and crossed her arms. Her eyes welled as she looked to the ceiling, searching for the right words to say to me. "I'm sorry, Hasting. I didn't mean to sound so cruel. You have to understand, we have a daughter together. Ever since you learned she was yours, you've shown no emotion toward her, and not once have you spoken of her as part of your plans. Don't think she hasn't noticed. It's like she doesn't exist to you."

"Not at all." My heart sank at her words. She was right: I had ignored my feelings about Ulfrúna. "I don't know how to approach it."

"I don't know. A part of me hoped in time you and I would rekindle our affection," she said.

"Would that make you happy?" I asked her.

"No." Tears streamed down her face. "You haven't changed as much as I first thought. You're still doing the things that drove me crazy before, and you still have no idea you're doing them. And, with Ulfrúna, you—"

"I what?" I interrupted with fists clenched.

She wiped her tears with her apron and steadied her hands on her knees. "I will accept Bjorn's offer, with your blessing."

"If you marry Bjorn, will you still be my völva?" I asked her.

She scoffed at my question, as if I had done as she expected, and said, "Yes, but not because I love you; because you need me, and Ulfrúna needs you."

"Good, because I still need your help."

She glared at me for saying it, but it had to be said.

"I am hopeful you can help me convince more Danes to settle Vindreyland so I can make a legitimate effort of building a true kingdom here."

Skírlaug shook her head and chortled in a complete shift of demeanor. "You surprise me sometimes with the things that come out of your mouth. Vindreyland is not a place Danes will want to settle; if it were, I would not have needed to name you king. The only way this works is if you ally with the Celts. They will make your wealth, and your wealth and reputation will attract warriors such as Ragnar and Rune to sail with you in the summer. But you will never convince them to stay." She stood, crossed the tent to me, and put a hand on my shoulder. "I will stay with you, for Ulfrúna, and Bjorn will stay with you as he did before."

A moment later, one of our warriors barged into the tent and cried, "A fleet on the horizon!"

We put away our differences and stirred to action. I urged Skírlaug to leave everything in the tent and said we would return after the battle to collect our things. I girded my sword and met Tariq outside. He vanished inside for a moment, and when he emerged again, he had his own sword fastened around his waist and a shield on his arm.

We marched toward the ships to find that Ragnar's fleet had already rowed beyond the rocks to open ocean. A fleet drifted toward us, hugging the horizon. They were Vikings.

Skírlaug, Tariq, and I boarded a small rower to the *Riveted Serpent*; its crew was ready to set sail. Across the small, calm cove, Rune's ships meandered through the rocks to catch up with Ragnar.

When we passed the wall of semi-submerged rocks, we found ourselves fighting against a forceful current that twisted and turned our ships in ways we could not control. A few of the vessels collided but were undamaged. It took some hard rowing to move past the current, but our sail finally caught the stiff breeze and carried us onward. We had the wind at our back that morning, and it gave us an advantage over our enemy. As we moved closer, I could make out their red and black sails and shields. It was Rurik, and no one else.

Our fleets appeared similar in size and strength. Rurik had left a few dozen of his ships behind after he had fled my island, taking only the vessels he needed for his Danish troops to escape. The other ships, we had surmised, had carried the Frankish reinforcements he had brought from Frisia, and they had retreated with their Nantais allies after the battle.

Rune led his fleet to the left, Bjorn to the right, and we followed Ragnar up the middle. Rurik's ships had all lowered their sails and taken to rowing.

We had the sun at our backs, which made it harder for our enemy to see us. The previous night's storm had passed, leaving a clear blue sky and a tranquil, albeit choppy, ocean. Our ships skidded across the water, and when we reached the enemy fleet, we lowered our own sails and drifted toward them. The fleets merged together, sending grappling hooks to pull each other in, and the boats locked together to form what soon looked like a wooden island.

Skírlaug commanded her men to guide our ship toward the peripheries and hook to one of our own so we could escape if needed. The vessels in the middle of the huddled mass of iron and wood stood no such chance.

I had never fought a sea battle before, but everyone else seemed to know what they were doing. Warriors formed lines of interlocked shields above their gunwales and pressed against the enemy's line of shields. They repelled arrows overhead and spears thrust from underneath, and they thrust with their own spears in the hopes of opening up a hole in the enemy line. Since our ship had latched onto one of our own, we were not inundated with an enemy attack. We mustered our men and leaped from boat to boat until we arrived at the line of battle.

Some of our ships had pressed forward too eagerly, and they found themselves latched to an enemy ship on both sides. Rurik's men swarmed those ships and made quick work of them. Bjorn and Ragnar's fleets had converged in a similar way to trap some of Rurik's ships, and we could hear the furious clatter of metal on wood and metal on metal.

As the battle unfolded, seagulls and cormorants circled overhead, eyeing the entrails of the slain for their first meal of the day. The fighting progressed from an initial standstill to a raging, chaotic brawl. The way the ships had interlocked had allowed crews to rove around and behind shield walls. In that way, each crew formed its own small war band of a few dozen or so men and moved from ship to ship. The victor of each of these little battles moved on to the next, leaving a trail of corpses in their wake. In such close quarters, neither side had time to take prisoners, nor the luxury of letting them go. My war band of one hundred men swooped left behind Ragnar's and consumed smaller clusters of Rurik's warriors.

Tariq stayed at my side every inch of the way, helping me ward off stray spears and arrows as I stabbed and slashed my way forward. Skírlaug fought at my side, throwing her shield around to block enemy thrusts and to lure them into a vulnerable position where she could finish them.

In the fray of the fight, it was hard to tell if my skill as a swordsman had any effect—we fought in such close quarters I could not swing my blade. That I could not move sent me into a panic. The men behind me pushed me forward into the enemy line, and the enemy drove forward, pressed by the men at their backs. The complete madness and disorder of the fight led me to feel I had lost all control over my fate. For most of the battle, I felt sure I would die.

When I least expected it, the rim of a shield appeared from nowhere and struck me on the forehead. I fell backward into the arms of my men, dazed, and they sat me back against the gunwale of the ship we had boarded. In front of me, all of my men were falling back to a powerful charge by the enemy. Our group scattered, and a slew of Rurik's men leaped onto the ship, seething at the chance to run their blades through me.

Two of them lunged forward to finish me off, and I did not have the wherewithal to stop them. Tariq dove to my defense and surprised them with a quick swing of his blade. They seemed more surprised by the look of him than his moves, and when he howled with a deep, raspy voice, they tripped over each other to escape. He helped me to my feet, and as I stood up, our men rallied forward around us.

The many small war bands consolidated into two broad groups, and the ferociousness of the fighting lessened. A lull in the battle allowed everyone to catch their breath, but across the sea of bodies swaying with the waves below, Rurik called out to me.

"Hasting! Come and fight me!"

My men made a path for me to move forward, and I strode across several ships to face him. He stood on a rowing bench near the mast of one of his boats with his arm wrapped around the wooden beam to steady his footing, and his Dane ax extended over the heads of his men.

When he saw me, he hopped down and twirled his ax with both hands. I raised my shield to face him, and he lunged over the gunwale to strike at me with the momentum of his fall. The rocking of the ships unsteadied my feet, and when the broad head of his ax hit my shield, I fell backward. My men caught me and pushed me forward again, and I stabbed at him with my sword. Its tip grazed his belly. Tariq tried to join the fight, but I shoved him back and shook my head. He understood and stepped back, though I could tell he wanted to help. This was my fight, and mine alone.

Rurik swooped his ax around again, the blade almost catching the warriors around us, and it landed square on the metal boss of my shield. The metal rang out, and the vibration made my arm ache. A large swell rocked the boats and we both fell over, as did many of our men. I stood up again and flexed my knees to steady myself, and Rurik did the same. His chest rose and fell with labored breaths. I adjusted my fanged helmet and charged at him. All around us, the fighting had stopped. Both camps watched as their leaders fought in a single duel that would determine the outcome of the battle.

I swung at him with my sword, right, left, and right again, and each swipe he blocked with the shaft of his ax. He sprang up onto a rowing bench and skipped across another, then swiped down at me from above. Raising my shield, I blocked every blow, but now I could not reach him with my sword.

With my shield over my head, I swung at his ankles, but he danced out of the way before I could cut him down. My swipes did, however, unsteady him, and he jumped back onto the deck with me. In anticipation of my attack, he reached down for a wooden bucket on the ground and launched it at my head. I raised my shield in time, but the distraction had allowed him to move around me and swing at my shoulder.

The edge of the blade glanced off my maille. Had the metal not protected me, I am sure he would have taken a chunk of my arm clean off. With another jab of the ax head, he locked the blade's beard on the rim of my shield, but before he could pull it back, I clasped it with my sword, thrust it down to the ground, and stepped on the shaft to disarm him. He fell into the arms of his warriors, stunned by my move, and they pulled him back and raised their shields to protect him.

The battle raged on, and Rurik's side struggled to repel my army's momentum. I was weak and exhausted, so I pulled back from the fighting and sat on a rowing bench to catch my breath. Tariq was at my side and he patted me on the back.

Rurik's men cut at the ropes that tied their ships to the island and launched off in retreat. The battle had begun with an equal number of boats, but now they left with fewer than ten. My men cheered at our victory, their voices echoing across the ocean so the whole world might hear them. The gods, at least, heard them.

With the strength I had left, I joined Ragnar on one of the ships near the edge of the battlefield. We watched Rurik's remaining fleet glide away toward Frisia, no longer a threat to Vindreyland or Armorica. On their heels, however, were several ships with black and gold sails. Grjotgar had launched his boats in pursuit of Rurik to seek revenge for his brother's death.

"Should we help them?" Ragnar asked.

"No," I said. "We fulfilled our end. It's up to Grjotgar, now, to kill Rurik, if he can."

"To Vindreyland?" Ragnar asked.

"I'll meet you there. I have someone I need to see while I'm so close to Armorica," I said.

Ragnar nodded, and we set about dismantling the island of ships. Our fleet towed the boats left behind by Rurik back to my island, each worth a small fortune in Jutland and the North. Nothing quite compares to the spoils of war.

I, on the other hand, prepared a ship and crew to sail to the Morbihan to meet with Nominoë. We had the important matter to discuss of winning the war against the Franks once and for all. Skírlaug did not join me this time. She sailed back with Bjorn while I took her ship and some of her crew.

"You fought well today," I said to Tariq as we pulled away from the fleet with the wind at our back. "You saved me more than once."

Tariq bowed his head.

"To thank you, I will give you your freedom."

Tariq grinned and said, "You mean, I am free now?"

"Yes. You are free, and when we reach Vannes, I will give you silver so you can purchase supplies for your journey home," I said.

Tariq hung his head in thought. "What if I want to stay here with you?" he asked.

His question surprised me. I was sure he would want to leave us. I crossed my arms and said, "Do you have oaths, where you are from?"

"We do," Tariq said.

"Among our people, oaths are very important—so important that oath-breakers are killed," I explained. "If you want to stay, you will need to swear an oath to me, to fight for me, to defend me, and to follow me. Is that what you want?"

Tariq knelt down. "Yes, I want to serve you. There is nothing left for me in my homeland. I swear my oath to you that I will serve you well."

It was a bit of an awkward oath, but in my eyes, it counted. I reached underneath my maille shirt and pulled out a silver arm ring—I had learned to always keep a few on me for these exact situations—and gave it to him. He stood with chest high and filled with pride, and he slipped on the arm ring. The crew, who had listened in on our conversation, cheered. Tariq had earned their respect for how well he'd fought.

"You said free men have earned names," he added.

"Sometimes," I said. "But not always."

"Do you have one for me?"

I gave it some thought and asked him, "What is the deadliest animal in your homeland?"

"The viper," Tariq said without thinking.

I nodded and stroked my beard. "What do you think of the name Tariq Viper-Venom?"

Tariq frowned at the title. He looked down at his arms and hands and glanced at the rest of the crew, then said, "What about the Black Viper?"

I put my hand on his shoulder and smiled. "The Black Viper it is."

15

The Enfeoffment

Our ship arrived in Vannes at dusk. The Celts met us at the dock with dozens of soldiers, both mounted and on foot. Nominoë led them, to my relief, and when he saw me, he rejoiced. No sooner had I stepped off the plank than he leaped forward to embrace me. I could tell the weight of war had worn him down, and he needed any excuse he could find for joy. Tariq followed me off the ship, drawing the gaze of all the soldiers on the pier. Even Nominoë paused to look at him.

"You have a Saracen on your crew?" he asked.

"His name is Tariq," I said.

Nominoë tilted his head with a frown and nodded. "How did you end up with him?"

"It's a long story."

"Of course," Nominoë muttered. "Please, come. I will have my servants set up beds for your men in the old barracks. Will you join me for dinner tonight?"

"Absolutely."

"Good. And bring Tariq," he said.

Tariq and I followed him back to his hall, while the others followed his soldiers to the empty barracks. They did not converse, nor could they have—they did not speak each other's language. Nevertheless, I was sure my men would enjoy a dry place to sleep and fresh food, and I did not fear for their safety, nor did I think any of them stupid enough to start a brawl.

Once at Nominoë's hall, we climbed the stairs to the second floor to find the same hearth I had known since my youth, and the same tables arranged in the same manner. We sat where the Celts asked us to, and they brought platters of meat, bread, and a cauldron of vegetable soup.

Nominoë started the evening by asking about everything that had happened since I'd left. He listened to what I had to say about Rurik and how he had brought his troops from Frisia to support an army of Franks from the continent. That the Franks had tried to retake the island surprised him. He had not thought them strong enough to risk sending soldiers so far to reclaim land that held so little value to them and had always proved impossible to keep. Though he rejoiced that we had defeated Rurik and sent him running and that I had earned the loyalty of the other warlords prowling in the region, giving the coast of Armorica a reprieve from the raids, he seemed troubled by the actions of the Franks. After a short while of eating and chatting, a familiar face entered the room and sat on the other side of Nominoë.

"You remember Lambert?" Nominoë asked me.

"Of course," I said. "But last time I saw him was in Nantes, with Ricwin and Renaud. How is it he is here with you again?"

"Renaud expelled him," Nominoë said.

I took a bite of bread and leaned over the table. Lambert averted his eyes, seemingly incapable of acknowledging my presence.

"So, the first part of our plan failed," I said.

"So it has," Nominoë affirmed. "Now we have to kill Renaud to install him as count."

"I was planning on killing him anyway," I said.

Nominoë glared as he poured himself another goblet of wine. "So, tell me, how many warriors do you have under your command?" he asked.

"It's hard to say."

"Surely you must have some sense of your numbers."

"I have several fleets who have followed me and fought for me, but they are not from here and not interested in settling on the island. By summer's end, most of the fleets will have returned home. As of now, it appears I will have two fleets stay the winter if I am lucky."

"I see," Nominoë said. "What is it that brought them here in the first place? Just wealth?"

"Yes, and once I pay them, they will leave," I said.

"What I am hearing is that you have an army, but it is impermanent." Nominoë took a sip of his wine to think through what I had told him, and when he put the goblet down, he continued, "It is not so different from us. When I raise an army, I can only afford to keep it so long, and once it has served its purpose, the men return to their homes. The difference is that I can call them back on short notice. It is for the best, Hasting. We don't want Northmen settling the islands of Aquitaine."

His assertion made me uncomfortable. I had fought hard and risked life and limb to keep my land and title, all so I could help him in his fight against Renaud. Part of me wanted to scold him, but I remembered why I had embarked on my latest journey in the first place. Being called king had started going to my head, and I found myself wanting the things I had wished for before my captivity and revival. Had I drifted away from all I had learned in Bouaye and afterward?

"It sounds like you are having a hard time governing the island," Nominoë said. "I do not mean to be harsh, but trying to attract Danes to settle your lands so you can keep warriors close seems impossible. Better to accrue wealth and hire the fleets that come here in spring as sell-swords, like you've done this summer."

What he said made sense to me. I had tried with every tool at my disposal to convince my followers to stay. Still, the men who sailed from the North were Vikings—bold, restless, and with a burning desire for adventure. They would never agree to settle down in such a foreign and dangerous place, and certainly not with their families. Bjorn might stay for Skírlaug's sake, but his followers, too, would desire to return to the land of the Danes. More and more, it seemed I would need to look to the Celts to establish myself.

"I agree," I said.

He sat up a little straighter, adjusted himself in his chair, and said, "Good."

"I have a plan in mind if you'll hear it," I said. "I will keep a war band at my side and retain the title of a king among the Danes and Northmen. When fleets arrive in the spring and summer, I will recruit them and direct them away from Armorica, or wherever I am needed. Warriors will hear of the wealth I have given Ragnar and Rune, and they will flock to me to fight, or so I've been told. In the meantime, I ask that you recognize me as the ruler of Vindreyland and accord me whatever title suits that position. I'll also need a greater share of the salt trade to pay for the summer fleets."

"I had already thought of it." Nominoë snapped his fingers and one of his servants brought him a long parchment filled with writing. He pointed to a section of the text, and said, "Hasting, *Fidelis* of Nominoë, Duke of Vindreyland."

I marveled at the document and asked him, "What is it?"

"It's an enfeoffment, a grant of land in exchange for your loyalty and service. It gives you official ownership of the island and all the income associated with it," Nominoë said. "The village runs itself, and more of my people will flock to you when they learn how bountiful trade is there, especially for those displaced by our war with the Franks. It's a bit complicated how it will work, but in essence, the salt farmers will pay a tax to you, and the merchants who buy it from them and sell it in Armorica will pay one to me. The charter also stipulates that you will pay a tithe to the church."

"A tithe?" I scoffed.

"Yes, and it will directly benefit the church in your village," he said.

"Fine, fine," I said with a wave of my hand.

"You will also answer my calls to war." He coughed into his sleeve and said, "Perhaps you can whip this lazy son of mine into fighting shape."

I sniggered and bobbed my head. "That I can agree to."

Nominoë handed me a quill. "Sign your name at the bottom, and it will be the law of the land." I took the feather and drew a rune since I had never signed my name before and did not know how. Nominoë stared at it for a moment and said, "What is that supposed to mean?"

"It's the wolf's hook," I said. "It is used in the North to ward off danger."

Nominoë smiled and nodded, and I believe he understood what I had meant by signing my name with it. He rolled up the parchment and handed it to his servant, who returned to his place on the other side of the hall.

"You are now a nobleman," Nominoë said. He raised his goblet to offer me a toast. "To Hasting, Duke of Herio, or Vindreyland, and loyal vassal to Armorica!"

After our meal, I excused myself from the table. I walked to the church to find Conwoïon, my oldest friend and confidant. Nominoë had taken an interest in Tariq and asked him to stay a little while longer so he could learn more about his homeland. That they spoke to each other in the language of the Danes struck me as comical. Neither had mastered it, but they both knew enough to communicate.

I found Conwoïon scrubbing some grime off the stone floor on the far side of the chapel. My shadow in the candlelight eclipsed him, and when he turned to see who stood over him, he jumped back against the wall.

"Ah, Hasting! You scared me, my boy. I heard you had returned."

"Do you have a moment to talk?"

He nodded and left his brush on the floor to join me on the first row of pews.

He read the sadness on my face and asked, "What is troubling you?"

"You were right," I said. "It was too soon for me to go back. I'm starting to feel as if I'm losing touch with my purpose again."

Conwoïon scratched at his chin and said, "Losing touch, hm? What makes you say that? Do you feel things are not going your way?"

"On the contrary, they're all going my way, almost too well." I leaned forward and held my head in my hands. "I'm supposed let go of my wants and needs, and of fearing the future, but now I find myself drowning in those things."

"You are too hard on yourself." He put a hand on my back and rubbed it around to comfort me.

"You don't understand; I've done terrible things again. I've killed," I whispered.

"Had you not, would you have been killed?"

"Yes."

"There is your answer. You did evil out of necessity, to ward off evil," he said.

"I'm supposed to be acting for the good of others."

Conwoïon continued to rub my back. "I believe I see where you are struggling, my friend. You have trapped yourself in a way of thinking that is at odds with how the world works, and I do not blame you. Every day, my flock comes to pray in my church, lamenting the evil in their lives. It is as if they assume the world is naturally good, that they are naturally good, and evil plagues them."

"That sounds about right."

Conwoïon laughed. "Alas, that is not the case. Good and evil cannot exist without the other. Without evil, we would not know good. The Bible tells us we are all born with both. When we were cast from Eden, it was for our evil, and that evil stains us from the moment we are born. We all want to believe we were born good, but if that is true, we must be born evil as well. The same is true of the world around us. That every creature born into this world must struggle, suffer, die, and decay tells us evil is the natural order of things. Good emerges as a remedy to evil, and not the other way around."

"I don't see how this helps me."

"What you are feeling is normal in light of what you've lived through. I'm sorry to say, Hasting, that before your capture in Nantes, you lived a life of evil, and you were unwilling to look within yourself to see it. In Bouaye, you saw the good in you, and I admire that you desire so much to focus on it. Yet, had you not been evil, you would never have seen the good in yourself, and had you not uncovered the good, you would not have acknowledged your sin. What you need to do now is reconcile the two.

"It is a blessing for a man to see both in himself, and to know that he can neither disown nor live without evil. It is also a blessing when a man learns that his achievements are bound to the conflict between good and evil and that the course of his life ebbs and flows between those two forces. Hasting, there is no such thing as pure good and no such thing as pure evil. Our lives are not about achieving good apart from evil but in spite of it."

I sat with his words for a moment. The course of my life seemed to have taken a wrong turn, though Conwoïon did not think so.

"What about redemption? How can I atone for the evil things I've done?"

Conwoïon smiled and said, "My friend, it is far simpler than that. God is most forgiving of those who have looked within, reckoned with their evil, and humbly asked Him for His forgiveness. The fact that you sought me out to tell me how you are feeling—and that you have not given up on your new journey despite setbacks—tells me you are on the right path."

"Thank you," I said.

"Pray with me."

He took my hands, closed his eyes, lowered his head, and uttered a prayer in Latin. I breathed deep breaths, listening to his prayer. His words soothed and cleared my anxious mind, and a wave of euphoria wash over me, starting with my head and running down to my fingers and my toes. It is a difficult thing to explain, except to say that for the first time in my adult life, I was able to let go, abandon all thoughts of past and future, and glory in the serenity of a clear head and heart. It felt as if the god of the Christians had reached down from above and released me of my guilt for all the evil I harbored in my heart for those who had wronged me.

I let go of the hate I felt for those who had slain my father and abused me on their ship; and of Hagar for all the evil he had done to me and those I had loved; and of Eilif for abandoning me in Armorica; and of Renaud for murdering Asa and luring me with the hope that she still lived. Where I had believed the wolf Fenrir had invaded my spirit, I now understood he had been a part of me since the beginning, and I no longer feared him.

To Conwoïon's astonishment, I fell to my knees and clasped my hands, my eyes filled with tears, and I laughed.

"What is it, Hasting?"

"I felt him," I said. "Your god, I felt him just now, like a cleansing wave."

Conwoïon put his hand on my shoulder and smiled. "He is your God now, too."

Nominoë sent messengers to the seven counties of Armorica to invite his vassals to a war council. He asked me, too, as his newest vassal. He brimmed with confidence in the days leading to the arrival of the other Celtic noblemen, encouraged by how I had neutralized the Viking threat, at least for a while. His war with the Franks had not gone well, so the good news I brought from Vindreyland had lifted his spirit.

I, meanwhile, sent my ship back to Vindreyland to carry word of my plans to attend the council, and I asked them to send a boat to retrieve me in no less than a fortnight. Only Tariq remained with me in Vannes, and I valued his company. He had received a great deal of schooling in his homeland, and he had a refreshing penchant for history I had not found among the Danes. I thought at first that he and Conwoïon would have much to discuss, both of them fascinated by the past. Unfortunately, Conwoïon refused to speak with Tariq, complaining of the treatment of Christians by the Moors. Nominoë, on the other hand, did not seem to mind. He and Tariq spent long afternoons discussing the history and relations between Christians and Muslims, among other subjects.

I would have joined them, but Ratvili's representative arrived a mere four days after the messengers left Vannes, and as luck would have it, Ratvili had sent his daughter Morgana to represent him.

News of her arrival sent my heart into a flutter. My reaction caught me by surprise. I had faced innumerable enemies, survived impossible odds at sea, and lived through abandon and starvation, and yet none seemed quite as frightful as meeting a woman I hardly knew, and to whom I felt a powerful attraction. To my surprise, she found me first, sitting alone in church on the day she arrived, and I jumped when she sat beside me. Her eagerness to seek me out told me she felt something for me, too.

"Are you a Christian now?" she asked.

"I'm not sure." I glanced at the cross on the altar.

"Sitting alone in a church is a good sign." Her back was rigid against the pew. She straightened the bunches of her green gown across her thighs. "It's good to see you."

I looked at her and smiled. "It's good to see you too."

We sat in silence. I wanted to say more, but I also did not want to say too much. She had seemed so terrified by our last encounter, I was unsure what she thought of me. I leaned back to mirror her posture.

"I hope you will forgive me," she said.

"For what?"

"You saved my life and I never thanked you."

"I think you did thank me," I said.

"I didn't," she insisted.

Her eyes were brilliant emeralds. She tilted her head and grinned. "I heard Nominoë gave you land."

"He did, although it was mine to begin with."

She chuckled and put a hand on my leg. "What you have done is truly exceptional."

"How so?"

"You are a Northman, and you have earned the trust of our king. He has gifted you land and title. No one has ever done what you have," she said.

"What about you?" I asked. "Not every lord sends his daughter to a war council. Sounds exceptional to me."

"Me, exceptional?" She ran her hand through her hair and looked back up at me. "I am nothing without the land and title my father will give me when he dies."

"You sound unsure of yourself," I said.

"I am. I've had suiters since my father fell ill, but none of them want *me*. They want my father's land. And Nominoë insists I marry. He does not want the Rennais governed by a woman."

"Idiots, all of them."

"What makes you say that?"

"First, women govern all the time in the North, and frankly they do better at it. And second, as beautiful as you are, men should be lined up to die and kill for you," I said.

She averted her eyes at the mentioned of killing. "One did," she said.

Morgana angled toward me. Her hands found mine, and she pulled me in close. She had more to say, I could tell, but she did not utter another word. Our conversation had tiptoed around her purpose in seeking me out.

"I've thought about you, you know," I said.

"I've thought about you."

We had drawn so near that our noses nearly touched.

"Hopefully this time no one interrupts us," I said.

She pressed up against me, and we kissed. Her warm lips sent a shockwave through my whole body. I lost track of the world until a voice behind us started shouting. We both pulled back to find Conwoïon storming up the aisle between the pews.

"This is a house of prayer!" he exclaimed.

Morgana took my hand, and we made a run for it while tripping over the stone floor, both of us giggling the whole way. We bolted out the side door into an alleyway and slipped around the adjacent building and out of sight. She leaned against the wooden wall and tugged on my tunic to pull me in. Her breasts pressed against my chest, and my hand found its way down to her leg. I held her thigh to my hip and pressed my weight between her legs. When I kissed her neck, she took a deep, gasping breath and lifted her other leg to grapple me around the hips.

"We have to stop," she whispered. "Hasting, we can't."

Her actions did not match her words. She kept squeezing me with her arms and legs, gasping and groaning as we kissed. I felt no resistance until, without warning, she dropped her feet to the ground and pushed me off. She fixed her gown, ran her hands through her hair, and sauntered back toward the church.

"Someone will see us," she said. "Come."

I stood dumbfounded as she drifted away. Before she turned the corner, she beckoned me with her forefinger. Her coy smile and alluring eyes triggered my hunting instincts, and I chased after her. At the moment, I felt like a starved wolf, desperate for a catch. In truth, I was an unsuspecting butterfly floating into a spider's web.

She wanted me as much as I wanted her, but she also desired more than a fleeting affair. My heart could not resist her. Somehow, against all my expectations, she had made me feel the way I had felt with Asa. Passion drove me forward, and I followed her from the church to the guest quarters Nominoë had given her, and we vanished out of sight.

Later in the day, I heard men shouting my name, searching for me in the city streets. Nominoë had called for me. Morgana was cuddled up against me, her naked skin entangled with mine. I ran my fingers down her back. She caressed my face and, with her head resting on my chest, said, "I think we're in trouble."

"Why?"

"We're not supposed to make love outside of marriage."

I chuckled and said, "That hasn't stopped anyone I've ever known."

"What will Nominoë think when he learns two of his war council members are lovers?" she mused.

"Is that what we are? Lovers?"

She slapped the top of my head playfully and said, "You scoundrel."

"I've been called worse," I said.

"You should go."

I took in a deep breath, reluctant to move, and continued to run my hand up and down her back. She did not move either. When the voices calling my name drew nearer, she sighed.

"What do we do now?"

"I'll go see what he wants," I said.

"No, I mean with you and me. You have to return to your land and I to mine. What do we do from here?"

"I don't know," I said.

She pulled away from me, sat herself up on her knees, then straddled me like a horse. I ran my hands up her thighs and held her waist.

"I think you know what I want," she said.

"To marry?"

She nodded.

"You don't want to marry me."

"Why wouldn't I? All the men my father has tried to marry me off to have been witless mongrels. And now that you have land—"

"But I'm still a Viking," I interjected. "I fight and raid and sail to faraway lands. We would hardly ever see one another."

She leaned forward, grasped my wrists, and held them against the bed above my head. "Imagine what our reunions will be like after a long absence."

She arched her back, shifted her hips, and rubbed her body against mine. Her breathing quickened. I sunk my fingernails into her flesh. When I thought we might start again, she stopped me.

"No," she said.

She rolled to the side and hopped to her feet. Before I could say anything, she threw her dress back on and sat at a small table with a bronze mirror to work on her hair. As she fiddled with the different brooches in front of her, she called out a name and an old woman barged through the door. I grasped for the blankets to cover myself.

"Don't mind my servant," she said. "We can trust her to speak nothing of what she's seen."

"Has she been here the whole time?"

"Well, yes, and the others too."

I had been so focused on Morgana that I had not noticed the servants in the main room outside the bedchamber. They must have heard everything. One of them, I was sure, would report to Nominoë.

"I should go." I grabbed my clothes off the floor.

Morgana turned on her stool to face me, her servant still working on her hair. "I'll see you later?"

I pulled my clothes back on and stumbled over to her for a kiss, then darted out of the room to find the men who were searching for me. I thought it strange they had not checked Morgana's quarters. When I found one of the men, he bade me return to Nominoë's hall. I followed him in and up the stairs to find my benefactor sitting at the table across from the hearth, where he spent a great deal of his time.

"Ah, Hasting, good. Come, sit with me," he said.

His son Erispoë sat next to him. He had started to look more like his father, with short brown hair and thick eyebrows, but fatter. To my surprise, he wore the uniform of a soldier, as if he had trained as a warrior all his life. I knew he had not. At Nominoë's behest, I sat at the chair closest to him.

"How can I help?"

"It is a sensitive matter, and one I would like to keep between us." A sudden bout of coughing gripped him, and he leaned forward in his chair with a handkerchief pressed against his mouth. I scooted my chair back to give him some space and to put some distance between us. When the coughing subsided, he continued, "Apologies. My cough has worsened these past weeks, and it doesn't seem to be improving. Anyway, I want to talk to you about my succession."

I thought he had wanted to talk to me about Morgana, and that he did not gave me great relief. "I am listening," I said.

"Erispoë is my only son and heir, and should I die, God forbid, I need to make sure those who are loyal to me are loyal to him," he said.

"I understand." I looked past him at Erispoë, who seemed to have other things on his mind.

"Hasting, your allegiance to me is particularly precarious," Nominoë went on. "I want assurances that whatever we decide in the war council, you will follow even if I am not around to see it through."

I crossed my arms and glared at him. His lack of faith disturbed me. "My word is my bond. I would never break it," I said.

"Good. So, you will not mind if I amend your enfeoffment to say you are a vassal of Erispoë?"

"No." I did mind, but I did not see how arguing with him would help my cause. "Do you plan to die soon?"

"Heavens, no. But one can never be too ready. Erispoë still has much to learn. With that, I also want to say that I have canceled the war council. I have been feeling unwell and am not up to hosting my noblemen."

"Cancel the war... but Renaud, and the—"

"Relax. The council was just a formality. I already have a plan in place, and my noblemen will fall in line with what I have decided," he said.

Nominoë's cough returned, and the second fit was worse than the first. A servant scurried over to help him, and while he struggled, Erispoë hardly seemed to notice. When the coughing stopped, Nominoë slumped against the backrest of his chair, exhausted.

"It does seem worse," I said.

Nominoë smiled. "You have my thanks for noticing. On another subject, I heard from Conwoïon that Morgana arrived earlier today."

"He told you that, did he?" I glanced out into the dark hall, as if I might spy the priest lurking about.

"Among other things. I must confess something: I had hoped the two of you would get along." He leaned over the table and grinned. "Morgana is a beauty unlike any other in Armorica. Ratvili has always been proud of her. But then, she has always been a problem. Her height has not helped her. She towers over most of her suitors, and coupled with her beauty, men quiver in her presence."

"I can see how they would."

Nominoë laughed as he said, "We thought God had blessed us when we found the Neustrian prince who agreed to marry her, but he died in the civil war not a week after the wedding. Such a shame." He reached for a silver chalice and took a sip. A purple streak ran from the corner of his mouth to his chin, and he wiped it with his sleeve. "Now, she is almost too old to marry."

"Can women over twenty-five even have children?" Erispoë asked.

"That's a ridiculous question." Nominoë shook his head.

Erispoë shrank at his father's disapproval. "Everything I say is ridiculous to you," he said.

"Then perhaps you should think through your words before you say them," Nominoë spat.

"I'm not as stupid as you make me out to be," his son retorted.

Nominoë sighed. "I didn't say you were stupid, only that you need to think about what you say before you say it. How can you hope to take my place when I die? Do you think the noblemen will take you seriously if you go around spouting nonsense?"

"That's what it's always about. You don't think I have what it takes to rule Armorica," Erispoë said. Nominoë shook his head. "I'll prove you wrong. You'll see."

Erispoë stormed out of the chamber. Once he was gone, I relaxed into my chair and sighed.

Nominoë chuckled and said, "You see how much work I still have to do with him?"

"So... Morgana." My mind had latched onto her and would not let go.

"Right," Nominoë replied. "Ratvili is also ill. He has a cough worse than mine. If he dies without a male heir, his lands will pass to me."

"Why wouldn't they pass to Morgana?"

"Our laws say the land will pass to the closest male relative of the deceased lord. I am Ratvili's nephew, and so I would inherit his land and title," he said.

"It seems unfair. In the North, women can inherit land and rule," I said.

"That would be something," Nominoë said. "But the lords of the other five counties would never give a woman their respect, not without a husband, or a son."

The pieces started to join together in my mind. I knew him too well to think Morgana and I had found each other by chance. Nominoë had planned the whole affair. What I did not know was if Morgana had knowingly taken part.

"You want us to marry."

Nominoë slapped his leg and cried out, "That's the boldness I remember!" His outburst made all the servants around us jump. "It's up to you, but I urge you to think about it carefully. Marrying Morgana would make you husband to the most beautiful woman in Armorica, and any children you have would inherit the Rennais. Who knows, your descendants could one day rule Armorica."

"And my loyalty to Erispoë would be assured in the interest of my new family."

"Your acumen has always impressed me," he said.

I closed my eyes and took a deep breath. What Nominoë proposed would draw me further into Armorica and away from the Vikings. At the moment, I thought about what Skírlaug might think, or Bjorn, or Rune. I then thought about what Morgana had said, that I'd done what no other ever had, and marrying into the nobility of Armorica would be one step further. Celts and Danes would sing my name for what I had accomplished, and I relished the thought. What stories would the skalds sing if I managed such a feat? What Vikings would hear of this and try to conquer by enfeoffment rather than invasion?

"Yes," I said.

"Yes to what?"

"I'll marry her. And I will sign your new enfeoffment to swear fealty to your son."

Nominoë snapped his fingers and one of his servants scurried down the stairs behind us. While we waited, Nominoë poured me a cup of wine. He placed it in front of me and sat back in his chair. Without thinking, I had the wine in my hand, and we tapped our drinks together in celebration. I had not had a drink in years, and I had almost forgotten the taste. Its warmth filled my belly. I felt enlivened. While we drank, Morgana entered and joined us at the table.

"I heard the two of you made a deal without me," she said.

"My servants talk more that I would like," Nominoë lamented.

"I'm not mad about it," she said. "I just wish I could have been here."

"You are here now," I said. "Nothing is set in stone yet."

"So, you've reconsidered my proposal?"

"I have." I took a long sip of my wine before speaking again. "Nominoë helped me to understand your circumstances, and how we would benefit each other in marriage."

Morgana snatched my arm and pulled me away from the table. She led me to the corner of the hall and whispered, "I don't want you to marry me because it will fill your pockets with silver."

"That's not it at all," I said. "From the moment I first laid eyes on you, I felt something larger than myself pulling me in your direction."

"When was that?"

"When I came back with Lambert. You were in the church sitting next to your father. We'd never met, but somehow I already knew you. I'm sorry, I'm not trying to scare you—"

"No," she said. "It's very kind. You must understand; I have too much to lose if I pick the wrong husband."

"You said it yourself: marrying each other will give us both what we want, while still leading the lives we have."

Morgana glanced at my goblet of wine. She seemed to have sensed a change in my voice. However, she shook off her hesitation and said, "All right."

We returned to the table and I took my seat at Nominoë's side. Morgana stood over him with her arms crossed. He poured himself more wine and took a hearty gulp, and when he turned to her, he smiled with purple teeth.

"We will be betrothed," she said. "But I don't want a wedding until next year. The last thing I want is to marry another man who will die at war before we can have children."

"I think that sounds like a wise plan," Nominoë said.

"She seems to know more about the war to come than I do," I said. "What happens next year?"

Nominoë wiped his mouth with his sleeve and leaned toward me. He had a slight sway in his shoulders and his head bobbed as he looked at me.

"I plan to besiege Nantes next June," he said.

"And me?"

"I had hoped you would lead a fleet up the Loire to distract Renaud."

"The timing will need to be perfect," I said.

"I have a plan for that, too. Until then, I ask you to keep your followers together on the island and keep other Vikings off my back. When you have gathered more men to your cause, we will join together to destroy Renaud."

16

Call to War

"Do I look all right?" Bjorn's fingers trembled as he adjusted the collar on his tunic.

"Never better," I said.

He took a long sip of wine from his goblet and sat next to the window on the far side of my bedchamber. The sky was dull grey; wind and rain battered the monastery's stone walls. It had been an unusually cold and wet spring.

"It feels tight. Does it look tight to you?"

"Relax," I said.

"What about you? Aren't you nervous? Have you ever seen a wedding before?"

"Of course I'm nervous, but it is a happy occasion," I said.

Ulfrúna burst through the doorway. Ingrid called for her from down the hallway, and when it seemed she might catch up to Ulfrúna, the little girl darted off again. She had kept all of us busy all winter. Some days I had taken her under my charge, and at first I was hopeful I could teach her the Celtic language and how to read, among other things, but she proved a difficult, impatient student. I suppose children of that age are all difficult students. To my relief, candle-making held her attention, so some days I took her down to help the local priest, a small-statured man named Roland who had moved in during my absence from a border town on the Breton March that Renaud had raided and burned. Roland did not need help, but he let us join him, I think out of a need to show me appreciation. I had begun to tithe that winter, and for the first time since he had arrived on the island, he had the resources he needed to serve his congregation.

"That girl will be the death of Ingrid," Bjorn said.

I chortled and agreed. "I think she gets it from me."

One of Skírlaug's men stepped into the doorway, his clothes soaked from the rain. "We're ready," he said.

Bjorn shrank in his chair. His nails dug into the armrest and muscles tightened in his jaw. I grabbed his arm and helped him to his feet.

"I'd rather face an army of giants," he said.

We walked out of the monastery, into the rain, and down the path to the village. A new Danish quarter occupied the northern end, with square houses made of oak logs, and steeply pitched roofs sealed with soil and clay.

Bjorn and I had directed his men to build permanent structures for themselves, rather than let them suffer in their tents all winter. Among the buildings they had constructed, Bjorn had asked to have a proper longhouse built for his betrothed, and she had since moved out of the monastery and into her new lodgings.

The entrance to the longhouse had a steep gable with thick oak pillars and a large double door carved with Skírlaug's family emblems of stags, ravens, and bears. As we entered the longhouse, we had to duck below several garlands of flowers. Skírlaug had waited all winter for the spring blooms. Further into the hall, we found ourselves shrouded in lavender incense. Two men played lively music with a flute and a drum, and some of the people who sat and drank on the long benches on both sides of the hall tapped their feet to the rhythm.

I led Bjorn through the fracas to the far end and stood him by a tall wooden fylgja carved in the likeness of cats surrounding a nude woman. We did not have to wait long before the music stopped and all the people sitting at the benches got to their feet.

"Who enters this hall?" I said so all could hear.

"Skírlaug, daughter of King Horic, seeress of the mist and sea," said a voice from the other side of the room.

"I bid her enter and take her place at my side," I said.

Bjorn leaned toward me and whispered, "You seem well rehearsed."

"I've been practicing."

Skírlaug entered the room wearing a long green gown with golden embroidered trim. She was flanked by her servants on both sides, and she held a bouquet of lilies still dripping from the rain. A few steps into the hall, she paused to let her servant place a silver crown over her braided hair, one of the many treasures from my trove. She had asked my permission to use it since she did not have her family's traditional bridal crown. Once the crown sat securely on her head, she inched toward us and took her place facing Bjorn by the fylgja, with me standing between them.

"Welcome all to this joyful Frigg's day." I paused to clear my throat. "May the gods watch over this ceremony and give their blessing to the union of Bjorn, son of Jarl Ragnar, and Skírlaug, daughter of King Horic."

Skírlaug kept her eyes on me through the whole ceremony. She and I had practiced the lines to exhaustion, and the look on her face told me I had better remain faithful to what she had asked me to say.

"First, we must exchange the dowry. Since I am the benefactor of both—"

"Don't do it," Skírlaug snarled.

I took a small satchel of silver coins off my belt, shook it for the audience to hear, and passed it from one hand to the other. It was a joke I had planned, since neither Bjorn nor Skírlaug had families interested exchanging dowries in the traditional way. Skírlaug scowled, but when the audience laughed, she relented with a smile.

"Now that it's done, on to the next," I said. "Bring in the goat while the bride recites her vows."

Skírlaug recited a skaldic poem to Bjorn, who listened with a pale face. She evoked the protection of the gods and the need for a sacrifice. A warrior from Skírlaug's crew led a goat to the front of the hall and handed the rope to Bjorn.

Bjorn pulled a hunting knife from his belt and knelt by the goat. He waited for Skírlaug to finish her poem, and when she did, he wrapped his arm around the animal's neck to hold it in place and then cut its throat. Skírlaug held a wooden bowl to catch some of the spewing blood, then carried the bowl to a shrine to Frigg behind the fylgja. Servants dragged the slain goat away, leaving a trail of blood along the ashen floor.

"With the sacrifice made, we now pass to the rings," I said.

Ulfrúna appeared behind her mother and, with Ingrid lurking watchfully behind, handed her mother a silver ring. Bjorn's brother Ubba stepped up and gave him his ring and a sword.

"I offer you these gifts as a sign of my devotion to you. A ring to bind us as husband and wife, and this sword for you to keep for our son," Bjorn said.

He placed the ring on the hilt of the sword and held it out for Skírlaug. She took the ring, and then the sword.

"I offer you this gift as a sign of my devotion to you," she answered.

She held out the ring Ulfrúna had brought her, and Bjorn took it. They placed the rings on each other's fingers and stepped back again.

"Let these rings serve as reminders of the unbreakable vow you have committed. Now it is time to seal the bond with a kiss."

Bjorn took Skírlaug's hands and leaned in with pursed lips. She closed her eyes, and when their lips touched, the hall erupted in cheer.

I was supposed to say something more after that, but the room was so loud I could not hope to be heard. The musicians played, and as Bjorn and Skírlaug walked through the hall, the crowd showered them in red poppy petals. Ubba stepped around the pillar where he had hidden during the ceremony and stood at my side to watch them. For such a large, well-trained warrior, he was oddly nervous in front of a crowd.

"I wish my father had stayed," he said.

"I have the sense he is a hard man to keep around long," I said.

Ubba bobbed his head and shrugged. "All of us brothers have different mothers. That's how we ended up so close in age," he said.

"All of you? How many brothers are there?"

"There's me, Bjorn, Ivar, Sigurd, and Hvitserk," he said. "Those are the ones we know about, at least."

I laughed. "We should all be so lucky. I haven't had a woman's affection in ages."

"Neither have I," Ubba said with a long sigh.

I patted him on the thick of his back and smiled. "You need a drink."

We followed the wedding procession out of the hall and into the rain. Men and women alike howled at the downpour and everyone took to running to reach the feasting tent. Skírlaug and her servants had spent the better part of a fortnight preparing a massive tent in the fields beside the village to accommodate as many guests as possible. Her new hall, spacious as it was, did not have enough room for everyone she had invited. It had taken over a dozen smaller tents sewn together to make one as large as Skírlaug wanted, and inside it was spacious and warm, except for the occasional gust that blew through the entrance flaps.

The Christians had chosen to skip the ceremony in the hall, but we'd made it clear to them that they were welcome to join us for the feast afterward. Both Skírlaug and I agreed the gesture would help bring the different camps in Vindreyland closer together. To my delight, many Celts had already arrived by the time we reached the tent and the feast kicked off to a cheerful start.

We ate and drank our fill all afternoon, and the rain did not dampen our spirits. Ulfrúna sat in my lap while she ate roasted chicken and some pottage, and her foot beat against my leg to the rhythm of the music. Tariq sat at my side wearing a white tunic and a flower in his ear. We had become inseparable since the battle, it seemed, and as Skírlaug drifted away from me toward Bjorn, Tariq moved closer. Ulfrúna had taken a special interest in him, too, and she had even learned a few words of Arabic, his language, although it was only to say hello.

"*Salam aleikoum,*" she said to him as she settled into my lap.

"*Maleikoum salam,*" he said back with a smile.

Bjorn and Skírlaug sat several places down from us, flanked by Ingrid on one side and Ubba on the other. They seemed genuinely happy, smiling and giggling, and whispering in each other's ears.

Some of the men entertained us with unique skills. One of Bjorn's warriors balanced a knife on his nose. With the blade teetering over his face, he received a roaring cheer. Next, the new Celtic priest, a local man named Loànn who Conwoïon had sent to take over the village's church, juggled three apples, then two in one hand, then three again. Everyone cheered him on and, spurred by our support, he added a fourth apple and managed to keep them all in the air at the same time. When he let them all fall to the ground and gave the newlyweds a bow, he was met with thunderous applause. I noticed Ingrid leering at him as she clapped. Something about his balding grey hair and time-worn face had drawn her attention.

After a few hours of laughing, eating, and drinking, Ingrid stood and raised her hand to silence us.

"To bed," she shouted.

We had reached the part of the ceremony where the couple had to consummate their union, and they had to have two witnesses. Ingrid had initially said I needed to attend, but I thought, given my history with Skírlaug, she should volunteer someone else. To my relief, Loànn had learned of the tradition, which apparently happens at Christian weddings as well, and he volunteered to take my place. Bjorn and Skírlaug walked out arm-in-arm, followed by Ingrid and Loànn. Once they'd left, I had the privilege of watching over Ulfrúna, who darted off with some other children across the tent.

"Where I am from, they do that too," Tariq said.

"Do what?"

"They must have witnesses for the first bedding," he said. "I remember when I married my first wife. It was a happy time."

"I thought you said you weren't married."

"Not anymore. My family banished me from our land, and my two wives were remarried to others."

"Two wives? You can have more than one where you are from?"

"Yes, my brother has six," he said.

"Why were you banished?"

"For the same reason you did not mind when Rune sailed home," he said.

I understood his meaning. Evidently, his people frowned on man-lovers as much as Northmen. The more I learned about his home and his people, the more I thought we sounded alike.

"What happened after you were banished?"

He crossed his arms and sat back in his chair. "I joined the emir's army. We fought against the Christians of Asturias. They fight with dirty tricks, the Christians. They hide in the hills and mountains and ambush us in the narrow paths. And after they make us retreat, they raid our villages on the border and slaughter our people."

"I am sure your people raid, too," I said.

He locked on me with focused, angry eyes.

"I meant no offense, my friend. It has been my experience that, in matters of war, no one is completely innocent."

He had not talked much about his homeland during the winter. Perhaps it was the wine that loosened his lips.

"Tell me more about the emir," I said. "Is he like a king?"

"He rules over all of Al-Andalus," he said. "Except Asturias. Allah gave our people a sacred mission to bring the world under his teaching by the spoken word or the sword."

"Sounds familiar," I joked.

He did not laugh.

I took a sip of my milk and looked out into the crowd. "The world seems to be full of people trying to change other people to be more like them."

He seemed to consider my words for a moment and then nodded. Ulfrúna appeared again and tugged at Tariq's tunic.

"I want to show you something," she demanded.

He looked at me and, when I smiled, he followed her. I found myself sitting alone at the table, watching everyone else talking, drinking, and laughing. We did not have enough tables for all of them, so most stood, making it hard to see across the tent from my seat. The Celts had dressed for the occasion and wore garlands of poppies around their necks. They kept their distance from our warriors, although a few mingled. The language barrier made it hard for them to communicate, but some of them managed.

Sitting there, far-and-away in my own thoughts, I jolted back into the present moment when a man in soaked leathers barged through the front flaps. His entrance caught the attention of everyone in the tent, and the musicians stopped playing. When the man saw me, he charged up with a parchment in his hand. Several warriors held him back, but I motioned him forward, and he knelt before me at the table.

"A message from the continent," he said. His hands trembled as he held out the parchment.

I took it from him and broke the wax seal. It read:

Hasting,
Nominoë has fallen gravely ill. The summer campaign against the Franks should be put on hold, but his son Erispoë and Lambert have resolved to march on Nantes. Erispoë wants to prove himself to his father, but I fear Renaud will kill him. I have convinced them to wait for you and your fleet to arrive, as you and Nominoë planned. They will meet you on the banks of the Loire by the fortified bridge on June 21. Remember, your purpose is to support. Under no circumstances are you and yours to take the city. The only way Lambert can be installed legitimately is if he earns it himself.
God be with us.
~ Conwoïon

I thanked the messenger and sent him away to rejoin his ship. The message brought ill news indeed, but I did not want to ruin the wedding with it. Everyone stared to gauge my reaction, and when I swirled my finger to tell the musicians to play on, the festivities picked up where they had left off. Tariq emerged from the crowd without Ulfrúna, and he sat at my side. He wore a long frown as if he had also read the letter I'd just received.

"What's happened?" he asked.

"Our ally on the continent is ill," I said. "His son wants to march in his place this summer when we move on Nantes."

"Is his son a warrior?"

"I hope for his sake he is." I look a long sip from my goblet and stared at the crowd in thought. "Conwoïon says we are to move forward with our plan."

Tariq scoffed. "Can we trust his son?"

I took a deep breath and slumped in my chair. "There's not much I can do. The plan is already in motion. Only an act of God can stop it."

I wondered what had happened to Ingrid and Loànn. The bedding should not have taken so long, and I needed Ingrid to mind Ulfrúna. When they did finally return, at least half the guests had slipped away. Loànn held the flap for Ingrid, and they both grinned. They gave each other a parting hug before returning to our table, and they lingered in each other's embrace. When she sat down, Tariq and I leaned forward and gawked at her.

"What?" she asked.

"Nothing," I said, leaning back in my chair, Tariq and I both chortling.

"Where's Ulfrúna?" she asked.

"Back there, with the other children," I said. "The bedding went well?"

"No surprises," Ingrid said. "I cast the runes; they will have a son."

I raised my eyebrows. "The gods told you that?"

Ingrid nodded. I did not want to press the issue, so I swiveled slightly in my chair to face the crowd. Tariq filled his goblet with more wine. I stared at the rolled-up parchment, anxious at how Nominoë's ill health might ruin my chance at facing Renaud. We were less than a fortnight away from the planned return of Rune's fleet, and without the Celts we did not stand a chance in the world of taking Nantes.

"Do you have your runes?" I asked Ingrid.

"I do," she said.

"Would you cast them for me, quietly, at the table, to see what they have to say about the war to come?"

She scooted her chair over to me and pulled a leather satchel from under the table. "I thought you believed in the Christian god now," she muttered as she emptied the contents of the satchel on the table.

"I believe in more gods than I should," I said.

"Are those finger bones?" Tariq asked when he saw the runes.

"They are," Ingrid said. "Only the bones of the sacrificed will tell us the will of the gods."

"So, you killed people to make those?" he said.

"I didn't," she said. "There is a temple far to the north where many are sacrificed, and the bones are collected and sold. I bought these at market."

"Anyway," I interrupted them, "what can you tell me?"

Ingrid sorted through the runes. She scoured the pile, looking for the right angle from which to divine the will of the gods. Ulfrúna bolted out from the crowd, chased by the other children, and she barreled into the table, giving it a massive jolt. She fell to the ground and started to howl, and Ingrid darted over to comfort her. When Ingrid returned to her seat beside me with Ulfrúna in her arms, she looked down at the runes I had caught in my hand as they had fallen off the table from the impact.

She gave me an ominous smile and said, "Those are the ones that will tell you what you seek."

I closed my fist and held it out over the table in front of Ingrid. When she nodded, I dropped the runes and said, "Read them."

She leaned forward as much as she could with Ulfrúna spread out on her lap. Her brow furrowed as she leaned back in her chair with a solemn scowl. "You will find victory in battle," she said, "but at great cost."

"What kind of cost?"

"I don't know. The gods will only say as much as they think you should know. Ulfrúna needs a nap. I must leave you now."

I sat back in my seat with my arms crossed. Tariq stared at the runes. He took another long sip of his wine.

"You must be careful with dark magic like that," he said.

"You think?" I scoffed.

"No, you do not understand. Where I am from, if you try to use dark magic to divine the future, you can invite in spirits you did not intend to invite," he said.

"What kind of spirits?"

"We call them Gin. When a Gin finds you, he will haunt you, and he will not go away until someone you love dies, and that is the only way to make them go away."

"Hardly seems frightful compared with the monsters in the North," I joked.

Tariq did not laugh. His eyes remained fixated on the runes; he had the look of a man who had just seen death.

I patted him on the shoulder and said, "Relax, my friend. The runes are harmless."

No sooner had I said this than the carafe of wine next to Tariq spilled over onto the table. We both jolted to our feet and stepped away. I looked at him, terrified by both what he had said and what had happened after, and wiped at the wine that had spilled on my lap. Tariq started to laugh.

"What's so funny?"

"You!" he howled.

"What? What do you mean?" When I realized the whole thing had been one big joke, I laughed with him.

"You have been too serious all day, Hasting," he said. "I had to snap you out of it."

"I hate you right now," I said still laughing. "So, the Gin aren't real?"

"This is a story we tell children to make them behave," Tariq said.

One of my servants scurried up to the table and wiped away the wine with a damp cloth, and when she left, we sat back down.

Bjorn passed through the entrance flaps a moment later. He sauntered over with a grin, and we cheered him as he approached. He rested his hands on the table and leaned close to speak with me. "There's a ship in the harbor," he said. "Anything I should know?"

"Nothing you can help with today," I said.

"Don't worry, you won't ruin my wedding day by telling me," he insisted.

I sighed and looked at Tariq who shrugged at me. "Nominoë is ill," I said. "Erispoë and Lambert, it seems, have decided to march on Nantes without him."

"What about us?" Bjorn sneered. "They were supposed to wait for us, to meet them on the Loire."

"I know," I said. "And they will meet us where we planned. I had hoped we would have time to wait for Rune."

"When are we to meet them?" Bjorn asked.

"June twenty-first of their calendar, or ten days from now," I explained.

"So, if we wait for Rune, we will arrive late and the Franks will cut the Celts to pieces," Bjorn said.

"That's about right. We should prepare to sail as soon as possible."

Bjorn smiled and stood tall. "I can't wait to take the city. The skalds will sing forever of this, and we will be heralded as heroes among our people."

"Actually, they've asked us not to touch the city," I said. "They will pay us handsomely for our help, but for the plan to work, they need us to steer clear so Lambert can take control of Nantes legitimately."

Bjorn scowled. "That was the whole point for us, wasn't it? It has been our dream, since we sailed with Eilif, to take the city. No Vikings have ever taken such a prize. And now you are telling me we cannot?"

"I am sorry, my friend, but believe me when I say the rewards for patience will pay off tenfold in the future."

Bjorn spat on the ground. "Fine," he growled. "When do we sail?"

"You still need your wife's permission," I said with a chuckle. "What will she think if you agree to sail to war on the day after your wedding?"

"She thinks you shouldn't treat her differently because she got married," Skírlaug said, walking suddenly through the flaps.

"I am sorry, Skírlaug, we had not meant to exclude you," I said.

"And you had better never make that mistake again," she derided me. "I'm still your völva, and you still need me."

"Of course."

"Good. Bjorn, you have my permission to go with them," she said.

It was hard for me and Tariq to hold back our laughter. Even she seemed on the brink of it.

"What about Hasting?" Bjorn cried out. "Why am I the only one who needs your permission?"

"He's the king, and you're my husband," she said. "Get used to it."

"I almost forgot to ask; would you like to join us?"

She shot Bjorn a coy look and said, "I would love to."

Bjorn knew not to protest, but his crooked smile told me he did not want her to come along.

"It is settled, then," I said. "Tomorrow, we sail for the Loire."

17
Where Wild Beasts Roam

When the first arrow-strewn body floated past our ship, we knew we had arrived too late to save them. After spotting several more bodies in the river, all of them in Celtic clothing, I knew Erispoë had fought and lost to Renaud.

We had rowed hard to reach the Loire's riverbanks in time. His eagerness to prove himself to his father had led him to calamity. I wondered how the battle had unfolded. It seemed strange that they fought near enough to the river for there to have been corpses dumped in it. Or perhaps these were stragglers cut off from the retreat and chased down by Renaud's cavalry. I did not know, and it made me nervous to think the Franks were out there somewhere, potentially stalking us as a cat stalks an unwitting bird.

Not far from the crumbling, abandoned fortified bridge—the one we had accidentally burned down—I sent scouts out on foot to learn of the movements of the two armies and to assess their strength. So close to Nantes, I thought, Renaud would have surely returned to the city after the battle. All of my scouts returned far sooner than I expected, and all of them reported the same thing: a Frankish army was camped near the river not far from where we had paused in our journey.

"What do you think they're doing there?" Skírlaug asked.

"Maybe it's a trap," Bjorn suggested.

"Hard to say." I sat across from them on one of the rowing benches. "It depends on whether or not they know we are here."

"I can't think of any reason they would camp so close to the city," Bjorn said.

"Perhaps they are resting after a hard-fought battle," Tariq suggested. "The bodies we saw had not bloated up yet; they were killed this morning."

"So, we missed the fight by barely half a day," Skírlaug said.

"It is possible." I scratched at my chin. "If it is true, we have an opportunity to strike at them while they are weak and undefended—and tired."

"They would not see us coming." Bjorn's eyes opened wide with excitement.

"That's not what we came here to do," I said. "We need to wait for the scouts to return with word from Erispoë."

"Damn Erispoë!" Bjorn blurted out. "The gods have delivered Renaud to us on a silver platter. We must act on it."

"I agree," Tariq said. "Take down the beast first and find our allies after."

"I feel like I am blind," I said. "We have no idea if their scouts have spotted us. Renaud is a cunning man; he could be luring us in to destroy us. He's done it once already this morning."

"What about the runes?" Bjorn asked. "Remind us what they said?"

"Ingrid read them, and they foretold that I would have what I want, but at great cost," I said.

Skírlaug moved to sit beside me and said, "I can cast the runes again, if you'd like."

I was unsure if that was what I wanted. For the first time in a long while I felt paralyzed by fear. Nothing about what we had found on the Loire felt right. I have never been one to indulge in premonitions, but that day I felt something terrible was about to happen.

Tariq shook his head when she offered to cast the runes. He had made it clear that he did not believe in her magic. As I looked around at our crew and back at the other ships, I saw the angst in their eyes. They had also seen the bodies in the river, and they had the look of an army on the brink of breaking and running.

"Cast the runes," I said. "Show the men that the gods are with us."

Skírlaug smiled. She darted to the back of the ship where she kept a trunk of belongings, and she returned with a handful of bones with runes carved upon them. As she cast them, more of the crew gathered around behind us, craning their necks to get a look at her working her magic. It took a few tosses onto the wooden planks for her to discern the will of the gods.

"I see victory," she said, and the men behind us cheered. "The gods will give us glory in battle. But—"

"But what?"

She looked at me and said, "I am not sure how to interpret this other part." She stood and stepped over her runes to sit next to me again. Leaning into my ear so I alone could hear, she said, "The runes say there will be a betrayal."

"Who?" I asked.

She shook her head. "The runes did not show me who. It could be one of us, or it could be you. The gods only—"

"They only show as much as you need to know; yes, your mother said the same," I snapped. "Bjorn, prepare your men. Let's go win this war."

"Yes!" Bjorn cried out.

He clapped his hands together and stormed off barking orders. Our ships rowed past the bridge toward the city, careful to avoid the stones protruding from the water where the bridge had collapsed, and all of us watched carefully for the enemy camp. We saw no smoke and no clearings where an army might rest. The thick underbrush of the forest and tall shadowy trees made it hard to see far inland from the river. Our hearts raced, and all of us prayed to one god or another that our foe would not spot us. After a short while of searching, Bjorn spotted a man on the riverbank rinsing his hands in the water. He called up an archer who knocked an arrow and took aim. When the arrow loosed, we held our breath.

"Did it hit him?" I asked.

"No, it missed," Bjorn said.

Bjorn nudged his archer to fire again, but before he could draw a second arrow, the man on the riverbank spotted us and pointed in our direction. He remained frozen in place, as if under a spell. The archer took aim at him again and loosed an arrow, which met its mark. We heard the thud of the steel arrow tip slam into the man's chest, and he fell face first into the water.

"That was lucky," I said.

"Too lucky," Skírlaug added.

Our ships formed a line along the riverbank and our warriors assembled on the shore, all of them itching for a fight. Bjorn led a third of the men into the forest to the left, Skírlaug took a third of them to the right, and Tariq and I led my third up the center, moving as quietly as we could through the muddy forest.

To my astonishment, the Franks seemed completely unaware of our arrival. Their men were sitting in a grassy opening on the edge of a dirt road. On any other day, it might have been a pleasant outing, with warm air, a slight breeze, and no rain. We caught them so unaware, we did not need to make a shield wall to face them. Along the trees, on the edge of the forest, closest to where my men and I crept up on them, their crossbowmen lounged idly in the midday sun, crossbows and conical steel helmets piled in a heap beside an oak tree. I waved to start our attack, and I pointed to the crossbowmen as our first target. I waited for a moment before ordering a charge to see if Bjorn wanted to attack first. I could not see him or his men in the shadow of the forest.

"Charge!" I howled, and we sprang like wild beasts at our unsuspecting foe.

The ambush worked. Bjorn cried out from his side, and his men thundered out of the forest, and Skírlaug, too. We swarmed through their camp, and our victims hardly had a chance to get to their feet before we cut them down. I realized once we charged forward that they heavily outnumbered us, but our sudden appearance had so surprised them that we had made ourselves seem far greater in number than we actually were. Those who saw us from farther away did not bother to pick up their arms; they ran for the trees on the other side of the road.

That's when I saw him.

Renaud, with his long black hair and scarred face, hopped onto his horse and screamed at his men to muster a response.

"Hasting! There!" Bjorn yelled out, pointing at Renaud, but I had already had him in my sights.

We hacked and slashed our way forward, and the closer we drew to him, the stronger the resistance we met. Frankish warriors with heavy iron shields and lances banded together to form a line in front of their master. They struck down any of our men who ventured too close. The tide had turned. What had started as a slaughter turned to a pitched battle.

We brought our men forward to form a shield wall, shoulder-to-shoulder, hip-to-hip. I did not join the wall; I had never trained to fight in one, but Bjorn's men knew what to do without my help. I stood back with Tariq and Skírlaug at my side, and we followed the Danes forward.

Renaud pulled his horse back and forth frantically, looking for his crossbowmen, but we had killed them all.

Across the battlefield, our eyes locked. He laughed in disbelief when he recognized me, and his smile soon turned to a growl. Drawing his sword, he barked at his soldiers to join the fight, and to my dismay, hundreds of men moved up from behind him, their numbers obscured by the shadows of the forest. We had sprung the trap.

"We are outnumbered!" Bjorn cried out.

I took stock of where we stood. We had barely lost ten men, and we'd killed more than I could count. Half of Renaud's army fled down the road, and the other half looked shaken. They had mustered a response, but we had them on their heels.

To break the standstill, I drew my sword and ran through our shield wall and at our enemy. My warriors watched in awe, and when it was clear I would not stop, Bjorn roared at them to follow.

The Franks had not expected us to charge again, and their line was faltering. Some of their soldiers broke formation and ran, leaving gaping holes in their line. As I neared their shields and spears, I darted for one of the holes and lunged through, slashing at their necks with my sword. Before they could move to stop me, my army crashed into them. It was not the prettiest battle I'd ever fought, but we had to act boldly if we hoped to defeat them.

Once I had passed through the line, I found myself facing little resistance. Renaud had not noticed me, and he led his horse up and down the line behind his men to encourage them.

I stopped for a moment, and at my feet was an abandoned lance, as if placed there by the gods so I could throw it. Though I had not thrown a lance in many years, I had been one of the best among Nominoë's warriors. The Celts called me the Hero of Pontivy because I had thrown the lance that had wounded Tristan and led to his capture. Now, it seemed, Renaud would face the same fate.

I picked up the lance and took aim. The moment I threw, I knew I had missed. The lance flew past Renaud and alerted him to my presence. He looked down at me and bared his teeth. Something on the battlefield drew his attention, and he put on a menacing smile. He barked orders at the men near him, and one of them handed him a loaded crossbow. He took aim over my head and fired. In the same moment, I heard a bloodcurdling scream from behind our line.

"Hasting!" I heard Bjorn cry out.

I stared at Renaud, who was now laughing. The enemy line had all but crumbled, and most of the Franks had abandoned their shields and fled. Renaud pulled hard on his horse's reigns and kicked the beast forward down the road.

His men looked back to see he had fled, and they broke their formation to follow. Without their leader, they had no resolve to fight.

I searched for the source of the scream. Bjorn's warriors had formed a protective circle around Tariq. I ran up to them and they let me through. Bjorn held Skírlaug in his arms, his hands covered in blood. Skírlaug looked up at me with tired eyes.

"What's happened?" I asked.

"An arrow," Tariq said.

I knelt by her side as Bjorn pointed to a crossbow bolt lodged in her shoulder. She raised her hand to touch my face and said, "Now is your chance."

"I can't leave you like this," I said.

"You can," she insisted. "You will."

"We can take care of her," Bjorn said. "Go."

I stood and looked at Tariq and asked him, "Can you ride?"

Tariq nodded. The Franks had left several horses behind, so Tariq and I mounted two and started the hunt.

My heart bounded at the thought of catching Renaud, and I lost focus of everything else happening on the battlefield.

Our horses strode swiftly along the road through the trees and out into the green pastures of the fields beyond. Frankish war horses had always impressed me with their size, speed, and the quality of their training. Tariq also impressed me. He had evidently ridden many horses.

We passed hundreds of fleeing soldiers on our way, all of them exhausted and moaning. They never gave us a second look. Where we emerged from the forest, we could see much farther down the road, and I spotted Renaud.

He had slowed from a gallop to a trot, but his escort warned him of our approach. He shot a quick look back at us and kicked his horse forward. We galloped with all the speed our horses would give. Renaud turned with the road into the open fields that surrounded the city.

We charged across rolling hills of cultivated pasture as far as the eye could see, and at last we took sight of Nantes and its shimmering limestone walls. The city spurred my urgency to catch Renaud before he could reach it.

I gradually closed the distance. As I came up behind Renaud, my horse's snout brushed against the backside of his. The small touch unnerved the beast; it took a hard turn off the path against Renaud's wishes and lurched forward on the uneven, rocky terrain. Renaud flew from its back and rolled on the ground.

I rode up to him and drew my sword. He drew his and swiped with all his strength at my horse's neck. Though he missed, my horse reared, and I slipped off its back.

I rolled out of the way of the beast's hooves, which slammed down inches from my head. The horse ran off into the field, leaving me behind in the grass. I rolled onto my stomach to push myself up, still dazed by my fall, and scrambled for my sword.

Renaud charged at me. Tariq rode up and moved between us with his horse, and he swung down with an ax at our enemy. Renaud staggered backward. Tariq's horse jolted forward, leaving me to face Renaud again, but it was time enough to retrieve my sword.

"We've never actually fought before, you and I," Renaud said.

Tariq turned his horse around and looked as if he might charge again.

"Stay back," I said. "This is my fight."

As Renaud and I faced each other, a dozen Frankish soldiers ran up behind me, so Tariq galloped off to slow them down. Renaud used the distraction to thrust at me with his sword, and I swiped it away from my chest.

"You've studied with a swordsman," Renaud said. "I should have expected as much. Of course Nominoë had you train."

"His name was Yann," I said.

We circled each other, both of us holding our swords above our heads with two hands—in the stance of the falcon, ready to strike from above. When he stepped forward, I stepped back, and when I stepped forward, he stepped back.

I was losing my patience, so I swiped down at him to the left, and he swung forward to block me. Our swords twanged when they collided. With my next stroke, I aimed left again, and he moved to meet me. My sword's momentum brought it down over my hip, and when I swung back up at him, he swung down to block.

As we fought, I realized I was holding back. I knew how to swordfight better than that, yet I was somehow hesitant. Now that I was staring Renaud down, something changed in how I carried myself. Thoughts of failure filled my mind. I would never have another chance such as this, I thought, to avenge Asa, and to remove the blight that he was from the land I had come to think of as my home. He saw the hesitation in my step and in my strokes, and he used them against me.

"What's happened?" he asked. "Lose your nerve?"

His words enraged me, and I charged at him. I swung hard, but he parried to the side and slipped his blade under my guard. The cold steel ran over my leg, and I felt the warm dribble of blood on my knee. I limped backward and held the wound. A darkness of spirit loomed over me. I felt hopeless, as if I had already lost the fight. With a wound on my leg, I thought, I could not hope to defeat him.

As we fought, the wind picked up, and with it a flurry of dandelions swirled around us. I closed my eyes and took a deep breath, praying silently for the strength to endure.

And then I heard her. Her voice was as clear as the day was bright.

Let go.

Yes, I thought, I needed to let go of my fear; let go of my anger; let go of what the future might bring, and of what the past had wrought.

I opened my eyes to find Renaud swinging his sword at me, and I swung my mine to meet him. Every move he made, I met with skill and precision. The pain in my leg left me, and I walked calmly toward him, my chest held high and my eyes aimed at him like daggers.

My renewed confidence unnerved him. He inched backward and tripped over some rocks. When he turned again to face me, I had launched an assault he could not repel. My sword bore down on him with the strength of several men. It slammed his own blade against his shoulder and cut into his neck. He howled like a fox in a trap. Holding his neck, he turned and fled.

Exhausted, he could hardly run. He yanked on his overcoat as he jogged and pulled it off to shed some weight. Next he tugged on his maille shirt, and he tripped as he tried to slip it over his head. On his knees, he pulled harder and managed to free himself of its grip.

I nearly caught him then, but he launched the maille at me and darted off again. Seeing his distress, I did not feel the need to run. I stalked across the field, seething at the chance to nip at him. The wolf Fenrir's spirit possessed me, and I was a wild beast in pursuit of my prey.

We crossed over a wicket fence into the next field, and the inhabitants of the farm stepped outside to watch us pass by.

Renaud ascended a hill toward a lone oak in a barren, burnt wheat field. At the crest of the hill, we could see far and wide over the farms surrounding the city and the Loire meandering to the east and west. Renaud could no longer run. He fell to his knees and crawled to the tree, heaving to catch his breath, blood running down his arm

He sat against the trunk and looked down at the city. I stepped around the tree to face him and lifted my sword.

"You're supposed to be dead," he muttered between labored breaths.

"In a way, I was."

"You must be very proud," he said. "You will have your revenge today." He wiped his running nose with the sleeve of his undershirt and stared off into the distance. "What will you become after you kill me?"

"A king," I said.

Renaud scoffed. "A king of what? The wind? Charles will avenge me. Your island will perish, just as the first settlement of Northmen perished."

"You killed them," I said.

"And I enjoyed it. Your kind has been a plague on our lands."

"I have seen what you do to your lands. Your wars have cost your people much," I said. "The empire is corrupt, and you are part of the problem. That you blame us, that you would scapegoat us—this is why my blade strikes you down today."

"Spare me the lecture," he growled. "Get it over with, then. Kill me, in the name of your girlfriend."

I swung my sword.

His cleaved head rolled down the hill and his body slumped over into the grass. My sword stuck in the tree's trunk, and I left it there for a moment. I looked up to the sky and opened my arms, waiting for a sign from the gods, or even the Christian god. Tariq rode up behind me and dismounted.

"It is done?"

"It is," I said.

"For this, you will be remembered for a long time."

I looked over my shoulder to see if the Frankish soldiers had continued their pursuit, but Tariq had chased them all off.

"Did I do the right thing?" I asked him.

Tariq grabbed me around the shoulders and said, "Right or wrong, today everything changes, for all of us."

"Shit," I said, and Tariq stepped back as if he had done something wrong. I pointed at the river. "Look."

A Viking fleet of several dozen longships rowed toward the city. From their colors, I knew it was Bjorn. He was going to take Nantes against my wishes. The runes had spoken true: I had my victory, and I was betrayed.

With Renaud dead and his army scattered, the city was defenseless. Bjorn was about to steal my glory and ruin my plan to be the first Viking to take a major city in the Carolingian Empire.

"What should we do?" Tariq asked.

"What can we do?"

I stood on the hill and watched, helpless, but Tariq had other ideas.

"Come," he urged me forward.

I followed, and together we started the long walk to Nantes.

Historical Note

In the historical note of *The Lords of the Wind*, I was purposely vague in order to avoid spoiling too much of the story of the future series. The first book gave me more creative license to structure Hasting's early life so that the rest of it, which is far better attested in historical sources, would make sense. Again, I will focus only on the parts of my research relevant to this book and avoid oversharing any elements that might spoil the next tome.

HASTING'S EARLY LIFE

In this second volume, I followed historical events more precisely and used as the primary basis for the start of the narrative the works of Raoul Glaber, a medieval chronicler who gives us more information on Hasting's early life than any other. Though historians often call into question his testimony, we can cross-reference so much of what he says about Hasting's later life with other sources that we may consider his earlier work partially relevant.

Glaber writes in his *Historiarum* that Hasting was born in the region of Troyes, in France. His assertion stands in contrast with all other contemporary sources, which describe Hasting as a Scandinavian. Nevertheless, the idea that he might have been born in France but of Scandinavian parents is not incompatible. We know the Danes and Saxons had close connections, particularly among the elite. The Saxon chieftain Widukind, defeated by Charlemagne at the battle of Verden, was the brother-in-law of the Danish king Sigfrid. We also know that the wars in Saxony displaced many people, and Charlemagne had entire villages moved farther into his empire to convert them to Christianity and cut them off from the pagan North. Hasting's parents may have lived in Southern Jutland and been moved to the Troyes region of France by the Carolingians.

Glaber puts Hasting's birth between 810 and 820 (in *The Lords of the Wind*, I placed his birthdate in the year 816, for reference) and tells us that by age fifteen, he abandoned his family's farm to return to his ancestors' homeland. He traveled on foot to Frisia, perhaps to the trade port of Dorestad, and then took a ship to Denmark. There he enlisted as a sailor and began his long career at sea. We cannot verify any of these events through other sources, so for the most part we have to take Glaber's word for what he says. When considering other sources on Hasting, the approximate date of birth, at least, seems about right, but we must call the rest into question.

Glaber's telling has Hasting start as a crewmember of a trading vessel that followed warships from place to place. When he grew big enough, he enlisted on a warship and quickly rose through the ranks. His peers quickly recognized his courage, determination, cunning, and intelligence, and his authority grew. Although Glaber alone tells of Hasting's early life, he assures us he worked from credible sources, and nothing to this point appears implausible. That Glaber avoids many of the problems that plague other medieval sources may lend a sliver of credibility to his narrative.

Why did I not begin my saga with Glaber's telling of events, you might ask? Simply put, it disagrees with a few core events that I needed to reconcile for the narrative. Chiefly, Hasting spent the better part of his life in the Aquitaine and Poitou regions of France, and textual and archeological evidence suggests the men who raided in those areas were predominantly Norwegian. The *Annales d'Angoulême* describe the men who sacked Nantes in 843 as *Vestfaldingi* or Men of Vestfold. Such testimony indicates that the Vikings who raided in Aquitaine may have been from Norway and not Denmark. It also suggests they had trade contact with the local population before raiding, since the only way the authors of the annals could have known they had come from Vestfold is if they had introduced themselves first. If true, the most likely route taken to reach Aquitaine would have been around the north of the British Isles and through the Irish Sea, where Norsemen from Norway had already established a heavy presence on the Irish coast. A silver horde found in Ireland confirms contacts between the Norsemen of Ireland and those who raided in France. The horde contained Carolingian coins minted in Aquitaine, called the Mullaghboden Silver Coins, thought to have been brought back from trade with Southern France. In the opening of *The Lords of the Wind*, therefore, I felt I needed Hasting to start his career as a Viking in Ireland.

VINDREYLAND: THE ISLAND OF NOIRMOUTIER

Hasting makes his first appearance in Aquitaine sometime in the 830s. At the core of the Vikings' activities in the region is the island of Noirmoutier, then called Herio, and in the novel, the Vikings call it Vindreyland. The island was home to a wealthy, well-connected monastery called Saint Philibert, and it had suffered repeated attacks since the first raid in 799. A letter written March 16, 819, by the abbot Arnulf of Saint-Philibert, complained of frequent and persistent raids on the island. The *Vita Hludovici* and the *Annales Regni Francorum* confirm the frequency of raids and tell of a particularly gruesome episode where a fleet of dozens of ships appeared suddenly and sacked the *vicus* on the neighboring island of Bouin in 813, and again in 820.

In light of the growing number and frequency of raids, Arnulf asked Emperor Louis for permission and money to build a new monastery at Déas, on the shores of Grand-Lieu Lake about forty kilometers inland. Each spring and summer throughout the 820s, the monks abandoned Herio and returned in the autumn when the risk of raids had abated. Strangely, evidence exists to suggest that the economic output of the island, which was by no means negligible before the Viking raids, did not suffer too terribly from the arrival of the Norsemen. A royal charter from the year 826, given by Emperor Louis, offered the monastery an exemption on taxation of their exports. The tax exemption suggests a certain level of economic output persisted throughout this period, and the Carolingians wanted to encourage continued growth. Conspicuously absent from mention are the other inhabitants of the island; all the sources focus nearly exclusively on the fate of the religious order. These two pieces of evidence suggest the other inhabitants of Herio did not leave the island during the raiding season and instead remained to farm and export the island's resources. Chiefly, they exported salt.

By 830, the situation on the island had grown desperate. A royal charter from Emperor Louis permitted the monks to fortify the monastery grounds, described as a *castrum*, to defend themselves from the repeated raids. Despite their best efforts, the fortifications did little to stop the Norsemen's incursions. Between the years 831 and 835, the monks continued their annual migrations to Déas. Over time, Déas grew in size and reputation to outshine the monastery on Herio. The monk Ermentaire, who bore witness to these events, described in his writings a last attempt to repel the Vikings. One of the local lords, Renaud d'Herbauges, traveled to Herio in 835 to defend the island.

That he traveled to Herio explicitly to fight the Vikings, and that they appeared and fought him, reinforces the notion that the raids had, by this time, become astonishingly regular. It may also suggest the Vikings had established some kind of settlement or camp nearby to which they returned each spring and summer to continue their activities. Ermentaire describes the battle as a glorious victory for Renaud in which he slew over four hundred Northmen and lost only one man. Such a gross exaggeration hurts the credibility of the account, but a mention in the *Annales d'Angoulême* affirms a battle likely took place and was, in fact, a victory for Renaud. No sooner had Renaud left for home the following September than the Norsemen returned and captured the *castrum*. The following year, the monks petitioned the ruler of Aquitaine, Louis' son Pepin, to exhume the bones of their patron saint and carry them to Déas for safety.

At this juncture, when the monks definitively abandoned the island in 836, contemporary mentions of Noirmoutier declined. Sole Glaber suggests the island's fate: the Vikings took possession of it as a base to launch raids in the Loire River Valley, a notion echoed in the *Chronique de Nantes*. According to Glaber, Hasting was a member of that fleet and a follower of a king named Horic. Horic died in 838 while in the region. This event marks the start of the narrative of *In the Shadow of the Beast*.

DISSOLUTION OF THE CAROLINGIAN EMPIRE

Europe remembers the Carolingians fondly. Charlemagne, the most successful of their dynasty, is claimed by both France and Germany as a foundational figure. Throughout the Medieval period, the ruling class in Western Europe sought to legitimize their place and power by tracing their lineages in an unbroken line back to him (much of which was fabricated). His was a story of divine provenance, of conquest, and of spreading Christianity to the pagan people of Europe, or so his chroniclers would have us believe. Few argue the impact of his reign. Europe as we know it today would not exist if not for him and his family. It is no surprise he has found a permanent place in the histories of his day.

Nevertheless, despite all he accomplished, his most significant achievements and triumphs unraveled within less than a generation. His empire crumbled as his son and grandsons battled in repeated civil wars that culminated in the Frankish nobility's utter destruction at the Battle of Fontenoy-en-Puisaye in 841 and the permanent division of his lands. Though he did not live to see his work undone by his successors, he witnessed a threat that would one day put at risk everything he'd fought for. His biographer, Notker the Stammerer, tells us Charlemagne greatly feared the raiders from the North, whom he called the Northmen. In a passage about a journey he took to Southern France (whose date is not explicitly mentioned but is presumed to have occurred in the 790s), he witnessed the sudden appearance, raid attempt, and disappearance of Viking ships. His men did not capture them, but the incident inspired tremendous trepidation:

"Charlemagne, who was a God-fearing, just and devout ruler, rose from the table and stood at the window facing East. For a long time, the precious tears poured down his face. No one dared to ask him why. In the end he explained his lachrymose behavior to his war-like leader. 'My faithful servants,' said he, 'Do you know why I wept so bitterly? I am not afraid that these ruffians will be able to do me harm; but I am sick at heart to think that even in my lifetime they have dared to attack this coast, and I am horror-stricken when I foresee what evil they will do to my descendants and their subjects.'"

The incident in Southern France is often disputed as perhaps not having taken place because it cannot be cross-referenced with other sources of the day. However, it remains relevant insofar as it informs us the Carolingians had an awareness of the potential for increased raids by the Vikings long before the more extensive, more organized raids of the mid-ninth century began. Indeed, Charlemagne's alleged prediction proved disastrously right. Beginning in 799 with an attack in Aquitaine, thought to have struck at the monastery of Saint Philibert on Noirmoutier, among other coastal islands, wave after wave of raids plagued his empire. They chipped away at the edges of what had been during his rule a well-defended coastline and an impenetrable river system. Political upheaval among the empire's nobility after his death opened the door for opportunistic outsiders. Like wolves stalking their prey, the Vikings waited patiently for their chance to take down the largest prizes. Over three centuries, the Vikings established a significant presence within the Carolingian sphere of influence. They allied themselves with the Franks' enemies, such as the Bretons and the Basques, and they played a cruel game of politics to achieve their aims. The leaders of their armies grew in renown and reputation. Many of them made their mark in the chronicles and histories of the time. Both of Charlemagne's greatest fears—the division of his empire and the Viking invasions—upended his vision for the world after his death.

The first significant raid south of the Loire took place in 799, attested in a letter written to the archbishop of Salzburg, Arno, by the monk Alcuin:

"As you may have heard, pagan ships have done much harm to the islands of Aquitaine. Some of them were entirely lost; five men were slaughtered by hundreds of marauders on the beach. A great chastening is upon them unlike any the ancient Christian world has ever seen; perhaps it is because they have not kept their vows to God."

Almost immediately after the 799 raids in Aquitaine, Charlemagne ordered the construction of a fleet of ships and fortified bridges to guard the rivers. His efforts seem to have worked for a short while. After his death, however, his son Louis struggled to maintain the same level of organization. As Viking raids intensified along the coast of what are today Normandy, Bretagne, and Aquitaine, he failed to rise to the challenge to repel them. He also failed to maintain the integrity of his empire through a process that can only be described as poor estate planning. The Franks had not yet conceived of the idea of primogeniture, or the passing of one's lands and title to the eldest child. Instead, the Carolingians, by law, had to divide their possessions equally among their surviving sons. Louis was Charlemagne's only legitimate son, so the empire remained intact after his father's death, but his sons Lothaire, Louis, and Pepin had a claim to an equal share of the empire.

According to the primary source on Louis' life—the *Vita Hludovici Imperatoris*, whose author signed his name enigmatically as Astronomer—a near-death experience in 817 prompted Louis to settle his estate with his three sons. The empire's first partition gave each son a more-or-less equal portion of land and title, which included the lion's share of the rents from those lands. Had Louis died in 818, the empire might have clawed its way back to a unified whole. The Carolingians were not so lucky. Instead, Louis' first wife Ermengarde died in 819 and, on the advice of his councilors, he remarried. Louis' second wife, Judith, gave birth to a fourth son, Charles, in 823. Charles' birth rocked the foundation of the original partition of land. For six years, Louis and his eldest three sons argued over how to divide the empire fairly. Lothaire, Louis, and Pepin did not want to lose any income from their lands, particularly not to a half-brother. In 829, Louis convened the Council of Worms to settle the matter. He imposed his will on his sons and forced them to accept the terms of the new partition to include Charles. All three sons rebelled against him the following year.

By the year 830, civil war had become endemic in the Carolingian Empire. When Emperor Louis the Pious died in 840, any hope for unity died with him. Plots, rivalries, and shifting alliances plunged one of the most powerful empires Western Europe had ever seen into chaos. As the Carolingian state crumbled, outsiders lurked on their borders, hungry to exploit their weakness. None would prove more dangerous than the Viking Hasting.

REBELLION ON THE BRETON MARCH

The Carolingian civil wars emboldened rebels. The Obotrites, Slovenes, Bretons, and Basques, among others, pushed back against the austere rule of Charlemagne's successors during infighting. In Bretagne, the Bretons had failed to break free from Louis' grip in the preceding decades. Their greatest hope, a leader named Wihomarc, had surrendered to Louis in 823. Throughout the early ninth century, the Bretons maneuvered politically and militarily to claw nearer to their independence. When the war between the emperor and his sons broke out, they saw an opportunity to break away. A young leader named Nominoë took up the cause. Unlike his many predecessors who had failed to achieve independence, he played an astute game of politics rather than foment a fruitless armed rebellion.

Regino of Prüm wrote in his *Chronicon* that Emperor Louis had named Nominoë duke of Bretagne in the 830s. While many aspects of the testimony have received scrutiny by historians, particularly for the date the *Chronicon* mentions the event, it demonstrates the more calculated approach Nominoë took to achieve his goals. He attended court, received the emperor's favor, and managed to earn a Carolingian title. Good relations with the Carolingians helped ease tension along the border between Breton and Frankish lands, which is known historically as the Breton March. Nominoë also spearheaded an effort to found an abbey at Redon, along the River Vilaine. After all, the Bretons were Christians, and Louis believed the establishment of abbeys and donations of land to the church along the Breton March would reduce the frequent raids carried out by Breton rebels. In essence, he thought the church would act as a buffer between his lands and those of the Bretons. Nominoë backed the founding of the abbey of Redon to gain further trust from Louis.

When Louis died in 840, his son Charles, who took control of Neustria (roughly what is today France), asked for Breton's support in his war against his older brother Lothaire. He initially received it. However, following the battle of Fontenoy in 841, where a significant number of the Carolingian gentry lost their lives, including Ricwin, the count of Nantes, Nominoë saw an opportunity to achieve independence, and he launched a rebellion against Charles.

NANTES STRUCK BY THE APOCALYPSE

The final chapter of *In the Shadow of the Beast* sees Hasting and his companions stumble by chance upon a resting Frankish army. In the *Chronicle of Nantes*, the *Annales d'Angoulême*, and the *Annales de St. Bertin*, we learn of a battle between Renaud d'Herbauges and Nominoë's son, Erispoë, at a place called Messac. Renaud won the battle, but while his army rested and celebrated their victory, they were ambushed by Erispoë's ally Lambert, who destroyed the Frankish army and killed Renaud.

Lambert himself is a fascinating character. His father, Lambert I, had been the count of Nantes but was exiled for joining Lothaire's first rebellion against Emperor Louis. Lambert II spent his whole life clawing up the ranks of the nobility to retake Nantes, and he used any means necessary to achieve his goal. We see across many sources that he allied himself with Nominoë, who gladly took him under his wing. Nominoë saw in Lambert an opportunity to sew further discord among the ruling class of the empire.

At the battle of Fontenoy, the sitting count of Nantes, Ricwin, fell. Lambert had backed a victorious Charles and hoped the opportunity to regain his father's title had arrived. Charles passed him over and instead appointed Renaud d'Herbauges as count. The betrayal sent Lambert straight to Nominoë for help. Again, Nominoë saw an opportunity to help his cause and supported Lambert's claim. There was no love lost between Nominoë and Renaud. According to the *Cartulaire de Redon*, Renaud and Ricwin had opposed Nominoë's bid to establish the abbey at Redon.

In 843, Nominoë fell ill and could not lead the campaign he had planned against the Franks. His son Erispoë led the army instead, supported by Lambert, and they marched toward Nantes to take it. Renaud met them at Messac and handily defeated the Bretons. Lambert's forces arrived late and, according to the *Chronicle of Nantes*, surprised Renaud's army while they rested and slaughtered them. The composition of Lambert's forces remains somewhat a mystery, since he did not have the support of the Carolingians. However, the *Chronicle of Nantes* suggests he had been in league with Northmen, and it has been suggested, albeit dubiously, that Hasting killed Renaud.

For the sake of the novel, I had to sort out the ambiguity surrounding these events. Of course, with Hasting as my protagonist and Renaud as the antagonist, I made sure there would be a showdown between the two of them. I also needed to give the Vikings more cause to join the Bretons than just Hasting's alliance with Nominoë. So, I moved the date for the battle of Messac forward about one month and placed it closer to the Loire. I did this to facilitate the transition from the battle to the sack of Nantes, which I believe was the direct result of the Bretons losing control over their Scandinavian allies.

When the Vikings sacked Nantes on June 24, 843, during the festival of St. John (*la St. Jean*), Christendom paused. Never before had a major city in the Carolingian Empire fallen to the pagans. The *Annales d'Angoulême* describe the attack as an apocalypse, and the *Chronicle of Nantes* echoes that sentiment. Little did they know in the wake of the catastrophe that the attack signaled a new modus operandi for the Vikings, one that cities large and small would prove powerless to repel.

HOW MANY HORICS?

In *The Lords of the Wind*, I suggest Hasting was in league with King Horic of Jutland, who contested his throne against a rival named Harald-Klak. That same figure is the one I bring to Noirmoutier at the beginning of *In the Shadow of the Beast*. There is a disagreement, however, in the sources about Horic. The early kings of Jutland are reasonably well documented by the Carolingians, who had frequent contact and involvement with them. Horic begins his fight for the throne of Jutland in the mid-810s, and according to the Chronicler Rimbert, who wrote a biography of the the missionary Anskar, he remained in power until his death in 854. Fifty years is an unusually long reign for any king, let alone a Danish warlord with a dubious claim. Glaber's suggestion he died while raiding is both in character for Horic (Horic frequently raided the Obrodites and the Frisians) and more reasonable of a lifespan for the type of career he had. How

I reconcile the disagreement between the sources in the novel is to suggest Horic's son, also named Horic, took over for his father sixteen years earlier than previously thought. Rimbert, like Glaber, was a later medieval chronicler working from contemporary sources that no longer exist, and so from a historical perspective, it's possible Rimbert confused which Horic was in power and when.

A NOTE ON PLACE-NAMES

While many authors of early medieval historical narratives attempt to create a measure of authenticity by employing names and place-names as they might have been in the day, I have chosen to forgo such an endeavor. My goal with these novels is to make them accessible to a full breadth of readers, from the high-schooler with a tenth grade reading level to the retired Ph.D. professor. Considering my novels took place outside the anglophone world when English and French were not yet languages and that I write for modern English- and French-speaking audiences, I think that using ambiguous ancient names is neither authentic nor useful (to say nothing of the fact that ancient place names are often spelled differently in different sources, often leading to more confusion). Instead, I have chosen to use modern names for the most part so that a curious reader who wants to learn more about a place mentioned in the book can plug it into Google, and Google will return coherent information. The notable exception to this is the island of Noirmoutier, which Hasting named Vindreyland in the narrative, and which Celtic and Frankish characters refer to as Herio, its original name.

Primary Sources

- Letter from Alcuin to Arno, ed. MGH, *Epistolae Karolini Aevi*, t. II, no. 184, pg. 309.
- "Annales Engolismenses " *MGH SS XVI*. Ed. Holder-Egger, O. Hanover1859. 486. Print.
- "Annals of Fontanelle (Annales Fontanellenses; Chronicle of St-Wandrille)." Ed. Laporte, J. Rouen and Paris: Société de L'Histoire de Normandie, 1951. Vol. 15. Print.
- "Annals of Fulda (Annales Fuldenses)." *MGH SRG*. Ed. Kurze, F. Hanover1891. Print.
- Nelson, J.L. *The Annals of St-Bertin.* Manchester University Press, 1991. Print.
- "Annals of St-Vaast (Annales Vedastini)." *MGH SRG*. Ed. Simson, B. Von. Hanover1909. Print.
- Maguire, C.M.M., et al. Annals of Ulster: A. D. 431-1056. Ed. By W. M. Hennessy. H. M. Stationery Office, 1887. Print.
- "Annals of Xanten (Annales Xantenses)." *MGH SRG*. Ed. Simson, B. Von. Hanover1909. Print.
- Robinson, Charles H. Anskar, the Apostle of the North, 801-865, Translated from the Vita Anskarii by Bishop Rimbert. London: SPCK, 1921. Print.
- Rogers, B., and B.W. Scholz. Carolingian Chronicles: Royal Frankish Annals and Nithard's Histories. University of Michigan Press, 1972. Print.
- Prüm, Regino of. "Chronicon." *MGH SRG*. Ed. Kurze, F. Hanover1890. Print.
- Ermentarius. *De Translationibus Et Miraculis Sancti Filiberti*. Ed. Poupardin, R. Paris: A. Picard, 1905. Print.

- Sturluson, S., et al. *Egil's Saga: Penguin Classics*. Penguin Books Limited, 2004. Print.
- Thegan. "Gesta Hludowici Imperatoris." *MGH SS II*. Ed. Pertz, G. Berlin1829. Print.
- Flodoard. "Historia Remensis Ecclesiae." *MGH SS XIII* Ed. Waitz, Ed. I. Heller and G. Hanover1881. Print.
- Nithard. "Historiarum Libri IV." *Histoire des Fils de Louis le Pieux*. Ed. Lauer, P. Paris1926. Print.
- Merlet, R. La Chronique De Nantes (570 Environ-1049). BiblioBazaar, 2008. Print.
- Finlay, A., and Þ.E. Jóhannesdóttir. The Saga of the Jómsvikings: A Translation with Full Introduction. De Gruyter, 2018. Print.
- Stammerer, N. *Two Lives of Charlemagne*. Penguin Books Limited, 2013. Print.
- Ermentaire. *Vie Et Miracles De Saint-Philibert*. Eds. Delhommeau, Abbé Louis, Claude Bouhier and Préf. Jacques Oudin. Noirmoutier-en-l'Île: Les Amis de l'Île de Noirmoutier, 1999. Print.
- Astronomer. "Vita Hludovici Pii." *MGH LXIV*. Ed. Tremp, E. Hanover1995. Print.

For a list of secondary sources, visit:
https://cjadrien.com/selected-bibliography

About the Author

C.J. Adrien is a bestselling author of Viking historical fiction novels and has a passion for Viking history. His Kindred of the Sea series was inspired by research conducted in preparation for a doctoral program in early medieval history, as well as his admiration for historical fiction writers such as Bernard Cornwell and Ken Follett. He is also a published historian on the subject of Vikings, with articles featured in historical journals such as *L'Association des Amis de Noirmoutier*, in France. His novels and expertise have earned him invitations to speak at several international events including the International Medieval Congress at the University of Leeds, the Oregon Museum of Science and Industry (OMSI), and conferences on Viking history in France, among others. C.J. Adrien earned a bachelor's degree in history from the University of Oregon, a master's degree from Oregon State University, and is currently searching for the right university to complete his doctoral thesis.

To learn more about the author, visit www.cjadrien.com

Did you enjoy Hasting's story? Leave it a review: https://www.amazon.com/product-reviews/B07TWSLWG6/

Printed in Great Britain
by Amazon